READERS' PRAISE FOR NICOLE COLLET'S *RED*

RED, a quarterfinalist in the 2014 Amazon Breakthrough Novel contest, was originally posted on the digital platform Wattpad, where it became an international sensation. At the time of publication, it had received two million hits.

"I absolutely love *RED*. It has substance and the perfect balance between warm love and fiery passion. Brilliant plot, well-rounded and engaging characters... Collet creates worlds and enlivens the senses while encouraging readers to think critically. Bravo!"
—PATRICIA FRANCO, PHILIPPINES

"*RED* is rather amazing: one of the best, most intricate and consuming books I've ever read. It explains romance in such a captivating way, portraying love like everyone feels it. It's hard to put it down for even one second. Unlike any love story I know... it should have its own genre because there's nothing like it."
—AMELIA LILY HUGHES, ENGLAND

"Nicole Collet has a beautiful literary imagination. Her writing is unbendable gold, with unique imagery that comes to me almost too suddenly. I really enjoy this novel—the world needs to read it."
—EMILY KENT, ENGLAND

"*RED*'s words slipped through my mind like a moving image. I felt enveloped by the writing and couldn't quite get it out of my head."
—SHOUA HER, UNITED STATES

"Amazing... Fresh and new, something I would read over and over again."
—MARIJANA ĐURIČIĆ, SERBIA

"Terrific story, told poetically and with great cultural references. It's rare to see the sexuality of an 18-year-old portrayed in such a realistic manner."
—**ELENIRA NASCIMENTO, BRAZIL**

"Absolutely fantastic. I'm so glad to have found a bearable teacher-student romance, although this far exceeds bearable and breaches a 'phenomenal' characteristic."
—**ESTELLE STYVE, UNITED STATES**

"Spicy and funny but at the same time educational. Marco blew my mind with his talk about instinct and reason."
—**CRISTINA DE PAULA, UNITED STATES**

"A beautifully written piece. I was carried by the words and emotions. Right words, the anticipation—everything! Wonderful."
—**KIM SALDO, PHILIPPINES**

"*RED* is an absolutely riveting read, so different from other teacher-student romances. I have actually learnt something from this book… I love that the author added intellectual aspects to the storyline."
—**MAHRIA BASHIR, ENGLAND**

"Awesome. The author is able to transmit, in an unparalleled way, the development of the story and the feelings of the characters, whom we grow to love."
—**GABRIELLA SUZART, BRAZIL**

"The pages of *RED* are filled with so much talent…
I get chills from reading it."
—**ROSE MOLEUS, UNITED STATES**

"*RED* is wonderful and exciting and I love it."
—**EDIDIONG GODWIN EMAH, NIGERIA**

NICOLE COLLET

RED
A LOVE STORY

SOMETHING
OR OTHER
PUBLISHING

ISBN 13: 978-0-9846938-4-9

Library of Congress Control Number: 2015946566

Printed in the United States of America
First Printing: 2015
19 18 17 16 15   5 4 3 2 1

Cover design by Eleanor Leonne Bennett
Interior design by James Monroe Design, LLC

Info@SOOPLLC.com

For bulk orders e-mail: Orders@SOOPLLC.com

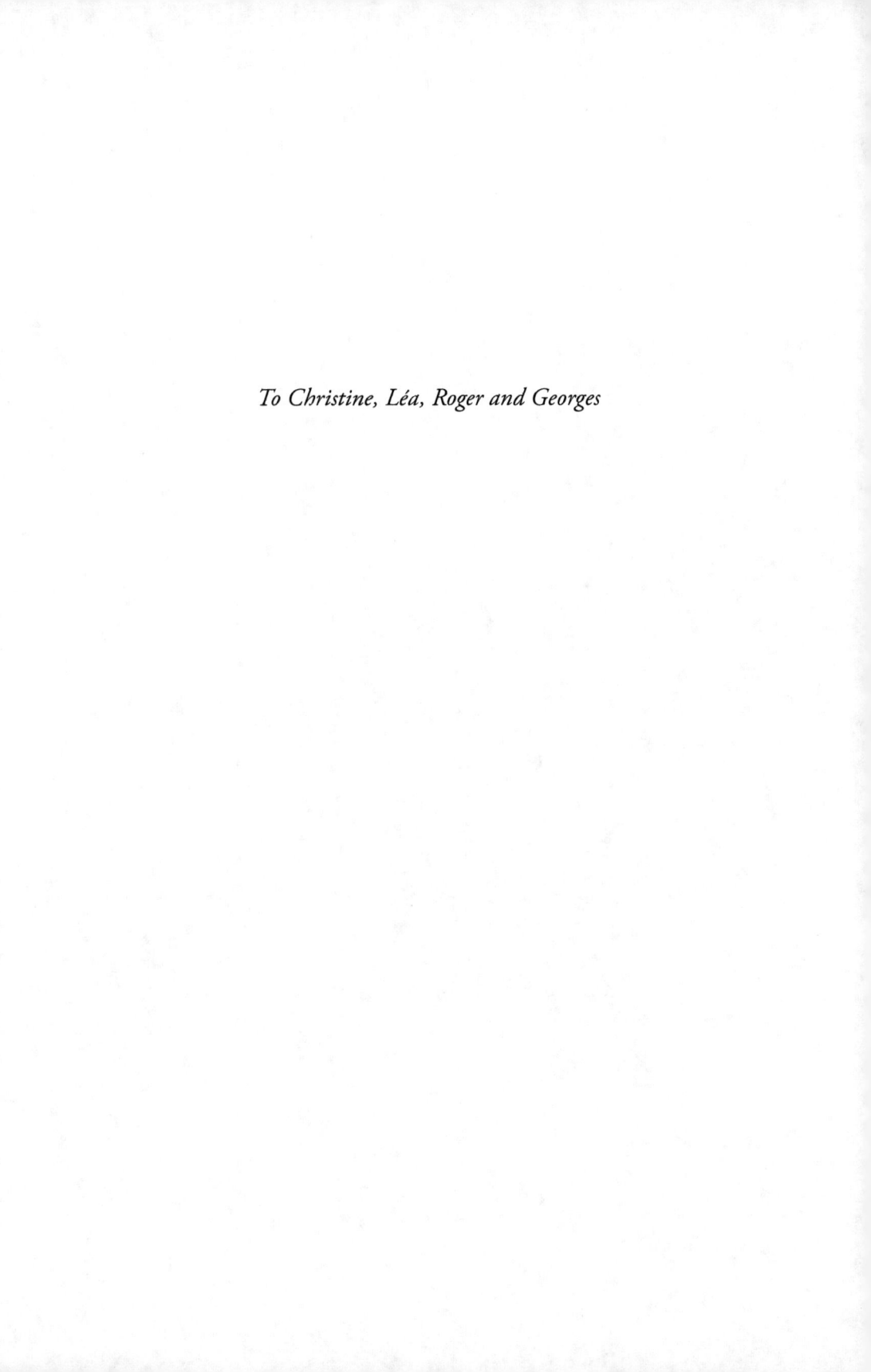

To Christine, Léa, Roger and Georges

CONTENTS

A Note About Music / *ix*

PART 1 | White: Welcome to the Surface

1. Drink This Moment to the Last Drop *3*
2. Hobbits and Sexual Deviations from A to Z *10*
3. What's Up With Sartre *20*
4. This Is the Text *28*
5. Signs, Bonbons and Siderodromophilia *32*
6. Strategic Pause *37*
7. Tropical Rain *44*
8. Rolling the Die *51*
9. Dream a Little Dream of Me *60*
10. A Prank *64*
11. Close Encounter of the Third Kind *70*
12. Duet Story *78*
13. There Won't Be Roses *83*
14. Carnival *89*
15. After Hours *96*
16. The Graduation *104*
17. Behind the Peephole *114*
18. A Shadow of Doubt *121*

PART 2 | Black: A Plunge Into the Abyss

1. A Well Stares at the Sky *131*
2. The Chase *136*
3. The Taming *141*
4. Doctor Spitzer *144*
5. The Number One *148*
6. White Circle, Black Square *152*
7. Something Different *157*
8. Miracle Fruit *163*
9. In the Bedroom *170*

PART 3 | Red: Black and White Converge

1. Turning the Page *177*
2. The Light Inside Your Eyes *184*
3. Serendipity *195*
4. Wear Flowers in Your Hair 198
5. The Kashmir Lounge *201*
6. A New Day *210*
7. The Leather Dream Fair I *214*
8. The Leather Dream Fair II *221*
9. The Ball at the Devil's Lair 226
10. A Little Surprise *231*
11. Dopamine + Pheromone = Nonsense *235*
12. The Devil Laughs 243
13. Nostalgia 250
14. Frontiers 254
15. Vertigo 258

CONTENTS

16. Speaking of Love. *261*

17. Two Ships Sailing the Night 268

18. Denial. *275*

19. Full Circle. *276*

Appendix: Poems & Works / *281*

Acknowledgements / *283*

A Word from the Author / *285*

A NOTE ABOUT MUSIC

I love music and when I'm writing I can't help it: songs pop into my head and migrate to my story. I had initially included many lyrics when I wrote this novel, some of them even threaded into paragraphs. I removed them all to avoid copyright infringement. But those emptied portions still ached for lyrics, and the solution was to create my own lyrics or use public domain material.

As an exception, small portions of Brazilian lyrics are included, under fair use in accordance with Brazil's copyright law.

I still mention song titles and artists for an obvious reason: they comprise the soundtrack to this story and I invite readers to listen to them. Most are favorites of mine, beautiful songs that touch the soul or fun tracks that make you want to dance.

I do not wish to misinterpret the lyrics of those songs, so please keep in mind that the lyrics used in this story (except for Brazilian material) are not the actual lyrics of the songs mentioned nor hold any similarity to them, except for occasionally adopting the same general theme. They are used to enhance the atmosphere of certain scenes, or translate what characters feel and think while listening to those songs.

The four words in Urdu are merely a translation of the English title of a song with Urdu lyrics. It's included here to give an idea of how that language sounds.

The full credits and sources for quoted material are found in the Appendix.

By the way, the paraphilia encyclopedia mentioned here is fictitious. The sexual deviations in it are not.

Red symbolizes extremes: it dresses the Pope just like it paints the Devil. The first visible color in the light spectrum, it signals passion—which is nothing more than the extremes of joy and pain.

PART 1

WHITE:
WELCOME TO THE SURFACE

Spring, November

1. Drink This Moment to the Last Drop

The night was an empty house. Its lights bore lone reflections, and its sounds, belated echoes of a distant thunder. Those who came in and walked out at daytime hadn't left any marks. Now a bluish mist lingered there carrying a green smell of moss, the herald of the storm with its unseen horn.

From the pricked-up trees, leaves fell whirling around in a rain dance that mirrored Marisa's disquiet. Cautiously, she advanced on the deserted street with a sudden knot of apprehension. Adrenaline gripped her chest like the claws of a predator. She shivered when her coat half-opened and flapped, ready to take off. Her Mary Jane shoes stamped a solitary voice on the asphalt. *Clog, clog, clog...*

They seemed to be saying: *Stop, stop, stop...* She sped up the pace.

A grayish rat with bloodshot eyes leaped from the curb and startled Marisa. She looked to the sides as she cursed herself for not taking a cab. Rushing around the corner, she followed a wide avenue in downtown São Paulo. Her steps left behind locked buildings and dormant store windows in pitch-black slumber. Marisa only stopped when she reached a quaint building with a blue-tiled façade typical of the fifties.

She rang the bell, all the while pounding one fist on the glass door. The porter recognized her and pressed a button behind a shiny cedar counter. As the door opened, Marisa nodded to the porter and quickly crossed the green marble lobby. On her face blossomed a smile he did not see.

Marisa waited for the elevator, one Mary Jane shoe tap dancing discreetly. She ascended to the fifteenth floor, where she arrived with a slight pant. In the vestibule with no ornaments, the door did not offer resistance when Marisa pushed it to sneak into the dark living room. A shy rectangle of light guided her to the hallway. She stopped before the office, caught her breath, went inside.

As Marisa advanced, the walls lined with books receded into dimness, leaving behind the smell of paper and lavender furniture polisher. The tic-tac of a pendulum clock—methodic, impatient—dotted the silence. Marisa paused in the middle of the room, the sight of Marco imprinted in her retina. All anxiety, all guilt, all fear was forgotten.

The glass shade of the lamp on the desk glowed like a jade lighthouse in the sea of shadows. Behind the green reflection, seated on a high-backed chair, he waited. His eyes, a solid brown on the brink of black, contemplated Marisa even before she entered, picturing her at the sound of each step. In its stillness Marco's body held a torrent, denounced by the gleam in the irises and the way one hand curled on the desk's edge. He bore a dark rather than fair complexion, meditative forehead and mouth drawn with firm lines. His straight, black hair was parted on the side, with a hint of formality that matched his gray slacks, narrow leather belt and white shirt with a loosened silk tie.

Now he rolled up his sleeves in a deliberate manner.

"You are late," he finally said in a stern tone.

"I apologize, Master. It won't happen again."

"This time I'll let it pass. In the future, however, I will not tolerate it. Is that clear?"

"Yes, Master," she replied in a feeble voice.

"You can remove your coat."

She obeyed, revealing what hid underneath—a short navy blue skirt, indigo T-shirt, thigh-high white socks. In that pretended school outfit, her compact build was of a woman. Feeling exposed, slightly abashed, she played with the end of the braid hanging over her shoulder. The luscious hair was straight, the same golden brown as her lowered eyes. The visage emanated the beauty and glow of her eighteen years.

"Now turn," he commanded.

She did as he said, but was reprehended in a sharp note.

"*Slower.*"

Marisa finished turning in a tense motion as he studied her. His incisive gaze paused on the interstice of naked thighs between the skirt hemline and socks. It then trailed up to the breast contours below the V collar and lingered on the lips that she nibbled. His eyes darkened; the pupils dilated. He beckoned her to move closer. Then he stood to his feet and advanced to meet her in front of the desk. Now the two were only a few inches apart.

"On second thought, I am not going to forgive this indiscipline," he said, and now his voice almost dropped to a whisper: "Your behavior disappoints me, Marisa."

"Master, I promise it won't happen again."

"Nevertheless, it already *happened*, Marisa. You have disregarded punctuality. What do you suggest I should do about that?"

He spoke in an affirmative tone—it became clear the answer did not matter. His gaze remained unfathomable. The well-drawn mouth, however, was pressed in a line signaling the path of his intentions.

Marisa stared at him spellbound. Voluptuousness. Uncertainty. The voluptuousness of uncertainty. *Something* would happen soon and she didn't know what it was. She tingled as if hands tantalized her body in no hurry, lingering here and there... here and there... Marisa had no time to react when, without warning, he made her bend over the desk. With one hand, he held her wrists behind her back. With the other, he traced the curve of her hip, first in the front, then on the back, moving around, going up, going down. Up again. And down. Beneath the skirt. Caressing her inner thighs.

With her face on fire and chest heaving, she kept still. The slap landed on the right buttock, then on the left. Marisa clenched her teeth and suppressed a surprised gasp, which was followed by the languor of a sigh: now his fingers touched her feverish skin with the lightness of a breeze, tracing the marks as if contemplating their work. Then they followed the shape of her narrow waist, strolled on the back and twisted the braid, pulling it close to the nape of her neck.

Marisa shivered when his breath caressed her ear: "Next time I won't be so complacent. Don't say you weren't warned."

Marco released Marisa and made her turn around. He framed her face in his big hands, dark eyes sending sparks into hers, mouth hungrily inching closer and closer, until it took hers in a fervent kiss. His left hand searched for the breast over the blouse; the right one found the vertex of the thighs under the skirt. He deepened his fingers there, making her moan, devouring her moan with his tongue and teeth. He knew exactly how to touch her, in the exact measure to counter a firm move with softness. He coaxed, advanced, withdrew to make her want more.

Marisa wanted it. She wanted Marco above everything. Encircling his waist, she drew him nearer, hands sliding beneath his shirt to feel the bare skin, the well-defined muscles, the triangle of the shoulder blades. With her eyes half-closed, she drank the scent of the man and discarded the cologne's. Marisa inhaled the air sharply as she allowed her hands to spread adrift across the strong torso, scratching the skin until they reached the fine hair on the chest… and, farther down, the navel and the zipper line.

The kiss a blaze, tongue against tongue instinctively replicating the gestures of hands, a mad spin inside the mouth consuming the entire body in successive flames that reached further and further—the body's thirst, the body's liqueur. Breasts pressed against the wall of the wide chest, intertwined thighs in a perfect fit. Everything was orchestrated in a sinuous synchronism: lips, tongues, fingers, hips and legs.

Slow legato. Crescendo. Staccato.

With a quiver, he lifted Marisa and sat her on the desk. He pushed aside the clothes in his way, fingers entangled in cotton and lace. Then he completely abandoned himself in her flesh. Marisa opened up to him with a fitful sigh. Her muscles molded to him, contracted around him, clenching and clenching, and he wanted more, deeper, denser, ethereal. More. In the eternity of an instant, the fused bodies pulsed with a spasm, from the core to the solar plexus, to the fingertips, to the roof of the mouth, to the vault of the sky…

They remained in each other's arms and exchanged a long look as their heartbeat quieted.

"Happy birthday," Marisa said, stroking his face.

"That was the best present ever."

Smiling, they finally parted and straightened up their clothes. Marco fixed a russet strand that had broken free from her braid. Marisa pulled him closer and kissed him, still craving. She then picked up her coat from the chair.

"I have to go home, Marco."

"So soon? I've prepared dinner for us."

"Oh, what a shame."

Frustration transpired on her countenance. It wasn't lesser than his frustration. Marisa tried to be practical: "But it's late, and my mom is getting increasingly suspicious of my absences. And I still need to study for the literature exam tomorrow, remember? Truth is, I shouldn't even be here tonight, but I had to see you… I think we're both a bit crazy, eh?"

"Yeah… I think so, love." Now he gave half a smile. Only half. "I wouldn't want to harm a model student like you. Let's go, then."

Let's go. Neither of them moved toward the door. They inhabited a fragile crystal terrarium, a landscape within the landscape that could come crumbling down at any moment. The coat returned to the chair, and they embraced like castaways.

"On Saturday we'll celebrate properly. I got you something, but I couldn't bring it along because it would draw attention." Marisa paused. She blurted out: "I can't stand this anymore. Having to hide is just horrible. I feel like a criminal. And what have we done, after all? We didn't kill or steal or covet the neighbor's wife…"

"I know, Mari, I'm not happy with this either. But didn't you say yourself that a few weeks were nothing compared to eternity and we should enjoy the present?"

"Did I say that? See, love, the problem is sometimes I don't listen to my own advice." She laughed with faint conviction. "I wanted you so much, and now I'm scared of what may happen."

"Let's be patient. It'll soon be over."

Marco caressed her hair with one hand while his gaze caressed all of her. His Venus. The star that brought the colors of a new day and kept surprising Marco with the familiarity irradiating from her face. He had recognized it since the beginning, even though he had never seen it before. It was the face of someone he had sought for a long time. In her arms the turbulence of the past dissolved into a distant clamor. He had a partner now, and that certainty still stunned him. Marco never grew tired of gazing at her because he never grew tired of recognizing her. His partner.

Marisa relaxed for a moment as she looked into his eyes. She saw so many things in them that the mere possibility of being apart from him made her gasp for air. How could she describe everything contained in those eyes? Inside them played a music box with the melody of endless conversations, furtive escapes to eat in Arabic delis, plans to visit a valley sprinkled with quartzes that glimmered in the moonlight. And the bedroom games, as he called them, in which she discovered herself more and more—a woman.

He blinked. In that lapse, the last quartz glimmered, died away, and all vanished. Time to go. The world outside awaited with the usual reproach. She looked into Marco's eyes once more to say goodbye to everything they contained, and pulled back at last.

"Well, I'm gonna put the wig on. I almost forgot it."

Marisa grabbed her purse and disappeared down the hall to check herself in the bedroom mirror. She returned with her long hair hidden under a mass of false black curls: she had to wear the wig every time the two went out together. Once in the elevator, they stood side by side and shut off any eye contact until finding themselves inside his silver Lexus in the garage. At that time of night there was no traffic, and the streets flew by the car window during ten minutes that passed in ten seconds.

They reached their destination in the traditional Higienópolis neighborhood—trees of generous shade and dogs, bars and universities, a large population of Jews and seniors. Marco stopped on the corner without turning off the engine. Marisa glanced around, removed the wig, stuffed it into her purse. She exited the car and walked down the street past bored porters in their posts while Marco waited for her to get home safely. Marisa paused at a modernist building of geometrical lines emphasized in pastel hues. She discreetly waved at him and rang the bell to the porter.

An electric buzz, a click, and the door opened. Marisa entered the building with reluctance. As soon as she crossed the lobby, the door of the apartment in the back started to open. From the crack emerged the face of an old woman, then her black robe. It was Ms. Rosaura, a small and boney widow of pleasant manners and gray hair with a faint purple tinge. No one could tell, but behind her innocent appearance lived a real professional of domestic intrigue. She resembled a carrion crow croaking with a deep voice, her robe puffing out as she gesticulated, her eyes always attentive to the flicker of an unusual event.

"Marisa, darling, how have you been?" She looked over her shoulder and checked the carillon in the living room. "You're coming home late tonight, huh?"

"Well, Ms. Rosaura, I was studying at a friend's. You know, for college admission exams…"

Marisa gave her a polite smile and mentally traced an escape route. On one side were the stairs; on the other, the elevator and a potted flaming sword plant. If she acted fast, she could reach the elevator parked on the ground floor… or, in a bolder move, begin fencing with the flaming sword to deter her nosy neighbor.

The elderly woman stared at Marisa with determination. They studied each other, initiating a choreography that seemed meticulously rehearsed: one advanced and the other backed off, one went right while the other went left. Desperate, Marisa drew the cell phone from her purse and excused herself to take a call, all the while waving and hurrying into the elevator.

After the sliding door closed, Marisa put the dead phone back in her purse. Ms. Rosaura had been thrown off the scent—now came the worst. Marisa saw thunder shaking walls, electric discharges ricocheting on the chandeliers, lightning bolts falling on the furniture. As she reached the eighth floor, Marisa clasped the coat to her body. She already knew a storm waited for her at home.

2. Hobbits and Sexual Deviations from A to Z

"The Germans are here!"

That precise sentence shook off the rust from the Wheel of Fortune and bumped it into motion in the unstable month of August that year, triggering the events until the paths of Marisa and Marco crossed in latitude -23° 32' 51" and longitude -46° 38' 10" at an altitude of 2,500 feet—that is, in São Paulo, Brazil. In order to understand what the heck the Germans had to do with them, first it is necessary to meet the author of that sentence: Aécio Palamedes, the former literature teacher at the Amaral High School. A ruin of flabbiness, he was almost ninety and had become a local folk character. Despite being retired, he insisted on teaching. The old man just lingered in the school, the years went by and no one ever questioned his permanence there.

It should be noted that in his youth—a long, long, long time ago, before he even discovered his inclination for teaching—Palamedes had fought the Germans in Italy during the Second World War. That fact scarred him for life, and lately brought back memories more vivid than his cloudy present tense. During class, with a trembling hand and one pointy finger, he would get lost in digression that inexplicably circumnavigated the Parnassian poetic to call at the Battle of Monte Castello amid a pyrotechnical grenade explosion.

One morning, in the end of August, a couple of cars collided in front of the school. Hearing the loud crash, Aécio brayed, "The Germans are here!" and entrenched himself under his desk until two janitors managed to extract him one hour later.

The school administration finally released him from his duties for an indefinite period. Hired to replace him, Marco Aurélio Fares stepped into the scene three weeks later. It was a dull Thursday—the students texted and yawned with their eyes already set on the weekend—and thus it didn't take long for the buzz to spread throughout the corridors like a shot (to use his predecessor's favorite terminology).

"Did you see the new literature teacher, Val?" Marisa asked her friend Valentina during intermission.

"Not yet. But I'm sure I'm gonna love him. I couldn't take another word about the Battle of Monte Castello."

"Well, I just saw him going inside the teachers' office. The school did the full upgrade: he's hot," Marisa said.

"As long as he doesn't talk about the war nor show me grenade injuries on his foot, I'll find him hot too," was her friend's reply.

Marco certainly brought a breath of fresh air to the school's strict environment. The institution's physical space alone spoke volumes. Built like a prison surrounded by tall walls, it bore a soul of cement. For the circulation between the three floors in the main building, there were two stairways: in the past, one reserved to the girls and the other to the boys. Decades and decades of traditionalism were ingrained in the walls and floors of the institution.

The progressive aura of the new literature teacher, paired with his privileged intellect, irradiated an irresistible brilliance there. During his very first class, nine out of ten high school girls began lusting for him. Marco was exactly twenty-nine years old and had a disconcertingly charming dimple on his square chin. Tall and well-proportioned, with charismatic eyes rimmed by black eyelashes, he played the role of a deus ex machina appearing onstage with his educational methods (and other extracurricular endowments) to save the girls from endless boredom.

There he stood on the podium, a Clark Kent with long legs and emphatic hands opening his shirt to reveal the Man of Steel with a dab of the Dark Knight's tormented sensuality, the God of Thunder's Olympian majesty, and... (here, each student would sigh and fill the blank with their own preferences, which could encompass anything from Johnny Depp's smirk to a juicy bowl of strawberries with cream). In his first class, literature was reborn from the ashes of the Second World War as Marco guided the students on a journey through different eras—starting in Homer's ancient period, when words were capitalized and strung together in manuscripts, until reaching the digital era, characterized by the atomization of language in unimaginable contractions.

"Think about how far we've come, from words strung together to text messaging," Marco concluded. "How does that affect our brain and our behavior? Today everything is not only ephemeral but changes too fast. Nobody can predict what the world will be like in five years and how future technologies will affect people's lives. Now the challenge is producing literature capable of defining our time."

Marisa listened in fascination, soaking in his words. Her passion for books had bravely survived the massacre promoted by Palamedes and now grew stronger in that class. She gazed at Marco with gratitude. More than gratitude: enchantment. While the class fell into silence, Marisa raised her hand and spoke:

"According to your reasoning, wouldn't indefiniteness be the very definition of our time? Literature today, as a reflex of those accelerated changes, already defines our time precisely in its difficulty to define it." Her voice trembled imperceptibly as she felt suddenly shy before Marco. Clearing her throat, she continued: "That would be the same as omission, for example. Just like action, it also brings consequences and therefore can be considered a form of action... right?"

He smiled and thought for a second before answering. Then the bell rang announcing the end of class and several students surrounded Marco to ask questions. Marisa stood up in an impulse but refrained from approaching him and sat down again.

"Val, I think I'm in love," Marisa joked, and for an instant she couldn't tell if that was really a joke or if it was serious.

"Then go talk to him, Miss Constant," Valentina encouraged her, not without a note of amusement. "The girls are like demented groupies around him. Next thing you know, they're gonna be asking for autographs."

"I'd rather wait till the next time. Too many people over there. It's pathetic. Look how Camila leaps forward... There she goes... pushing past Andrea, in between Júlio and Helena... Bingo, she throws herself at the teacher."

"Typical."

"Typical," agreed Marisa with a sting of jealousy.

The following class, Marco mentioned *The Lord of the Rings* and piqued her interest in the books. Such a classic work deserved to be read in print, accompanied by authentic English tea served in Royal Worcester porcelain, Marisa thought. So during intermission she rushed to the school library to get the trilogy and found the first two volumes. She savored them for exactly thirteen days along with a half gallon of Earl Grey. Sunday ended with the last chapter.

To her despair, when Marisa went back for the third tome on Monday, it hadn't been returned yet. She hurried to the city library right after the last afternoon class. There, the much sought tome was happily found. She intended to ask for it at the counter when she remembered a compendium of sexual perversions Valentina had mentioned.

Moments later Marisa requested both copies from the librarian on duty, a thin old man with thick glasses who eyed her gravely and, without a word, disappeared into a maze of bookcases. He returned with the third volume of J. R. R. Tolkien's trilogy and vanished again.

Avidly, Marisa leafed through the book and was so absorbed she didn't hear her own name being called. Someone touched her shoulder. Someone with long legs and narrow hips, broad shoulders and a gleam of onyx in the eyes. With a startle, she found Marco leaning against the counter. He looked different. In his jeans and black leather jacket, off the teacher pedestal, he seemed more accessible yet more intimidating now that he stood so close.

Her voice faltered and her heart pounded. Everything happened too quickly. He showed the rare edition of lyric poetry he was returning, a blue-cover book with yellowed pages that Marisa barely registered amid her surprise. Before Marco's inquisitive stare, she indicated *The Lord of the Rings*. He grinned and asked if she was enjoying the book.

Marisa didn't have time to answer, for the librarian emerged from the dusty shadows carrying the compendium of erotic eccentricities (black cover, bright red title) and placed it on the counter with a dry *thump!*

Marco's gaze fell on the huge letters of the title: *Sexual Paraphilia from A to Z*. He frowned. Marisa blushed and immediately hid the compendium under *The Lord of the Rings* while clumsily filling the forms for both books. Marco pretended not to notice her embarrassment and resumed talking about fairies and elves. Marisa shoved the books into her handbag, and they left the library. As the two were heading in the same direction, they walked together on the busy street, and she noticed he assumed a protective attitude by staying on the outer part of the sidewalk. The teacher was a gentleman, concluded Marisa with a secretive smile.

They turned the corner and zigzagged along pedestrian streets overflowing with people and booths stuffed with colorful clothes. Under old lampposts covered in ads for jobs, sat men in vests that read "I buy gold." At certain spots, clearings would open up where street artists performed surrounded by a curious crowd. The soundtrack kept changing, along with the artists and food smells from snack bars and restaurants. Here the aroma of cheese bread and a loud funk beat accompanying a female dancer in shorts, there a vapor of Greek barbecue and the chant of three Hare Krishnas, further down Kung Pao chicken, Andean music, pizza, samba, Portuguese pastries, African percussion…

In a given moment, Marco retained Marisa. They stood in the middle of the pedestrian whirlpool on Barão de Itapetininga Street.

"Have you noticed in Downtown there are two superimposed cities? Look," he said, pointing up.

On the ground level sprouted the chaotic São Paulo of contradictions: siren song, well-oiled machine, pit of dirt, stage for beauty, box of surprises. In the upper floors, however, a different city came to view in a landscape of historical buildings that sheltered the heaving stores below. It was like emerging from a tank packed with fish to reach the quiet azure. Up above, the sounds silenced and time took a step back in a realm of sober balconies with iron railings, arched windows, neoclassical capitals and imposing towers. Against the sky, a centennial tree top evoked the days when São

Paulo was greener.

"That's the Peace Building from 1913, which used to host the Viennese Pastry Shop. It was the spot for the high society and the intellectuals involved in the Art Week of 1922." Marco indicated a four-story neoclassical building with a light brown façade and ornate balconies. He then pointed to a modernist edifice opposite to it, which exhibited large V columns and a white façade of perforated blocks. "And that's the California Gallery, an Oscar Niemeyer project from the fifties. Inside, there's a mural by painter Cândido Portinari."

"It's incredible how we can walk in such a hurry and never look up," commented Marisa as she admired the gallery. "It's as if São Paulo were a lady from the waist up and a slut from the waist down. Can you imagine if *The Lord of the Rings* was set here?"

"That's impossible. The plot would take a thousand years to advance."

"Why?"

"Because of traffic."

Both laughed and kept walking. They resumed the conversation about Tolkien's trilogy and, when passing by a bar, Marco invited her for a cup of coffee. The two went inside a tiny, old-fashioned place like so many downtown, with dark wooden paneling and a U-shaped counter. Behind it, shelves laden with bottles containing beverages of extravagant colors and obscure provenance. The bar also offered a true Italian espresso machine, which dispatched white cups exhaling arabesques of fragrant vapor.

Marisa noticed all those things without dwelling on them. Her attention focused on what Marco was saying and, at each word, her admiration for his intellect grew (now he told that Middle Earth had actually been created to serve as a cradle for all the languages invented by Tolkien). His company gave her... contentment. Yes, she felt content, and wondered: what did that invitation for coffee mean?

Marisa couldn't deny she was a bit nervous, but the conversation flowed with such an ease that soon her nervousness dissipated. They sat at a small table on the sidewalk and Marco ordered lemon pie with the coffee. The two of them pushed the meringue aside at the same time (too sweet) and, as they ate, talked about the upcoming college admission exams.

Playing with the end of her braid, Marisa complained about the pressure to choose a profession. She didn't have a clue: she liked literature, dance and psychology; her mom insisted that she study law.

"Sometimes I think of Pierre Anthon, the character from *Nothing* by Janne Teller," Marisa said. "He climbed a plum tree and refused to come down, stating nothing mattered. He did the math: if we live to the age of eighty and deduct all the time spent sleeping, studying, working, cleaning and taking care of our children, we're only left with about nine years to enjoy. Then why worry so much?"

"The secret is to enjoy everything, Marisa, even the most ordinary moments. Neither the greatest joys nor the greatest sorrows last, so it's no use getting attached to them. All things pass, right? What remains is ourselves. So balance and motivation should come from within us."

As Marco spoke, she nodded slowly, absorbing his words. She liked what he said.

"True." Marisa emptied her cup. "Life is constantly oscillating and we oscillate with it. Like puppets. The string of an event lifts us up and we are merry, then another string pulls us down and we fall into depression. We have no control over life. The only thing we can control is our own selves."

"See? There you go. You've already answered your own question. Cultivate your inner balance so you no longer oscillate. And, if everything else fails, remember the first law of the galaxy: don't panic."

"Oh, it's the line from *The Hitchhiker's Guide to the Galaxy*! I love that book, Marco."

"Me too. In that case, we both know the answer to the meaning of life and everything else, eh?" he said with a solemn expression, contradicted by the humorous note in his voice. "But seriously, don't fall for the temptation of choosing a profession just to please your family. As Sartre once said, hell is other people. You could take a vocational test for guidance. The main thing is finding what motivates you. What's your passion?"

You, Marisa thought, gazing into his eyes. The thought just clicked but did not surprise her. It filled instead each empty corner of her mind and of her heart. *You*. And overflowed. She left his eyes and began observing him from that new perspective, which was not so different from the perspective a few minutes ago, just more complete. Complex.

She observed how Marco laid his elbows on the table, projecting the strong arms toward her. Marisa got distracted at the sight of the dark hands with long fingers—while they moved, his hands showed accuracy, and in a resting position, like now, they were comforting. She imagined what their touch would be like, the warmth of those hands on her body. Maybe in a dance, slowly sliding on Marisa's waist and back, welcoming her with a stroke from top to bottom... from top... to bottom... to top... until crowning her queen with the diadem of a caress on her hair.

Marco smiled encouragingly, kindling her imagination further— what it would be like to feel his mouth, his kiss... maybe in the bedroom, tracking every inch of her, the dress asleep on the rug while Marco awakened the female in her against the wall. The world spinning and spinning out of control...

Marisa bit her lip and tried to concentrate on the conversation. Marco offered to send her a list of professionals who would be able to help her define a vocation. He asked for her email, which she spelled out as he typed in his cell phone.

And little by little the world went back to normal.

"Be cool," he said, dropping the phone on the table. "Once you are on the right path, the Universe will make things happen and all pieces of the puzzle will fall into place."

There was a pause. Be cool? Marisa no longer knew what that meant. The twinges of disquiet created small scars that kept merging and spreading and covering all of her. Then she tried to ignore the disquiet and pretended everything was fine in the hope that the world would convince her of that. It didn't.

"You're quite mature for a seventeen-year-old, you know?" Marco said, breaking the silence.

"I just turned eighteen last month," Marisa rectified quickly, and blushed at his intent gaze.

"September." He reflected for an instant. "So you're a Libra?"

"Uh-huh. Now I only need some balance. What about you?"

"Scorpio. Maybe I could use some balance too."

They exchanged a smile.

"Anyway," she added, "I probably look older because I'm an only child raised among adults and books. My dad was a bookworm. He used to read stories for me as far as I can remember."

"And you live with your parents, Marisa?"

"No, it's just me and Mom. My dad is deceased."

Marco nodded and said nothing. Marisa was grateful that he would spare her of the embarrassment. She hadn't even attended the funeral. It had been six months since her father passed away, and the last time she saw him, he was perfectly well. He even joked about mosquitoes: *If one bites you, my dear, don't kill it or else ten more will show up for the burial.*

The day Marisa received the news, it was a shock. The empty hours went by like a surreal dream. Her mother wouldn't say it, but she clung to the details evoking his presence. The blue robe and the toothbrush in the bathroom. The unfinished crosswords on the desk, next to a half-empty cup with cold coffee. None of that could be touched: the objects came to a standstill, as if in wait for him to return. Then Marisa, unknowing, washed the cup and put it away, causing her mother to have a nervous breakdown…

"Hey, would you like another cup of coffee?"

It took her a few seconds to understand what Marco was saying. She acted as if trying to decide.

"Yes, please. Now tell me about yourself."

He signaled to the passing waiter and ordered more coffee. Then he lit up a cigarette before answering. He was the third son in a family of mixed Italian and Lebanese roots, quite Brazilian at that point after three generations. His mother possessed Calabrese blood and a big personality that rivaled his father's stubbornness. That triggered huge, sometimes even comical quarrels, but in the end they would always work things out. Marco had many aunts and uncles. His favorite, Uncle Jamil, owned three farms, where Marco and his brothers spent their vacations when they were boys. Marco had been raised in the countryside, catching blind cave fish, riding horses, and eating jabuticaba berries from the tree until he almost burst. He moved to the capital on his own at eighteen to study letters: he loved literature.

"They're playing your song," said Marisa, as she listened to the delicate chords coming from inside the bar.

"Which song?"

"Bebel Gilberto's *Jabuticaba*."

And the atmosphere of the music involved them.

If you were a fruit, it would be jabuticaba…

A small sphere of soft honey the color of the night, a summer whiff to be savored under the stars.

"Jabuticaba eyes. Dark and shiny like yours." She smiled. "What else?"

"Ah. I married a college mate, then got divorced, completed my Master studies here in São Paulo and went for my PhD in San Francisco." He recited the list as if handing a resume, then proceeded to the current occupation and relaxed. "After I returned from the US earlier this year, I moved to an apartment close by. I like the stories the old downtown buildings tell. And I love walking to the second-hand shops to dig up classic jazz albums. Do you like jazz?"

Summer breeze in the sweet fruit, and in your gaze the stars…

The day slipped away quietly. Their cups emptied, the bar filled up and the waiter became slightly annoyed that the two wouldn't leave. It was not summer yet, but up above, way beyond the strings of lights intersecting on the streets—the stars were glowing.

3. What's Up With Sartre

"Four hours… thirty-one minutes… nine seconds… That is when… the world will end," Sam muttered pensively.

"What are we gonna do?" Rachel swallowed up her own desperation.

Sam did not respond straight away. He needed to think. Massaging his temples, he kept his eyes fixed on the implacable Control Room chronometer. The countdown continued: eight seconds… seven… six…

Rachel glanced at the door.

"We better leave before the guards show up, Sam."

"Wait a minute. I think I know how to cancel the attack."

Sam pressed a blue key on the control panel. Then he suddenly hesitated. Right below it, there were a yellow key and a green key. Which one validated neutralization? Now that he had initiated the command sequence, if he stopped the alarm would go off.

He couldn't fail. The fate of mankind rested on the next key.

Lean and tall, Sam had trained in martial arts for the past decade. His body translated into pure muscular mass, but all his strength was useless now. He scratched his well-trimmed beard, and his dark eyes sparked. Noticing his frustration, Rachel stared at him with a pair of eyes as perfect and blue as snips of autumn sky. Since the facial reconstruction to change her identity, she felt like a Barbie doll. She missed her old face, more asymmetric, more like herself. It was the price to stay alive, though.

"What if you tried the red key?" she risked.

"I don't know which command it activates. I thought of the blue and green keys because the secret code mentioned *jungle* and *sea*. Now I recall it also mentioned a great *sun…*

As Sam and Rachel studied the keys on the black panel, the speakers built into the ceiling hummed a Mozart sonata, muffling the guard's approach. He sneaked behind them and drew his gun…

Rachel's scream echoed through the Control Room.

Marisa woke up with a startle and paused the film streaming on the computer screen. She had dozed off with her head on the physics text book, next to a plate holding the mortal remains of a bunch of jabuticaba berries. Dizzy, Marisa scratched her eyes and checked the clock: almost half past ten. She reached out to turn the computer off, and then remembered…

The mouse cursor steered away from the Shutdown button and, with the eagerness of a sniffer dog, advanced through fields of folders, bypassed flowery shortcuts and trotted to the canopy of tabs in the browser. There, it finally burrowed into the inbox and gave her another startle upon finding a message from Marco Aurélio Fares to Marisa Constant.

Hi, Marisa,

As promised, attached is a list of recommended professionals.

This period of life can be difficult, I know, but you'll overcome it. Here's another phrase to inspire you. In Existentialism Is a Humanism, *Sartre quotes Descartes: Conquer yourself rather than the world.*

Good luck!

Marco

Now, how should she respond? Talk about writer's block. She would begin a line, change her mind, and erase it. It had to look casual, but not *that* casual… Hmm. Perhaps she should deliberately include a typo to convey spontaneity. Hmm. Better not, or Marco might think she couldn't spell. One thing was certain: she wanted to impress him.

Marisa quickly checked out Wikipedia and learned that, according to Jean-Paul Sartre's philosophical system, existence preceded essence. What did it mean? People began to exist at birth and only then their essence formed, so a person had total freedom to mold their essence as they wished, through actions and thoughts. Hmm. *Freedom.* At last, Marisa came up with a reply that satisfied her.

Hi, Marco,

Thanks a lot for the list and the words of encouragement. I really liked the quote by Sartre.

The quote you mentioned earlier, "Hell is other people," got stuck in my head. Other people can really make our lives hell with their demands. We shouldn't become slaves to that, but mold our essence according to our rightful freedom.

Regards,
Marisa

Would Marco write again? Only then it occurred to her she should have asked him something in the email, that way he would be compelled to reply. Marisa hurried to undo the sending of the message, but to no avail. Her words were already swiftly sailing through cyberspace.

Now she was wide awake...

There were only three hours left to the end of the world. Three hours. And then the Earth would be cremated with no right to a funeral wreath or memorial service. The future of the planet lay now in the hands of two improbable fugitives.

After disarming the guard and locking him in the Power House, Sam and Rachel burrowed in the tentacles of an underground tunnel complex. Suddenly, the alarm bawled with a continuous siren and the lights went out. Then an eerie silence reigned.

"They found out we're here!" Rachel flattened herself against the wall, trying not to panic.

"They're gonna kill us to make sure we don't ruin their master plan. We need a place to hide," said Sam.

He turned his cell phone on to illuminate the tunnel, and the metallic walls shimmered under the device's cold light. As the pair advanced, the darkness kept devouring the dim clarity and regurgitating more shadows. Sam's experienced eyes, however, located a door ahead. Taking Rachel by the hand, he rushed to it.

"Sam, where are we—"

Rachel tripped and fell onto the stone floor. She grimaced and bit her lip to avoid screaming. Tears meandered across her face.

"Are you okay?" Sam helped Rachel stand up, while she shook her head.

"I twisted my ankle… It's really hurting. I can't walk."

"Hold the cell phone to shine the way."

Rachel did as told, and Sam lifted her in his arms with ease. They reached the door and entered a weaponry storage room with piles of crates up to the ceiling. Sam found a niche in the back and carefully laid Rachel on the floor, sitting next to her.

She uttered the question he didn't want to ask himself: "So this is how it all ends?" Her face glistened in the dim light. "We're gonna die here like rats?"

A silence charged with meaning followed.

Sam held Rachel's hand while more tears welled up her eyes. They were cornered. Inside the mousetrap.

In that moment, desperation fueled the mutual attraction they had felt since the beginning. The warmth of their bodies was like a balm, a reaffirmation of life in the deadly setting around them.

In the quietness of the storage room, they sought each other's lips…

The close-up of the impending kiss froze on the screen when Marisa interrupted the film again. Her inbox tab had just highlighted incoming messages: a Facebook friend inviting her to watch a movie, a petition against the use of fur forwarded by Valentina, a dance class promotion and… yes, Marco Aurélio's reply!

Marisa,

I'm happy you're interested in Sartre. That's a quote from No Exit. *Its interpretation, however, is a bit different from what you've imagined.*

Let's start with a couple of basic philosophy concepts: subject and object.

The subject is that who observes. The object is the observed thing. In other words: when you look at another person, you are the subject and they are the object of your gaze. But the opposite is also true: if another person looks at you, they're the subject and you become the object. That's when things get tricky.

As a subject, you're the center of your own subjective world and are able to control it. As an object, you lose control and thus your freedom of choice: you cannot control the subjective world of who's looking at you nor can you choose how the other person sees you.

Hell is other people because it's unsettling not to have control over what people think about us. A typical example of this would be racism, as well as prejudice in general.

Another line from No Exit *illustrates this idea:*

Now I'm going to smile, and my smile will sink down in your pupils, and heaven knows what it will become.

M.

Marisa felt embarrassed for delivering such a simplistic interpretation in her previous message and decided to research the matter more extensively. While reading a long article about the existentialist theories by the French philosopher, she was introduced to the *being-in-itself,* the *being-for-itself* and (as if there weren't already plenty) the *being-for-others.* Her brain, knocked out in a dark alley by a gang of physics formulas, did not stand a chance and shuffled it all... Oh-oh, she shouldn't follow that route or she would write some *larger-than-existence* nonsense. Marisa decided to call Valentina for an emergency consultation.

"Check out Marco's email that I forwarded to you, Val. Tell me what you think."

"He has already emailed you?" asked Valentina, who was aware of their encounter at the library that afternoon. "Wait a sec. I'm gonna read the message thread... He's repeating that hell is other people. What's the big deal?" Her skepticism would discourage even a stony statue.

"What's the big deal? In the last quote he's *smiling at me!"*

On the other end of the connection, Marisa heard her puff... or maybe it was the TV on.

"My dear, your imagination never ceases to amaze me. Marco is talking about Sartre. There couldn't be anything *less romantic.* Hellooo, do you remember Sartre, the guy who wrote *Nausea?"*

"I was the one who told you about that book. I tried to read it during my last vacation and couldn't stand it."

"That's it, say no more. You took *Nausea* to read at the *beach.* It's the glaring proof of your lack of discernment."

"I was curious, is that a crime?" Marisa retorted in a resentful tone. She defended herself: "Don't forget, later I downloaded that Gabriel Emerson book."

"Okay, it's all in the past. It doesn't change a thing, though. Only you could find romance in a discussion about *hell* and *nausea*."

Ignoring her remark, Marisa insisted—what should she reply? Desperate, she had resorted to a quote website. She found, respectively, two phrases from *Nausea* and one from *Being and Nothingness*. The first went like this: "It's quite a job starting to love somebody." A bit negative... The second was "I exist, that is all, and I find it nauseating." Too dramatic... The third affirmed, "The sole power of the past lies in the future" (that one she didn't quite understand). Marisa talked and blabbered and insisted so much Valentina interrupted her with a lament.

"Ma, please, no more. It's past midnight, and I can't take this talk of love, nausea and power any longer. Why don't you lighten up? Choose some different author to quote."

Marisa's eyes gleamed.

"Which author, Val?"

"I don't know. Try something from *Jonathan Livingston Seagull*—"

"Seriously?"

"—or *The Little Prince*—"

"Val!"

The conversation went on like that, and it would have continued for considerable time if Valentina hadn't broken the dire cycle: "Listen, if you want to flirt with the teacher, it's no use buttering him up with saccharine. That way you'll only succeed in giving him diabetes. You know very well with which *head* men think. Be bold."

Marisa was going to ask for a proper clarification when there was a knock on the door.

"Wait a sec, it's my mom," she said in a low voice. Then aloud: "Come in."

The mother's head popped in—pale face, brown hair tied in a bun. Her body, wrapped in a faint pink robe, followed. She leaned against the door frame with one hand on the knob, her suspicious eyes roaming the room.

It was her daughter's territory, where she kept her secrets. All white, with sparse furniture consisting of a built-in closet, bed, nightstand, and bookshelf with a desk. That laconic whiteness, colored only by the books squeezed on shelves, offended the mother's aesthetic sense. She glanced with instinctive hostility at the only occupant of the bare walls: a black and white poster of a shirtless Jim Morrison opening his arms above the bed.

Then the mother turned to Marisa: "I thought you were already asleep, and then I heard you—"

"I'm on the phone." Marisa concealed her impatience, while the mother frowned and pursed her lips.

"With Valentina, is it?"

"Yeah. I have a question for her before finishing a physics exercise."

The mother looked at the book on the desk, made an analytical pause and appeared to be convinced. The muscles on her face relaxed, although uneven lines still showed on her forehead, which remained slightly creased.

"I'm going to bed. I don't know why, I feel so tired today." She cast another glimpse at the room, as if expecting to catch a silhouette hidden behind the curtains. "Good night."

"Good night."

The door closed. Marisa waited for a moment and resumed her consultation: "Bol—?"

The door reopened, this time at half capacity, and the mother squeezed her head through the gap.

"Before you go to sleep, take that plate to the kitchen and throw the leftovers in the bin so not to attract bugs," she instructed like a general, indicating the jabuticaba skins. Then her tone mellowed: "If you're hungry, I just baked some bread for tomorrow."

"I will, and thanks."

The mother retreated with a nod. Marisa listened to her footsteps trailing off in the hallway and concluded that the night watch was complete.

"Bold?" Marisa repeated anxiously to Valentina.

"Yeah." She yawned on the other end. "You pick a suggestive quote and go straight to the point, no detours."

Boldness was not one of the main traits in Marisa's personality—at least, not that sort of boldness exhibited by her classmate Camila, with her cleavage waving at all men that passed by. Still, Marisa researched other quotes by Sartre and eventually found one that seemed viable. She wrote a short message (straight to the point), took a deep breath and sent it.

Minutes later, she received a text message from Valentina.

On a second thought, don't send anything compromising. If the teacher doesn't like it, you'll find yourself in a tight situation. Now I'm going to bed. Hugs, Val.

Her blood pressure plummeted, and Marisa felt like the most inadequate of all creatures. She thought of a cheap hotel with a sad bathroom disguised as a bedroom: the porcelain fixtures replaced by third-rate furniture, a thin layer of paint on the tiles, and a reminiscent faucet by the bed beside a moldy painting from the dollar store... Her hands grew sticky, her blood turned into cold water gagging in creaky pipes. That was what she got for going against her own nature. She wasn't *bold*. Why hadn't she just sent a quote about the being-in-itself or something? Oh, no, she had to listen to crazy Valentina and send *that* quote...

Marisa hurried back to her mailbox and, in utter distress, tried to cancel the message.

Of course she didn't succeed.

4. This Is the Text

The next morning, when the two met in the hall, Marco walked past Marisa in a hurry and nodded without stopping. She entered the classroom with simmering thoughts and couldn't concentrate on anything. As she completed trigonometry exercises (she got them all wrong), Marisa kept asking herself: hadn't he read her message yet? Or maybe he had, and found it annoying? brusque? conceited? disappointing? exasperating? foolish? gauche? hilarious? infantile…? Oh dear. She could go through the whole dictionary and would never know.

The next-to-last class was literature. Marisa pretended to pay attention to the exposition, all the while scrutinizing Marco to see if he looked at her in any different way. He remained perfectly neutral. In truth, Marisa had the impression Marco hardly looked at her. As the class neared the end, she thought of going to the front of the room to probe his reaction. Why not? The situation couldn't get any worse.

Soon he gathered his belongings and prepared to leave the classroom. Marisa stared at him, uncertain, throat dry, heart pounding. She had only a few seconds to make a move. Marco had already closed his briefcase and was drawing away from the desk. In a flash, Marisa stood up and advanced amid the chairs, while furiously trying to come up with an excuse to approach him. Desperation suggested the perfect question: he had mentioned the sensation caused by the Modern Art Week of 1922 for breaking paradigms, which included the fact that composer Villa Lobos wore one shoe and one slipper at the event.

Very well, what was the meaning of that slipper? The mismatched footwear could signify, for example, either the fusion or contrast between the cushioned art of the elite and the spontaneous art of the streets. It would provide a good pretext to extend the conversation should Marco be open to that. *Good job, Marisa!* She had barely congratulated herself, though, when a mule at full gallop seized her carrot: Camila. Within one second, the girl monopolized Marco's attention. Indignant, Marisa hesitated, returned to her seat and watched the scene.

Camila was an older classmate nicknamed "Edible" by the other students because of her curves and the habit of wearing provocative clothes to enhance them. Edible always found an excuse to attend literature classes (like now) in some low-necked top, which served as a shop window to her pale bosom and the scandalous golden pendant anchored on it. So she, her cleavage and the pendant asked Marco why composer Villa Lobos had showed up at the Modern Art Week with a shoe in one foot and a slipper in the other. And as Camila spoke, she seductively tossed her long and brown hair—hair that would have been pulverized should irate stares possess minimal pulverizing power (for Marisa addressed the girl such a stare upon hearing her question).

Laughing, Marco explained the fact was interpreted as an affront to the audience, when in reality Villa Lobos had worn the slipper due to an inflamed callus. Marco left the room followed closely by Camila, who remained by his side like a guard dog and now was asking… Marisa couldn't hear the question because the two vanished into the hallway. Shortly afterwards, the physics teacher entered the room and grunted his way to the board as usual. Camila returned a little later, which earned her a lecture that offered Marisa a small consolation.

Nevertheless, Marisa remained furious. She only didn't know if she was more furious with herself or with Valentina. Taking advantage that the teacher had his back to the students, she texted her.

Marco is acting weird with me. Why did you have to give me that stupid piece of advice?

Seated on the chair next to hers, Valentina tried without success to pay attention to class. As soon as she heard her cell phone beep, she read the message and, concealing a smile, typed.

Don't be melodramatic, Ma. I warned you not to send anything compromising.

Yeah, you warned me AFTER you had advised me to send something compromising, countered Marisa.

Calm down. If what you showed me was all you've sent, it's no biggie, wrote Valentina.

It may be no biggie to you, Marisa retorted, typing with a heavy hand. *But Marco... I have no idea of what goes on in his head.*

You know what, Ma? I thought what you wrote was kinda cool.

Suspicious, Marisa gave her a sidelong glance. Valentina raised her eyebrows, shrugged and reciprocated it with an innocent look.

Val, you're a liar. Now you're trying to slip away.

Seriously, Ma, it was cool. Read it again and analyze it.

Marisa didn't need to read it. She knew it by heart: *Marco, I like this phrase by Sartre from* Being and Nothingness: *"To caress with the eyes and to desire are one and the same."*

Valentina could say whatever she wanted, it was no use. The more Marisa thought about it, the worse her embarrassment. Marco taught them classes on Tuesdays and Thursdays, so the following day there would be no literature class for them. Luckily. That way, maybe Marco would forget about her message and things could go back to normal. Maybe, who knows, in the meantime some major event would take place to divert his attention? Like a fire in the school or a nuclear war...

Nonetheless, if Marisa believed she could avoid an encounter with Marco that Wednesday, she was mistaken. The two bumped into each other in the hallway, and this time Marco paused to talk to her. Here, it's important to remember Einstein's wise words: time is relative. It varies according to the rhythm of one's heart.

In that moment, time unfolded in slow motion before Marisa. It could have accelerated to the blink of an eye, given her anxiety at finding herself suddenly face to face with Marco. Surprise, however, rendered Marisa dumbfounded, and all time could do was reduce its own rate while she remained in suspension.

Marco's attention fixed on her face. Marisa caught the hint of a smile spread throughout his countenance. No neutrality remained there. The mouth then displayed the row of white teeth; the eyes softened. Marco searched her face with an eloquence Marisa couldn't decide if it was amusement or curiosity. Or both. Without realizing it, she blushed.

Marisa drew her gaze away from his face as she followed the hands opening the black leather briefcase and producing a printed copy. Marco extended a couple of stapled sheets to her, and Marisa stared at the upside-down letters, which in her eyes resembled tiny ants carrying secret messages on their humps. Next, she lost herself in another eternity while contemplating the dark hands that neared her body, preceded by white sheets of paper...

Then two girls approached Marco.

Time jerked back into its habitual march, suddenly pervaded by the hallway rustle, by the grayish sky framed in the window, by the cold lights on the ceiling.

"This is the text you've requested," he said, filling her hands with paper before turning to her classmates.

With the sheets clutched in her hands, a perplexed Marisa levitated away in the corridor.

She hadn't requested anything from Marco.

5. Signs, Bonbons and Siderodromophilia

Later, during gym class, Marisa and Valentina exiled themselves in the restroom to escape the torments of a volleyball competition. Marisa finally had a chance to show the print Marco had given her: an excerpt with the phrase she had used in her message. While Marisa handled it with the reverence of someone holding a sacred talisman, her friend snatched it and began to read.

If Valentina possessed an undeniable virtue, it was objectivity. Her parents' divorce, when she was still a girl, embedded in her a visceral skepticism only surpassed by her sympathy toward all minorities. At the time of the separation, it came to light that her father had another woman. More than that: he had another family. Valentina never forgave him. She often said you couldn't count on anyone and uncertainty was the only certain thing in life.

To illustrate her point, Valentina mentioned the case of English suffragette Emily Davison, who, at the 1913 Derby, in defense of women's right to vote, leaped onto the racetrack and was trampled by King George V's horse. The next day, the big sensation reported by the press was not the accident that claimed her life, but the outsider horse winner of the race.

From her father whom she so passionately rejected, Valentina had inherited the prominent nose with a Catalan profile, the exuberant mouth and intense eyes, dark-brown like the curls that floated out of control around her face and down to her shoulder. From him, she had also inherited assertiveness and obstinacy. Being one of the few students immune to Marco's allure, Valentina could deliver an unbiased analysis of the case at hand. Or so Marisa hoped.

In the deserted lavatory, the only witnesses were the white sinks on the granite top and the mirror where some girl had drawn with lipstick a mysterious letter *D* inside a heart. The air carried a light pine smell, and from time to time the cries of students in the patio broke like a wave, rising, falling and curveting through the window. Under it, as they sat on the white ceramic floor, Marisa and Valentina confabulated.

"He's sending me a message in between the lines, Val."

"There you go again," Valentina reproached her. "Marco advised you the same way he would any other student. You can't keep imagining hidden motives in everything people do. You need facts, concrete evidence." Since Marisa started to protest, she silenced her with a raised index finger: "A print about existentialism does not qualify."

At each of her words, Marisa would grow impatient and disagree, shaking her head.

"You don't understand. The text includes the full quote by Sartre from *Being and Nothingness* that I sent to him. And what does it say following the phrase I used? *Desire is expressed by the caress as thought is by language.* Can't you see? First it was the smile, now it's the caress."

"Which means you found something in a text about nothing."

Valentina scratched her head, sighed and raised both hands flat, as if to physically prevent Marisa from committing a terrible, terrible mistake. To reinforce her words, she held Marisa's shoulders: "You're gonna drive yourself crazy if you keep trying to find encrypted messages in this text. You're gonna drive *me* crazy. Please, don't do that. I almost *miss* Palamedes and the war…"

"What about when he asked me to have a cup of coffee with him, huh?" insisted Marisa. "The way we clicked was amazing. You weren't there to see how he looked at me. He repeated my name several times and leaned toward me while we talked."

"So what?"

"Those are *signs*, Val."

"Says who?"

"Why, behavior experts. Did you know 93% of communication is nonverbal? There's the body language, tone of voice and other clues to suggest interest. Like, for instance, touching…"

Hey, hey. Marco had actually *touched* her? Valentina's curiosity rose above the icy waters of skepticism: now she wanted all the details. Marisa explained he had laid one hand on her shoulder when arriving at the library—and then she started braiding a lock of hair, lost in the memory of the conversation that had ensued. To which Valentina rolled her eyes and made an O with her mouth, in a mix of amusement and exasperation.

"Will you stop it already, Ma? The problem is, when a person falls in love, everything becomes a *sign* that requires interpreting. *Oh, he looked at me.* He loves me. *Oh, why didn't he talk to me?* He loves me not. *Oh, he had a cup of coffee.* Blah-blah-blah. Then you try to decipher every tiny gesture, as if the most mundane things had a hidden meaning. Let's be objective. Marco felt like having coffee and invited you out of politeness. He lives by himself, right? He probably wanted company for a chat. End of story."

"Do you really think so?"

"Yeah. Besides, getting involved with a teacher is a recipe for trouble. Let's assume (and note it's only an *assumption*) that something happens between the two of you. Then someone finds out. First, there will be big-time complications at school, meetings of the board of directors, memorandums, drastic measures. Then your mom will be summoned for a 'talk.' Can you imagine Ms. Adélia's reaction when she learns that you got involved with a teacher? She'll go berserk and chain you to the foot of your bed."

"Thanks a lot for predicting my future." Marisa grimaced. "I didn't know you had a degree in psychic abilities."

"I don't need to be a psychic to foretell your mom's reaction."

Marisa reached into her purse and produced a couple of bonbons, offering Valentina one. Sugar always helped keep spirits high. The chocolate melted in her mouth in a comforting way, and Marisa contemplated philosophically the pink cellophane wrap.

She had known Valentina for four years now, since her friend had been expelled from another school for challenging the history teacher in protest against a grade she deemed unfair. Valentina solemnly approached his desk during class and placed a box before him as she said: *This is what I think of your evaluation.* The teacher opened the box to find inside a pile of dog poop.

Valentina was transferred to Marisa's school, and since then they'd spent countless hours talking about everything from the meaning of life to the best waterproof mascara to wear on the beach. In spite of a certain inclination to eccentricity, the friend proved herself precise in her judgments about life and cosmetics.

"Maybe you're right," Marisa admitted, quite crossly.

"Elementary, my dear. I'm always right. Now we need to find you a guy so you forget that teacher once and for all." Valentina paused to savor her chocolate. "By the way, how do you like the book?"

"The one about paraphilia?"

"Yeah."

Well... with the cover black like the abyss of human sexuality, the title red like sin, and a certain flair for Greek, the encyclopedia held words as unprecedented as bizarre. Right under the letter *A*, the bulky *adstringo-penispetraphilia* combined in its syllables the male organ, a medium-size string and a bunch of pebbles for geological pleasure. Its distant relative *agalmatophilia* promoted romance with statues and found a correlate in *pygmalionism* (p. 305). Desert islands, aliens, ghosts, all had a guaranteed spot in the encyclopedia, and not even the Milky Way had escaped the wandering hand of sexual deviation.

Clinical cases abounded too. The teenage girl diagnosed with knismo-lagnia, who had suffered the embarrassment of climaxing during an innocent tickle session at school. The retired sergeant who obtained pleasure only when he wore his wife's panties. The incompatible couple of balloon fetishists—in the throes of passion, he wanted to pamper the balloons, whereas she enjoyed popping them with her stiletto heel.

In Marisa's opinion, the most curious example was the normophilic patient who casually found out he was a pervert after reading a medical journal. A civil servant and religious man respectful of laws and moral principles, he had to treat his excessive normality: a paraphilia too that was. In order to cure him, a colossal dose of pornographic magazines and videos was prescribed. The treatment, however, inadvertently degenerated into pictophilia.

"What about the couple with the statue?" Valentina exclaimed with disgust.

"Statue?"

"Oh, you haven't reached that part yet, so I won't deliver any spoilers. Suffice to say during a train ride they do all this crazy stuff with a statue and an avocado."

Marisa listened attentively and began folding the cellophane wrap with methodical gestures.

"Hmmm… It's a typical case of pygmalionist siderodromophilia with dendrophilic tendencies," she diagnosed, carefully spelling out each word. Then she dropped the cellophane paper with a naughty expression. "Do you know there's a sex shop near the library? We could stop by when I return the books."

"Oh, don't tell me it's the Lost Paradise."

Yep, confirmed Marisa. Valentina then told her it was the hottest sex shop in town. The store carried exclusive products, and its owner, a retired anthropologist, travelled the world collecting tribal mating artifacts. Marisa promptly pictured what those devices would be like. Valentina, with an ironic chuckle, told her the store sold inflatable serpents covered in gold dust. Inspired by the creatures of the Amazon jungle, they became such a hit in orgies that people kept comparing their snakes and even forgot to use them.

Marisa wanted to see the mating artifacts in person. Valentina preferred the erotic snakes. Amid laughter and chattering, they planned a visit to the shop. Their enthusiasm was well-justified: the Lost Paradise, indeed, held many surprises in store. More than they would have imagined.

6. Strategic Pause

On Thursday Camila circled Marco again and glued to him in the hall-way. Marisa began to harbor serious suspicions of La Edible's intentions: now it was no longer a matter of insinuations, it had become a frontal assault. At the end of classes on Friday, on her way home, Marisa saw Camila and Marco on the corner of the street. He was saying something and she smiled mesmerized, playing with the golden pendant in an obvious attempt to draw attention to her cleavage.

Unable to refrain her resentment, Marisa hid behind a newsstand and watched them. Camila had already repeated one school year and, in Marisa's opinion, she was simply *dumb*. What good were all those curves without a brain? Yet Marisa had to admit, against her will, that the other girl was pretty, with her lean body, long hair and big brown eyes. Camila personified the stereotype of seduction men seemed so keen on. And Marco apparently fell for that stupid, *primary* game.

Men are such idiots, thought Marisa. It was pathetic how biology spoke louder than reason. No, not speak, no: biology yelled and tap danced, while reason moaned and crawled in agony. When a man was around cleavage, hormones boiled in his brain and he could only think of procreation. Guys out there even attended *classes* to learn the shortest route between their hands and a woman's underwear. They claimed to be "pickup artists." It was cruel but true: the masculine world valued easy exuberance, not substance.

As for easy exuberance, Marisa couldn't prevent her eyes from roaming over Marco's figure. She paused on the back pockets with one of his extra-curricular endowments that brought joy to the school girls… Irritated, she steered her gaze to the sleeve of his shirt. Despite Valentina's advice, Marisa couldn't resist Marco. Why him? After all, there were millions of men in the world. But why *not* him? She had never felt such affinity with anyone as with Marco. She admired his knowledge, sense of humor, easy ways... his smile, his hands... (Here, Marisa let out an ambiguous sigh, half romantic, half annoyance: a sigh of annoyed romanticism.)

Very well then, Valentina had hit the last nail on the coffin of her hopes: all Marco meant with his coffee invitation was an amicable conversation. The proof stood right there across the street. Marisa wanted to leave but couldn't stop looking at the pair on the corner. Now Marco spoke again in that assertive manner of his. Now Camila fidgeted again with the damn pendant... And now... the fatal blow: Marco retrieved a bunch of papers from his briefcase and handed it to Camila. *So he did that for all the girls.*

Feeling betrayed, Marisa aimed a poisonous stare at the pair and inadvertently leaned forward. She knocked over a pile of knitting magazines with a merry woman on their covers. They landed with a *plump*, and now eighteen women with their knitting needles smiled at Marisa from the ground. The old newsvendor glared at her as if saying: *Aren't you gonna fix that mess?* Marisa gestured an apology and recoiled behind a wall of newspapers. Since she didn't move from the spot, the man grunted and knelt down to retrieve the magazines carpeting the sidewalk.

Marco and Camila interrupted their conversation to observe the old man talking to himself. Marisa, from behind the cover of a finance publication, took a peek at the two. Marco indicated the newsstand with a motion of his chin. Camila shook her head. Marisa froze: Marco rotated his body to face the newsstand... he took one step... another step... *and began crossing the street.*

Her heart fussed like a frightened bird. He would follow a diagonal route and, upon reaching the newsstand, he would see her. Marisa's first impulse was to run. The second, to hide under the newspapers. The third (a flash of reason), to pretend she was reading some article. Yes, of course, that was it... Marisa stared at a headline about the Federal Reserve and feigned deep concentration. She fervently promised the Almighty never to be daft again if she escaped that one with her dignity intact.

Her cell phone ring, a techno version of The Doors' *Break on Through*, almost gave her a syncope. She retrieved the phone quickly from the outer compartment of her purse. It was a call from her mother. Marisa thought of turning the device off, but she had already ignored the mother's previous call.

She answered in a whisper.

"Hi, Mom."

"I had tried reaching you before and left a message, did you listen to it? I wanted to ask you to get some olive oil on your way home. I need it for lunch." Her voice carried an edge of impatience. "Where are you?"

"At the newsstand," Marisa replied as she monitored Marco's advance from the corner of her eye.

"Then hurry up, otherwise you're going to be late for your afternoon classes. You know which olive oil, don't you? Don't get the light one, as it has no flavor…"

"Uh-huh. Light." At each step he took, her heart thundered.

"… and bring passion fruit for juice too. Ripe."

"Sure. Ripe."

The mother didn't notice Marisa's distraction because she was distracted herself, waiting for the propitious moment to approach a subject of the utmost importance.

"Do you know I met a very distinctive young man at church? Lucinda's son. His name is Tato and he's studying law. He's so pleasant and responsible. I thought maybe you could come with me to mass on Sunday. He'll be going too."

"I have to study."

"But it'll be just for an hour…"

"Mom?"

"I'm here."

"Mom, the connection is breaking… Mom? I can't hear a thing…"

Marisa turned the phone off with a pang of guilt. Lately the mother had been impossible to handle, always trying to shove her into the arms of the first "good catch" that happened to materialize. It was as if the mother didn't know what to do with her and sought reinforcements. Unfortunately, the two of them didn't share the same tastes—her mother seemed to have a fascination for dorks.

But right now a more pressing matter demanded her attention. Whoa. What was going on across the street? Hmmm...

Camila moved forward, hooked a very long arm to Marco and held him back. She then brought her face close to his, sibilating something that made him draw back and smile awkwardly. The Messalina wanted Marco all for herself, thought Marisa, outraged. Once more, the chin-head dialogue. (Oh, heavens, was that ever going to stop?) Marco muttered something and Camila finally recoiled the serpent's arm. Then he aimed again for the newsstand and took one more step...

This was not the place for Marisa to discuss her own faith or the existence of God. But the fact is, before traversing the street, Marco asked the newsvendor if he needed help. The old man said no. Marco hesitated and rejoined Camila. They exchanged a few words, and he seemed ready to take off when the ophidian arm retained him once more. Marisa huffed. Luckily, the two parted soon after that.

When the enemy was gone, Marisa marched from behind the newsstand with an imaginary knife clenched between her teeth. She marched away with her dignity intact and a mood bitterer than the newsvendor's. *Seriously, men deserve the Nobel Prize of idiocy.* She couldn't believe Camila's boldness and Marco's endless paper supply. She couldn't believe, above all, her own idiocy.

Another week passed, and Monday brought one more gym class. Marisa and Valentina sought refuge in the usual lavatory when Marisa announced she had finished reading the paraphilia book. Valentina proposed skipping the last afternoon class so they could go to the library and the sex shop. Marisa hesitated, but the friend's scientific rationale persuaded her: no class in the world could compete with the Lost Paradise. Thus, later that day the two of them made a quick visit to the library and proceeded briskly to the sex shop.

"I'm so excited!" said Valentina when they arrived. "I read on the Internet that the store owner suffers from priapism, of all things... Can you imagine?"

"Where on earth do you dig up that sort of information? It's gross," Marisa protested, pulling a face.

At the store, the two found a number of bizarre items sure to make lots of people's hair stand on end. Besides the tribal artifacts, there were all sorts of publications, films, toys and intimate jewelry (hypoallergenic). Not to mention a vacuum penis expander made with German technology, which was just plain scary.

The inflatable dolls offered a special chapter in the store's inventory. Commercialized with exclusive distribution, they were ordered from an American company and sent to an Italian artisan in order to receive the finest finishing that would make them stand out from the crowd. Their silky texture invited the touch, and their complexion was so fresh it could even fool an inattentive user.

As the Lost Paradise's flagship, the inflatables offered the portability their heavy silicone counterparts lacked. They used to be exposed at the entrance of the store, until a depraved customer ran away with a doll that served as a model in a re-enactment of the film *When Larry Ate Sally* (the store owner, besides being priapic, had a soft side for romantic comedy). The thief dashed on the avenue with the doll under his arm—naked as it came into this world, covered solely with a red miniskirt flapping like a flag.

After that, the inflatable collection migrated to the back of the store. Valentina and Marisa had to forge their way through shelves and counters to reach the dolls. They were arranged in varied poses against a painted scenario reproducing the Garden of Eden. Valentina quickly turned sour at the sight of them. While Marisa admired the collection, Valentina approached the clerk and filled a form before returning with a triumphant expression.

"What was that?" Marisa asked.

"A complaint form. They have a suggestion box."

"And about what did you complain?"

Valentina pointed to the inflatables with evident disdain.

"Can't you see what's going on here?"

Marisa gave her a quizzical look. She couldn't find anything wrong with the lot: a serpent coiled on an artificial apple tree and half a dozen female dolls (blonde courtesan, futuristic beauty, etc., etc.) around a bared-chest, Latino macho-style doll in tight leatherette pants. All ready to start an orgy and be dispatched nonstop to the seventh circle of hell. But to Valentina, naturally, the circles of hell hardly mattered.

"Marisa, Marisa. You're so heedless." Her admonition linked to a rally-style discourse. "Do the math. They release several female dolls and *only one* male doll. This is typical of the segregation minorities suffer on a daily basis. Don't female and gay audiences have equal rights when it comes to variety?" She gesticulated, taking an imaginary stand: "As Anaïs Nin wrote in her book *In Favor of the Sensitive Man*, eroticism is one of the pillars of self-knowledge, as indispensable as poetry!" Then she checked her cell phone and suddenly worried. "Oops, gotta go or I'll be late for my dental appointment."

Valentina left quickly, but not without first addressing a glare of reproach to the clerk. Marisa still remained in the store for another half-hour. Without someone to share impressions, though, the whole thing became a bit pointless and Marisa decided to go home. At the exit, she fished in her purse for the MP3 player, adjusted the earbuds and selected a Doors remix (Infected Mushroom). Jim Morrison began singing *Light My Fire*.

She was about to move away from the store when she saw an enormous silicone penis that a clerk had just placed in the display window. Marisa leaned over to study the large triple-ended article: with its greenish color and red protuberances, it looked like a cross between a stegosaur and an alien. She perused its instructions card. Horrified but unable to stop, Marisa read it wide-eyed, then frowned, read on with even wider eyes, and grimaced.

At that point, her peripheral vision captured the motion of a silhouette coming out of the store and—without knowing why—she straightened herself up. The moment lingered in suspension when her eyes met Marco's.

Now, rather than having his jacket on, he carried it in his arm. Marisa's gaze ran from his square face to his light-gray T-shirt and jeans, trailed the jacket folds, and at last reached his hand holding a white shopping bag with the store logo. Finally, her eyes moved up, all the way back to the initial point. The two stared at each other without dissimulating their surprise—he still hesitant at the sex shop door, she completely baffled beside the gigantic triple-ended phallus.

And Jim Morrison always singing.

Marco moved his head in a short nod and walked away with a long stride. It was rush hour, and Marisa saw him burrow in the adjacent avenue amidst the crowd going back home. For a moment, she observed the unruly procession streaming in all directions. Then she turned back to the card. Her interest in the stegosaur-phallus, however, was (so to speak) extinct.

7. Tropical Rain

It was tempting to confide to Valentina the encounter with the literature teacher at the Lost Paradise. Marisa usually told her everything but this time had scruples. In the way Marco had looked at her, Marisa captured something she knew too well herself. Something that should be respected: susceptibility. The next day in class, every time the two exchanged a look, it betrayed complicity for one shared secret and curiosity for another unrevealed. Marisa tried to guess what hidden desire had led Marco to the store. He speculated the same about her.

October drew to an end, and that Tuesday was a typical springtime rainy day, still irresolute amid the last breath of winter and the neighboring summer showers. After classes, as Marco drove along the street, he spotted a silhouette in a lilac dress walking with bowed head on the sidewalk. He rolled down the window pane, and thick drops spattered on his face when he called Marisa to offer a ride. She rushed to the Lexus in a mess of notebooks, handbag and clothes clinging to her body. Her relief for escaping the rain lasted just long enough to become uneasiness: in the confines of the car, the window panes grew foggy with steam and tension.

After the encounter at the Lost Paradise, after the dissimulated looks in the classroom, here they were squeezed in a metal box. Just the two of them. Suddenly embarrassed. They talked about the weather and Marisa complained she had forgotten to bring an umbrella that day. Marco turned the heat on and opened the glove compartment, where he kept tissues. She muttered a thank you, picked up the tissue box and dried herself. The conversation dimmed out. The rain pattered on the car's silver-gray hood. Traffic dragged painfully.

"Did you do the vocational test?" Marco asked after a few minutes.

"No, I… forgot…"

It dawned on Marisa the extent of the apathy hidden inside her. In truth, she no longer cared about college or the future. Since her father's death, she had already quit dance classes and the choir. As she couldn't quit school altogether, Marisa numbed herself with studying to forget life had no meaning. Her soul perched on a plum tree like Pierre Anthon, silently shouting nothing mattered. Life was a parade of platitudes, wake up in the morning and brush teeth, say hi to the porter upon leaving the building and upon returning, finish one set of homework just to begin another and another, long for the future, get disappointed with the future, have meals, dress for the weekend, sleep and wake up again, until the day waking up was no longer an option. And in the meantime, everything a person loved the most ran out between their fingers until all that remained were empty hands.

The suffocated pain rose to surface. First a contraction in the chest, then the jolt in the throat and a burning sting in the eyes. She's there again. For the first time. Walking with her mother on the path paved with cement and dry leaves. They stop before a rectangle of fresh grass with a black granite tombstone. She reads in the inscription what she refuses to accept. The name and the dates. So that's it. From an entire life, all that's left. She'll never see her father again. Never again. The sky darkens, the pine trees bow in the wind, and the horns on the street come from afar—from a world to which she no longer belongs. The mother hugs her in silence, bleakly. Marisa cries. She looks at the sad saints watching the graves and promising eternal bliss. She's angry. Angry at life for robbing her of a most loved one and then continuing without him, angry at the father who had left her behind, angry at herself for not being able to save him. Angry. She swears not to shed another tear.

She almost kept her word.

Marco grew disconcerted when he saw her wipe away a teardrop. He tightened his grip on the wheel as he glanced sideways at Marisa. Better to keep quiet so not to make her uncomfortable. She was biting her lip, restraining herself. He relaxed… but soon she sobbed, and that first tear multiplied into many. Marco parked in the first available space.

"What happened, Marisa?"

She stammered incoherent things—the nothingness, the stone saints mocking her pain, the plum tree and her feet dangling in the void. Uncertain of how to react, he put his arm on the seat headrest, began a gesture, faltered and at last laid one hand on her shoulder.

"Hey, Marisa, easy... easy..."

"Sorry." She wiped her face with the back of her hand and attempted an awkward smile. Weeping brought relief and also emptiness. She felt hollow, a ragdoll without stuffing in a struggle to stand. "It's nothing. I think I'm just nervous with the coming college admission."

Marisa had a beautiful face, Marco noted, even with the sad smile... He noticed the scent emanating from her skin (vetiver?) and a birthmark half hidden on the nape of her neck—a small grayish form that reminded him of a diadem. Marco studied her turgid gaze, the pomegranate of her swollen lips, the pale face contrasting with hair darkened by rain. He thought of a sugar clump dissolving in water.

What could he do to comfort her? Be a good listener, or try cheering her up, or... Without thinking, Marco leaned over to kiss Marisa on the cheek, and in that instant she turned to face him. His lips almost touched hers. They exchanged an uncertain look—she was fighting a sudden quiver, he was backing off in equal surprise.

"Do you want to talk?" Marco quickly collected himself and, since she made a negative gesture, insisted: "Are you sure? Then I'm going to take you home."

"Please, no..." She became agitated. "I don't want my mother to see me like this. Can I stay with you for a little while?"

Marco hesitated. He needed to go home. Marisa assured him that he could take care of his matters and she would study in the meantime. Given her commotion Marco agreed, and Marisa called the mother to let her know she was having lunch with a friend. On their way to his apartment, the mute tension crept back between them. They took the elevator in silence, pretending to watch the floor-indicator panel. Tension brushed against Marisa. Marisa brushed herself against Marco. Marco did not avoid contact.

When the two entered his apartment, Marisa stood by the door. The property, old and spacious, had high ceilings, varnished parquet flooring and plaster cornices. She absorbed every single detail, trying to identify Marco's personality there. He obviously liked orchids: three vases adorned the coffee table with purple, yellow and blue flowers. What drew her attention, however, were the empty spaces. The furniture was scarce and—except for some normal wear and tear—almost impersonal, as if it had been transplanted straight from a store display.

A set of brown leather sofas and armchairs gravitated around the coffee table designed with reclaimed wood. A pair of side tables carried a pair of white-shaded lamps. In one corner, a stainless steel floor lamp tried in vain to break the hard symmetry of the furniture. The few objects there told stories that instigated Marisa's imagination: the small bronze sculpture curled up like a question mark, the green Murano vase, a framed picture of Marco smiling with the Golden Gate Bridge behind him. And there were also the jazz albums inhabiting the low rack spread across an entire wall. Hundreds of albums split into CDs, LPs and rare 33 RPM editions.

It was interesting to watch Marco there, in his kingdom. In black jeans and dark-gray shirt with rolled-up sleeves, he followed the route between the rack and the hallway with an ease that suggested habit. First he turned the sound system on, then he headed for the office to drop his briefcase. Marisa, in the meantime, distracted herself investigating the music collection. John Coltrane, Miles Davis, an entire section dedicated to Ella Fitzgerald, Herbie Hancock, Bessie Smith… and classical composers, too, such as Satie, Debussy, Chopin, Bartók… On the radio played the delicate melody of *The Pageant of the Bizarre* by Zero 7, with verses about crossed-star lovers and a tempest at sea.

> *Thunder blossoms gorgeously above our heads*
> *Great, hollow, bell-like flowers*
> *Rumbling in the wind*
> *Stretching clappers to strike our ears*

Marco reappeared in the hallway and told Marisa to leave her things on the coffee table while he fetched a towel for her. She thanked him and halted halfway to the table once she noticed the state of her notebook.

"I can't believe. The rain stained my notes."

"Big damage?" Marco turned around and came to stand before her.

"More or less. The top of it is wet, but I guess I can still read it," she replied, examining the pages.

He offered to leave the notebook to dry in the laundry area and, as he spoke, reached out for it. They had never stood that close. There were shapes and colors and warmth. *Presence.* A fragrance of cologne with woody notes. Vetiver mixed with rain. His skin, feverish like arid land. Hers, still glimmering with translucent droplets that rolled from her hair to her shoulders. Their hands touched and their eyes met in a pause. And then, very gently, Marco's gaze grazed Marisa's lips. He grazed the full curve of ripe fruit with his eyes and then with his mouth, nibbling on the lip, tasting it on the tip of his tongue. Marisa nestled herself on him and mirrored his movements. She buried her fingers in the fine, soft locks of Marco's hair, felt with a vestige of vertigo the fabric of the shirt hiding his flesh. She had longed so much for this moment. Her legs faltered…

> *Full-lipped flowers*
> *Bitten by the sun*
> *Bleeding rain*
> *Dripping rain like golden honey*
> *And the sweet earth flying from the thunder*

The books cascaded to the floor, and Marco pulled her closer, his arms adjusting to her figure with such ease it surprised him. His body had its own reason. Something stirred deep down inside, something that had been restrained and now just broke the barrier… He didn't know how Marisa could disarm him that way. Her kiss transmitted the sweetness of abandon that he desperately wanted to reciprocate. His hesitant, thirsty mouth expressed the dilemma between great doubt and even greater certainty. He froze on a sudden. That didn't feel right. She was his student, frail now, and he no longer knew what he was doing. Marco forced himself to back off as he registered with crystalline clarity Marisa's face standing out amid a smudge—the music rack, the window, the vortex of gray sky.

"I'm sorry... really sorry," he said in a hoarse voice and looked away. "I'm thirsty. Do you want some water?"

Marisa nodded, her legs shaky again. His taste lingered in her mouth and poured into her whole body. After a moment, she followed him at a numb pace.

Marco practically burst into the retro kitchen fitted with white tiles and black Formica. He opened the refrigerator, grabbed the water bottle and, as he filled two glasses, almost made the water overflow from one of them. Marisa stood at the door and waited. Marco turned around with a startle, laying the bottle on the counter. In a reflex, he offered her a chair at the head of the six-seat table.

After handing her a glass, Marco took the chair on the opposite end. When he spoke again, his voice sounded controlled—almost natural.

"Do you have any exams this week, Marisa?"

"Yes. Literature, don't you remember?"

He smiled, awkwardly, and she smiled too.

"Of course... I mean, do you have an exam in *any other* subject?"

No, fortunately, she didn't. It seemed she had exams all the time in that school. She was going crazy. It was school in the morning, college admission classes in the afternoon and preparation for exams in the evening. Sometimes she resembled a sleepwalker and needed buckets of coffee to keep herself awake. Before that year, she didn't even *like* coffee...

Marisa shushed, aware of her own nervousness. It had been a mistake to insist in tagging along with Marco. He felt uneasy, and she didn't intend to impose her presence any longer. She left her glass untouched on the table and stood up.

"I'd better be going."

"I'll give you a ride." He rose in such a haste that the chair protested with a shriek.

Marisa insisted she didn't want to disturb him; she could take a taxi. Marco insisted it was no trouble at all. The two returned to the living room and he helped her collect the textbooks from the floor. They barely looked at each other. Marisa balanced the books in one arm and hung her purse over the other while they headed for the door. Marco turned the key and laid one hand on the knob, pausing ever so slightly.

She would never know what got her in that instant: watching him hesitate, she stroked his face. And with the gesture Marisa's irises pulsed, turned into liquid and haze. In that moment there was him. Only him.

"Don't worry, Marco. I wanted that too…"

An indecipherable expression veiled his countenance. His eyebrows remained still but the eyes stirred with a slight tremor. His lips, the upper with its well-drawn shape and the bottom fuller, parted in a reflex as he sucked in the air. One second. Two. Three. His hand released the doorknob, ripping the air, circling Marisa's nape, bringing her closer.

Marco sought her mouth with sudden voraciousness. The kiss was intense, then tender, then urgent… The books fell again to the floor, and the purse soon joined them. Marisa fastened her hands around his neck, reciprocating with fervor.

Then Marco buried his face in her damp hair, breathed in its perfume, his eyelids half-closed, an odd intoxication. Inching back, he stared at Marisa.

She laced her fingers through his and spoke to him with one gaze. He replied.

That was how it all began.

8. Rolling the Die

They had a month and a half to go before the end of the school term: December 13th was officially the last day of classes, with the graduation party scheduled for the following evening. Marco wanted to wait. Nonetheless, it came to happen after one week, four furtive cups of coffee and a Sunday lunch that lingered in conversation through the afternoon. It happened naturally, like the rain that day and the sparkle in their eyes.

It was Marisa and Marco's first date in no hurry. He opened a bottle of Merlot and, while he finished preparing a vegetable tiella, the two shared family stories and memories. They talked about his large clan based in the countryside (two brothers, seven uncles and aunts, seventeen cousins, twelve nephews and nieces) and her kindred living in the city (second generation of French immigrants, two uncles, four cousins, no nephews or nieces). They talked about the first time he walked on the Champs-Élysées and the day she couldn't go to the top of the Eiffel Tower due to a protest march.

She told him of a lecture on the Buddhist Wheel of Life, he explained archetypes and the hero's journey toward consciousness. Those topics were alternated with platitudes such as his microwave in need of replacement and the horoscope in the newspaper left on a chair (the Libra woman should have a surprise and the Scorpio man would face a family problem). In their conversation, a simple comment about the weather carried the colors of enchantment: the words didn't matter as much as what lay between the lines—in that language known only by lovers, even the most trivial sentence forged kinship.

"We could go to Alto Paraíso for Carnival," Marisa was saying. "Do you know the place?"

"Only through photos. It has waterfalls, right?"

"It has the Valley of the Moon. One of the most beautiful spots I've ever visited. A stretch of rocks like lunar craters, with the cerrado tropical savanna around it and turquoise pools in the middle. The rocks have tiny green crystals embedded in them, which shine in the moonlight."

"Let's go there, Mari. If you like waterfalls, we can also visit Lençóis da Bahia on Easter... Oh, you don't know it? It's a lovely town with colonial houses and..."

Outside, the raindrops were rolling; inside, it was the notes of Chopin's piano. Marisa inquired what was playing. Waltz no. 14 in E minor. Let's dance, Marco. Ah, Mari, but I can't waltz. It's very easy, Marco, come here and I'll show you... He stood smiley and awkward, she brisk and didactic. Position: one hand on the partner's back (here, close to the shoulder) and the other away from the body holding your pair's hand. Let's go. One-two-three... And off they went whirling around the table, left-right-left, passing by the stove and the refrigerator, one step forward for him and another backward for her, now the cabinets and the counter, one-two-three...

The *Minute Waltz* kicked in and hastened the pace, and suddenly they were spinning in the romantic Paris of the 19th century, he in a black tail-coat, bow tie and waistcoat, she in an airy raspberry dress with shoulders bare. They danced in a blue ballroom with a vaulted ceiling and walls where flourished gold-plated reliefs and multicolor rose bouquets. The notes hopped amid the scintillation of crystal sconces and chandeliers, one, two, three, twirling and twirling in blue golden crystal inside the rainbow abloom. In a given moment, the aroma of fresh basil spread in the kitchen: in São Paulo of the 21st century, lunch was ready. Marco removed the dish from the oven and lit up a candle to enliven the table.

The two sat down contentedly and, while eating, talked about books and favorite authors, so many they even lost track. Marisa recalled *La Petite Fadette* by George Sand, which her father had read to her when she was little. Marco was surprised by the coincidence: the author was one of Chopin's lovers. The conversation moved on to poetry and he headed for the office to fetch a book before dessert—which they would only savor much later anyway. It was a collection of visual poems by Augusto de Campos, and Marisa really liked it. *Pluvial* (the word falling like rain to become a river). *Timespace: A time from space to space, a time, a space from time to time...* They leafed through the book, one more sip of wine, one more kiss. Debussy and *Clair de Lune* in the air, the taste of grapes and something else, another poem, the time without time of a caress. Then it happened.

Here are the lovers.

Here they are with nothing but their bodies. Lovers relatives. Here are the lovers, with no relatives but their bodies...

The bedroom submerged in dimness when Marco shut the curtains, blocking the sight of the lead-gray sky streaked with beads of glass. Marisa vaguely captured the rain sounds, the incandescent colors of the painting at the headboard and a flash of antique silver from the rectangular mirror across the bed. Next, all her senses were siderated by Marco's closeness, his skin, warmth, scent. Embraces, whispers. One half-smile mirrored on their lips and multiplied in the mirror.

Have you ever tried that, Mari? You can be whatever you want...

A princess from a distant land. Kidnapped. At his mercy.

Marco covered Marisa's eyes with a blindfold and, in a fluid motion, impelled her to the bed. She felt the silk of the spread on her back and his body next to hers. A faint aroma of aftershave lotion followed by warm breathing against her neck when he spoke in her ear: "You're on a desert beach swept by a storm. The sand borders a forest. In the middle of the forest there's a cabin. You're a prisoner inside, at the mercy of a stranger. You don't know how you got there and try to guess what your captor is going to do. You fear... anticipate... and can't suppress a shiver when he touches you..."

Marco's hands grazed from her legs down to the ankles as he removed her sandals. Then they initiated an ascent to the waistband of her denim skirt that bordered the white bodice. His voice was like thick velvet and sometimes would punctuate the words with a stronger note.

Words.

The voice rustled in her ears, words grasping the senses, trailing the skin to make it vibrate like a musical instrument at each syllable, each meaning, letters entering her pores, hands-words stretched on her body, in the core.

"You try to protest, but your captor covers your mouth..." Marco placed one hand on Marisa's mouth, while the other advanced. "He unbuttons your skirt. His hands explore your body. Evaluating... the thighs... the hips... They play with your navel. Sprawl all over your stomach, your flank. They go down. And further... You feel chill bumps. You want more. He refuses it. His hands glide to your bodice neckline and pull the fabric. He lowers the straps. Little by little. Then the whole top at once."

At each word followed the action. Hands tantalized the blossoming skin. Marisa quivered. Fever budded where he touched and irradiated to every inch of her body.

So that's how it was. His touch.

Marisa moaned faintly when Marco slid his tongue on her breasts, collarbone, shoulder. His teeth sunk softly on her neck, lingered on the earlobe.

A whiff on the sensitive skin. Again the hand against the mouth.

A whisper in her ear.

"Inside, the cabin is hot. The rain pounds on the roof. Through a gap in the window comes a cool draft... the smell of wet ground and sand mixed with the scent of the man manipulating your body without permission. You feel exposed. Want to cover yourself but are afraid of crossing his will. You can't do a thing when his hand descends to the last piece of clothing..."

It was white and lacey. His hand insinuated under its smooth and coarse surface, slithering on the line above the pubis. Coming and going, coming and going.

"The hand hooks in the fabric. It yanks it off. You're naked. You feel the cooler air as you sense the stranger's eyes caressing your whole body, each curve, each hiding spot..." Marco heaved, his breath a shiver on her skin. "You tremble from head to toe, chest rising, legs weak, a tingle up your thighs. He likes to watch you. Watch the desire on your face."

The hand that silenced her traced the contour of her lips. Two fingers were inserted in her mouth. Marisa let her tongue roll around them, sucked, tasted. One more instant. The fingers dismissed, his lips on hers. Firm hands that pinned her arms against the mattress. That groped her hips with hardly restrained hunger. The kiss, increasingly thirsty.

And on a sudden, his tongue was not enticing her mouth any longer. Now it travelled an impromptu path to her navel, dived in it, surrounded it, kept moving… The flattened hands on her thighs, a fiery touch on her sex. The tongue. The fingers: first one, then the other. The tongue on one part, the fingers deepened in another, retreating to deepen more. She circled her hips with a sigh, dominated by a liquid sensation that ran across her limbs, spiraled over her breasts and swirled low in her belly. Slow, fast, deeper and deeper.

And then these hands, this mouth abandoned her. The sound of his clothes, T-shirt, belt, zipper, condom wrap torn with teeth. The blindfold removed. The craving.

His eyes in hers.

His body in hers…

The afternoon oozed away with the rain while they remained in the bedroom—captive and captor, inside the cabin in the forest. Then it was two silhouettes under the circle of light from the nightstand lamp, lying together, contently spent—so close to each other it was hard to tell where one ended and the other began.

"Did you like it?" asked Marco as he stroked Marisa's hair.

"I loved it. I enjoy experiencing different things." She half-closed her eyelids, nuzzling his neck.

"Then you found your match. We got along well, didn't we? It's as if we already know each other. And it'll get even better as we have more intimacy."

"The funny thing is, I didn't feel nervous with you the way I felt the first time with my ex Sérgio. It took me a while to be at ease with him, even though he was more traditional… You always do that?"

Marisa contemplated him with renewed curiosity when he said: "To me, sex is a channel of expression. And I like to explore fantasies." His hand now traced the line of her hip. "Desire is mystery, a constant discovery. You never know what's gonna happen and may discover things about yourself that you weren't even aware of. Between four walls anything goes. The bedroom is not politically correct."

"Hmm… politically correct… *That* would be a hell of a kinky fetish."

"Yeah. With an ISO 9000 guide for best practices and ecological solutions."

"Mr. Fares," Marisa cleared her throat and pitched her voice, "I have already disinfected my hand with alcohol. Allow me to shove it inside your pants."

"It would be a pleasure, Miss Constant. If you don't mind, I want to reciprocate your kindness. Pass me the alcohol, if you may…"

Marco pinched her bottom and suppressed a laugh when she wriggled, protesting, *Mr. Fares, please!*

Then he changed his tone.

"But we shouldn't have done it, Mari. For one thing, we shouldn't even be seeing each other."

"Why not?" Marisa tipped her head back to stare at him. "In a few weeks' time I will no longer be your student. What are a few weeks compared to a lifetime? To eternity? This is just a matter of form. Oh, we shouldn't be together because it's morally wrong. Yeah, right. Do I look like Lolita? Nabokov must be laughing in his grave." She gesticulated impatiently. "It's easy to judge someone when you're not in their shoes. But you can only understand something once you have lived it. Until then, it's just an abstraction based on stereotype. Each case is different. Besides, we're not hurting anyone. Let's not forget hell is other people."

Marco's clouded expression cleared with a smile. Lolita. No, she was his Marisa. And yet… *Light of my life, fire of my loins, my soul…* Marco recited Nabokov silently as he placed a kiss on her forehead. *I love you.* Without warning, those three words budded in his thought. They almost budded on his lips. Their sudden intensity stunned him. He hadn't felt that way in such a long time he almost forgot what it was like. It was wonderful. It was terrifying. He swallowed up the words and joked instead: "Now you got into quoting Sartre. I've created a monster."

"Seriously, Marco. The future hasn't arrived yet and the past is gone. Happiness is in the here and now. The present is what threads the past and the future. Let's make the most of what we have *now* to create our memories and our tomorrow. We're feeling a strong bond, and it happened. And

I'm very happy with you."

"I know what you mean. I just think that when in Rome... but I'm happy too, Mari, more than you can imagine. It's the first time I've felt like this since my divorce... no, actually way before that, because things between me and her had not been working for a while. Then, when I was on my own, I had a number of one-night stands that meant nothing. I just felt numb. Heavy. Like a hundred years old."

"Your separation was that bad?"

The marriage had lasted seven years. It started off happily in spite of difficulties, and little by little dimmed out almost without them realizing. In the last year the relationship became unsustainable. Constant fights, often for no reason. The problem was not what they manifested but what they hid. He still hoped to salvage the relationship. When it ended, it was like a hurricane sweeping his life away and turning everything upside down.

A shadow crossed Marco's face—the expression settling in belonged to another man. Marisa was alarmed: she didn't recognize him. More than that: she lost him. The traits were the same, albeit somehow different in the imperceptible contraction of the muscles and in the shield covering his gaze. Then the shadow dissipated, and the Marco she knew reappeared, but still on time's high wire, with one foot behind and the other in midair, slowly returning.

"That was what it felt like. A hurricane. I lost weight, couldn't sleep, drowned myself in work. I tried picturing life without Lorena and couldn't. It took me quite a while to pick up the pieces. I got divorced two years ago and, in a sense, I still have some bits scattered around... But let's not talk about that. It's in the past, and what matters is the present, right?" His mouth curved in a smile as he stared at her. "Now it's like I'm twenty again. I must look plain silly."

Marisa smiled too, caressing his hair with tenderness for everything he was and had been. Like rock sediments telling a history, she read his existence in various layers: the teacher who she knew in class and the man with whom she now shared her intimacy; the doctorate student with a stubble beard composing his thesis behind a barricade of books; the man married to a college mate (and here, dark spots on the stone prevented a clear picture);

the University of São Paulo freshman plotting great plans with his mates at the King of Mixed Drinks... and finally, on the last layer—behind the shield of adulthood and the idiosyncrasies she could sense—Marisa caught a glimpse of a boy in shorts, with a bandage on his knee and hands covered in dirt, running carelessly to the river and the barn with his brothers, far from imagining what the future had in store. Childhood was an eternal now: it captured yesterday with the lasso of a very short rope and tomorrow with a stone thrown too far to be seen. In the enchantment of childhood, everything shone brand-new, and Marisa saw through Marco's eyes silvery fish in the silver of the river, unicorns with hazel manes and the sky where fat herds of clouds grazed.

And Marco, as he looked at her, saw the summary of childhood and adolescence with all colors in mutation, increasingly hybrid and complex. In the beginning it was pink for strawberry candy and plush teddy bears, then the deeper pink of the first kiss, the dusky pink of the first great question without an answer, and finally the deep blue of disquiet. Marco contemplated the blooming face and, in the eyes, behind the amber glow, something opaque like oxidized copper. Marisa had learned what existed beyond dolls, family vacations and the latest cell phone model: pain. She had lost her maternal grandfather to a heart attack when she was little, but that didn't compare to the loss of her father. Would it be easier if he had been obliterated by disease, giving her time to get used to the idea of his absence? Marisa said she still saw him everywhere. At home, she startled when a cloud concealed the sun or a curtain undulated in the wind—in those moments, light shifted and she would turn to find, instead of her father, only a shadow slipping away through a slit in the air. Marco knew in that farewell her life too had been turned upside down. He kissed Marisa's left eyelid and then the right one, and held her close.

There, in the bedroom, their lives were intervolving along with their bodies—like two tired travelers who saw a window shining in the middle of the night and, as they drew nearer, realized they had at last reached home. In a way, it was a return to the colors of childhood, for everything became a new discovery. Dinner time had arrived when, wrapped in twin gray robes, they proceeded barefoot to the kitchen to honor dessert. Amid giggles and icy kisses, they spoon-fed each other fruit salad with a mountain of ice cream.

While they were at it, Marisa saw the die on the counter behind a jar. Curious, she stood to pick it up and brought it to the table. It was an ivory piece with hand-carved dots, each exhibiting one circle that spiraled within another. Like eyes. Marco explained it was a replica of a die used in the time of the Roman Empire.

"It's very beautiful. It should be in your living room. Why do you leave it here?" asked Marisa, rolling it between her fingers.

"I keep it in the bedroom, but when I'm on my own I like to throw it on the kitchen table. I totally forgot about it. It's been here since the last time."

"And was the last time good?" she asked with a twinge of jealousy.

"It doesn't matter. That was before you."

Marisa felt reassured by his gaze. Then her curiosity returned.

"But why the kitchen?"

"It's a neutral space. It helps me think."

"About what?"

A glint of mischievousness colored his eyes, and he avoided the subject with a kiss—ice, warmth, a taste of apple. Marisa insisted, sat on his lap and threatened to tickle him.

Marco laughed.

"You know. The die is for bedroom games," he said.

"Let's play, then."

"Maybe some other time."

"Oh, Marco." She puckered her lips. "Let's play…"

So they did. Marco opted for the most basic method and set the parameters. Then Marisa had to guess which number would turn up. She thought for a second. Five. The die was thrown. Two.

Marco's caressing gaze found Marisa.

"It looks like I'm the winner, Mari."

He gave her instructions she was supposed to follow to a T for their next tryst.

9. Dream a Little Dream of Me

Early evening. Marisa arrived at the apartment and, as expected, found the door unlocked. When she entered, she heard the duet by Ella Fitzgerald and Louis Armstrong in *Dream a Little Dream of Me*. Birds of starry plumage blowing love promises in the breeze. The diffused light from the table and floor lamps accentuated the song's nostalgic feel, spreading out in soft circles like a thin, golden veil that could fray at the slightest neglect.

The ample window framed the forest of buildings and the sky blurred by city lights. Marisa glanced at the scenery, and her attention was soon drawn to the coffee table, where a white shopping bag jutted out among the bronze sculpture, a computer magazine and a pile of books. The paper bag carried the familiar logo of a red apple with one bite mark and two words: *Lost Paradise*.

With burning curiosity, Marisa sat down on the edge of the sofa and picked up the bag. She took out from it a pair of black high-heeled sandals and a wide belt weaved with metal plates, round and shiny like brand-new coins. The last item retrieved was a package wrapped in pink paper and tied with a red ribbon. Marisa undid the wrap with impatient hands to find a square box holding a bed of tiger-pattern silk paper. In it lay a black strip ornate with strass, linked to a chain that featured a leather loop end. A collar on a leash for her to wear tonight.

Marisa studied it for a long moment without touching it. She undressed, put the sandals on and fit the belt around her hips. Only then she removed the collar from the box, feeling the softness of the leather and the hard sparkle of the strass. It smelled of something new. Marisa admired it with her eyes and fingertips, thought about its meaning and what Marco was going to do to her. She blushed, and the flushing descended from her face to her chest to her thighs. She fastened the collar around her neck in a gesture that betrayed fatality. Holding the leash with reverence, Marisa headed for the bedroom.

She found it illuminated by the faltering flames of a dozen candles, which multiplied in the mirror next to the bed, saturating the air with a fragrance of sandalwood. Above the mahogany headboard floated an abstract painting in fiery hues. On the nightstand, an almost empty glass of port. On the chair beside it, Marco—dressed in black, legs crossed and a delicate flogger resting on his knees.

His relaxed posture dominated the ambiance. He contemplated her in silence, mouth touched by an almost imperceptible smile. His gaze caressed her nudity with satisfaction. It concentrated on the collar, then on the snowy breasts and the glimmering chain. It searched her face. Inflexible eyes, as smooth and voracious as time.

Marisa approached him slowly. As she advanced she became more pliant. Ready to surrender herself completely. That night. The high heels click-clacked on the floor, the chain links whispered faintly at each step, the belt tinkled to the soft swing of hips. Her body created music as it moved toward him.

The unspoken words, his and hers, cut through the air.

Come with me to this dreamscape...

I want to know by heart the rhythm of your heartbeat. I want to drink of you until I quench this thirst that won't leave me in peace, devour your body with my hunger, turn it inside out and outside in, let your blood and your soul invade me, make up for the lost time of all days and hours and seconds I've lived without you, rip all the armors sheltering your treasures, penetrate in light and darkness, up to the last recess... I want to know by heart the rhythm of your heartbeat.

Marisa paused before Marco and looked deeply into his eyes. She quivered at her own reflection in his irises, quivered as she crossed the border to the unknown, quivered for what she was about to say.

Her legs faltered, the belt a whisper.

She handed him the chain.

"I am all yours."

And dropped her gaze.

And the game encircled them with its whims, an invisible whirl carrying the perfume of the candles, shadows on snippets of skin, murmur and melody, the flog strips, soft hands, a drop of port slithering down to the navel. The hours twirled and twirled. Later everything dispersed like fog in the wind, the candle put out released a black thread of smoke, the music died and the voices quieted. *Shhh...*

Marisa lifted her gaze.

In the following date silence reigned, and a secret smile on her lips. She tossed her coat on the couch and, sitting on the armrest of a chair, began her preparations. Unbraiding her hair, she fixed it with her fingers and picked up a makeup kit from the purse. Marisa applied heavy colors on her eyes and red lipstick on her lips (Fantasy #5, waterproof). Lastly, she put on high-heeled sandals in a gracious motion, straightened up and smoothed her scarlet dress—it barely covered her legs, a generous neckline in the front and the back.

This time, when entering the bedroom, she found Marco stretched on the bed. With his back against the pillow, he was wetting his lips in a glass of port and lighting up a cigarette. Barefoot, in jeans and a white T-shirt, his face was shadowed by the dim bedside lamp. His dark eyes gleamed as they took in her body.

The open window beckoned the breeze and the echoes of the night. Cars, voices, distant laughter—for a moment it was all that could be heard in the bedroom. Marco put out the cigarette, and the last streak of smoke spiraled until dissolving in the curtain diaphanous white. Marisa sat on the edge of the bed, provocatively crossing her legs. Then she tapped on the mattress.

"C'mon here," she said in a flutelike voice.

And when Marco did it, Marisa stroked his hair and ran her fingers across the narrow sideburns. She flexed one hand on his chest, scratched the T-shirt cotton with her red nails and went sliding down to rest her hand on his thigh. But not for too long. With her index and middle fingers, she walked to his belt, trailing the jeans waistband.

He raised one eyebrow and smiled.

"What are you doing?"

"*Shhh...*" She pressed her index finger to his lips.

Marisa kindled him with half-caresses all over his body. She moved around his hips to concentrate on the inner thighs, her fingers skimming ever so lightly there. Without touching him where he wanted the most, she changed course and proceeded to explore what lay underneath the T-shirt.

Marco pulled Marisa closer and tugged her onto his lap, nestling her against his chest. His strong hands enveloped her waist. One remained in place while the other glided possessively across her bare thigh.

"That's better."

Marisa detained his hand.

"If you want some more, you'll have to pay."

Marco stilled for an instant. Another wicked smile.

"I need to know beforehand if the service is good."

"I guarantee it's first rate..."

She gave him a sample. He gave her a bunch of bills. They played all night long.

10. A Prank

Valentina was the only one who knew. Marisa had told her everything on the day following her involvement with Marco, when the two of them were walking home after classes. Valentina almost tripped upon hearing the story. Then she poured a bucket of questions, advised caution and, eventually, reacted to the news with enthusiasm: she even suggested that Marisa use the paraphilia encyclopedia in future erotic games.

On weekends, Marisa would make arrangements with Valentina and tell her mother she was sleeping over at her friend's to study. Then she spent time with Marco. It had become increasingly difficult to dribble her mother though, and the arguments multiplied. One Sunday morning, Marisa woke up late and returned home apprehensive. She decided to use the kitchen entrance for precaution; if she was lucky enough, that would give her a chance to reach her bedroom without being seen. And if she was really lucky, her mother would be in the bathroom getting ready for church.

Marisa turned the key in the lock a fraction of an inch at a time, gently pushed the door and stepped inside. She tiptoed, but halfway into the kitchen she could already hear the TV blabbering. Marisa surrendered. When she entered the living room, the Louis XIV-style décor unfolded its prairies of Savonnerie rugs abloom. The place held more paintings than walls, and the excesses were disorienting like a stereogram. The question was which unexpected image would emerge from that entanglement of sideboards covered in embroidered mats and china, cabinets pregnant with relics, and small tables eclipsed by a constellation of Czech crystal miniatures.

Perhaps a monster with two Sèvres cups for eyes.

In the bookcase, a collection of framed pictures competed for real estate with the TV. Opposite the bookcase was the blue sofa, and on the blue sofa was the mother. Stiff as a rock, she watched a romantic comedy on the cable channel. Her hair bun, so tight it almost called for self-punishment, compensated for the folds of the beige robe that lately had become too loose. Her eyes resembled her daughter's, their light-brown hue highlighted by thick eyelashes. The difference resided in the irises, which darkened visibly along with her mood.

At that very moment, the mother fixed on Marisa a pair of very dark eyes.

"You are late."

"I had to stay a little longer at Valentina's to review math equations. You know I have a hard time with trigonometry."

The mother didn't tolerate well points of view diverging from her own. And, in her view, the equation at hand had nothing to do with trigonometry. She didn't even need to open her mouth to announce the bad weather coming. But naturally she opened it.

As the star couple reconciled amid tears on TV, her voice rose above the saccharine soundtrack: "This is becoming unbearable. You're hardly home these days and never answer my calls. Do you think I was born yesterday? I *know* you and that *weirdo* are up to something."

"Will you stop calling my friend like that?" Marisa forgot about her intent to smooth things over. She could barely restrain her exasperation. "We've had this conversation a million times. Is it so hard to understand I need to *study* if I ever want to get to college? I'd *love* to spend the whole day watching TV like you do."

"Show me some respect, girl. If your father were alive—"

Onscreen, the movie couple now exchanged a passionate look and declared: I love you.

"I know, I know." Marisa rolled her eyes and assumed a sarcastic tone. "But Dad is not alive, is he? And you didn't even allow me to attend the funeral. How could you do that to me? Do you know what your problem is? *You just don't get me.*"

At those words, the mother's eyes sparked and her nostrils quivered. She punched a cushion.

"I've had it up to here with your taunts, do you hear me? After all I've done for you... Well, let me tell you: if you can't, or won't understand what happened, just pack up and leave. I wash my hands of this."

"Yeah, wash your hands of everything, as usual!"

The music soared to a climax of violins, and the TV couple walked hand in hand on a beautiful Tuscany plain.

Marisa bolted to the bedroom. It was her temple, all white, with the view of a lavender trumpet tree from the window. Next to the Jim Morrison poster above the bed lingered the inscription Marisa had recently made after watching a Werner Herzog film. The big letters, scribbled with a thick black marker, leaped out from the wall.

Every man for himself and God against them all.

Her face burned. Her eyes burned. Trembling, Marisa grabbed the cell phone from her purse and called Marco. As soon as he answered, she emptied her heart. When her dad was alive, he acted as a point of balance in the family with his easygoing smile. If Marisa and the mother quarreled, he soon made them laugh with a joke or took the two out for ice cream, which could cure any hurt. He possessed the serenity of a man who didn't need to prove anything to anyone. For years Marisa's relationship with her mother oscillated between harmony and friction, but now her mom was like a stranger. Even worse, she seemed *hostile*. What kind of mother told her own daughter to pack and leave?

"Your mom didn't mean it, Mari," said Marco. "She must be feeling lonely and insecure. She wishes you well and worries about you, but doesn't know how to communicate that. If you step into her shoes, it's easier to understand. She's very unhappy. And when people are like that, they *dry out* because they feel deprived: they can't even be generous toward themselves, let alone toward others. Your mom will eventually get over her grief and this will pass."

"Do you really think so? I wonder... when I see Valentina's mom, always so affectionate..."

"I'm sure. For the first time, both of you are learning to live with each other without your father. Look at the situation as an opportunity to get closer to your mom. Everything is going to be fine, and one day you won't even remember this. But now you need to calm down. Want to go for a walk?"

Marisa agreed with relief. While changing to go out, she turned the MP3 player on and chose a selection by the band Air. *Once Upon a Time* began playing. She raised the volume until drowning the sound of the TV in the living room.

Marco took her to the distant Park of Carmo, which sheltered centennial trees and native Atlantic Forest. They went around the lake and sat under a palm tree, watching the herons, swans and teals in the water. Marco pointed to a grove on a hill in the distance and explained it was cherry trees. They blossomed for two weeks in the beginning of springtime. So Marco and Marisa planned a picnic there for next year, under the blooming cherry trees. They dreamt of a poem with rosy branches on the blue page of the sky, of wine and fruit, artisan breads and chocolate… and got hungry. They decided to have lunch at a Japanese restaurant he knew.

"Thanks, Marco," said Marisa when they reached the parking lot at the Carmo entrance. "I'm feeling better already."

"Family quarrels are normal. In the end, you and your mom will be okay, believe me."

"I don't know. After her fit she kept a long face and wouldn't even ask where I was going." She sighed. "Maybe she was calmer."

The restaurant occupied a house surrounded by residences and other establishments in the Liberdade Asian district, which bordered Downtown. A white sign with black ideograms identified the place for those who knew Japanese. Marisa proceeded first, walking along a stone path in the garden with a fountain. The murmur of water merged with clients' low voices when she stepped into a compact room. A golden fish aquarium shone near the entrance, and dim lights trickled across the sushi counter and a dozen tables. Following Marco's instructions, Marisa climbed the stairs in the back and chose a private room on the upper floor. She left her shoes outside, as required by custom, sitting down on the tatami to wait for Marco.

He showed up minutes later. They ordered a sushi special, then watered it with cold sake. The alcohol turned Marisa's heart into a merry song and her hands into butter. In the competition that ensued between Marisa and the chopsticks, three were the rounds. In the first the chopsticks, agile gymnasts forged in Eastern soil, executed an acrobatic turn and flew from her hands. Chopsticks scored one point. In the second, she tried using them again and gave a demonstration of clumsiness. Chopsticks scored another point. In the third round, a sauce stain the size of Australia covered Marisa's white dress. Chopsticks won with flying colors, *clap, clap, clap, clap*.

She headed for the restroom to clean herself. It took her a while... and another while. Marisa returned with her dress white again and her face flushed with excitement, two shades above sake-pink.

"Marco, guess who's in the room next door."

"Who?"

"The Siamutt. And here comes the best part..." She made a dramatic pause. "He's got company."

A Siamutt would be the cross between a Siamese and a stray cat. That's how the school director, Breno Belvedere, carried himself with his expensive suits and aristocratic pretension. He bore watery blue eyes, a stature that remained indecisive between tall and short, and thinning brown hair. The difference between a Siamutt and Belvedere was that the Siamutt looked cute.

Marco didn't seem too impressed with the news.

"Let me guess. You saw Belvedere with the new librarian, right? Pale, black hair, old-fashioned clothes and thick glasses?"

"That's right. Celeste. How did you know?" Marisa sounded disappointed with his lukewarm reaction.

"I'm not blind."

Marco had once caught Belvedere morphing into the leading man from a bad soap opera as he discreetly performed a romantic scene in the library.

"He should get a lesson," said Marco. "Such a hypocrite. Posing as a saint to the shrew he has for a wife. Preaching the virtue at school and intervening even in the female students' clothes. Who does he thinks he is? The Pope? Christian Dior?"

Marisa laughed and almost spilled more soy sauce on her clothes. Then her face clouded over: they'd better leave. She feared being recognized in spite of the wig. The check was requested, settled and returned to a Brazilian lady in a geisha disguise, owner of smooth hands and swift feet.

When they were about to exit, however, Marco retained Marisa. He put one index finger to his mouth, asking for silence, and whispered: "Let's give him a fright."

"What?"

"Let's hide his shoes," said Marco, and pointed to a pair of black moccasins lying in the hallway.

They exchanged a look of complicity, then smiled. Marisa returned to their private room. Marco glided over the floor with the stealth of a ninja and snatched the shoes. They split their prize. Marisa searched for a place to hide the left shoe assigned to her. She slid it under a pile of cushions in the corner, but the pile tipped over like a ridiculous Leaning Tower of Pisa and denounced the shoe.

Marisa retrieved the moccasin and turned back as Marco flung his load out of the window. A muffled noise signaled when the trajectory of the footwear was interrupted by an awning. Marisa's jaw dropped. Marco snatched the other shoe from her hands and, before she had a chance to close her mouth, threw it over the neighbor's roof. Another thud, sharp this time, consummated the crime.

The two of them tiptoed across the hallway, accelerated down the stairs and said goodbye to the geisha in the reception without pausing. They darted onto the street and only came to a halt on the corner, panting and laughing. Then they exchanged a cinematographic kiss.

The school director, on the other hand, found himself in a very tight corner while trying to explain to his wife where he had lost his shoes.

11. Close Encounter of the Third Kind

It is said the prohibited is exciting. In their case it wasn't. At school, Marco and Marisa barely spoke to each other, for they feared their intimacy would transpire in their eyes and in their voices. In certain moments, though, when no one was watching, they sent caresses at a distance. And text messages.

Marco: *You look gorgeous in turquoise. I like your top.*

Marisa: *It's new. I bought it thinking of you.*

Marco: *Drop your pen on the floor.*

Marisa: *What for?*

Marco: *I want to admire your cleavage.*

She smiled, raising her eyes. Around her, the other students filled out a form about Clarice Lispector's works. With her head slightly lowered and her eyes fixated on Marco, Marisa brushed the pen off with her forearm until it rolled to the floor. Then she leaned forward, allowing one of the top straps to slide off her shoulder. She retrieved the pen, straightened up in no hurry and pretended to concentrate on the form.

At his desk in the front of the room, Marco concealed his cell phone behind an open book (*Coldness and Cruelty*, a study by Gilles Deleuze on the works of Sacher-Masoch, purchased the day before). He directed a silky gaze to Marisa before typing.

Marco: *Would your top be up for an evening out tonight?*

Marisa: *It needs to finish some writing when it gets home. But that shouldn't take too long.*

Marco: *Great. I'd like to invite it to dinner at a bistro out of town. A place with antique décor and candlelight. Do you think your top would be up to that?*

Marisa: *Absolutely. Btw, do you know it made you that dessert you like and bought you a gift? My top found something on ebay that you were dying to get.*

Marco: *Don't tell me it's that rare album by... oh, no, it can't be... and lemon cheesecake...?*

Marisa: *Sorry, honey, now its lips are sealed.*

She raised her eyes to find Marco's twinkling with enthusiasm and curiosity. He was very, very curious. Marisa always played that game. She liked to watch his reaction. It had been long since Marco had a relationship, and he welcomed her attention with almost exaggerated contentment. She loved it.

That evening was an exception—the two of them under the sky speckled with stars, driving along the deserted road to Embu das Artes, a town eighteen miles away known for its arts and crafts. The tiny bistro Saint Pierre held half a dozen tables and lay by a quaint set of steps linking two streets on a hill. There, Marco and Marisa tasted vintage wine, shared chocolate soufflé for dessert and forgot all worries of being seen together: it was Tuesday, an improbable day for romantic dinners out of town. Before returning, they took a stroll near the town square, along alamedas of purple and white lasiandra trees.

As a rule, when Marisa could steal a few hours in the evening, the two of them would go to bars, eat at Arabic delis or spend time at the movies: they watched hand in hand Woody Allen's *Whatever Works* and *Midnight in Paris*, as well as a special session of Hitchcock's *Psycho*. The pair usually remained in the Downtown vicinity, for the crowd from school seldom visited the area at night. The heart of the richest metropolis in Brazil pulsed there, beating madly at daytime and hibernating after working hours.

In its origins, the city founded by Jesuits in 1554 was no more than a grain of dust that any fiercer wind would sweep off the map. By sheer luck a tiny coffee seed—descendant of another brought clandestinely to the country—fell on the state's purple soil. With the explosion of the "black gold", the capital entered the 20th century like a wealthy lady with Old World flair. Its motto became *Non ducor, duco*: "I am not led, I lead." From the downtown area, São Paulo kept stretching. It stretched so much there wasn't enough time to include in the map all new streets mushrooming month after month. A number of vintage mansions were demolished to make room for high-rises and, twelve million inhabitants later, the city kept shape-shifting.

In Downtown, however, the past persevered. Marco and Marisa liked a bar called Ambrosia from the late forties with art deco columns, checkered flooring and pastel-yellow walls fitted with wooden panels. The décor displayed antique furniture, crystal chandeliers and mirrors that stretched in a long, narrow space. A hardwood counter flanked by leather stools followed most of its length, featuring golden draft beer taps and the inevitable espresso machine. Above it, a curved mezzanine with a piano bar levitated in half-light.

One warm Friday evening, as usual, Marco and Marisa were having a beer on the mezzanine. He wore light pants and a white T-shirt, she wore a little flowery dress with her wig tied up in a ponytail. They had come on his black Ducati: summer was right around the corner with all of its delights.

"Tell me that poem," Marisa asked him.

"Which poem?" Marco inquired, reaching for her hand over the table.

"The one I like. About truth. By Carlos Drummond de Andrade."

The Divided Truth. He thought for a moment, eyes wandering across the mezzanine to glance at the piano with its quiet player and at the walls lined with old sepia photographs of the city, many of which portrayed places that no longer existed. Then he turned his gaze back to Marisa and declaimed: The door of truth cracked open but only gave way to half a person at a time. So the half-persons went in and each brought out their profile of half-truth. People compared the profiles, and they did not match. Distressed, people broke down the door and found out the truth bore two different halves, neither entirely beautiful. A debate ensued to elect the best half. No verdict was reached.

"So each person chose according to their own whim, their illusions, their myopia," Marco concluded.

"I love it even more when you recite it." Marisa sighed, leaning over the guardrail.

She recoiled with a nervous gesture.

A couple sat downstairs at a table opposite the bar, and Marisa recognized them straight away.

"Don't look now." She lowered her voice. "The school principal is here. Apparently with his mistress."

"Oh please, give me a break. Can't he go somewhere else with that librarian?" Annoyed, Marco pressed his lips together.

"Here's the thing. He's not with the librarian. He's having a drink with his secretary."

"Jane?"

"Yep."

Marco cast a glimpse downstairs. Yep. The school principal, in his corniest performance, held the hand of a young blonde in a pink dress. She wore red-framed glasses. Maybe it was no coincidence he'd found another mistress with high-prescription glasses. There you had well illustrated the old saying that love was blind.

Marisa wanted to leave quickly. That posed a technical problem, however. On their way to exit they would pass by Belvedere and his rosy princess. Marisa considered waiting until the couple left, but Marco rejected the idea. Belvedere and Jane could be there for hours.

"I'll tell you what. I go first, and you exit ten minutes later. I'll wait for you on the corner," Marco instructed.

She instinctively brought her hands up to the wig, making sure it was in place. "What if they recognize me?"

"When you're passing by them, lower your head and pretend to search for something in your purse."

"What about you?"

"I'll be fine."

They requested the check, brought by an employee nicknamed "Jorge Express" who frequently waited on them. A thin man from Northeastern Brazil, he had curly hair and skin the color of mocha coffee. He lived by himself and loved talking with Marco about literature. Marco recommended and gave him books from time to time, and now the waiter was dying to discuss his latest finding, *Tower Struck by Lighting*, by Spanish author Fernando Arrabal.

The last thing Marisa wanted was for Jorge to begin a literary discussion. Express, my ass. She had to endure the usual rigmarole. Isn't it a fascinating book, Marco? Yes, it is, Jorge. See, Marco, even if I don't understand a thing about chess, I'm following the story and want Tarsis to defeat Amary, as he's such a weirdo with all those people talking inside his head. Yeah, Jorge, chess is merely an artifice for structuring the plot in a logical manner while the backstories of both protagonists unfold in a blast of color and paradox…

Etcetera, etcetera, etcetera.

After the fates of Tarsis and Amary were dissected to exhaustion, Marco paid the check and stood up. Then he stroked Marisa's hand in a tranquilizing manner.

"Relax, my love. Everything's gonna be fine."

Marco brushed his lips on hers and headed for the stairs, leaving Marisa dazed. She kept the warmth of his touch, which pulsed inside her chest like a sun. It sparkled and throbbed and exploded.

My love.

Marco had never called her that way. Several thoughts bumped into one another in Marisa's brain. Belvedere and Jane, wait ten minutes. What Marco had just said. Lower head, fumble with purse. Her mind spinning, her body tingling. And what she had wanted to say back to him.

Love of my life.

When Marisa realized, it was almost time to meet him outside. She waited a few more minutes and risked a peek at the bar: Belvedere and Jane had started dinner, and he shoved a forkful of stroganoff into her mouth. Marisa descended to the ground floor and tiptoed forward. Belvedere had his back to her. Jane managed to steal a glimpse at Marisa's face and frowned, a spark of familiarity surfacing in her eyes.

Marisa flustered, furiously fumbling with her purse. Things became more interesting when she approached their table and saw from the corner of her eye the silhouette of a man in black pants and a white shirt… Jorge! Here he came, attached to a tray overflowing with beer tulips.

"Everything okay?" he asked, his face solemn.

Marisa nodded with no intention of stopping… and stopped: Jorge parked right in front of her with the barrier of glasses. Marisa assumed a contortionist pose to talk to him and simultaneously prevent Jane and Belvedere from seeing her face. She stood in an ambiguous position, neither frontal nor lateral or posterior, like the statue of some exotic divinity.

"I saw Marco leaving earlier, and… I hope you two didn't have an argument because of me," Jorge went on, mortified, the tray tilting slightly to the right. "I noticed you were nervous and I should have quit talking. I'm so sorry!"

"It's okay, it's okay," she said in a low and incisive voice.

Keep quiet, you chatterbox.

With one stretching eye Marisa could see Jane with an intrigued expression as the director prepared another mouthful for her. The secretary told him something. He glanced at Marisa and shook his head. Jane shrugged and opened her mouth to receive the food. On her face, though, a question mark lingered. *Oh-oh.*

"Are you sure?" insisted the immovable waiter, and now the tray tilted left.

"What?"

"Is everything really okay between the two of you?"

"Sure, Jorge, *he* left ahead to… get the bike," she improvised.

"Oh, thank God. And sorry again for my intrusion. It's just that it's such an interesting book. Have you read it?"

"No, I haven't, Jorge…"

Marisa fixed one hypnotized eye on the tray that oscillated like a ship on the waves of an increasingly turbulent sea… *Oops… oooops.*

"If I may suggest, read the book. It's riveting. Me, I can't wait to end my shift here and go home to finish reading it. I'm crazy in anticipation with—"

CLINK, CLInk, CLink, Clink, clink, clink, clink! He was going crazy, all right. Here, his animation became such that while gesticulating he caused a blast of glasses—the glass tower struck by the lighting of his enthusiasm. To the impassible checkered floor they all tumbled, the only survivor being the tray. Marisa jumped back. The floor before her was covered in shiny shards, golden puddles of beer, and personal effects falling in single file from her gaping purse. She and Jorge crouched to collect a cell phone, lipstick, an organizer, a ballerina key holder, a creased receipt, a folding toothbrush, a leather wallet… and two bright yellow condoms that jovially sprung out of it.

Now Marisa just wished she could disappear into the nearest manhole. Patrons at neighboring tables, including Belvedere and Jane, watched with great interest the condoms afloat like buoys on the wet floor. Marisa hurried to shove the dripping items into her purse and zipped it up with exasperation. Jorge helped Marisa get to her feet amid profuse apologies—he bowing a thousand times, she dying to get the hell out of there. In the midst of commotion and haste and demented gestures, the wig got displaced. That was the last straw, or rather the last drop of beer. Grasping the wig, Marisa gave an Olympic jump over the broken glass and ran away.

She chewed her heart up to the newsstand on the corner. Marco serenely read a gardening magazine with tips for growing *Vanda coerulea* orchids. He returned the copy to the pile, concerned with Marisa's distress. She told her version of the facts while fixing the wig with a nervous tick.

"I survived, but now I'll probably need a Prozac. Maybe two." She caught her breath. "What about you, how did it go?"

It was easier than expected. A waiter carrying a platter of stroganoff showed up and covered his back as he passed by Belvedere's table. That was it. No glass cascades or special effects. It was a shame she had to go through such a stressful situation. Relieved, Marisa urged they leave straight away. Marco didn't move. Then he smiled—mouth twitching upward in a reflex while his eyes ignited like a pair of flames. Marisa knew that smile. He wasn't happy at all.

"What's the matter, Marco?"

"Wait for me here. I'll be back in a minute."

He didn't give her a chance to protest. Marisa saw him retracing his steps and couldn't believe when Marco reentered Ambrosia. Her gaze, on alert, hooked to the entrance as if to pull out the door and peer inside. The possibilities stretched out on the horizon: a conspiracy with Jorge to sneak laxative into the director's beverage (*anything* was possible with Marco), an

altercation between Marco and Belvedere, a full-blown fight, Marco fired…
And there was nothing she could do now. Actually, there was *one* thing she
could do: destroy her manicure and bite her nails to death.

Marisa began meticulously with the right index.

12. Duet Story

When Marco finally returned from the bar, Marisa had already ravaged three nails to perfection and was preparing to attack the fourth. She dropped her hand and aimed a microscope-like eye at him, investigating the white clothes with no rips or blood stains (check), the hands, arms, neck and face unscathed (check), the hair impeccable as usual (check). Marisa cheered up, then frowned. Marco not only showed up in one piece but barely hid his satisfaction.

"Why did you go back there?" she asked, anxiously fiddling with one jagged nail with the tip of her thumb. (She needed a file badly or she would go crazy.)

"I couldn't forget my good manners, could I? I had to say hello to Belvedere. I even took a picture of him and Jane for the school blog."

"Marco Aurélio! You're crazy!" Marisa kept feeling the jagged edges. (Where could she find an open drugstore to get a nail file?)

"Not me. I don't intend to post anything on the blog, but that should teach Belvedere to stay away from *our* bar."

Upon seeing Marco, the director choked on a piece of steak and turned redder than the tomato flower decorating his plate. Jane, as white as the plate itself, stood up and started punching his back. At that point the piano player, now performing Frank Sinatra's classic *My Way*, sang the lines about biting off more than one could chew…

Marco cracked up, and Marisa couldn't help but laugh too (nothing like some comic relief in a disaster film… and speaking of disaster, where again could she find a drugstore to buy a file?). They walked around the corner to get the Ducati, and she proposed going to Marco's apartment. He refused. They would head for another bar he knew in the vicinity.

Marisa slowed down to a halt.

"I'm not sure, Marco. If Belvedere happens to pop in..." (A nail file! Pleaaaase!)

"If I know the guy, he'll rush back home with his tail under his legs. Besides, the place is safe. It's located in a dead alley and, trust me, our friend would never set his delicate foot there."

"Really?" (Do you think Marco would have... Ah! She must have a file in her purse... hmm... wet.)

"Wanna bet?"

The bar Extreme Tigress presented itself with modesty: a few tables around a pillar and, in the back, a counter flooded with black light. Although the white walls were naked, the owner had taken care of adorning the tables with plastic flowers. A jukebox starred the evening wrapped in the soft luminescence of a dream, playing old hits by tacky Brazilian idols. Exuberant women with big feet, boobs and hair fluttered around.

It was a transvestite bar.

Marco and Marisa indulged in the luxury of choosing one of the four tables aligned on the sidewalk. To the sound of Sidney Magal's *If I Catch You with Another Man I'll Kill You*, a waitress in a skintight yellow uniform slinked to their table to take the orders. Two vodkas and tonic with lots of ice and one order of fries. Oh, of course, and a nail file, please.

The two of them amused themselves imagining what Breno Belvedere would do now that his affair had been unveiled. Maybe, Marisa speculated, the director would try to save face by pretending he was with the secretary to talk about work.

If I catch you with another man, I'll kill you
And send you some flowers before fleeing

Marco got extreme. Inspired by the lyrics of the song, he concocted a Nélson Rodrigues sort of tragedy in which the shrew found out about her husband's infidelity while having a drink with a girlfriend at the piano bar. In shock, she squeezed the ketchup hard over her fries, and a red stream crowned the pale mound that looked like a heap of bones. The shrew envisioned the corpse.

With a vengeance, she sent her sons off to their grandmother's (they didn't know a thing about Nélson Rodrigues anyway) and proceeded to plot her husband's death in a paradox of calculation and culinary passion, by adding ground glass to the bastard's tropeiro beans. The director agonized slowly. His innards bled as much as his wife's heart. The shrew called him a cheater, then hugged him and begged him not to leave her— until in a paroxysm she spat on his face and yelled that he made her sick to her stomach.

They say I'm wrong
But whoever says it has never loved

Marisa also gave her contribution to the drama: after dispatching Belvedere to the Otherworld with her macabre delicacy, the shrew posed as an inconsolable widow and, for the deceased's funeral, purchased the most expensive carnation wreath in store. Then she eloped with the gardener, an ardent young man with whom she had been having an affair, as the director was no longer able to please her (he couldn't get it up).

The widow and her lover traveled to the Caribbean to enjoy an illicit honeymoon. Once there, however, the young man met the waitress from a local spa, a fake blonde with oblique eyes and hard flesh that bewitched him with her slink. So for dinner the shrew spiced up Creole-style shrimps with an extra measure of ground glass. She then tried to decide which flowers would be appropriate for a gardener's funeral.

When Marisa and Marco saw the waitress place plastic daisies on the neighboring table, they exchanged a smiley look.

"Very nice. Still, our story has a discrepancy," said Marisa, nibbling on a potato stick.

"What's the problem?"

"The lyrics refer to *a man* catching his wife with another guy."

"Poetic license."

"No, sir. Things need to be accurate. Your turn."

He emptied his glass and thought for a moment.

"Okay. The shrew, disillusioned with men, those useless cheating bastards, decides to have a sex change surgery and later winds up in a torrid affair with the spa waitress. Then, one day, she catches the girl in bed with another man, prepares a special dish for her, etc."

"I don't like this take."

"Hmmm. Yeah, it's a bit contrived..." Marco glanced at a ghastly drunkard that stumbled into the bar. "I'll tell you what. In a dark and stormy night, Belvedere's *ghost* appears to the shrew. She blacks out and her heart gives in. Few people attend the funeral because at this point she's already earned the reputation of Black Widow. Belvedere's ghost, for old times' sake, leaves a bunch of purple carnations at her grave. Then he escapes to the afterlife realm—"

"Good move, Marco."

"—where he has an affair with the spirit of the waitress murdered in the previous version."

"You've spoiled it all over again."

Marco stared at her gravely.

"I think you're jealous of the waitress, Mari."

"Which one? The girl who had a ground glass overdose or the girl who served us this second-rate vodka here?"

Marisa looked at the waitress with bleached hair and red nails, who now talked to the bartender. Her breasts seemed about to perform a somersault right out of her low collar.

"Does it make any difference?" asked Marco, following her gaze.

"Hmmm... nah. Either girl would merit a seal of approval by Nélson Rodrigues."

Meanwhile, the urban fauna was circulating in the area. Here, on this side of the street, a couple of students hurried to the movie theater and a lady of the night winked at a lonely wanderer. There, on the other sidewalk, a noisy group of play actors headed for an Italian restaurant. Further away, a platinum-blonde transvestite tried to entice clients with her Marilyn Monroe contours in skimpy clothes.

A man of strong build, the sort of guy who lived at the gym, passed by her in a tank top that emphasized his phenomenal biceps, triceps and pectorals. The transvestite approached him with curvaceous words, but her baritone revealed her true anatomy (a woman imprisoned in a man's body, with an inconvenient five-inch appendix).

Outraged, the man rebuffed her. The transvestite retaliated with her fake Prada purse and an outburst of insults. She called him a closeted sissy. The man gave her a slug in the face and stormed off in a huff. Astounded by the action of those phenomenal biceps, triceps and pectorals, the Marilyn Monroe from the tropics wobbled, floated and landed her tender fanny on the harshness of the pavement.

The forceful union of silicone and asphalt wasn't amicable: the diva stood up with her dignity not only outraged but quite sore. She cursed, put her wig back in place and composed herself on the curb. Soon a black sedan stopped, with a well-groomed gentleman behind the wheel. The two of them talked briefly and the transvestite climbed in the car.

Marco and Marisa exchanged looks as the sedan disappeared on the avenue. That was *sooo* Nélson Rodrigues. They made a toast to the writer and asked for the check. When Marco presented his credit card, the waitress apologized for the malfunctioning wireless device and asked him to pay at the cashier. He went inside to settle the check while Marisa waited at the table.

Across the street, a blue neon sign flickered already in the after-hours mood. The bar was virtually deserted and the jukebox began playing a slow track (*Stop Taking the Pill*). The chords mingled with a couple of beeps from Marco's cell phone. Marisa stared at the phone on the table. Who would be contacting him that late? She picked it up and saw the notification of an incoming email. Without a second thought, she touched the screen. Marisa turned livid when she read the name of the sender.

13. There Won't Be Roses

Blue and black the neon flickered across the street. Tremulous blue, then black with the ghostly outline of the letters composing the establishment's name. From time to time, a letter would faint amid the blue flash. Kiss Club… Kiss Club… K ss Club… Kiss Club… K ss Cl b… With the cell phone clutched in her hand, Marisa stared at the neon sign, immobile like a waxen statue. She heard Marco saying goodbye to the waitress and quickly returned the phone to the table. Within instants, Marco sauntered out of the bar with carefree Sunday demeanor: arms swinging to confident strides, a smirk on his lips—the alpha male in leisure mode, as Marisa noted sourly.

"Shall we go then?" He grabbed the cell phone, noticing her insistent gaze. "Everything okay? You look pale."

"It's nothing."

"Are you sure?"

"Yes." She shrugged and stood up. Her brain was spinning and spinning and spinning.

Marco put his arm around her shoulders and they went for a promenade in a nearby square, where a flower market was open until late. On a sudden he halted, turning to Marisa. He ran one hand on her hair and contemplated Marisa in silence as he sensed her turmoil. His eyes were serious under the thick cape of eyelashes, and when they narrowed like that they acquired an almond shape, a crease on the corner of each eye while another, deeper, appeared between the brows—a small gash on the serenity of the forehead. His jaw first clenched, then his mouth half-opened. Marisa stilled her breath and waited. The words never came.

Marco blocked the lamppost light, bathing her face in shadow and her lips in kisses. Soft, brief. Until he threaded his fingers in her hair and lingered to explore her mouth with an intimacy that made Marisa melt. The kiss always soft but now slow in each recess, on the tip of the tongue and further in. She kept reluctant hands on his shoulders while he pressed the small of her back and brought her closer. The breeze surrounded them with the scent of flowers, and from an apartment window sneaked out a drowsy song from the fifties. *I Don't Know*, in the voice of Ruth Brown. Marisa questioned if she should give her heart to him. And the chorus replied: I don't know, I don't know…

Marisa extricated herself from Marco's arms, feigning interest in the roses displayed beside her. For a moment they admired the arrangements on the shelves of half a dozen booths along the sidewalk. Flowers with all colors of the day, from gold at dawn to blood at dusk. Flowers as blue as the wings of a bird tinted by the night. On an impulse, Marco picked up a bouquet of red roses. They were Colombian, larger and more fragrant than ordinary roses. With no thorns.

"Do you like them, Mari?"

"Very pretty."

"They're for you."

Marisa hesitated and shook her head as her disquiet increased. Why that whim now? Marco had never given her flowers precisely because they were impossible to hide. Maybe he felt guilty and was trying to relieve his own conscience.

"Thanks, but my mom will get suspicious if I show up with them."

"You can leave them in my apartment. They'll always be yours."

"Will they?"

"Of course." He half-smiled, frowning.

"Better not."

'Why?"

"They're gonna *wither*, that's why," Marisa replied curtly.

Taken aback by her tone, Marco returned the flowers to the stand with an air of frustration. He studied her face, reaching for her hand. Marisa retreated rigidly, unable to hinder her thoughts.

"We've never discussed our situation," she blurted out, and her voice carried such an edge he lifted an eyebrow.

"True. I've never been involved with a student before, and I admit: sometimes I'm confused."

"Why confused?"

"Because, strictly speaking, I should have never—"

The sentence hovered incomplete as Marco sidestepped to make way for a couple approaching on the sidewalk. He waited for them to move away and, when he turned his attention back to Marisa, he found a pair of somber eyes.

"You should have never done what, Marco?"

"I'm your teacher, Mari. I'm more experienced and, in my position, I can't afford to be irresponsible." He sighed, improvising a tired smile. "I *couldn't* have afforded, but now the damage is already done."

"I didn't know you regarded our relationship as *damage*."

"That's not what I meant—"

Wasn't it, really? And, here, Marisa emptied her chest of the suspicion consuming her. Maybe Marco would rather be with a woman his own age, someone with more *experience* and less problems at home. Maybe even *Camila*. How could she be sure he wasn't seeing the other girl? Marisa tightened her arms across her chest to hide a tremor. She waited for him to speak out—to say anything, anything that would appease her.

"There are plenty of opportunities. That Camila is already nineteen, attractive, and more than available," insisted Marisa.

Marco remained quiet, in search of words. Until now, he hadn't mapped the consequences. When doubt or insecurity rose, he closed his eyes. But reality was sinking in and he needed to face it… While he followed the rugged topography of his musings, Marisa's words diverted him. He frowned.

"Camila? What's with her?"

"I see you together at school. On one occasion, you two were chatting on the corner and you handed her some papers. Yesterday she gave you a ridiculously expensive box of chocolate. And she *emails* too. I saw it in your cell phone," Marisa retorted in an accusatory tone, which sparked a furious glare from Marco.

"So that's it." He paused. "I can't believe you've spied on me."

"Are you seeing her?"

Marisa sustained her gaze and waited for an answer with ambivalent expectation. Fear and hope. Because there was no denying the email in his cell phone and Marisa needed to know. Because she wanted to believe there must be a plausible explanation for that message in the middle of the night...

But which explanation?

She thought of the messages she had exchanged with Marco in the beginning and of the text he gave her and of the smile that came with it. She remembered how exhilarated she was with the first message and the first kiss, thought of the happiness she felt with Marco. Would that all be a mistake? Marisa tried to decipher his face. Maybe he wasn't who he appeared to be. She imagined him saying to Camila the same words he had said to her, and panicked because the world as she knew it might not exist. When would she learn? Believing what people said didn't work. The only thing that mattered was their actions.

They were evidently on different pages, languages, planets. Tightening his lips, Marco said nothing for a moment. His face reddened as he shook his head. A lock of hair rolled onto his forehead. He didn't take notice of it.

"I expected more from you, Marisa. What you did was *low*. Your question doesn't even deserve an answer."

"That's how it is?"

"If you don't trust me, we're on for a bad start. I don't tolerate that kind of behavior. You should be ashamed of following me and searching my things."

"Yes, we're on for a very bad start." She pointed one finger at him. "You refuse to answer a simple question and then make accusations so you can steer away from the subject. Do you think I don't get it? Sérgio used to play this game to make me feel guilty, whereas *he* was the one cheating."

"I am not Sérgio," Marco retorted with barely restrained exacerbation.

"Then answer me."

Marco's expression and voice became harsher at each word he spilled out: "I won't answer because it's *useless*, Marisa. Did I ever doubt you? The fact that you asked me this question is proof of your lack of trust. If I answer no, will it change a thing? Tomorrow you'll find another message, another box of chocolate, and if it's not chocolate it's gonna be something else. Then we'll have this conversation again. And over and over again."

"Oh, so you admit there will be other messages and more *chocolate*." Exhausted sarcasm. "There's my answer, right?"

"Listen—"

He directed a furious glare at the owner of a stand a few feet away, who looked from one to the other. The man started fussing with a bunch of tulips and virtually buried his face in them.

"Listen, have you ever heard me talk about Camila?" Marco's voice, a coarse whisper, grew louder. "I *never* mention her. I couldn't care less for that girl."

"Really? Maybe you don't mention her to avoid suspicion. You're dating *me*, why wouldn't you date Edible too?"

"*Edible?*"

"Camila, Edible, *whatever*. While I kill myself studying, she doesn't mind idling and has all the time in the world to jump into your bed. Not to mention her mother doesn't cause half the trouble mine causes. It's quite convenient, isn't it?"

Now Marco's eyes shot sparks. Only the eyes. Under the street lamp, his face became a frigid mask drawn with angry charcoal lines. Marisa could no longer reach him. How odd, she thought, the way relationships could be so fragile. One moment you were in someone's arms sharing your heartbeat. The next, all that remained was distance and a track of words lost in translation.

A flower brochure dragged by the breeze produced an intermittent rasping on the cement. It rolled to the curb and fluttered by the mouth of a manhole. Then it vanished.

"I have no control over your thoughts, your suspicion, your jealousy, Marisa. We can talk and be good today, but it'll be just a temporary fix, because your lack of trust will manifest sooner or later. Do you recall Sartre? If that's what you choose to believe, there's nothing I can do," he reasoned in a sharp tone.

"Don't you drag Sartre into this!"

"Are you going to make a scene now? That's the next move?"

She was about to protest; however, Marco ignored her and averted his face, looking fixedly at a light sign across the street. He remained still while his indignation imploded in locked fists. Marisa felt a dagger being thrust into her heart and twisted with impassible meticulousness. She didn't recognize Marco. As in a diorama, light shifted to reveal shadows in the cheerful colors of the canvas.

The sidewalk under her feet seemed to crack, a sudden web of fine veins that branched throughout the cement, veins dilating in all directions, pieces of ground breaking and sinking down. And her in the center. The sidewalk on the verge of swallowing her just like the manhole had swallowed the brochure. She couldn't believe it. Just a minute ago, the two of them laughed together in a fifth-rate bar. There was love in the laughter, joy in the plastic flowers. Love and joy made of plastic—was her mistake that huge?

Marisa strived to keep standing. She grew dizzy. Intoxicated with pain.

"Do you really have nothing else to say to me, Marco?"

Her voice sounded like broken glass. His tore the air.

"No, Marisa. I don't feel like talking to you."

"The truth is, it doesn't make any difference, does it? I'm only a pastime. I should have realized it sooner. But, as you said, I'm not as experienced as you. Goodbye, Marco."

Marisa spun on her heels and moved away, a splash of flowery dress waning amid the trees in the square, then farther down the street. Marco—his eyes immersed in the light sign—did not move.

14. Carnival

Marisa drifted disoriented. Everything empty. The streets, the hours, her heart. Her head spinning. Marco. The connection she felt with him was so strong it hurt. So strong it scared her. He understood her in a gaze, a caress, a word. He *mattered*. Not the others now inhabiting her past in small storage rooms locked with the key of indifference. They weren't that many anyway.

Louis, the older school mate with sandy hair who had taken her virginity when she was sixteen. The two of them had been dating for a while and were listening to music in his bedroom that day. Marisa remembered—The Beatles' *Revolution*, the curtains closed, the odd sensation of having her intimacy touched by another person. But Louis erected an impenetrable block: in truth, he only had eyes for himself. Months later, when he departed to study marketing in France, there wasn't much room for longing.

Then Sérgio came into the picture. Handsome and dark and tall, alluring like a colorful gift box. An empty box. The perpetual bliss lasted exactly nine months, the time for a gestation and for Sérgio to replace her with his diving instructor. Heartbroken, Marisa refused to get involved with anyone again. Then along came Marco and she lowered her guard. She had *presumed* their relationship meant something to him but was clearly mistaken.

A sob sprouted from deep down inside and tears flowed freely from her eyes. *I was nothing more than a toy to him.*

And Camila… Marco's falsehood triggered a wave of nausea in Marisa. She searched her recollections for an indication of his lies—and found many, since memory fabricated its own treacheries. Marisa felt torn between the hope of being wrong and the even stronger suspicion that he concealed something from her. One could only know a person when an extreme situation forced them to disclose their true nature. Marco had finally revealed his. Worse, he didn't even show the decency of looking after her safety, leaving her to wander into the night on her own. Marisa yanked off the wig angrily, shoved it in her purse and let her hair loose.

As if guessing her thoughts, the cell phone vibrated with a call from Marco. She didn't answer. Another call, followed by a message: *Where are you?* Marisa ignored both. Now it was too late. To use Marco's words, the *damage* had already been done. And, in that moment, a practical matter required her attention. She couldn't go home because her mother believed she was at Valentina's, and she couldn't show up at two in the morning at her friend's doorstep either.

Marisa needed to find a hotel for spending the night. She hastened her pace—actually, she first needed to find a safe place in order to check her cell phone for a hotel. Glancing at the cars passing by, Marisa hoped to get a taxi. The few that went past her were already taken. A bar caught her attention yet soon discouraged her with its filthy counter surrounded by drunkards.

At that point, she recognized the engine sound at her back and, squaring her shoulders, kept on walking. She set her eyes ahead and wiped the tears with a furtive gesture.

"Mari!"

Marco tagged along after her, and Marisa advanced at a brisker pace. She went around the corner and he followed her in the counterflow, with the black Ducati close to the curb.

"Mari, stop. I'm sorry, let's talk."

"We have nothing to talk about. You made yourself clear," Marisa said without pausing.

"You don't understand."

"Oh, yes, I do. You can go back to your apartment and fool around with whomever you want. I will mind my own business, which I should have done from the beginning."

"Will you listen to me?"

His voice echoed on the deserted street. The imperious tone brought Marisa to a halt. She turned around to face him, crossing her arms.

"Come with me." Marco strained to sound calm. He seemed about to explode. "I won't leave you roaming the streets by yourself at this time of night. Let's go to the flat, and tomorrow I'll drive you home."

"That's what hotels and cabs are for."

"Mari, don't be stubborn."

"Leave me alone!" she nearly yelled. *"I'm not your toy."*

Marisa resumed walking and then, on a sudden, was running to the next avenue. There, like an oasis in the urban desert, she spotted the glass façade of a bar with interiors enlivened by candles and strings of multi-colored lamps. Marisa read the yellowish sign as she crossed the street. It displayed a frame of suns, moons and stars around a name written in old-fashioned letters: Carnival.

She entered the place in a state of daze, hardly noticing the counter across the wall and the round tables in the center, many surrounded by empty chairs. All Marisa registered was an out-of-focus snapshot as she headed to the bar in the back. She perched herself on one of the stools, tapping her fingers on the red Formica counter. Only then did she look around.

The walls displayed vintage posters featuring a gallery of characters painted by hand—a magician with a top hat and a fortuneteller with a headscarf, a dwarf and a bearded woman, Siamese twins and a lizard-man. Near the entrance (Marisa just noticed) stood a natural-scale tin bear sporting a golden-trimmed red coat and cap. A drum hung from its neck.

The house still entertained twenty or thirty patrons. Marisa ordered a vodka and tonic and decided to stick around until dawn: better to be miserable in that bar than alone in a hotel. A slow music selection began playing, and she recognized the track by Amadou & Mariam, *Sans Toi.* Her shoulders sank along with her thoughts. *Without you there's no song, no dance, no rest...*

The bow-tied bartender brought her drink and a miniature merry-go-round with seats filled with peanuts and potato chips. Marisa half-heartedly munched a chip and took a long sip of vodka and tonic. Retrieving the cell phone in her purse, she typed a message to Valentina.

Call me asap, I need to talk to you. Marco and I broke up. You were right, I shouldn't have dived head first into this…

Marisa had a startle when she heard a roll of drums announcing… what? She turned in the direction of the sound and realized the tin bear had started its number, blinking a pair of sky-blue eyes and maneuvering the sticks with its mechanical arms. Next to it, a girl in puffy pink pants laughed out loud as she pressed the control connected to the bear by a plastic cord.

The toy continued to play until it stopped brusquely, paralyzed with a stick in the air, one irresolute eye half-closed and the other wide open. The bar fell once again into a discreet rustling. The after-hours quietness, pervaded with weekend activity exhaustion, crept into the building. Much like the circus it mimicked, the bar already signaled its fatigue after hosting the crowd. On the now-empty tables, the candles exhaled one last sigh before dissolving into a bed of melted wax.

When Marisa turned back to her vodka and tonic, she noticed a young man with dark hair and olive skin staring at her from the end of the counter. She ignored him and resumed typing.

I'm so shocked. You wouldn't believe Marco's coldness. I'm almost positive he's seeing Edible. How come I was so naive…

Someone took the empty stool by her side, and Marisa raised her eyes to face the dark-haired guy. Thin, medium height, he wore black clothes, red suspenders, a green belt and colorful sneakers. *A clubber stranded amid the carnies,* Marisa deduced.

"Hi, what's up?" He rested his elbows on the counter. "I've never seen you here. First time?"

Oh-oh, here came an after-hours shark trying to score. She assented stolidly and returned to her unfinished message.

"Nice to meet you. My name is Felipe. May I ask you something?"

Marisa looked at him as if she had received an unsolicited call from a telemarketer at dinner time. Any other guy would have been intimidated. Not Felipe.

"Are you waiting for someone?" he inquired in a nasal voice. Before she could answer, he added: "My girlfriend would like to talk to you."

Caught off guard, Marisa realized Felipe was gay. He indicated a tall blonde with short hair at the end of the counter. The girl had three silver hoops in each ear, and her black tank top exposed a pair of bracelets tattooed on her forearms. Her blue eyes widened as she grinned.

Marisa grinned too. It would be good to have company that evening. She would feel more at ease with those two than with some shark hitting on her. In a couple of hours it would be light outside and she could go home— her mother would be already asleep after watching half a dozen films.

The girl approached Marisa and stood before them, introducing herself: Daniela. The three formed a circle and spent the next few minutes in small talk, until Felipe left them to speak with an acquaintance.

Daniela was an art student in the third year of college and, just like Marisa, loved TV series. She argued that TV, not cinema, created true innovation. Cinema had been pasteurized in order to assure return of investment from a global audience. Television, on the other hand, could be daring. For example, the most amazing series of all times was…

"*Breaking Bad!*" Marisa said in unison with her.

"That's it!"

"Simply unbeatable."

"A work of art."

They smiled with complicity, and Marisa said: "I wish I were more knowledgeable about art. One day I'll attend a course like you."

"Formal education isn't necessary to appreciate art. References are important, but too much theory kills spontaneity and intuition."

Marisa stared at her with a doubtful expression and told a story. When she was fifteen, she had visited the MoMA with her parents to check out an exhibition featuring all sorts of installations. The family stopped before an assembly consisting of a dark-gray cleaning cart with colorful bottles, an electric-turquoise bucket and a yellow wet-floor sign. They observed all details and tried to interpret the work. They stood there for ages. The father thought it criticized the moral filth in the world. The mother believed it sang an ode to cleanliness. Marisa considered it a homage to pop art. They were at it when the museum's cleaner showed up and took the cart away.

Daniela laughed. The boundaries of art were blurred. In a museum somewhere in the world, there might be a gray cart in display referring to moral filth, cleanliness or pop art. She talked about performance artist Marina Abramović, who during three months occupied the atrium of the same MoMA where Marisa had her encounter with the cleaning cart. Marina would keep still and silent, seated opposite an empty chair. That summed her work: the artist's presence. More than 750 thousand people spent hours in line just to sit on that empty chair and exchange a look with Marina.

"People must have gone to the museum compelled by curiosity or to show off," refuted Marisa. "It sounds like she wanted to do something eccentric so everybody would think she's a genius. The woman decides to spend three months sitting on a chair without moving or opening her mouth, and that's supposed to be art?"

"It's seemingly so simple, isn't it? Now think of all the physical and mental discipline required for that. Especially mental. It's easy to get dispersed, but she remained *present* there, with her body and soul. Thus people saw their own humanity in her. The artist became a mirror. Many people cried. Many returned. The most inspiring moment was when the love of her life, Ulay, sat on that chair. It had been more than twenty years since the two last met. Marina, concentrating to receive the next visitor, kept her eyes closed. When she opened them and recognized Ulay, he became her mirror..." Daniela paused and held Marisa's hand. "You're sad. What's the matter?"

"It's nothing," Marisa lied to her as well as to herself. "I'm already getting over it."

Daniela stroked her hand, and the two exchanged a look—in that instant, two mirrors gazing into one another. A dive into the same reflex, the soul imprinted on the iris glow. So many stories in there wanting to come out, and a silver drop falling onto the mirror of the lake—a tear? Marisa tried to find something to say but was at a loss for words. Daniela simply asked: "May I kiss you?"

Marisa didn't reply. The lips caressed hers. She kept still, eyes wide open. It felt strange to be touched like that by another woman. Soft. A drop forming circles in the water. So soft. Daniela broke contact, ran her fingers on Marisa's cheekbone and hair. She drew her lips close again...

Marisa heard someone clear their throat and snapped her head to find Marco standing next to her. The tin bear rolled the drum and the girl in the puffy pink pants spilled peals of laughter.

Ba-dum-tisssh! Ah, ah, ah, ah, ah...

15. After Hours

"Can we talk?"

Marco's voice was hard. His eyes, mercurial. Marisa assented mutely while Daniela stepped back and peered at him with curiosity. Marco pulled the tab from under the glass and suggested they go to a quieter place. Still under the bear's drumming, he paid for the check and exited the bar towing Marisa by the hand.

Marco barely glanced at her as he climbed onto the Ducati parked across the street. Handing Marisa the helmet, he waited for her to mount and took off without as much as a word. She felt the cool wind on her face and his taut muscles against her body as they sped up along empty streets with a succession of buildings and intermittent lights.

He rode faster than usual and the trip was a short one. Marco's silence made her increasingly uncomfortable. When they entered the apartment, he moved straight to the kitchen and returned with two bottles of mineral water. He offered her one and emptied half of the other in one draught.

Then Marco sat on the sofa with one ankle on his knee and one arm stretched over the backrest. He stared at Marisa for the first time since the two had left the bar.

"Are you gonna stand there? Why don't you sit down?"

Each word transpired aggravation. She agreed and settled for the other end of the sofa with all dignity while repeating to herself she was free to do as she pleased. Marco had no say about it. If anyone there owed an explanation, it was him. The jerk.

After a pause, Marco inquired what she was doing at the bar. Marisa shrugged. The quarrel began.

It's none of your business. I'm not allowed to ask a simple question? You didn't answer *my* question, why should I answer yours? Marisa, enough of that. What do you think people do in bars? Who was that girl? A friend. Since when do you kiss your girlfriends on the mouth? Since I turned single.

The two had reached a crossroad. At that point, they could take the path of mutual accusations, dig trenches and unearth resentments. It was a wide path. As they walked it the distance between them would broaden just like their deafness, until they lost sight of each other as they embraced the belief that being right was more important than being in harmony. And so each one would keep going on the opposite margin of the road, clinging to their own truth—flawed, incomplete, human truth.

Marco and Marisa vacillated and, in silence, gazed at each other. Her irises burnt with an amber tinge, as if a flame throbbed behind the retina. His were darker, circled by bloodshot white. Marco let out a sigh.

"I don't own you, neither do I believe in cages, Marisa," Marco said with a sigh. "I respect your decisions. You should go for what suits you best, but with consciousness, for a legitimate reason. Not out of anger."

"Who said I didn't have a legitimate reason?" She jutted out her chin. "You're so fond of your games and now want to play the moralist?"

"This has nothing to do with morals. Exploring your sexuality is not a problem as long as no one gets harmed. You acted without thinking."

"Marco, just forget the lecture. I'm not interested."

He directed a sideways glance at the wooden floor, drumming his fingers on the sofa. Then he stared at her again.

"If you keep throwing stones we'll never come to an agreement. Is that what you want?"

"You don't have to worry about your professional reputation," she assured in a calm tone, contradicted by the flash in her eyes. "I'm not reporting you to the school board. All I want is to forget what happened between us. Soon I'm gonna graduate, and I'll never have to see you again—"

Marisa bit her lip. Now he was getting to his feet and closing the distance between the two of them. She winced, perturbed by his composed countenance. She knew it was a mask but couldn't read beneath it. Marco sat next to her as if trying to decide what to do.

"I've said it already, I'm not telling anything." Marisa's voice sounded high-pitched. "What else do you want?"

She nearly jumped when he leaned over to lay his parted lips on her neck, stroking the skin with a whiff. His long fingers drew invisible patterns across her collarbone, with the lightness of another whiff, and Marisa felt just like she would always feel under Marco's spell: spiraling, spiraling, spiraling... She made an effort to collect herself and slapped him on the shoulder—she wanted to get back at him, hurt him too. Marco held her wrists, and she couldn't counter his strength. His fingers closed around her flesh with an ease that only served to infuriate her. The ragged sounds of their breathing permeated the room.

Marisa cursed, her face flushed, eyes sparking. She was immobilized under his weight. The wide chest crushed hers. The large hands pinned her arms against the upholstery. She struggled, attempting to kick him. The skirt of her dress slipped up, the neckline slipped down, and Marisa felt on her bare skin the texture of Marco's clothes. They left in her an imprint of his warmth with a vestige of cologne. She weakened but resisted.

"Let me go!"

"I'm trying to calm you down," he said unperturbed.

"That's all I need. You're so *pretentious...*"

"I don't like to fight with you, Mari. Let's make peace."

"... *pretentious and controlling!* If you think that... What did you say?"

"Let's make peace, my love..."

And, with that, Marco sealed his lips over hers. Marisa kept her mouth tightly shut. He insisted: with the tip of his tongue he courted and taunted until she gave way to him. Sensing Marisa relax, Marco released her wrists and caressed her nape, flexing his fingers, barely touching her, touching just enough as to sow a trail of trepidations—small seismic waves here and there, minute volcano eruptions in the pores, and the imaginary lava winding all over the epidermis...

"Marco... you get on my nerves..." she sighed as he began nipping at her ear.

"I know." He smiled against her skin. "You should set me straight."

"Hmmm, that's what I'm going to do... sometime..."

Marisa enveloped Marco's neck when he kissed her again, and her caresses wandered on his back and on his hair until wrapping his nape. She felt Marco's quiver on the palm of her hand and his dampened moan on her lips. The sensations intensified, as anger was still a memory in their cells. They devoured each other now, tongues nearing, inching back and entwining in a sinuous dialogue. The punishment of a bite on the lip mingled with the flirt inside the mouth.

And then Marco pulled back and inhaled sharply, his gaze still cloudy over her body—the long legs revealed by the dress, the meandering line from the hips to the waist, the chest that heaved under the flowery pattern. He imagined his mouth on each of those flowers and then his fingers ripping them to attain other gardens. He ached to fill his hands with her shape, play at the threshold just to tease her. And feel those legs wrapped around him while he submerged in the satiny, moist, tight warmth and spent himself there to the last drop. The rhythmic sound of their bodies colliding, billions of atoms dancing and shuffling their scent—pheromones, fragrance, sweat, sap. Marco suppressed the urge to lift her skirt and penetrate her like that, half-dressed, the urgency impelling him to thrust hard, harder, the urgency of fusing into her and having her cry with release. To see her face blend a smile, a sob, a blaze at once transfixed on him and already enraptured by pleasure.

Not now.

With reluctance, Marco straightened up and helped Marisa sit. He held her hands.

"What is it?" Her eyes widened, apprehensive.

"We'll continue this later." His smile emerged, hovered for an instant and faded. "But we need to talk because it's no good to leave things pending. I've learned that the hard way, and I don't want to make the same mistake." He pressed Marisa's hand. "I owe you an apology. I shouldn't have allowed anger to take me over. But in that moment I was in no condition to talk. Without realizing, you touched a wound. I'm sorry, Mari. I didn't mean to hurt you. I looked for you everywhere... I'd never forgive myself if something happened to you."

"It didn't seem that way."

Noticing Marisa's wounded expression, Marco cocked his head as his eyebrows joined. He stroked her face.

"Where did that come from, Mari? I stood across that bar like an idiot only to make sure you'd be okay... I thought about what you said and understand your suspicion. But Camila means nothing to me. I don't know how she got my email. At first I replied to be polite, then I ignored her and she stopped emailing. Yesterday, for some reason, Camila left a box of chocolate in my pigeonhole along with a card for National Education Day. It was pathetic. I made up an excuse and returned it this morning."

"She bragged about it yesterday and I thought she'd made that up. Why didn't you tell me?"

"Why would I tell you something that has no relevance whatsoever? To be perfectly honest, I had forgotten all about it."

Marisa told him about the email Camila had sent that evening, and Marco seemed surprised. He picked up his cell phone from the coffee table and slid his index finger on the screen. The message was brief: "This reminded me of you. I started reading *The Selected Prose of Fernando Pessoa* and would love to talk with you about it. Maybe one of these days after school?" Attached to it, the photo of a sunny forest and a quote by the poet: "Organize your life like a literary work, putting as much unity into it as possible." Marco shook his head and pressed the trash icon.

"Done," he said, emptying the trash. "I don't know what got her to start harassing me again, but I'm gonna keep my distance."

"She's really trying hard, eh? It's the last chance to hook you before the end of the year." With her curiosity satisfied, Marisa was now indignant. "And what's the deal with Fernando Pessoa and the forest? Are the trees supposed to provide paper for the literary work of your life?"

"Beats me. Now let's forget about Camila, okay? Mari, you've got to promise you will never spy on me again. You have no idea how much that affects me. My marriage was destroyed by mistrust. I want to build an honest relationship with you."

Marisa clarified she had seen him with Camila by chance. She apologized for checking his cell phone and, after some hesitation, asked if he wasn't attracted to Camila.

The question disconcerted him. He thought about the possibility, which had never crossed his mind until then. Granted, Camila was pretty, but her looks did nothing for him. It was rather like a photograph in a catalogue that you would flick through and soon forget. Camila bombarded him with questions and followed him in the hallway, making it almost impossible to get rid of her. She had asked for research help once and he gave her a print, but that was all.

"To me, Camila is just a student like any other," he concluded. "With you, things are different. And I'll never cheat on you because I don't accept cheating. If we were to see other people, it wouldn't make sense for us to be together. The intimacy we share is unique. It belongs to the two of us alone. Dragging someone else into the relationship would violate that, and it's not what I want." Here, Marco stared at her with such intensity it alarmed her. "If you ever fall for another man, you've got to be honest and tell me."

"Marco, I don't do to others what I don't want others doing to me." She sustained her gaze with equal intensity. "I hate lies and would never betray your trust. I know how it feels to be awake at night imagining the person you love in the arms of someone else, imagining they were together behind your back, cringing for having kissed a person who was just out of someone else's bed. I couldn't do that to anyone. Especially to you. But tonight I felt so insecure when you mentioned *damage*..."

"Please, erase that. I wasn't talking about us. You are the best thing that's happened to me. But I don't want to cause problems with your family and be an obstacle in your life."

"An obstacle? My love, I've never been so happy as I am with you."

Her eyes confirmed what she said. She put her arms around him. They remained silent for a moment, each with their own thoughts.

"Thank you. I needed to hear that," he whispered. "Everything will be easier once you're no longer my student. We'll figure a way of smoothing things out with your mom. With time, she'll eventually get used to the idea."

"I hope you're right..."

At that point, Marisa blurted out her concern. Her mother was a difficult woman. Maybe she was like that because of her own father, an irascible colonel who had driven her two uncles away from home as soon as they turned eighteen. All severity reserved to the uncles, however, turned into complacence when it came to Marisa's mom. If none of what his sons did was ever good enough, everything his daughter did was perfect. She grew up not knowing what it meant to be contradicted.

At twenty, she was engaged to a senator fifteen years her senior. She obsessed with the perfect wedding and her willful ways brought the relationship to an end. The senator called the engagement off one week before the wedding and, a month later, Marisa's mother learned he was with another woman. That carved a deep wound in her pride. She recovered upon marrying Marisa's father, but then she dreamt of having a child and tried for five years to no avail. When she gave up, she got pregnant.

"My mom spoiled me a lot. She wanted me to be like her. When I grew older, I rebelled and she started criticizing me. We had many ups and downs until things cooled off. But since my dad's passing she's been so neurotic. I don't know how to be closer to her and I feel guilty for not giving her more support."

"We can take your mom out on the weekends, and then the two of you will spend more time together, Mari."

"That's the problem. My mom obsesses with finding me a perfect husband. The failed engagement to the senator made her suspicious of older men, and I fear her reaction when she learns about you."

"She could change her mind once she realizes you're happy and it's a steady relationship." He smiled and added: "I've always been good at charming my girlfriends' moms."

Marisa's face remained somber.

"My mother is stubborn, Marco. If she doesn't approve of something, that's it. She didn't like my ex Louis because he's Jewish. My dad attempted to appease her, but she wouldn't leave me alone." Marisa shook her head at the memory. "One day, at a family lunch, my uncle Carlos took my side and said she was prepotent. They quarreled, and my mom wouldn't speak to him for almost two years. *Two years.* She only got back in touch after my granny's funeral."

"We'll find a solution."

Marco didn't allow his uneasiness to show. He had his own reasons to worry—but those he kept to himself.

16. The Graduation

Springtime dwindled and December reached the summertime threshold with a scent of warm rain and the end of high school. The 13th was a lucky day: when the last class of the year ended, major relief jump-started students back to life. Extra assignments still waited for those who needed to improve their grades, and the course for college admission would continue for another few weeks. But for now, for a brief intermission, no one worried. The class had already planned a trip to Cancun for celebrating, lulled into a sunny daydream with stretches of turquoise water and seas of tequila.

In the evening following the end of classes, a Friday, the school's Rotary Club promoted its traditional graduation party. Marisa had no intention of going, and twisted and turned to dodge her mother.

"What happened to the long blue taffeta dress? What you're wearing is so *plain*." The mother studied her in disapproval and pursed her lips.

"The blue dress got stained," Marisa said cautiously, smoothing her black minidress. "But this one will do."

The simple, sleeveless model featured details in silver thread that sparkled as she moved, accentuating her figure and her legs, elongated by high-heeled sandals. It matched the sapphire necklace and earrings that had been her father's gift for her birthday the previous year.

"I'm not so sure," the mother insisted in a sour tone. "Black is such a *depressing* color. I can't believe you ruined that blue dress. It was so elegant."

Marisa hated the taffeta gown her mother had bought for her. Right now, though, she didn't want to keep talking, or an argument could erupt. When her mother was upset, any word, even the most innocent, turned into an elephant paw on a minefield.

With the excuse that she didn't want to be late for the photo session at half past six, Marisa picked up her purse and said goodbye. She then initiated a marathon: she took a taxi, got off at the party venue, ensured her appearance in the graduation photo book, sneaked out, slipped into another taxi, slipped the wig on, and proceeded to meet with Marco at the Jardins area.

Marisa passed by mansions and upscale buildings, bars and restaurants exuding a deliberate casualness perfumed with money. She disembarked before an impressive façade in the shape of an inverted arch that seemed to float above the glass-walled lobby. Similar to the profile of a ship covered in copper plates, the place was an architectural landmark in the city. Spherical windows dotted its six floors, and the entrance door at the side, as imposing as a cathedral's, opened up to a lobby with impossibly high ceilings.

Once in the atrium, Marisa had the impression of crossing the bottom of the sea as she passed by designer furniture disposed like coral clusters in the wideness of clear water: black and white chaises lounges, here a sculpture of Saint George and the Dragon in a niche, there an anemone of flecked flowers. The reading area, delimited by a semicircular bookcase, boasted red fan-shaped armchairs and a gigantic navy blue puff that spread like a sleeping shellfish on sandy marble. Up above, the rooftop water mirror undulated in crystal reflections.

Marisa's thrill at meeting Marco intensified with the singular beauty of the hotel, which not by chance had been baptized the Unique. It was strange getting together with Marco away from Downtown—a thrill mixed with disquiet. They *should* be safe, for the school crowd would stay at the graduation party until late. But what if an acquaintance happened to show up at the hotel? (Marisa lowered her head and glanced at the executives, tourists and models circulating in the lobby.)

She neared the bar in the back featuring a concrete wall with gleaming shelves that piled up high, guarded on each side by a golden statue. One way or another, Marisa went on thinking, she had scored good grades and the school term was officially over. Freedom was almost within grasp for Marco and her. A future with no more secrets or guilt. Only one dark cloud still hovered on the horizon: her mother's reaction once she learned about Marco. Better not to think about that now.

One, two... eight, nine... fourteen, fifteen... She counted sixteen shelves in the bar before taking the panoramic lift that, immersed in a faint haze of light, took her straight to the rooftop. There, a vestibule wrapped in dimness led to a corridor fitted with translucid onyx of yellow veins. The stone emitted diffuse clarity like an ethereal tunnel.

C'mon closer
Close the gap
Jazz up over
C'mon closer

As she proceeded through the corridor, Marisa discerned the whispered singing of a deep house track. *Come on Over* by Neolectrique. With soft notes of guitar, the music grew louder toward the restaurant, where a brunette in an impeccable blue dress waited. When Marisa mentioned the reservation under the name of Mr. Fares, the hostess grinned.

"Oh, yes, Marco." She pointed to the far end of the restaurant. "He's waiting for you on the terrace."

Marisa advanced through the long room in half-light, throwing a glimpse at the large windows that leaned over the Ibirapuera Park right across the street. Once the water mirror was transposed, the room expanded onto the elevated deck beside a rectangular swimming pool with submersed red lamps, which drew fairy circles of color in the water. On the opposite side, pairs of white loungers lined up under lanterns and square parasols. At that point, a flutter of butterflies and jazzy notes overflowed in her heart...

Marco idled on one of the loungers, his shoulders relaxed, one leg folded and the other stretched. He too wore black, with a new shirt that emphasized his broad shoulders. She rehearsed a sideway approach and, without making any noise, covered his eyes with both hands. Marco inhaled deeply—vetiver—and smiled. Marisa lifted her hands, sitting next to him. She pressed a kiss on Marco's lips and then on his neck.

"Hmmm. I like it. What cologne is that?"

"Acqua. I decided to go for a change. According to the ad, this fragrance is gonna emphasize my virility and give me an irresistible aura of refinement."

Marco's playful expression vanished when he took his time to admire Marisa, pausing on the curves shaped by the dress and on her mouth. For a moment, he envisioned the two of them in a room of the hotel, where he would be able to yank off her dress and lipstick. He flirted with a change of plans but forced himself to dismiss that thought. Tomorrow they would have the whole night for themselves.

"You look stunning. It's a shame you must hide under that wig."

"*Psst*... I'm a spy in a secret mission and I have some top secret information. Next spring we'll have that picnic under the cherry trees, with a special cheesecake just for you." A pause, another flutter of butterflies. "Hey, Marco, did I mention I love your company?"

"I love yours too, Mari Hari." He stroked her hand. "And your cheesecakes."

She took those words with laughter, looped her arm in his, peeked around. The flickering glow of white candles poured onto the deck center, and a dotted line of lights followed the plant beds on the sides. An island in the heights, the terrace floated amid the urban forest with its neon towers and lit-up windows twinkling in the distance.

"This is beautiful."

"It's one of my favorite spots in São Paulo," he said.

"You are like one of those Russian dolls that hold another doll inside, and another and another. I didn't know this side of you."

"Which side?"

"Your eclectic tastes. Traditional bistros, transvestite bars, trendy restaurants."

"I like places with a personality. They can be simple or sophisticated, modern or old-fashioned, it doesn't matter." He traced her jawline with the tip of his finger. "I'm happy you're here with me. Speaking of which, this calls for a toast."

Marco picked up a champagne bottle from an ice bucket on the side table. He uncorked it and pulled a linen napkin, uncovering a couple of black crystal flutes. He poured the golden liquid into them and offered Marisa one of the glasses: to your future, Mari, drink it all in one go for good luck. They toasted, and the echo of crystal blended into the music. *Finally vs. Love Story* by Kings of Tomorrow and Layo & Bushwacka. The music about worlds colliding and the march of time and the beginning. Finally.

> *And we gazed and dreamed*
> *Till our spirits seemed*
> *Absorbed in the stellar world*
> *And we sailed over seas*
> *Of white vapor that whirled*
> *Through the skies afar*
> *Angels our charioteers*

Radiant, Marisa did as he said. When she reached the last drop, the glass clinked, surprising her lips with a cold metal kiss. Marisa widened her eyes. She tipped off the flute, and the ring rolled onto the palm of her hand, platinum lace embroidered with diamond, ruby, tourmaline, emerald…

She felt her throat blocked and her eyes cloudy with a veil that for an instant made the world waver out of focus. She wavered with the world, muttered his name and couldn't voice anything else. Marco dried the ring with the napkin, sliding it onto Marisa's third finger.

"I was leaning toward a solitaire, but thought these colors go well with you. Do you like it?"

"A lot… thank you, my love. You didn't have to do that."

Marisa placed a kiss on the palm of his hand. Marco caressed the lacey finger and covered her hand with his.

"Of course I had to. Don't cry."

"It's just that I've never received such a beautiful gift from a boyfriend. And your gesture—"

"*Shhh*, you deserve it. Now let's go inside. We can't take too long to dine."

The waiter brought the champagne to their table by the window and, as they drank, Marco and Marisa enjoyed the view of the park. Just like the city, it hosted a diversity of ethnicities, from the native jatobá to the Australian eucalyptus, and huge trees dressed up in Christmas lights poured their reflection onto its lake.

Echoes of classical music reached the restaurant, and the dance of the waters began: the fountain in the lake projected jets that rose, dropped down and entwined, changing colors. Suddenly a thunder dampened the music. And, as if someone had pressed a button, the whole scenery blurred under the cape of a summer rain. In the park, commotion burst. In the hotel, those on the terrace stampeded into the restaurant amid exclamations and laughs.

Marisa glanced at them and turned to Marco.

"This will be my first Christmas without Dad," she said pensively. "Although I still miss him, today for the first time I could picture the possibility of being happy again. Now I realize the pain was the last thing my dad left for me, the last memory. I got attached to it for that reason. It was the only stable thing remaining in my life, the only thing no one could take away from me. The pain was *mine*. Since my father's passing, I've been carrying around a weight. This morning I looked at myself in the mirror and knew straight away something had changed: the weight was gone."

"Consider that everything in the world is energy, Mari. Quantum physics has already demonstrated that, when you reach subatomic particles, the physical contours separating things are no longer visible: all is part of the same sea of energy. Your father just shifted into another form. He continues to exist and, most importantly, he continues to live in your heart. What's left is the longing, which only time can cure. But I'd like to help you get over it."

"You've already helped me and are still helping me, Marco. If it weren't for you, I don't know where I'd have ended. I was devastated when we first met. Many times I pretended to be fine but deep down…"

"I know. I know you."

They gazed at each other, communicating silently. It was as if they had lived together their entire lives. And in a way they did, in dreams and thoughts.

"I wish I could reciprocate all you do for me, Marco."

"You do reciprocate, more than you think. I am the one in debt with you."

His words lingered between them. The waiter brought them bread, moved away, and the echo of the words still persisted.

"How come, Marco? You give me all the loving and support."

"I'm not sure if it would be the same with another woman. You bring out the best in me, and I *want* that to surface more and more because it brings me peace. By giving me your love, you give back to me my own love, which I thought I was no longer able to feel."

Marisa reached out over the white tablecloth to hold Marco's hand. As she did so, she admired the ring on her finger with new awareness. Marco sometimes wouldn't speak out his innermost.

"Your ex-wife did hurt you a lot, didn't she?"

"Certain wounds take time to heal. Sometimes they never mend completely." He got lost in a pause. "When I look back, I understand Lorena. We were too immature. To make matters worse, we lived in turmoil. But a part of me still can't accept what happened. I always think that, had I behaved in another way, maybe we could have been happy and…" He shook his head without finishing the sentence.

Marisa stiffened and released his hand. She folded her arms, and behind them there were clenched fists. She felt the ring's texture against her palm—a ring whose meaning she could no longer interpret. It seemed suddenly hollow and brittle, an empty shell. Fear seized Marisa, for she felt she was being emptied herself.

Noticing her reaction, Marco leaned over the table, his gaze trying to reach her where she had sought refuge.

"What is it, Mari? Why are you suddenly angry?"

"I hadn't realized you were still so attached to your ex-wife. Maybe you still love her? You need to seek the answer in your heart with utter honesty. Not only for my sake but for your own."

"Give me your hand." His tone revealed apprehension.

Marisa shook her head and kept her arms crossed. She could have remained quiet and pretended it was nothing. Pray all would be fine and, above all, act *pleasant*. She used to behave that way. It had never led to anything.

"I prefer to have everything in the open, Marco, no matter how brutal the cut. It's better than living a lie. You know how it was with Sérgio. A lie. I don't ever want to go through that again. Even if I wanted, it wouldn't work. One day the house of cards goes tumbling down anyway."

"Give me your hand. Please." When Marisa finally stretched her hand out, Marco cradled it between his. "I know exactly what it's like to live in a crumbling house of cards. I don't want that either. I'm not implying I'd still want to be married to Lorena. What I wish is to have prevented so much pain. When I got involved with her, I had no idea of the problems I might cause."

"I'm sorry if I got you wrong. I guess I have my own traumas." Marisa sighed. She wanted to help him and didn't know how. "After all, what problems are you talking about? I know you two dealt with a lot of friction and arguments were escalating."

"To say arguments were escalating is an understatement. Our marriage turned into hell. We said horrible things, hurt each other way too much. The contradiction is that, while we argued, there was hope. One way or another, we still cared about the relationship. *Lorena* still cared. Then we silenced. She stopped complaining. I clammed up in my resentment. There's nothing worse than feeling lonely when you are with someone, Mari."

"But for sure something else was going on?"

Marco would rather not go into details. He distanced himself. Contrary to the usual, his voice droned.

Lorena's family didn't approve of the marriage and broke contact with her, stirring all sorts of tension. The irony was they rejected Marco because he possessed no wealth. A year after the divorce, he and his brothers inherited their uncle's coffee farm. That alone would not be enough to appease Lorena's family, but time has passed, the road was paved and the city expanded to the farm perimeter. The year before the last, they split the property into lots and sold it per square foot to a luxury condo.

He still recalled the last time he had coursed the coffee plantation with his brothers, under the deafening song of destitute cicadas fleeing the urban offensive. Their shadows stretched in the sunset and streaked the path as tiny white flowers waved goodbye in the breeze: goodbye to childhood memories. The next day the bulldozers took it all down.

Every gain came at a price.

After investing the money, Marco settled in a comfortable situation. He studied for his PhD and, for now, taught for the enjoyment of it and to test new educational methods. He wanted to found his own school. If it were today, Lorena's family wouldn't have any problem in accepting him. During the marriage, though, the situation was different. Lorena became increasingly frustrated and unhappy. The few relatives who still kept in touch fed lies. Marco blamed himself for not having sufficient maturity to give her support the way she needed. He just wished he could have avoided what happened later.

And, at those words, color ripped through his voice. It was red. Crimson, scarlet, coral, rosy, almost white... and then the cut sealed up again. In silence, Marco stared at the window pane where rain teardrops spattered.

Marisa entwined her fingers in his. The stones on the ring sparkled.

"You know it's a lost battle, Marco. We can't change the past, only accept it and learn from our mistakes. Then everything is worth it. All experiences, good and bad, shape us into what we are today. You try to suppress your hurt, but it's no use keeping it in a drawer under lock and key. You need to open that drawer, forgive Lorena and yourself."

"I've tried, believe me. I tell myself I'm gonna erase it all and pretend none of that happened. But it's hard."

"Forgiveness isn't a magic pill that you take and instantly changes everything. It's a process. You can forgive gradually and in your own terms. But you have to forgive. Otherwise resentment will grow deeper roots." Marisa caught herself half-smiling as she thought of Sérgio. "When I say that to you, I'm actually saying it to myself too, because sometimes I don't listen to my own advice. But forgiveness is the only key that unchains us from the past and unlocks the door to the future. Wasn't it Lao-Tzu who taught that if you feed your resentment and seek revenge, you better dig two graves?"

"I believe it was Confucius." Marco smiled, and his gaze softened. "I know, my love. I'm learning. You're teaching me. Please, I don't want you to fill your head with nonsense. You're the one I want, not Lorena, not another woman, do you understand? Sometimes I feel…" He stared at Marisa for a long moment and picked up the menu, changing his tone: "Shall we order our food?"

Marisa respected his reticence. They checked the menu and, as had already happened on several occasions, the two ended up choosing the same dish, this time salmon in a ginger and lemon sauce. Then, as a habit, they shared dessert, a chocolate mousse with Grand Marnier and orange zest. By the end of the meal, both were relaxed and content.

As they exited the hotel, they faced traffic. An impatient Marco consulted the clock on the car panel and took a backstreet. He now zigzagged across town to avoid busy streets. It was a computer game: the car, a silver rectangle in a glistering grid of asphalt, gliding, halting, bypassing, threading. Marco entered another backstreet and accelerated. Marisa asked why the rush. Concentrated on the wheel, he didn't look at her. But he smiled.

"*Shhh*. I can't tell you. It's a surprise."

17. Behind the Peephole

Marco threaded his way from the hotel to Downtown, dropped the car in a parking garage and, taking Marisa by the hand, dashed along the sidewalks still damp with rain. The two followed an avenue. At the end of it, converging to an overpass above the valley, they reached the illuminated frontispiece of the Municipal Theater. Renaissance statues perched like angels on the façade that stood out against the backdrop of skyscrapers and a starless sky. The lobby sparkled with art nouveau and baroque minutia in a profusion of marble, bronze, mirrors and stained glass.

"Here we are, right on time," Marco announced. "I thought the opera would be something different for celebrating your graduation." And since Marisa was getting all excited: "But hold on, you may not even like it that much—"

She silenced him with a kiss.

They took a box seat near the stage. Above them, the ornate dome supported a massive chandelier, poised like a sun with the radiance of thousands of crystal pendants. It slowly dimmed out until the rows of red velvet seats submerged in shadows. The stage came to life, revealing a 19th-century Japanese residence sided by a cherry tree. Madame Butterfly's tragedy began.

Cio-Cio San is a fifteen-year-old geisha who falls in love with Benjamin Pinkerton, a US Navy officer visiting the country. He weds her in a marriage of convenience and soon departs to the United States, promising to return. Pinkerton then marries an American woman, unaware that Cio-Cio is pregnant. She waits for him for three long years. Pinkerton eventually comes back with his new wife for his son. Desperate, Cio-Cio bids farewell to the child and commits hara-kiri.

At the theater exit, as they walked to the parking garage, Marisa remained quiet, shaken by the presentation. At the time of the story, not few American naval officers visited Japan and married Japanese women, abandoning them upon their return to the United States. According to the records, Madame Butterfly was real.

The sidewalks had dried up, streets filled with people and laughter punctuated conversations in bars. With the thermometer registering eighty-eight degrees, the air was like a viscous mantle that smelled of concrete, beer, sweat and perfume. Marisa contemplated the half moon with a halo of frayed clouds—a ghost enveloped in tatters. With sudden uneasiness, she squeezed Marco's hand.

As usual, he stopped the car on the corner of her street. Marisa crammed the wig into her purse and picked up a bunch of textbooks that had been left on the back seat at their last tryst. In the morning she had a practice exam and, as always, still needed to finish her notes before going to bed. With her hand on the door, she paused and stared at Marco. In an impulse, she dropped the books, kissing him somewhere between his chin and mouth.

"Hey, what's up?" he asked in flattered surprise.

"Thank you, Marco. For everything."

The two did not want to part. Their hands said it when they entwined. Marco touched Marisa's face. She brushed her cheek against his. Their hands met once more, fingers mingling, imprinting caresses on the palm and back, mingling again—waking up the body. Heat, shiver, hot, cold. All the things imagined. Their bodies couldn't be united in that moment. Their hands could, and that's what they were saying.

See how I caress your flesh on the mount of Venus, here below the thumb? It's just that I'd like to do the same to all of you. See how the tip of my index trails your fingers one by one, going up and down like this? That reminds me of the curves of your body, which I would so much like to kiss now, like dew on the petal of your skin… picking with my mouth the bud on your breast and the blossomed flower on the plane down below, until you quiver inside your dress…

And me, I feel my body pulsating at your touch, I brush my palm on yours in circles, this is what I would like to do, brush my belly against yours while I feel you in me, as a part of me, giving me so much pleasure like only you can give... I scratch your palm to give you a shiver. Afterward I stroke your hand with the back of mine, and it's as if we were lying together, skin with skin, arms and legs entangled, and me touching your face...

A world at the fingertips, in the palm of the hand.

"See you tomorrow night, then?" she finally asked with a sigh.

"That's right."

"Dinner and a movie?"

"Dinner and a movie. Then the flat," he added in a suggestive tone.

"How about we stop by before dinner?" Marisa caressed his nape and nibbled on his earlobe. "Just to check if your orchids are all right."

"Do you reckon they'll need watering?"

"Lots of watering. Before dinner. And afterwards."

"We have to look after the orchids, don't we?"

"Yeah. That *Selenependium* alone requires some care."

"*Selenipedium*," he corrected, wrapping a lock of her hair around his finger. "Ah, we need to do something about your Latin, Marisa. Such a shame. A promising student like you. Tomorrow we'll revise a couple of terms that I find particularly enjoyable. While we water the orchids."

"I'd love a private lesson, Professor Fares. Your diction is perfect. You're so intelligent, so cultured, so strong. You know so many things."

"Hmm. I like that. What else, Miss Constant?"

"Well..."

Marco didn't wait for the answer. He demanded Marisa's mouth, one hand rolling from her hair to her shoulder and following a slow path down her arm. It lodged briefly on the waist before ascending to skirt her breast. And there it remained, splayed, as it kindled the flesh in a circular motion. With an impatient gesture Marisa pulled his hand. It closed around the crown of her breast and then opened to envelop all of it.

She moved her thigh against his pelvis, against the beginning of the erection, as she girdled Marco and pulled him closer. He reclined the seat and covered her with his body.

"I've wanted to do this since you arrived at the restaurant," Marco whispered, brushing his lips across her shoulder.

"Me too. If it weren't for the physics practice exam…"

"Tomorrow I'll book a room in that hotel. How about we celebrate again?"

Her acquiescence was implicit in the way Marisa fondled his body against hers, inhaling the new cologne and closing her eyes for an instant to detect his scent. She proceeded to investigate underneath his shirt, felt the smooth flanks and then the abdomen down and the soft hairs on the chest. With a sigh, she slid her hands to the back pockets of his pants, far from being satisfied. She desired more. To sip everything hiding beneath those clothes while his mouth travelled over her body. The two of them turning and turning, until her head was between his legs and his head was between hers. And then, at some point, the two would turn again and become one.

Just the thought of it… Ah. Damn practice exam.

"I know what you're thinking," Marco said in her ear, his warm breath awakening a shiver in Marisa. He stamped a moist kiss on her neck, eliciting a languid hum from her.

"You do?"

"I can give you a hand."

Marco leaned back and, hooking his index in her dress neckline, tugged it downward to her midsection. He kept it like that and, with his free hand, ran his fingers on the exposed groove between her breasts. Marco moved north and south, and now he strummed her skin with his fingertips. Very lightly, taking off and touching down, taking off again and touching down on another spot. He sent tiny shocks at each passage, and her flesh tingled in anticipation, uncertain as to where that energy would drip like a thick and hot liquid. Honey melting on his fingertips. Honey strewed across her belly, thighs and loins. Honey on the fingertips harvesting her honey.

She arched back, half-closing her eyes. Her head tossed from side to side, until her upper body stiffened when his hand quickened the motion simultaneously within and without. A jarred moan. Marisa hovered on the verge of climax. She plunged into a whirl, floating adrift on her senses, expanding in vibration. Climax rippled through her. And rippled and rippled.

Marco teased Marisa with a raw lunge of his hips as he sought her mouth and filled it—the way he wanted to fill her body—in a hypnotic swell that ebbed and flowed, stroking lightly, slithering, deepening. They danced in place, his solid build in contrast with her softness, together to the right and left, slowly slipping in opposite directions to intensify the contact. Then Marco smoothed out Marisa's dress and returned to his seat. He licked his fingers, smiling.

"We better stop," he said in a husky voice. "Or I'll have you naked right here."

"Marco, you're mean," she murmured, readjusting the seat. She still felt his presence on her body. She wanted all of it. To take it with her mouth, hands, core. To make him float too.

His smile became sinful. His obsidian gaze.

"Tomorrow night I'll show you how mean I can be."

Deep house on the radio, H2O's *Nobody's Business* track with lyrics from the 1920s.

I'm going to do just as I want to, if I should take a notion to jump into the ocean, ain't nobody's business if I do...

Reluctantly, they said goodbye and Marisa went down the street. Marco noticed one of her books under the seat and called after her. Since she didn't hear him, he picked it up and chased her, reaching Marisa as she entered the building. In the deserted lobby they exchanged a brief kiss and, the moment Marco was about to leave, he turned back and they kissed again, this time in a long promise for their next date.

After the two parted, Marisa stepped into the elevator, her expression aerial and her thoughts still with him. The first thing she heard upon entering the apartment was a scream followed by a burst of gunshots: her mother watched a gangster movie on TV.

"How was the party?" she asked.

"Great. The principal delivered a moving speech and I danced a lot."

While two men in dark suits exchanged punches onscreen, the mother studied Marisa from head to toe.

"That dress fits you well after all." She smiled. "And your dad's gift matched it. For Christmas, I'm going to get you a sapphire ring to complete the set."

Marisa smiled back and remembered to hide in her purse the ring from Marco. Concentrating on the TV, she asked about the film, to which the mother shrugged: she wasn't very keen on Mafia stories but couldn't find anything better on. Marisa offered to help her out and they explored the TV guide together. There was a German-Turkish comedy her mother hadn't watched yet.

"Soul Kitchen: In a suburb of Hamburg, Zinos struggles with his restaurant on the verge of bankruptcy, the departure of his girlfriend to China and the swindles of his ex-convict brother. As if it weren't enough, he gets himself a hernia, health inspectors are on his back, and his apartment catches fire. Yet the worst is still to come..." Marisa's mother made a doubtful face. Was that actually *a comedy?* Yes, lots of fun. So they tuned into the film: funk music soundtrack, a pile of destroyed plates and a gawky Greek, all wrapped up to go with a side order of fries—soon both mother and daughter were laughing and sharing a pack of caramels on the couch. Until Marisa remembered she needed to be up early the next day and kissed her mother goodnight.

When she closed the bedroom door, Marisa heard the cell phone beep. She sat on the bed, fumbling with her purse to retrieve it. There she found the text message from Marco.

Check your email.

She accessed her inbox and saw it: the photograph of a red rose bouquet wrapped in Mário Quintana verses from *The Everyday Song*. It was about how good it felt to live day by day, enjoying the moment like the clouds in the sky—with a crazy wind rose tied to his hat and without giving a name to any river, for the waters moved and thus it always became a new river flowing in an eternal beginning: *"And with no memory of former lost times, I cast the rose of the dream into your distracted hands..."*

To which Marisa replied, with the pen of poet Carlos Drummond de Andrade, that one should not take the word *love* lightly, for it was delicate and beautiful like a soap bubble, a sacred name that held perfection on earth and should not be desecrated. *(We keep this sacred name between us, my dear Marco, and the truth in this poem comforts me.)*

As she undressed, a bossa nova song came to play on her lips. It must be noted that Marisa wouldn't be singing had she suspected the commotion that gurgled eight stories below. It had all started that very evening when Ms. Rosaura, the gossipy neighbor from the ground floor, faced a couple of very inconvenient mishaps. Her pot of soup burned while she rushed to the market for parsley, and the malfunctioning TV decided to convert the prime time soap opera into a silent movie.

The first problem Ms. Rosaura solved with a cheese sandwich (very tasty mozzarella, only $4.99). The second problem was skirted with one of her favorite pastimes: snooping through the peephole. All in all, Ms. Rosaura concluded she should buy more of that cheese. She also concluded that, sometimes, the attractions in the lobby of the building turned out to be far superior to those on TV.

18. A Shadow of Doubt

On Saturday, Marisa woke up early to study and went to school for her physics practice exam, which rendered her more dispirited than hopeful about her performance. When she got back home with Valentina, she immediately sensed something wrong: the TV was off. In the apartment hovered a dense silence, so dense it seemed like a living creature breathing within the walls. The mother sat on her usual blue sofa—this time, reading the Bible.

"*Very nice.*" She closed the book. Her mouth, no longer used to smiling, curved downward like a waning moon in a somber sky.

"What's the matter?" Marisa glanced around and frowned. "Did I forget the light on?"

"Don't you have something to tell me?"

The mother's irises sparked while she tapped her fingers on the Bible resting by her side. *Toc, toc, toc...* From the kitchen came the sudden sigh of the pressure cooker and a waft of lentils.

Marisa sighed too.

"Why don't you just say what the problem is?"

Toc, toc, toc...

Valentina looked from one to the other. Tension crept into the room under the vigilant eye of a congregation of Czech crystal miniatures. Marisa grew impatient and crossed her arms. A dramatic pause ensued, with welling eyes and a certain overcalculation when the mother raised one accusing finger.

"I heard that yesterday you were in the lobby making out with a man old enough to be your father. *What the heck is going on, Marisa?*"

Discomfited, Marisa wondered how the mother had found out her secret. Then it dawned on her and she became furious.

"Who told you that? Was it the gossiper neighbor from the ground floor?" Marisa acted offended. "That's an exaggeration. I didn't make out with anyone. A friend gave me a lift and kissed me goodbye on the cheek. That's all."

"So Ms. Rosaura was *exaggerating*, huh?"

"For Christ's sake, Mom. That woman is senile," Marisa ventured, but she could see skepticism all over her mother's face.

"Do you think I'm stupid or what?" she vociferated, red with indignation. "What have I done to deserve this? I try to give you a good education and that's what happens. You're really a lost cause."

Valentina stepped in, assuring her it was a misunderstanding. The mother's thin eyebrows joined in a scowl and she hissed: "And *you*. You're a lost cause too!"

"Will you stop it already? I can't stand your criticism anymore." Marisa flushed as much as her mother, whereas Valentina paled. "What if I am involved with an older man, what's the big deal?"

"*What's the big deal?* I want to know who's this man you're seeing."

"It's none of your business. You're gonna drive him away like you did with Louis."

"You bet!"

The mother stamped on the rug flowers and rolled her hands into fists. The speech Marisa knew by heart began. The mother talked about the ex-fiancée who had cheated on her and practically abandoned her at the altar. She reviewed the stab on the back, the humiliation, the shattered heart. How could Marisa be so naïve she couldn't see an older man would only want to take advantage of her?

"When are you going to forget the senator once and for all? It's *not* like that." Marisa coiled with a knot in the pit of her stomach... nausea, nausea, nausea... "The way you talk, it's like I'm incapable of winning someone's affection. Well, you're wrong. He *loves* me."

The mother vacillated but wouldn't take defeat.

"Oh really? And what does a pipsqueak like you have to offer to an older man besides easy fun? He'll soon leave you for another woman, that is, if he hasn't already found himself one."

"I bet you're crossing your fingers for that to happen. Just to prove yourself right. You're trying to live my life rather than taking care of yours. And you've always got to have things your way. That's what happened after Dad passed, right? Everything needed to be neat and over with because you hate to wait. How could you exclude me from my own father's funeral?"

Marisa's eyes clouded with tears. She saw the father for the last time right before her trip on Easter. *If a mosquito ever bites you, my dear, do not kill it or else ten more will show up for the burial,* he had said as he kissed her goodbye.

Her dad was like that, a born comedian, and his own life ended with the irony of a joke: struck by an ambulance. It was Holy Thursday and he died on his way to the hospital. The crossword magazine he had just bought flew from his hands in the moment of the accident. It landed next to a trash can.

During that extended weekend, Marisa went camping in a forest reservation with Valentina and her uncles, who lived in the countryside. There, in the paradise where they had burrowed, the cell phones were dead and Marisa forgot to turn hers off. She came back one day before Valentina, with the discharged phone in her backpack. Marisa arrived home content. Then the mother told her. In shock, Marisa asked why she hadn't waited for her to bury the father. There was no answer. The mother simply took her to the cemetery…

Now the mother cried and yelled. Her voice changed, as if she had a wounded animal trapped in her throat: "I called a million times to tell you about your dad and was unable to reach you. I had to bury him because I couldn't stand to look at him and imagine the accident. How do you think it was for me, waiting for him to come back home for dinner and receiving the news of his death? You weren't the only one in shock. And I wanted to spare you—"

"*Spare me?*" Marisa trembled. "You didn't even allow me to say goodbye to him. How do you think *I* felt? I go on a trip and when I return Dad's no longer here, just like a ghost, no closure. All I wanted was to touch his face for the last time, and you robbed me of that."

"I did my best… Now you're out of control and I can't deal with the situation. I can't!" She sniffled before continuing in a plaintiff tone: "I know you've always loved your father more than me. But if he were still alive, things would be quite different."

They stared at each other in sudden silence, their breathing ragged by an avalanche of resentment. To the mother, it was a shock that Marisa couldn't understand how she tried to protect her. To Marisa, it was a melancholic relief that the situation had reached the confrontation she feared—at least now there was no longer doubt. Each remained on the opposite margin of the road, each with her own hurt and incomprehension. And as they exchanged that look, they begin to lose sight of each other. On the surface simmered indignation. In the deep, great pain.

"You're right. Things would be quite different if my father was alive," Marisa said. "He *accepted* me instead of criticizing me all the time."

"I only want what's best for you. You'll stop seeing that man, do you hear me? As long as you live under my roof, you ought to abide by my rules. I will *not* allow you to be crushed like I was."

"That's it. I can't go on like this. You just won't accept me for who I am. It's beyond your control. Only you can't decide for me. I'm no longer a child. If I'm wrong, I'll face the consequences. But I *know* I'm not wrong. Maybe it's best if I get a job and move out. I don't want to leave you, but you give me no option." Marisa turned to Valentina and took her by the arm. "C'mon, Val."

"Where are you going?" The mother was alarmed, her eyes red, dark, wide. "Come back here, Marisa! You're the only thing I have left in the world now…"

Marisa stormed out in tears. She headed for Valentina's and the two locked themselves in the bedroom, where Marisa had a glass of sugary water for her nerves. Why did everything have to be so complicated? She couldn't be away from Marco. He was her sun, painting a rainbow in the dull sky with his pranks and that boyish air he sometimes had, like the boy that still lived within him eating jabuticabas from the tree. She learned so much from Marco. He had given back laughter to her. Marisa wanted to erase from his heart the scab of bitterness that surfaced when he was distracted and the mask slipped off.

If she must stand against her mother to be with Marco, it didn't matter anymore. Marisa called him and the two had a long conversation. They would meet later as usual and decide the best course of action. When they hung up, Marisa was much calmer.

Yet Marco vacillated.

It was all happening again. The past. That predator whose eyes were two precise points with the gloss of a black mirror, positioned close together for better aiming at the prey. Its mouth accumulated several rows of teeth as sharp as blades and, when it opened, it shredded and laughed.

The past had a peculiar sense of humor.

A middle ground with Marisa was impossible. Even knowing the risks, he had allowed things to go too far. He jeopardized his reputation and plans for the future. But the worst was that now Marisa's family life might crumble as a result of his irresponsibility. He wouldn't be in peace with his own conscience if that happened—not again. None of it made any sense. He needed to be rational.

Rational.

He had been married and divorced once—Lorena had taught him the toughest lesson. At the time, he lived in the intoxication of his first love. Impulsive and inexperienced, he didn't know contention. Or fear. Marisa was still too young to know what he knew today. Did he really want to drag her into that? Did he have the right to do it? He thought of Lorena at that age and the shattered dreams she made a point to throw in his face: *You have destroyed my life.* She apologized, then said it and apologized again. And again. And then apologizing lost meaning. *You have destroyed my life.*

Scenes from the marriage pulsed in his memory. Forbidden fruit in the beginning, then conflicts, insecurity, lies and bitterness until the end. It was incredible, he thought, the myriad of small and big reasons that would destroy a relationship. Divergences. Jealousy. Unfaithfulness… Small and big sources of pain, which the law coldly labeled as *irreconcilable differences.* He had tried to overcome his remorse, he had tried to forgive her. To no avail. His heart was a piece of glass cracked by seven years of pain and mistakes. When he looked through its lens, the world emerged distorted. Shattered.

Maybe it would be best if he and Marisa went their separate ways. He was no good for her. If they continued together, what were the prospects? Marisa already lived in a distressed relationship with her mother, which his presence only aggravated. This was the moment for them to consolidate a bond. The last thing he wanted was to cause a rupture between mother and daughter. Then Marisa wouldn't bear the pressure and would feel compelled to move in with him—a bad start on itself, as he could attest from his own experience. Marisa ignored what had really happened in his marriage. He, on the other hand, couldn't forget. Fairy tales did not survive frustration. With time, Marisa would miss her family and he would carry the blame. They would drink from the cup of estrangement and have accusations for dinner.

And soon Marisa would be ready to fall into another man's arms. It was always like that, right? The natural cycle of things. Flowers blossomed, their petals and leaves fell off, dried out, soaked in the rain, dried out again, until they brittled and turned into dust and into nothing. What remained were the fossils of nails and hair, pain and thorns. The ending of sunken romance did not change much, in literature or real life. It had been like that with Lorena, sooner or later it would be the same with Marisa. He had emptied his baggage of illusions long ago. The world was full of Madames Bovary.

Or was it?

His brain said one thing—perfectly sober, sensible, centered. His heart—that same one dazzling his thoughts since he had noticed Marisa in the classroom, that unrestrained, unreasonable, unstoppable heart—said something else. And what had he noticed? At first, just a girl-woman with a pretty face and a braid, one small and pale hand raised. When she said omission was a form of action, a tremor hit him. Without knowing, Marisa no longer spoke of literature. She spoke of broken glass and a man who had retreated from life without realizing. She spoke of him, Marco. From then on, he began to observe Marisa. He captured on her face the fragmented impressions of a mosaic, which he assembled day after day: sweetness, sadness, amusement, irony, interest, apathy, life, death. All overflowing from within her. And then, as if a blindfold had slipped off his eyes, he recognized in Marisa fragments of himself...

The brain. The heart. In a perverse logic, the more he resisted, the more entangled he became in that sortilege. Until the only thing left for him was surrender. Gosh, was he tired, so tired of feeling that way, fractured. The brain. The heart. In response to one and the other, Marco helped himself with a shot of whiskey. Soon a comforting warmth coursed through his veins, clearing his mind, making everything simpler. Dissolving the melodrama. Yes, that was it. Life shouldn't be taken so seriously. What was again the title of that film by David Mamet?

Things Change, he muttered to himself.

Marco took another sip, hesitated, and emptied the glass. He glanced at the kitchen table in search of the pack of cigarettes—the companion for coffee, port wine and disquiet—and his gaze fell upon the ivory die sitting in a corner. He stared at it. Grabbed it. Rolled it.

Three turned up.

A coincidence?

He looked at the orchid he'd left to air on the windowsill. A rare *Selenipedium,* Marisa's gift for his birthday. She had brought him the flower on a Saturday, when they dined in the apartment and spent the night rolling the die. They didn't sleep much because Marisa needed to go home to be with her mother and study. When he woke up in the morning, she was sobbing with her face hidden in the pillow.

What is it, Mari?

Happiness. Fear of losing him.

Approaching the window, Marco touched the orchid's red petals. The situation had reached a breaking point. He could no longer keep standing with water around his knees—he had to make a decision and take the plunge. Marco retrieved his cell phone from the table and searched for Marisa's contacts. With no more hesitation, he selected the number.

PART 2

BLACK:
A PLUNGE INTO THE ABYSS

Three months later
AUTUMN, MARCH

1. A Well Stares at the Sky

He waited for her in the living room. Sitting on the couch with a glass of scotch in his hand, Marco listened to a classical piece by composer Zoltán Kodály about the hussar who renounced everything to be with his sweetheart: *The Fairy Tale Begins*. An ironic title, he thought. Just out of the shower, Marco had wet hair and a black T-shirt clinging to his slightly damp torso. He took a long draft of the whiskey swimming in ice. Autumn arrived, bringing back the height of summer in one of those typical São Paulo mood swings. In normal temperature and pressure conditions, the thermometer would *not* be registering ninety degrees in the shade.

Marco looked at the entrance door as the knob moved. She entered and tossed her purse onto a chair. Her beige top sported a low cut, and the bandage skirt highlighted the sway of her hips. Circling the coffee table, she leaned over to brush her lips on his and sat on the sofa. She asked what they would be doing that evening. Marco pointed to a white shopping bag at the feet of the couch, bathed in the dim light of the side lamp. With barely restrained curiosity, she picked up the bag, laid it on the table and studied the contents. She lifted the items one by one, examining them with a critical eye. Her interest faltered.

"What's this?" she asked in disconcert.

"Didn't you say you wanted to try new things? I bought it for you."

She evaluated the web of black leather strips and metal rings. After thinking for a moment, she returned it to the bag with a brusque motion. She didn't like that. When he asked why, she grew irritated: "Why can't we be like *normal* people?" Her breathing became fitful. "This is... this is *wrong.*"

Her hands trembled—Marco couldn't tell if the reaction was triggered by indignation or by fear of herself and what she might do. He just held her hand. He offered her his glass of scotch and reassured her they would only do what she felt like. A bit calmer, she took a sip from the drink.

"Don't you enjoy our games?" Marco put his arm around her shoulders and held her chin, making her stare at him. She tried to avert his gaze but he insisted: "Don't you like them?"

She nodded, her own admission giving her a sting of humiliation.

"Then trust me," he said.

"What if the situation gets out of hand? I don't want to lose control, Marco…"

That would never happen, he assured her. Didn't she understand? Marco studied her face. He found a pair of inquisitive eyes as she moistened her lips with the tip of her tongue. That same tip devoid of answers.

No, she didn't understand.

"This is a trick of mirrors." Marco paused for his words to sink in. "But you need to look past the surface to capture its essence."

"You talk through riddles. I don't get it."

"I'll put it another way. Have I ever done anything you didn't like?"

Shaking her head, she brought the glass to her lips, hesitated and returned it to the table. Her fingerprints slowly blurred on the cold crystal.

Marco gazed at her with a smile in his eyes. He ran his index finger across the curve of her shoulder, going up to the neck, tracing the jawline until it reached her mouth. There, it lingered in a caress. She couldn't suppress the shiver that followed the gliding of Marco's finger.

"Things are relative. You arouse me and then satiate my desire. Now who's the active and who's the passive?" he asked, his voice as soft as his caress. "The game is ruled by your will and your boundaries. Now who's the dominator and who's the dominated?"

She opened her mouth and closed it again, unable to respond.

"Sometimes I think you're a strange man, Marco," she uttered.

She stared at him and superimposed the image of the first time she saw Marco. That day, she had the sensation a serpent coiled around her and dragged her to him. She wanted Marco. His body, his smile, his words. She wanted him complete. In the beginning she thought they had affinity. But the truth was she couldn't grasp him. It was like watching a coin flip: when you glimpsed head it was already tails, and the coin would continue the spin without revealing itself as a whole. She recalled when they went to the park, and Marco had the breezy taste of vanilla, playing with a dog that passed by, reciting haikais as they walked around the lake. Then, in the bedroom, he would darken and become strong, thick liquor that triggered dizziness. He dived into the game with furor as if he sought something, as if he wanted to investigate the bottom of the abyss—the bottom of himself? *The die keeps things on track,* he had said. Or maybe it was the opposite. Maybe he was running away. Marco carried the marks of his broken marriage, and she wanted to make him forget them. Yes, she could do it.

"I may look strange to the people you call 'normal,'" he countered. "Normality and abnormality, however, lie in different points of the same scale. Between them there's no gap, but continuity. Like the color spectrum: on one end you have white and on the other black, with all the remaining palette in between. Colors are not separated, they keep changing into one another. There are normality gradients, the same way there are color gradients."

"What about you, Marco, where do you stand in the scale?" she asked, and curiosity made her quit the defensive attitude.

Think of the gray color, he said. Sometimes it held more black; sometimes more white, albeit it still remained gray. He had an unconventional world view, that's all. There was nothing wrong with exploring the instinctive side. Survival depended on it. Mankind had the arrogance of judging itself superior to animals, when in reality people were guided by instincts rather than by reason. The primitive part of the brain developed along 500 million years. And the rational part? Not even 300 thousand.

"Don't start with those theories," she said, her body stiffening. She saw the coin flipping. Heads and tails, black and white. The gray that she couldn't grasp.

"I'm just stating the facts. Anthropologist Desmond Morris has an interesting definition for modern society. And if you thought of a concrete jungle, think again: jungle dwellers live free. We, on the other hand, are confined in our cubicles. No, this is not a concrete jungle. It's a *human zoo*."

He pondered for a moment before continuing: "People have lost touch with their instinctive side and, therefore, have lost an important part of themselves. What they call intuition is nothing more than the primitive brain in action, one step ahead of the conscious mind. And what about pleasure? Do you think it's your rational side that makes you want to lie with me? How many pleasures do people deny themselves in the name of a supposed rationality?"

"I won't lie. I enjoy what we do. But this *is wrong*," she replied feebly.

Marco shrugged. Wrong? To whom? To social conventions? Yesterday yellow ruled, today blue. Did it mean blue should be better than yellow? Maybe, or maybe not. There was puritanism and the porn industry, there was right and wrong and debatable, and there was hypocrisy. The establishment needed a mass of maneuver and for that purpose created conventions—today blue, tomorrow green, the day after tomorrow yellow again. In a world where power had become a compulsion, money was the motherland, and life didn't take priority, the famous Marquis' words rang truer than ever: there was no horror that hadn't been divinized or virtue that hadn't been execrated.

"Everything changes according to context. Moral, religion, behavior codes, all is relative. Forget the conventions. The important thing is to be free and respect your own boundaries. I know you better than you think. You have a natural curiosity; why don't you give it a try? If you don't like it, we'll stop. But I have a feeling you won't stop."

"Well…" she hummed with an ambiguous air.

"If you're not sure, we better forget about it," Marco said in a firm tone, which then mellowed. "Let's not spoil our evening. Come here, give me a kiss."

He held the nape of her neck with one hand, brushing his thumb on her face. His other hand ran across her thigh, very close to the shadowy triangle hinted underneath her skirt. The gestures were confident. Smooth as a lacey cuff skimming on the flesh to duplicate with a whisper the caress of the hand. Now Marco's mouth turned into velvet on hers and disarmed her. He was like that: capable of the most extreme sternness and the most gentle touch of all. In any instance, he always triggered sensations that carried her far away in their current.

Gliding, gliding far away in the current. Swept by the waters' sheer force. She lost herself in Marco.

His words swirled inside her head, and the hunger she feared unleashed. In her innermost, she could foresee the black vortex sucking her into its epicenter. An explosion of a thousand stars as she plunged into the abyss of no return. Emitting a low moan, she arched her back slightly. She flattened her hand against his chest, at first intending to repel him, and then in a circular motion that was the beginning of a caress. She saw the gap of her own abyss.

"Enough." She pushed him with sudden energy and composed herself. "I'm leaving."

Marco kept silent. In his dark eyes darted a sparkle, one moment there and the next gone.

She studied him, wondering if she had dreamt that gaze. At times she had the feeling she didn't know him at all. She took a few steps toward the door and came to a halt. Turning back almost reluctantly, she stared at him with her face red hot.

Without a word she slowly began to undress. Then, bare naked, she picked up the white shopping bag.

2. The Chase

She walked along the deserted street under an impending rain, the trees hissing in the wind with the chorus of a thousand voices. On a curve, Marisa saw a silhouette against a wall. A big man dressed in black with a hat pulled over his face. She traversed the street and, sensing his invisible gaze after her, broke into a run. She then heard footsteps.

The man was much taller and quicker than she. *Just keep going... just a little longer*, Marisa frantically repeated to herself. Soon she would reach Marco's building and be safe... Her legs hurt, heavier and heavier, now almost dragging. The man lunged at her, and Marisa fell down on her knees. She didn't feel pain, only fear while the iron hands immobilized her and the pavement scraped her back.

They were under a tree that blocked the street light and cracked whips of shadow across the concrete. The stranger's face was a black screen where sparkles flared as the leaves flailed. Marisa saw the metallic glint of the pistol. The barrel found her throat. Then the trigger lock clicked.

"Now you're going to die."

The future came to a halt. Marisa's eyes welled up, the tears holographic images of pain. Up above, indifferent, they swung. They had gathered in the trees and on lampposts to weave a gigantic web over the street. A furious gust shook them, casting them into the air. They floated and plummeted like rotten fruit. Black tears before the rain: hundreds and hundreds of spiders forming a dark stain that simmered with a multitude of eyes and legs.

The man jumped to his feet and left Marisa exposed. The hairy paws immediately scaled her body and expanded across her face, filling the night with further darkness. She tried to scream and the spiders plunged into her mouth, their sticky paws with a smell of dirt in her throat, nose, eyes...

The shots blasted in her ears. The man was discharging his pistol at point-blank to chase the spiders away. Marisa felt a sting in her arm, another on her shoulder, another on her chest. She was wrapped in the shroud of her own blood, with no voice and no air. She thought of everything she would never see again: Marco, her loved ones, the sun, the sea... Suddenly light blinded her.

Marisa struggled with a scream stifled in her throat. Gradually she recognized the familiar surroundings. Her bedroom. When she realized it had all been a nightmare, instead of relief, an ominous feeling ensued. The clock on the nightstand registered ten past six. Jumping out of bed, Marisa rushed to get ready. She was running quite late for her college presentation.

Still dazed, Marisa left home and hesitated by the elevator before pressing the call button. Upon touching it, a diffuse coldness tingled in her fingertips, spreading icy tentacles throughout her body. *Clanc, clanc, clanc... clanc.* The old service elevator stopped on her floor. The door opened to reveal steel walls and cold light. A morgue refrigerator. She entered it reluctantly, holding her handbag tightly to her chest.

As the elevator went down, she recalled the physics teacher and his lessons about free-falling bodies. Marisa closed her eyes with a shiver. She was plummeting toward her grave. She could feel the lift running loose from the cables, sinking into the guts of the earth, fast, fast... faster, faster... *Crash!*

Marisa opened her eyes abruptly as the door slid to the side with a moan. Ground floor. She got off with her heart racing and, once on the street, tried to focus on her presentation for the coming class. A few blocks ahead, she arrived at the bus stop. Soon a man in a black jacket materialized by her side. When he asked her the time, it was as if the wings of a monster had eclipsed the sun. The day turned instantly dark, and the stranger's eyes lit up with a flash. She took a step back, gripping her cell phone.

"Eleven past eleven," Marisa replied without thinking, and then became confused with the numbers on the screen. What had happened to the past hours? She couldn't be that late. She glanced at the man and noticed a scar above his eyebrow, which looked like a centipede cut in the middle by a razorblade. When she turned back to the cell phone, the numbers had changed. Marisa tried to suppress the tremor in her voice: "Sorry, I made a mistake. It's six-thirty."

Her bus arrived and, shaky, Marisa hopped onboard. She found a corner to lean on, producing a notepad from her handbag to review her presentation. At one point, the driver hit the brakes hard and the notepad fell onto the floor. As she bent to collect it, someone was already handing it back to her.

Marisa raised her eyes and had a startle when she faced the man from the bus stop. He returned her notepad in silence and Marisa nodded a thank you. The proximity of the stranger, however, caused her disquiet. She eyed him discreetly, watching his every move. On a curve, his jacket half-opened to reveal the grip frame of a gun in the inner pocket. Marisa's hands tingled with needles of ice while her heart melted inside her chest.

It was him. The man in her dream.

Marisa looked around, assessing how many people she would need to dribble in order to reach the back door. Then the bus stopped and boarded even more passengers without giving her a chance to disembark. In despair, she pushed forward across the tight mass, pressed the stop button and exited the vehicle before her final destination. As the bus proceeded down the street, Marisa leaned against a wall. Her legs faltered.

The campus of the University of São Paulo was crossed by wide avenues lined with trees and lawns. Fair-faced concrete buildings with glassy façades reflected the blue sky. Marisa took a secondary street, deserted at that hour, and went around the clock tower. Then time stopped when she found herself face to face with the stranger from the bus.

Where did he come from? Marisa could swear she had been the only passenger to get off the bus back there. The man's eyes stole the light of day, and in the bottomless well of his pupils pried a vulture blacker than the night, ready to open its wings and charge. Marisa quickly dodged the attack, fleeing through a shortcut to the back entrance of the Communications and Arts School. On her trail she sensed the man's footprints. And the fluttering of wings.

The complex occupied an entire block and consisted of a dozen units. Marisa dashed along the paved way, past a row of low buildings, and only slowed down at the next-to-last unit. She entered it and rushed to an ample classroom with one of the walls taken by large windows. Her study group waited for her next to one of them: two boys and three girls in jeans and T-shirts, ready to change the world. Panting, Marisa approached her pals and made a helpless gesture.

"Sorry for my being late. You have no idea what just happened—"

She couldn't finish the sentence, for right then the teacher entered the classroom. With khaki clothes and gray hair and beard, he resembled a Doctor Livingstone. Only the hat was missing.

"Good morning, everyone." The teacher leaned against the desk in front of the whiteboard. He had an open countenance and calm manners. "Today we're gonna talk about the *state ideological* apparatuses that perpetuate the dominant ideologies…"

Marisa hardly listened. She kept peering at the window and clutching the edge of the board attached to her chair. Her eyes darted back and forth, from the window to her notes; the words on the notepad, however, now scrambled before her like a clump of barbed wire.

The clock on the wall stared at her with a malign eye. The minutes dragged painfully in the stuffy room.

Tic, tac… tic, tac… tic, tac…

It was already the end of March and officially autumn, but the city had plunged into a hellish heat wave and the thermometer rose to ninety degrees. Nonetheless, Marisa felt herself freezing and, with a shiver, hugged her body. She dreaded the moment when the class would be over and she'd have to leave the room. Who was that man? Why did he chase her?

"Now I'm gonna give the floor to your classmates," the teacher said before taking a seat in the front row.

There were murmurs, coughs, expectation. Marisa's study group directed inquisitive looks at her. She stood up and sought shelter behind the solid desk. From there, she spanned the whole room, dozens of curious faces, the master's affable countenance—all those eyes on her, waiting. Her hands began to sweat.

Tic, tac... tic, tac... tic, tac...

Silence lingered.

"Marisa, you can start now," the teacher urged, his foot tapping.

She opened her mouth but was incapable of uttering a sound. Her lips dried out, her tongue seemed glued to the roof of the mouth. A cold sweat beaded her forehead, and her heart began pounding. She was still in the middle of a nightmare, that must be it. *I'm not feeling too well,* Marisa thought. She wanted to ask for help; her throat was closing. She averted her attention to the nearest window, where the view was obstructed by a large bush almost flat with the pane. Horrified, she discerned the man's form behind the plant. The next moment, he had disappeared.

Marisa fixed her eyes on the window for a long minute, oblivious to her presentation and the astonished stares from her classmates. The stalker must be hiding nearby. But where?

Outside, students strolled between the cafeteria and the main building. She searched for her own reflection on the glass and then, with insurmountable perplexity, saw her body dissolving. Next, her face disintegrated too. *Poof.*

And then everything sank into darkness.

3. The Taming

She had liked it and wanted to do it again tonight. In the shadows of the living room, her pale nudity became ribbed with reflections of the city lights sneaking through the window. She looked like a tigress. Removing the accessories from the shopping bag, she adjusted them with care. Gradually she metamorphosed into a long-legged filly in platform boots with toe boxes split as hooves. The harness on her naked chest framed her compact breasts and, on the left nipple, a minute silver ring flickered. The hips and the firm buttocks were emphasized by a black thong, from which hung a dark tail of satiny threads.

She fixed a red feather on top of her head. Then she started to roll her braid into a bun, but Marco immobilized her wrists with an abrupt gesture.

"Leave your hair like that."

"Careful, you're hurting me," she complained, lowering her arms and massaging her wrists. The long braid fell down like a hazel mane.

Marco did not acknowledge the protest. His big hands, however, moved with unsuspected gentleness when he fitted the mouthpiece and reins on her. Lastly, he covered her face with a mask that exposed only the eyes and the crimson lips girded with a bit.

He could now do several things. Skim over her body with his own. Caress her chest. Lash her flanks to kindle the flesh and stir the mind. Until she begged for more...

Previously it had been almost a playful session. To ease her into it.

This time Marco chose discipline.

He stood beside her and held the reins, leading her around the room. She took a step forward and he slid the whip behind her knees so she would lift her legs higher. They went on like that for a few feet. She maintained a rigid posture while trying to balance on the boots. Little by little, she relaxed and eventually resumed her natural walk. She startled and straightened up when the whip touched the back of her knees. One more lap, followed by another. He instructed her to concentrate on the rhythm of the gait. It needed to be elegant and fluid. The angle of the legs absolutely precise.

When she got it right, the pace became hypnotic and she lost herself in it, accepting the guidance of those hands that held the reins with total control. She no longer had free will and gratefully transferred the weight of such responsibility to him. She was nothing more than an animal. A beautiful animal with a majestic poise at the Master's mercy. The whip now and again rewarded her with a pat or corrected her with a fiery kiss. She learned how to kneel to perfection and then rise even more gracefully.

The furniture in the room retracted to the corners, vanishing into the shadows. The half-darkness gave place to the warm radiance of the sun. She found herself in the open air, the dirt under her hooves, the breeze against her body and the whisper of the trees pricking up her ears. With a keen sense of smell, she captured the scent of the man guiding her in the paddock. It was distinct from hers, a citric aroma mixed with that of wood and trampled grass. She inhaled it deeply to introject a part of the man into her body, creating a stronger bond between the two of them. She was now an extension of him, and both moved in sync. From time to time his firm hand would reach her body—slapping her flanks or buttocks, squeezing her nipple in the precise cusp of pleasure.

She couldn't tell for how long that went on, until the moment the reins tightened in a smooth motion. She stood obediently still and directed an inquisitive stare at Marco. He cocked an eyebrow, his face stern, and that was enough to make her shiver in anticipation. A surge of heat irradiated between her thighs. Her core pulsated, slowly getting moist. *What's next?*

As if he guessed the question, Marco outlined the shape of her lips with his fingertip and loosened the bit. He brought his tongue into her mouth in a soft and brief kiss. Next, she felt the coarse texture of a sugar cube where his tongue had been. She hardly noticed the white mass melting in her mouth, as now Marco started caressing her thighs with the handle of the whip. With a quiver, she clenched her hands.

The cylindrical handle sank into the valley between her thighs, which forced her to part her legs just a bit. The handle was then replaced with the supple whip's end—that end used to inflict pain. The leather strips glided across her skin in unpredictable routes, encircling her stomach and buttocks, insisting on the curve of the breasts, gently pulling the silver ring. She panted, closed her eyes and, without realizing it, crushed the sugar cube between her teeth. A perspiration line budded on her forehead. Her whole body, her whole being, throbbed for the promise of the next caress.

For a never-ending moment, nothing happened. She opened her eyes to find Marco's fixed gaze upon her. He had stepped back and toyed with the whip ends, twisting them between his fingers. His face did not reveal any emotion, but she could sense in his dark irises the vestige of a smile.

Marco moved forward and repositioned the mouthpiece against her lips. Then whispered in her ear: "We shall continue now."

That evening, her taming was concluded.

4. Doctor Spitzer

Marisa got lost on the tenth floor of an edifice on Paulista Avenue, which concentrated medical offices devoted to all kinds of maladies. Consumed with anxiety, she walked through a maze of hallways until finally reaching the door with a metal plate on it: *Dr. Rebeca C. Spitzer, Psychoanalyst – Alternative Methods*. Marisa pressed the intercom, identified herself, and the door opened with a buzz. A camera above it monitored her as she entered the deserted waiting room.

After a moment of hesitation, Marisa proceeded to sit down on the straw loveseat positioned between two chairs. She inspected the magazines on the coffee table but only found French psychoanalysis publications. So she let her eyes wander to the far end of the room, where she could see a door next to a sideboard with a vase of red anthuriums.

The sight of the swollen, shiny, blood-red flowers made her uncomfortable. She averted her gaze to the watercolor hanging right above them, a square canvas displaying a black circle against a white background. She stared at it, intrigued, until Doctor Spitzer emerged from the consulting room and beckoned.

The psychoanalyst was best defined by her eyes: two impenetrable green sparks magnified by thick tortoise-frame glasses. The white of her skin, almost transparent, sprung to life with the fiery hue of straight, short hair. The suit and scarpino shoes were gray. The age, indefinite. The posture revealed vigor. When preceding Marisa in the consultation room, instead of walking, she marched.

There, light-green walls suggested a soothing ambiance for handling the troubles of the psyche. Set against one of them was the divan topped by a painting almost identical to the other in the waiting room, except this one displayed inverted colors—a white circle against a black background. On the divan's edge, Marisa noticed a small blanket neatly folded and a box of tissues. A sober desk and two caramel leather armchairs filled the remainder of the small room.

Doctor Spitzer sat in one of the armchairs and signaled for Marisa to take the other. She had an astute expression.

"Very well," she said. "Now you are going to tell me what your problem is, without omitting any thought that may occur to you while you talk. Here everything is important. Do you see that painting?" She pointed to the watercolor above the divan. "What does it show us?"

Marisa reflected for a while. The sphere, she deduced, must have a meaning linked to the mysteries of the human psyche. She studied the image attentively, from top to bottom, from left to right. Then responded with caution: "A white circle."

Beaming with a smile that combined insight and triumph, Doctor Spitzer shook her head.

"You are mistaken. The image consists of a white circle *and also* a black square, but most people only perceive what's on the foreground. If we were to make an analogy, the white circle represents the manifest content of your thoughts. The black background hoards repressed wishes, neurosis, everything that is situated beyond the conscious level. The unconscious, you see, is the fertile ground for symbolisms. That's how it communicates with the conscious mind. In such a quicksand terrain, for instance, the female sex can be represented by a box. Or a crochet purse."

"Oh…"

"Now let's concentrate on the matter at hand. And remember: everything you think or say means something else."

"Oh…"

Not knowing exactly how to begin her account, Marisa moistened her lips, cleared her throat, fiddled with a strand of hair and started to braid it. In a belated reflex, she hid her crochet purse under the armchair. Doctor Spitzer observed her in vigilant silence while Marisa resisted the urge to join her purse under the armchair.

How to explain the inexplicable? One week had passed since the disturbing events at her college, and she still didn't understand what happened. Flashes brought to her memory a kaleidoscope of isolated scenes, which she had a hard time piecing together in coherent order... The confusion in the classroom after she had fainted. The mad escape through the campus. Her reflection on the window pane. The man behind the bush. Her mother despairing like in a bad Mexican soap opera. Valentina's visit that afternoon. The rush to the hospital, where a strong sedative was prescribed to both daughter and mother...

As Marisa described the incident, she relived the details with disturbing clarity. Worst of all were the comments that spread in her college afterwards. Classmates stated no one peered through the window. The college security guard said he saw Marisa running indeed. No man had even remotely chased her.

"So it was all a figment of your imagination," Doctor Spitzer concluded.

"Apparently, yes. But I could swear... that man looked so *real*." Marisa blinked, on the verge of tears. "Do you think I'm crazy, doctor?"

"Be calm. Desperation won't help, we need to tackle the problem with a rational approach. What triggered the crisis?"

The therapist entwined her fingers and leaned back solemnly, waiting for an answer. Marisa shook her head. She didn't know what to say. Her mind was spinning, once again peopled with disconnected images.

Dismayed, she clenched her hands.

"I'm scared," Marisa blurted out.

"Scared of what?"

"Everything."

"Be more specific."

Doctor Spitzer then cast a look at Marisa that almost pierced her soul. Marisa sunk in the chair and glanced at the evening sky through the window. She shivered. The night gave her claustrophobia. She would have preferred another time slot, but the psychoanalyst's schedule was full. Averting her eyes from the window, Marisa tried to reflect and say something that would make sense.

That *thing,* she explained, had started with a vague discomfort every time she entered an elevator. She became obsessed with the free-falling bodies theory, thinking the elevator would plummet. Her uneasiness then expanded to incorporate overpasses, bridges, cliffs. Now everything merged into one and the same terror. She was afraid of going near windows. Afraid of having a car accident. Afraid of the dark. Afraid of sounds, afraid of silence. An intangible danger lurked wherever she went.

There was nowhere to run. Danger lived within her.

"You're afraid of your own emotions and had a panic attack, that's all," Doctor Spitzer diagnosed without the slightest hesitation.

"A panic attack?"

"Calm down."

Calm down? Marisa stared at her in despair.

Doctor Spitzer gave back an unflurried gaze. She checked her golden wristwatch and announced: "Our time is up."

5. The Number One

Fortunately, June was coming to a close. Marco needed a vacation. Needed to disappear. His mood had been awful, and not even the long sessions at the gym helped. When he wasn't lifting the weight of the world along with the training gear, he'd burrow in downtown shops until he lost track of time. Searching and searching—for what, he didn't know. That nervous energy found no escape. With great difficulty Marco dissimulated his state of mind. At school, Belvedere threw small talk to establish a male complicity that didn't interest him in the least. He actually felt like punching the director in the face: Celeste, the rejected librarian, now wept in the corners. It was heartbreaking.

Earlier that day, when he had joined her in the cafeteria, Marco made an innocent comment about the weather. It looked like it was going to rain. That's all. Celeste nodded, then suddenly poured a deluge of tears into her coffee mug. She feigned to have a mote in her eye and he, pretending to believe it, offered a napkin to dry her face.

Marco hated playing the fool. Besides, women's tears always made him nervous, with their flood of indecipherable emotions. Not to mention the accusations. It was no coincidence the ancient Greeks had created a female archetype associated with the instability of waters: Aphrodite, conceived in the ocean foam, the goddess of Love and mother of Fear, beautiful and seductive, unpredictable and willful—and probably a crybaby too.

At the sight of the sobbing librarian, Marco thought of Marisa. Of that rainy afternoon, the car pervaded with vetiver, her face marked by weeping, the textbooks spreading on the floor… before things changed. In the cadence of memories, the recollection also stemmed somewhere inside his chest.

It had been a long time since he felt that void. He needed to see her. As soon as he arrived home, Marco grabbed his cell phone and placed the call. While it rang and rang, he could hardly keep his impatience at bay. He hung up at the first words of the automatic reply.

Pensive, Marco swung by his office and approached the bookcase to retrieve one of the copies he was currently reading (*Coldness and Cruelty*, a complex study by Gilles Deleuze on the works of Sacher-Masoch, which he was determined to finish). Then he changed his mind and took the first thing that came into his hands, opening it at random: "We are two abysses—a well staring at the sky." He issued a faint laugh. *The Book of Disquiet* by Fernando Pessoa. Thanks for the irony, Universe.

Marco pulled out another title without looking. *Beyond Good and Evil* by Nietzsche. Good, philosophy never failed to relax him: "If you gaze long enough into the *abyss*, the *abyss* will gaze back into you." Now this was getting just ridiculous, thought Marco. And then he dropped the book, which landed on the chair with a resigned rustle.

Reaching for his cell phone, he tried her number again. This time, on the second ring, she answered breathless. He went straight to the point.

"Can you come here?"

There was an imperceptible pause on the other end.

"When?"

"Tonight. The usual time."

"I can't. It's my mom's birthday, and there's no way I'll be able to escape it... Tomorrow night?"

"Tomorrow, then."

New pause. When she spoke, her voice faltered slightly.

"Did you plan anything?" she probed.

"Not yet. How about a surprise?"

"I love surprises, Marco."

"There you go. I'll do something special for you."

"I can't wait."

At those words, Marco smiled and glanced absent-mindedly at the urban landscape outside the window. His tension began to ease.

She, on the other hand, let out a contrived laugh. She wanted to show him she had everything under control. Sensing Marco's smile, she wondered what he had in mind and restrained the wish to be with him in that very moment.

"I'll stop by tomorrow night, then," she said in a nonchalant tone. "I need to take care of a few things, but I think I can make it on time…"

As soon as he ended the call, Marco became agitated again. She no longer filled the void. Before, it was different. But was it really? Perhaps he couldn't see. Perhaps he didn't want to. Marco closed his eyes. No, he didn't want to see. He still hoped. He ignored the fact that she had started to fade. Not even her name visited his thought now. It was simply "she."

Marco felt guilty. He decided to make up to her and concentrated on the plans for the following evening. After all, he had promised a surprise, right? Marco went to the kitchen, seized the die from the counter and sat at the table, fixing his eyes on the ivory cube for inspiration. A classic piece indeed, he thought. It must be worth far more than the ridiculous sum he had paid. Marco wondered why that relic cost so little. He wasn't superstitious but could swear the die sometimes pulled pranks on him. It had been like that from the beginning. In a plastic city with a plastic lover.

He and his friend Jeff had flown to Las Vegas for the weekend. It would be his first and last visit to the city. He wasn't impressed with what he saw—a shiny trap lulled day and night by the howling of jackpot. In the first evening the two headed for a casino after dinner. At eleven o'clock, they decided to return to the hotel but got lost. They entered a narrow gallery with bars and fast-food restaurants, planning to take a shortcut; the gallery, however, had no exit. What they found in the other end was an antique shop. In its window, between an old camera and a china teapot, Marco saw the die.

The place was open, and they entered a dim room covered in walnut bookcases darkened by time. It smelled of old paper with a faint trace of camphor. No one showed up to assist them, so they inspected the shelves populated with objects representing various decades, from vintage atlases to statuettes of Baroque angels. Marco clapped his hands and called out without a response. After a few minutes, he couldn't resist and picked up the die from the display.

"That's on sale," informed a voice at his back.

He spun around to face a woman with very white skin and very black eyes and hair. She wore a dark, long dress with sleeves down to her wrists that didn't match the July heat. She drew closer, limping slightly.

"It's a handmade replica of a two-thousand-year old Roman die used as an oracle. Elephant ivory. A great piece. Notice that each dot contains a spiral, a symbol of life's mysteries, which are formed in circles: the planets and their orbits, the cycles of creation, destruction and re-creation. Time itself is a spiral that twists between present, past and future."

"Interesting. So it's used for divination games," said Marco.

"In principle, yes. But the second die is missing from the set and the oracle turns out incomplete. Sometimes that generates strange results."

At those words, Marco thought of Lorena and tried to ignore the twinge in his chest. He gave a smile that mocked itself. An incomplete die for an incomplete man. It should serve him right.

They arrived at the hotel a half-hour later, Jeff empty-handed and Marco with a small box wrapped in green paper. They both felt tired but made a stop at the lobby bar. Amid the reds of soft upholstery and curtains, the patrons' discreet voices mixed with the playback of big band classics. The room smelled of alcohol and sleepless nights. The two of them lodged at the ebony counter, ordering whiskey for a toast. It wasn't long before she came by—spiraling the night, spiraling time.

Marco felt the spiral of vertigo and pushed her away from his thoughts. The preparations for that evening entailed his attention. He concentrated, shook his hands and tossed the die. It seemed to float in slow motion, describing a mortal leap that propelled it toward the edge of the table. A few more fractions of an inch, and it would have fallen onto the floor. When Marco saw the result, he reached out to roll the die again. He stopped with his hand in midair.

The rule was to accept the result established by whichever number turned up first. That was the beauty of the game.

Marco stared at the lone dark circle on the surface of the white square. He rolled the die again.

6. White Circle, Black Square

Marisa saw Doctor Spitzer on Mondays, Wednesdays and Thursdays in the evenings. On Fridays, as she digested the sessions of the week, she wouldn't go out: her head kept stewing. What about those emotions she feared so much? She thought of the unconscious' black canvas, then tried to focus on her own emotions. All she could think of was a white canvas, just like the one in the therapist's waiting room. An immaculate white canvas. Or maybe (following Doctor Spitzer's reasoning) it was a canvas whitened by the veil of fear: a white square concealing the black square of the unconscious. A white square somehow blackened because it dis-simulated. It could hence be interpreted as a black square that masked the white square that masked the black square...

All that thinking was giving Marisa a headache.

And she hadn't even gotten to the circles yet.

She would lie on the divan and talk about her mother, remember her father, draw recollections from the dusty drawers of memory. Doctor Spitzer wrote and wrote in her little black notebook—until, in the end of June, Marisa had a cathartic dream, a true watershed in her treatment that was torrentially interpreted by the dexterous psychoanalyst.

"It's a full moon night," narrated Marisa. "I'm following a firefly in the woods. I come to a white house on a lake surrounded by pine trees. The windows are boarded up, but the door is unlocked. I go inside... and soon find myself in a dark corridor with many doors... I try to reach the first door, and the hallway starts stretching..."

She moistened dried-out lips. Inside her chest, her heart shrank.

"Suddenly the door is right before me and a cave-like voice calls...

Marisa! I flee, frightened, to the second door. It gapes open, and I enter a room with a clear crystal tank... The door squeaks behind me and a black cat appears. It meows... and instantly the tank breaks into a thousand pieces. Among the shards, I find a scrap of paper with a weird equation... $V1^2 = V2^2 \pm 2\,g.h - \infty$... The paper expands in my hands until it becomes a sliding door..."

With a shiver, Marisa interrupted herself. She didn't like to remember that part of the dream. Doctor Spitzer mumbled it was interesting and, without lifting her eyes from the notepad, pressed her to continue. Marisa sighed and complied: "Then I realized... that was the formula for calculating the speed of my own falling body. I heard the physics teacher summon me with his cave-like voice: *Marisa, the experiment is about to begin! Get in the elevator right now...* The door slid to the side and I... I got in..."

"Then what?"

The door closed at once. Inside it felt cold and the air was a mist. Like a Holy Grail wrapped in a halo of moonlight, a bouquet of anthuriums floated in the middle of the elevator. She reached out to grab it and, as soon as her hands touched it, the light wavered. The shadows detached from the walls, towered up to the ceiling and formed a circle. Marisa frantically pressed the button to open the door until it popped out and rolled at her feet... Darkness grew deeper. Terror overwhelmed her, she despaired. Suddenly, Sérgio emerged from the ring of shadows. Marisa's first instinct was to back off... Then she changed her mind. Oblivious to the shadows and her own fear, she raised the anthuriums and landed them on the ex-boyfriend.

By the time Marisa woke up, she had destroyed the whole bouquet on his head.

Doctor Spitzer wanted to learn more about Sérgio. Marisa told her the two of them had met at a party. It was love at first sight. He seemed perfect: dark and tall, expansive, affectionate, a business management student. They had plans to marry once Sérgio graduated, and her mother was quite fond of him. Until Marisa caught him with the diving instructor. It had been one of the most dreadful experiences in her whole life. Sérgio was spending the weekend in the countryside, at a friend's bachelor party. He would be back in the early evening on Sunday.

"When we started dating, Sérgio had a Beagle. He needed to be away for three days, so I offered to take care of the dog. Sérgio lent me his spare key and I ended up keeping it even after he gave the dog away to his sister. That Sunday afternoon I headed for his apartment to make a surprise. Oh, doctor, I wore my best lingerie and brought along a carrot cake with choco-late icing…"

Marisa waited for him amid the silent mahogany furniture in the bedroom swept by a late afternoon sun. Sprawled on the bed with her tablet, she meandered through Pinterest checking out recipes when the front door opened. She left the tablet in the brown armchair and glued one ear to the bedroom door. Marisa recognized his voice. Then hers. Débora, the diving instructor. She heard chuckles. A silence, a smack of lips and another silence. Footsteps approaching. She looked around in a frenzy and dove under the bed. Too late, she remembered about the tablet. Marisa saw the door describing an arch as it opened to allow four wobbling legs entwined. Saw shoes skidding empty along with discarded socks, the rival's silver anklet, clothes falling on the floor like surrendered flags, each one a symbol of her defeat.

On one occasion at the beach house, Marisa had found two cock-roaches copulating next to the pantry. Linked by their extremities, they formed a long insect with an indented waist and several paws that moved sideways, three erratic steps here, two steps there. Disgusting. But this now was even worse. The four legs entwined, three steps here, two steps there. Four, three, two. Like a countdown.

No, no, please. *No.*

One pair of jeans, two pairs of jeans, a yellow T-shirt, a pink tank top, a white bra and panties, blue boxers… a *tuff!* that crushed her spirit when the naked bodies tumbled on the mattress. She heard everything. Kisses, moans, thrusts. The rhythmic screaks from the feet of the bed against the wooden flooring—strident little shrills growing louder and louder, splinters of sound perforating her tympanums. Then she heard the release with its sticky smell. Suffocated, Marisa closed her eyes. It didn't work because then she could hear better. She reopened them to the hideous mattress frame and covered her ears, but kept hearing. Conniving sighs, lazy talk, paper tissue. She was entombed under betrayal. The pair didn't even notice the tablet that dozed in the armchair, dreaming of assorted recipes. Luckily they headed for a pizzeria after the quick yet vigorous sport. Marisa crawled out of her hiding spot, seized the tablet and ran away leaving the cake behind. Never again did she speak to Sérgio. He called her several times. She didn't answer.

"Sérgio ended up writing me a mile-long email, confessing he was in love with another woman and didn't know what to do. He was afraid to hurt me. I felt like replying with a mile-long swear word, only in the end I didn't write anything. At the time I had the bad habit of keeping quiet because I wanted people to like me." Marisa shook her head. She had actually thought of mailing him a couple of dead cockroaches but didn't have the stomach to do it. "Afterwards my anger subdued, leaving the trauma. Today I understand Sérgio, he was probably just a chicken... a sensitive chicken. But I never wished to see him again. God only knows what I'd been though under that bed."

"Hmm. It seems you used that bouquet to regurgitate all the bad words you've swallowed up. That's what you needed to overcome your trauma, and now Sérgio rests buried beneath a bunch of smashed flowers." The psychoanalyst aimed a speculative look at Marisa, nibbling at the cap of her golden pen. "Anthuriums, you say. White?"

"Red. More or less like that flower arrangement in your waiting room."

Doctor Spitzer probed if they were the same shade of red. Marisa wasn't sure, as the light shifted. The psychoanalyst insisted that she make an effort to remember. There were many types of red, and each might symbolize a different thing: ruby, coral, solferino, scarlet...

"Blood red."

"*Ahh*," exulted Doctor Spitzer. "Fascinating."

She made an annotation followed by several exclamation marks.

Marisa forgot what she was saying and stirred with visible anxiety. The divan upholstery underlined her words with a nervous squeak. "What is it, doctor?"

Staring at Marisa over the brim of her glasses, Doctor Spitzer closed the notebook. She motioned to the painting on the wall with a meaningful expression.

"This is very good. Very good," she concluded triumphantly. "Your unconscious wishes and your conscious mind are in open confrontation. The wishes want to manifest, and the conscious mind tries to repress them. Your ego could no longer mediate the conflict and collapsed."

Collapsed? Marisa became rigid. And why did she say *very good?* That couldn't possibly be good at all.

For a long moment, Marisa contemplated the watercolor above the divan, in search of a sign to appease her fears. The square and the circle, however, seemed to stare back at her with the impassibility of a sphinx. She anchored her gaze there and, with a shudder, had the distinct impression of grazing the black bottom of the canvas. She even caught a glimpse of the secrets hidden there. Such impression lasted only a moment, though.

"It's symptomatic," Doctor Spitzer resumed, "the recurrence of black and white in your dream. We have the firefly in the shadowy forest. The moon and the night. The white house with a dark corridor (the boarded-up windows are the eyes of the unconscious refusing to see). Furthermore, we have the clear crystal tank, the ebony cat, the white paper... " She concealed a yawn with the back of her hand. "Frankly, everything is so obvious even a child would see it."

"What about the red anthuriums?" Marisa avoided the word *blood*.

Behind her glasses, Doctor Spitzer's green eyes sprouted to life, discharging inflamed sparkles.

"This is the most important part of your dream. I would even say it will change your life forever, but I don't want to sound like a movie trailer. We'll continue in the next session."

"Let me guess. Our time is up."

"Uh-huh."

7. Something Different

Ten holds one and zero, the harmony between opposites. Nine embraces three triangles: body, mind and spirit. Eight lies down in the infinite. Seven is heaven—seven musical scales, seven colors in the rainbow, seven virtues. Six contains the two triangles of dialectics. Five adds up the senses that capture matter. Four calls God's name with the elements of nature, the seasons and cardinal points. Three brings the synthesis of father, mother and offspring. Two is me and you. One is the genesis of everything.

A minute point suspended in the multidimensional space, the starting point for all lines of creation: the number One.

Marco held the ivory die between his thumb and index finger. Pensive, he contemplated the small white square with the dark dot in the center.

The game was a living organism. The rules and number of tosses changed, combining to create from simple variables to the most complex. Each tossing affected the next. It could also happen that the first toss would be the only one, locked within itself with a categorical meaning. With no escape.

That had been the case the previous day, before he cheated. Marco chewed on his bottom lip. No. He wouldn't cheat. He was tired of subterfuges.

He knew exactly what he needed to do.

Marco put the die back in the nightstand drawer and began preparations in an elaborate ritual—the devil, as they said, was in the details. Diligence became a trance. His mind wandered, making plans and anticipating, while his hands worked in an uninterrupted flux as if someone else directed them.

The valise with accessories remained forgotten under the bed while Marco arranged the bedroom. This time there would be no incense and port. Or whiskey, for that matter. He changed the linens and opened the window to invite in the fresh air. When everything was ready, he undressed—the odd sensation of peeling off an old skin—and stepped into the shower. Closing his eyes, Marco let the water run over his body for a long time. He felt all of a sudden exhausted.

Once he was done washing, he wrapped himself in a towel and proceeded to the bedroom. The ring of his cell phone yanked him out of his thoughts with a startle. He dried his hands quickly and answered it. It was her.

"Hi. I just wanted to hear your voice... I can't explain. You're different this time." She paused. "Have you started preparations?"

"Yeah," Marco answered in autopilot.

"Did you stop by the sex shop?"

"No. And I know exactly where you're heading with this talk." He couldn't help a smile.

"Hmm, coming from you, should we infer the plans for tonight involve a literary classic?" She gave a wicked chuckle.

"I generally don't use work material for leisure."

She mistook his contrived cheerfulness for amusement and tried guessing: if it wasn't a classic, then surely it was one of those dirty books... No, no dirty book. A film? Neither. Her strident curiosity got on Marco's nerves. When she finally gave up the guessing game, he remained quiet. And she, assuming he was too busy to talk, cleared her throat and said an awkward goodbye.

Marco took a deep breath after he hung up. Although he didn't like to admit it, he was anxious.

For the first time in quite a while, expectation dominated him. He hadn't the faintest idea of how the evening would turn out. His partner's reaction didn't worry him though: he knew how to maneuver and lead her where he wanted, predicting her resistances and needs, guiding her sensations to wake up dormant instincts she hadn't even dreamt of. He carried on effortlessly. It was relatively simple to deal with the other, for he could step back and see in perspective. The problem rose when he had to predict his own reactions. Come face to face with this other that was himself.

What he planned to do deviated from his usual procedure. Now he was the one exposing a vulnerable flank. He hadn't done it since Vegas. But then he was drunk, so technically it didn't count. Now, choosing that route led to a peculiar intermission: neither master nor disciple. Then what? The master dictated the rules and knew intimately their dynamics and goals, aware that he could change them any time—and there resided the difficulty of it. The disciple would trust the master and follow the rules without questioning, hence being spared from the pains of free will. It was a fair exchange.

Safe.

Well, not this time.

Marco thought about the die. Would it be pulling a prank? The memory of that night in Vegas taunted him.

He and Jeff had raised the first toast. The scotch went down, burning their throats, and the friend asked about the die.

"Why don't we roll it? See what happens," he poked.

"The clerk said the second die is missing from the set. The results are truncated."

"So what? It's just for fun." Jeff reflected for a moment, smoothing out a wavy strand of his blond hair. His blue eyes glinted. "We can improvise. We ask a question. If an even number turns up, the answer is yes. Odd number, answer is no. The higher the number, the stronger the prediction. C'mon. It's not every day a two-thousand-year-old die shows up."

"It's not two thousand years old. It's a *replica*."

"Still. It's antique and has a certain mysticism to it. Imagine Romans throwing a die just like that in biblical times."

With a sigh, Marco laid down his glass. He groped his pocket for the package and opened it.

"You do the honors first," Jeff said with a bow. "Ask a question."

Marco's brain remained empty. The only thing that occurred to him was the same thing that had been occurring for the past year since the divorce. Lorena. A longing tainted with anger. Where would she be now?

Maybe married to the rich heir that her family so eagerly applauded—with a standing ovation. Love was ironic. Before, at the mere thought of Lorena, happiness expanded within him. After the separation, he began associating her with pain, and the memory of her brought a bad aftertaste to his mouth. Psychologists stated that it was a normal reaction, that anger helps you get detached in order to survive a breakup.

The last time he saw her before the separation was the worst. No quarrel, no indifference, and yet infinitely more hurtful. He returned early from work, and she startled. Soon Marco understood why: Lorena had packed her belongings and planned to leave without saying goodbye. She wanted to shake his hand, but he refused. The relief Marco caught on her face, which she attempted to disguise with a solemn expression, opened a gash in his chest. Lorena was relieved that she would no longer be sharing that roof with him, that her family would accept her back and life would return to normal. From then on, instead of facing difficulties, she would be able to live her dream. Behind the mask, Lorena's face was radiant.

"Did you ask the question?" probed Jeff.

"Yes," Marco lied.

He rolled the die half-heartily, and they followed the pirouette of the ivory cube.

"Ah, six. Then the answer is definitely yes, Marco. Satisfied?"

Even if Marco knew what to respond, he didn't have a chance to speak: she sat by his side before he could utter a word. Blondish straight hair, a siren's body and brown eyes shifting into green according to the light. A deluxe escort inside a white halter-neck dress lacking many yards of fabric. She introduced herself as Stefania and started to chat. It was her night off and she wanted to have a good time. She was sick of love for rent, of old men gushing money proportionally to their impotence and spoiled brats who didn't know what they were doing. Sick, so sick.

The two drank the first glass together. Then another, and yet another. Stefania said she liked him. She wanted to have a good time with him. She spoke as she nibbled on his lips, one curious hand on his thigh. Oh, he was good for groping. What about the rest? Levitating in a cloud of scotch, Marco ran his index down her neck and descended until parking where the low-cut neckline ended. Between her breasts, he traced a spiral with his fingertip. Stefania held his hand, brought it to her lips and slowly sucked his finger.

They left Jeff throwing the die with a drunken saxophone player. The last thing Marco heard was the friend attacking *La Marseillaise*. His room was on the seventh floor, and inside the elevator time became elastic, running slow and fast at intervals: for hours his hands felt Stefania's body parts that mattered, and in less than a minute they arrived at the carpeted corridor. Suddenly they were in the room. First, Stefania had a good time, her eyes a green mist, a wavering striptease. Then her hands, experienced despite the alcohol, worked to remove his clothes.

She began to ride him with might and main, her firm hands on his hips, mouth ajar, dreamy expression. They shifted, he knelt and she suspended her lower body to press her feet on his chest. Then they balanced on the TV rack, her sitting on the edge with both legs around him, and him deep into her soft inside. Maybe it had happened that way. Marco couldn't remember the sequence of it all, only the torpid urgency and the smell of sex in the stuffy room. He recalled vaguely she'd nicknamed him hottie and praised his size before inserting it into her mouth like she had done with his finger. He returned the compliment but was almost sure he didn't reciprocate her courtesy for lack of inclination. The images flashed and faded to black until the next scene. She spreading out like a starfish against the wall and lifting her buttocks to him. Then again on the bed, on all fours. Until the last scene. They were lying amid the upheaval of sheets and he looked at the smoke alarm on the white ceiling, his body and thoughts vacant.

Stefania drew her lips close to his ear.

"I really like you, Marco."

"Me too," he said without paying much attention, his hollow stare still on the ceiling.

She laughed.

"You really like yourself?"

"You're right. Let's say it properly." Marco turned to gaze at her. "I like you too, Stefania."

"Oh, I guess we're intimate enough for you to call me by my real name. Lorena."

He was instantly sober. The name invaded each fiber of his body, shaking it with the echo of a dream that carried a nightmare. The clerk's words came back to him. *The die sometimes produces strange results.* He looked at the woman sprawled next to him, the perfect breasts pointing at him, the parted lips in an invitation, and didn't know what to do with her. That was the problem of bringing unknown women into his territory. He couldn't stand to his feet and depart. What he had left was the shower. Then a feigned sleep while the name still reverberated inside him. *Lorena, Lorena, Lorena...*

Marco turned into a prisoner of the memory. It wasn't he who couldn't forget it. It was the memory that wouldn't forget him: Lorena-Stefania evoking Lorena-Lorena, the contrast between the colors of an amusement park and the barrenness of an industrial park. Love ends one day, and his finally wore out. But the mark left by love, that never wore out. It remained buried in time and, when he least expected it, found the way to his heart. *I'm here. Remember me.* Yes, the mark was pain, and also the symbol of a dream. Marisa once told him she became attached to the pain because it reminded her of her dad. In Marco's case, forgetting the mark was the same as betraying a dream. Maybe that's why he couldn't forget it—maybe that's why the mark wouldn't forget him, either.

8. Miracle Fruit

"What about the red anthuriums?" Marisa asked as soon as she lay down on the divan.

Doctor Spitzer raised an eyebrow, and her expression became as hermetic as a vacuum-packed cigar box. Sometimes a cigar was just a cigar, like Freud would presumably say. Or was it? Doctor Spitzer acted quite enigmatic that day, plus she wore a surprising electric-blue suit. Not to mention her scarpino shoes were white.

"Later," she retorted with a note of impatience. "First I want to know more details about the teacher."

"Well…" Marisa stared at the ceiling. "The whole class dreaded him. He was always in a sour mood. He would fill the whiteboard with those physics formulas no one understood—"

The psychoanalyst interrupted Marisa with her usual assertiveness: "Physics formulas? I was under the impression he taught literature."

Marisa stirred and shifted position. In her reverie, the physics teacher with his gray moustache gave room to the vision of Marco before the whiteboard.

"Oh, Marco… I'm still in love with him, doctor. It's just beyond my control. I've made out with some guys from college but always end up finding them dull. Life with Marco had *more color*, you know what I mean?"

Marisa couldn't erase from her memory their last encounter. Marco's gaze told her everything even before he spoke: it was best if they stopped seeing each other. And then her body turned into a dead weight plummeting from a cliff. *I don't want to cause you more family problems, Mari. Moreover, the age gap between us will create divergences. I'm very fond of you, but I'm not the right man for you. I've got scars…*

And he said that she was wonderful and he admired her greatly. That he felt sorry they couldn't be together and was jealous of the man who would succeed in giving her everything she deserved and he was unable to give. He spoke with extreme tact. It did nothing to ease the pain. Marisa couldn't understand how things changed that way. It was as if she had never existed in this life.

Marco returned her belongings: clothes left in the apartment, a toothbrush, the strass collar. He put everything in a cardboard box and handed it to the porter in her building. Marisa got rid of the collar, along with Marco's gifts: poetry collections, CDs, a white lacy top, a black lingerie set. She didn't muster the courage to part with the filigree ring and put it away in her closet's last drawer, where the sweaters were kept.

The drawer remained untouched. It was finally opened when winter arrived. Sweaters left it, returned, some left again. The last garment from the pile, however, crystallized on the bottom of the drawer and never shifted. It was a shroud. Under it rested the ring.

Inside Marisa the days were quiet. And outside, wherever she looked, she saw echoes of Marco—one day, upon seeing a street cart selling jabuticabas, Marisa broke into tears. She needed to reclaim life without his marks. Make it her own again. Her own. Not theirs.

Except for the ring, nothing was left. She ripped off cards and notes, deleted emails and the smiley photo taken in his kitchen—she behind a bunch of herbs, he with a grater in his hand. She couldn't stand the irony of the words and that smile now devoid of meaning. Marisa erased all physical traces of Marco's presence. The only thing she couldn't erase was the invisible trace that lingered within her.

Marco never contacted her again. At first she couldn't help but make up excuses to call him. Marco always acted solicitous. But he had changed. On those occasions, they would talk with a distant politeness that was much worse than no contact. Marisa stopped calling.

"It was all too sudden. Since he decided to break up, I feel like a shadow... Valentina says he's an idiot and I'm a bigger idiot because I keep thinking of him. She's right. I can't help it, though. I wonder if I did anything wrong, if he left me for another woman... I'm sure the situation with my mom was the last straw," Marisa stuttered as her eyes blurred. "Oh, doctor, I've never been in love with anyone like this."

She couldn't go on. Whimpering weakly, Marisa blinked and sniffled. Doctor Spitzer offered her a tissue.

"Nonsense," she retorted in a professional tone. "Let us steer away from the scope of traditional psychoanalysis for a moment. What people call passion is merely a cocktail of dopamine and pheromones. A biological strategy for the perpetuation of the species." She closed the notepad, ignoring Marisa's attempt to object. "You are suffering from withdrawal symptoms, that's all. Stop filling your head with foolish ideas and harboring feelings of guilt and inferiority. It's all going to pass. But Marco ignites your desire, right? You think you're in love, when in reality it is the hormones dictating your reactions. Note that a dream is the fulfillment of an intrinsically sexual wish..."

The therapist made a suggestive pause as she shifted in the armchair. For a moment, her glasses reflected the blue from the suit and sparkled with fury.

"Observe, in your last dream, the abundance of libidinous references. The night associated with the primordial instinct. The curvaceous lake and the phallic pine trees. The full moon, a symbol of femininity at its prime. The corridor representing the female organ. The closed doors of forbidden desire. The room with a cat, the icon of sensuality. The tank as a receptacle (female organ) that breaks into pieces under the feline's influence (desire), releasing the water (body fluids). And what have we got inside the tank? The formula for calculating the *fall* (surrender to pleasure) that causes *death*, i.e., total abandonment (climax). Everything is quite simple and logical. Clear as day."

Doctor Spitzer didn't hide her satisfaction and added: "The conscious mind has barred your sexual drive as a way of blocking the emotions associated with it: fear of vulnerability and loss, and even fear of happiness, for happiness is also disturbing: you cannot blame it for failures as you do with depression." She sighed. "Don't forget your whole life has changed in less than a year. And that can be very frightening. You lost your father and your boyfriend, besides losing stability at home and at school with the end of the term. As a result, you shut everything off to protect yourself, and the repressed wishes provoked panic attacks. But the important thing is you overcame your fear and entered the symbolic elevator. Even better: you picked up the red flower bouquet. Do you know what that means?"

"I have no idea, doctor. I will be frank, though, this color of blood makes me uneasy."

"Why is that?"

"I don't know. It makes me think of things like… *accidents*."

"It all depends on the context. Blood, just like the red color, can have various meanings." Doctor Spitzer gazed at an inexistent dot on the wall. She seemed to speak to herself, oblivious to the patient: "It's a vast subject. Really instigating…"

"What's so instigating?" interjected Marisa, unable to stand the suspense.

"The red color, you see, possesses diurnal and nocturnal qualities. In the diurnal polarity, it incorporates yellow and refers to the radiant energy of the sun. In the nocturnal polarity, it incorporates blue and is spectral. Blood itself holds such duality. Outside the body, it means death. Inside it, blood is life. Note the paradox here: what's without suggests the occult, and what's within evokes the explosion of life itself."

"I've never thought about that. But the boundaries between what's within and what's without aren't always clear, right? Funnily enough, red is one of my favorite colors."

It was the favorite color of children, Doctor Spitzer stated with a benevolent expression. Then she focused back on Marisa's dream. It brought three primordial shades. Black and white, the first two colors named by men's ancestors because they translated the basic perception of day and night, of the conscious mind and the unconscious. Parallel to that, another crucial color stood out in the dream: red.

Doctor Spitzer silenced in meditation. She had her legs crossed, one foot waving up and down to the tempo of her thoughts. Marisa glanced at her out of the corner of one eye and waited. She imagined Doctor Spitzer's analytical brain processing data like a state-of-the-art computer. Her RAM memory must be huge.

"The matter at hand is simple and logical," she affirmed at last. "Red is the first color to appear in the spectrum of visible light, that is to say, it's the first color we discern amongst all the others. The tint of life and death. Cave men used it in their rupestral paintings to portray the hunt (the death of the prey that supports life), as well as to worship the gods. The red color had a sacred quality associated with the enigma of existence. Today it represents love and passion. It equally represents hate and suffering."

As she spoke, Doctor Spitzer raised one hand and described an arch in the air. Red encompassed a palette of many hues. It was the color of extremes and dressed the Pope just like it painted the Devil. It attracted by symbolizing desire. And repelled as it warned to prohibition. It was visceral: it signaled pleasure as well as pain, the two basic human drives which coincidentally shared the same neural circuits to reach the brain. That's why they walked hand in hand and sometimes got mixed up. It was no wonder the reddest emotion of all, passion, reflected the full richness of the human experience. A quick look in the dictionary attested that *passion* simultaneously meant a strong feeling, love, and pain—because it was impossible to set the three apart.

"In fact, love and hate, pleasure and pain all converge at one point. Red is the color of emotion boiling up to the surface of the skin... be it positive or negative, or a bit of each," reflected Marisa. As she dissected it that way, the red color she saw with the eyes of imagination became less intimidating. "What is the bouquet in my dream about? Does it symbolize my repressed emotions?"

Doctor Spitzer rewarded her with a smile.

"Exactly. Observe that the repression mechanism is not selective. It's not feasible to suppress *one single* emotion. It's all or nothing. If you repress pain, you automatically repress pleasure too. Now just think of what happens when *all* emotions are shut off. They get exacerbated and, sooner or later, need to surface. Actually, when avoiding an unpleasant feeling (that is to say, pain), you avoid facing reality and fantasize about it instead. But fantasy can be much scarier than reality because the imagination has no limits."

She leaned forward and assumed a professorial tone: "In the first volume of his *Letters*, Jung wrote that your vision only becomes clear when you look into your heart: *Who looks outside dreams, who looks inside awakes.* You have gone through all those phases, Marisa. You have plunged into phobia, faced repressed wishes and returned to the starting point."

"So... if I'm back to the starting point, what happens now?"

"A new beginning."

Doctor Spitzer beamed, her face sank into the background and her mouth levitated, teeth shining like glow-in-the-dark tape. And thus the cigar box opened with a whiff that made the bright-blue suit dance a rumba with a pair of white scarpino shoes.

Before the scene became too surreal, Doctor Spitzer announced: "You have completed a cycle. You are cured, Marisa."

Hearing those words, Marisa sat up abruptly. She felt in her mouth the taste of her own astonishment. And what it was like? It tasted like miracle fruit, an African berry that is a red circle and tastes of nothing. The miracle fruit, however, dazes the palate, converting the sour into sweet, the lemon into honey. Dialectic lemon, relative flesh, red skin. That was the taste of Marisa's astonishment.

Cured. For a few seconds, she remained speechless. It was good news, right? Yet Marisa felt lost. How could she be dismissed from therapy just like that, how would she cope without psychological support? Her mind spiraled in a thousand and one interrogation marks.

"But... tell me something, doctor... what are those repressed wishes after all?"

Resting the pen on the notepad, the therapist fixed her enigmatic eyes on Marisa.

"Only you can answer that."

Marisa admired for the last time the watercolor above the divan, now with a strange commotion: so that was it. Squares, circles. From black to gray to white and back to the start. Red. She had survived.

Doctor Spitzer wished her good luck and walked her to the door. They said goodbye without effusion.

At the exit, Marisa halted.

"There's one thing I've always wanted to ask, doctor. I've noticed the two paintings in your office are the same, only with inverted colors. What's the meaning of that? Is it a metaphor about the alternation between the conscious mind and the unconscious? A Freudian interpretation of the yin-yang principle?"

Marisa stared at her with high expectations. She knew the therapist, with the aid of her powerful psychoanalytic magnifying glass, would have some astounding revelation in store.

Doctor Spitzer narrowed her eyes and lingered them on Marisa for a moment. Then, as she closed the door, she finally replied: "I don't know. My interior decorator chose those paintings. Have a good evening."

And that concluded Marisa's psychological treatment.

Coincidentally, the next day that same interior decorator would replace the office's watercolors with cubist paintings—which, besides suggesting the human being's fragmentation, matched perfectly the new geranium arrangement on the sideboard.

9. In the Bedroom

The orchids on the coffee table were replaced with a silver candle holder and a lone flame. Around it, glass platters offered a variety of Arabic specialties Marco had prepared. The menu included dumplings in yogurt sauce, raw salmon kibbeh and fattoush salad, as well as sweets from a traditional deli. The aroma of honey and herbs lingered in the air.

When the clock turned nine, she arrived preceded by a floral fragrance. She wore a satiny strap top and black skirt, her high-heeled sandals matching a pair of pearl earrings and a golden necklace. Marco couldn't help but gaze at her in awe.

When she was absent, her beauty seemed to pale. He contemplated her young body, returned to her oval face, stared into the irises that sparkled igniting his own desire. Marco oscillated in the frontier of lust and disquiet. It was such an odd sensation that he savored it for an instant while attempting to define it.

"Why are you staring at me? It's like you've never seen me before," she said, smiling.

"It's nothing."

She approached Marco with an insinuating gait.

"Aren't you forgetting something?" She leaned toward him. "How about my kiss?"

Her lips greeted Marco's as her hands slid up his white shirt and rested lightly on his shoulders. Then she sat on the sofa and crossed her legs as she studied the surroundings with curiosity. She frowned at the sight of the food and sought an indication of what was to come. This time, however, nothing there hinted at Marco's intentions, so the center stage would probably be the bedroom.

"What are we doing tonight?" she inquired. Her pupils dilated.

Marco remained silent. This was his last chance to back down. He could always get the valise and improvise a game. It held all sorts of toys—she wouldn't even notice the change of plans.

He hesitated, glancing at the bedroom door. His pause dragged.

"Let's have dinner first," he said.

The two sat cross-legged on the floor around the coffee table, drinking arak to world music by Pakistani Nusrat Fateh Ali Khan and Michael Brook. The melody of *My Heart, My Life* brought to the living room a summer night—harp lute and stars, guitar and crickets, percussion and breeze in the foliage. The Pakistani artist sang about life in the form of a woman, wishing her to sit before him so he could gaze at her always and always. *Mera dil, meri jaan...*

In the meantime she sat there, tasting the food and throwing furtive glances at Marco. Until she was unable to refrain herself any longer: "What did you plan, after all?"

"Just wait and see. Didn't you say you like surprises? Be patient."

Marco emptied his glass and poured more arak for both of them. He was about to raise the drink to his lips when he changed his mind and returned it to the table. She took a long draft and pushed the plate, her hands on the edge of the table, fingers tapping with a reflection of golden nail polisher.

"I've had enough, thank you."

A smile.

Now what? was what her eyes asked and his didn't reply.

The air closed upon them. Marco reached out for the glass of arak but gave up once more. He rose to his feet, reached out and helped her stand up. He drew her near, leading her in the music cadence.

She nestled up against his chest, and they danced cheek to cheek in place. Marco shut his eyes and tried to capture the womanly scent masked by jasmine. He skimmed his lips on the exposed nape of her neck, kissing the shoulder slope, pushing aside the top strap with his teeth to nibble the flesh.

Little by little she started to reciprocate each caress with fluid symmetry. Her hands roamed over his wide back while he traced the line of her spine. Their mouths met simultaneously in the same route, at first lightly and slowly, then with impetuousness. A famished kiss that went on and on while hands clutched, squeezed, scratched...

They tumbled on the couch, and he removed her top with impatient hands, then stripped off his own shirt. Bare skin against bare skin, they tightened their embrace. Her pulsating warmth. His moan. In an impulse, Marco took her breast in the mouth as his hand glided toward the curve of her hips.

The hand lingered there to tantalize the hollow of the navel, tracing circles with the fingertips, in and out, around and about, making her sigh. It kept sliding down, sneaked under the skirt, explored the recess at the junction of her thighs. His fingers then hooked in a tiny cotton garment and removed the last obstacle between them and the naked flesh.

She tossed back her head and buried her nails on his back. Then she groped for the waistband of his pants, the button, the zipper. She held him as if weighing the erection and smiled satisfied with herself, for she was the one responsible for that. She began stimulating him with her hands and mouth. Marco closed his eyes, caressing her hair, bringing her closer. Successive waves of delicious tension concentrated in one single spot to reach an almost unbearable crescendo...

She stilled to look at him. Wickedness beclouded her face.

"Let's go to the bedroom." Her voice trickled like thick caramel, then her gaze. "I want to see what you've prepared for me."

He winced, waking up to reality with a shock, resisting the urge to retreat. Marco straightened his clothes with an absent air while his lover stood up, every inch female, and pulled him by the hand. She was flushed, hair in disarray, her half-naked body undulating in feline fluidity.

Like a sleepwalker, Marco allowed her to drag him to the bedroom, where a candle burned on the nightstand commanding the shadows. Above the bed, the reds on the painting shifted to golds and maroons at the whim of the flame. A thick black outline emphasized the furniture and objects, and in the antique mirror the forms gained depth as if the carved frame gave passage to another place.

She hesitated at the door, her eyes darting here and there in search of a clue, taking the time to inspect the furniture and the darkness in the corners. When she realized there was nothing in sight to satiate her curiosity, she turned to Marco with an interrogative expression.

"Where is it?" She smiled, increasingly puzzled.

For an instant, the breeze made the room flicker in a dance of shadows and yellow rays. Then everything froze again in the stagnated air.

Marco smiled uncertainly in return.

"Didn't you say you wanted to do *normal* things? There you are. Tonight we're not using anything, nor following a script."

"What do you mean?" Disconcerted, she leaned against the door frame.

He felt cornered by the intensity of her gaze. He knew she liked to experience different things. Well, compared to what the two of them usually did, that *was* different.

"Tonight it's just you and me," he said. "No accessories. No masks."

She remained silent. On her face flickered a range of emotions: astonishment, incredulity, finally disappointment. She could sense she was losing him. He had become increasingly apathetic and withdrawn. She wanted Marco, his body, his smile, his words, even those she couldn't understand. For at his side she discovered herself. So she made a point in looking pretty for him. When she seduced him, it was a small victory in a battle that seemed already lost. More and more often, she had the feeling he didn't see her. Not even the game, the only thing that still moved him, would entice Marco as before. Her heart trembled. His indifference had entered the bedroom. The last stop.

Marco read the disappointment on her face and wondered at which point she had become a discomfort. He didn't know the answer. It had been like a draft sneaking through a crack in the window, then one day the house dawned cold. The thread uniting them wove together her desire and his pain. And her want gave him the measure of his own emptiness. It was unsettling. It was Mars with its harsh fire in the black sky. Despite the differences emerging between them, Marco thought it might work. He wanted it to work. He owed it to himself and to her: a chance. He had already relinquished too many things, and it was time to yank off that crust from his body.

New skin.

At that thought, Marco felt strangely calm. He believed it was a sign he'd be closer to her. He didn't know in truth he had already distanced himself and severed the bond.

"Come with me," he said, leading her to the bed.

The two rolled over the velvety spread and he covered her body with his. Their scent mingled with the lavender fragrance from the candle, their erratic breathing filled the absence of words. The caresses reinitiated, legs intertwined, lips united with renewed eagerness. They finished undressing and Marco sought her sex with his mouth. He laid a path of kisses that made her squirm, moaning ever so loudly.

On a sudden, she forced him to stop.

"I want you inside me…"

She wriggled, lying on her stomach.

"Not like this," he murmured as he grasped her hips.

She acceded mutely. Lifting herself, she placed her flattened hands and knees on the mattress. Then waited. Marco, however, held her by the waist and turned her around. They faced each other.

She chuckled.

"Is this really what you want, Marco?"

"Don't you like it?"

He licked her neck, sliding the tip of his tongue down the cleft between the pale breasts and up again. When his eyes reached her face, they gleamed like a pair of obsidians. Dark, lustrous. It didn't take much to convince her. She parted her legs, ready to receive him.

Marisa once said the present was what mattered, thought Marco. True. But now he was looking back. And, as soon as he positioned himself, he lost momentum. His concentration faltered. The energy escaped his body as if a dam gate had suddenly been opened. Emptied of everything, he was left with frustration and embarrassment.

Marco rolled to the side.

"I'm sorry, Mari…"

She sat up brusquely, her eyes flashing a spark of indignation.

"*Mari?* Who's Mari?"

Marco closed his eyes. He felt drained, emptier than ever.

"I think you better get dressed, Camila."

PART 3

RED:
BLACK AND WHITE CONVERGE

One week later
WINTER, JULY

1. Turning the Page

The Wheel of Fortune is shaking off some rust again. After a joyless summer and the disquiet of autumn, winter's blank page unfolds. It's July, time for vacation and for airing the house within and without. The wheel spins. The wheel spins spinning life. What's up goes down. What's down goes up.

For the first time in several months, Marisa felt optimistic about the future. When Doctor Spitzer declared her love for Marco was nothing more than a hormone cocktail, Marisa had doubts. She thought she would never get over Marco because he was perfect. Gradually, though, she realized her pain resulted not only from the loss of a real man, but above all from the loss of an idealization she had made of him.

If there was a devastating feeling, it was disappointment. Hers surpassed words. From the start, Marisa had admired Marco's strength and integrity. But faced with the first obstacle, he proved himself weak and cowardly, turning his back to her when she needed him. He set a meeting at a downtown bar after her quarrel with her mom. An impersonal, noisy bar. He said beautiful words but had already distanced himself. Obviously Marco never intended to patch up the situation with her mother. The indifference with which he proceeded to treat her could only mean one thing: his feelings were fleeting. It was even possible he already had another relationship going on. With the nonchalance of someone changing clothes. With the disdain of someone who had never really cared for her. And that hurt the most.

What is like opening up to another person? Open up your heart and your body, dreams and thoughts. Dedicate time and energy, and the best part of yourself, the most generous, the most understanding, the most affectionate. And then hear one day: I've never loved you, it was a mistake. He didn't say it with words, but the message was clear. The cliché. *It's not you, it's me.* What Marco meant was not that he wasn't right for her. He meant *she* wasn't right for him. She and her young age, her inexperience, her crazy mother. Probably Marco concluded it would be easier to find another woman and get on with life without that pile of trouble. Why take unnecessary risks? He was handsome, intelligent, successful, and could have anyone he wanted. She didn't meet the expectations.

Marisa pictured him with a new girlfriend: a beautiful, well-dressed woman with an impressive career. She would live in her own penthouse, and in her brain would live an entire library to delight Marco. He would smile to her as the two enjoyed a candlelight dinner and admired the view from the penthouse. Then they would go to bed…

Those thoughts haunted Marisa, robbed her of sleep and appetite. She spent the summer on the beach, enveloped in her gloominess under the sun without really being there, far too engrossed in her own wound. One night, unable to sleep, she went for a walk.

In the serene landscape flowed a canal with grassy banks. A frog croaked. On this side a path and a lamppost surrounded by moths in a ring o' roses game. On the other, the back of a warehouse, its roof with two slanted panes pointed to the sky, and between them a white light that emitted star rays and drew in the dark water a specter made of shining dots. The specter danced.

Marisa reached the beach and strolled for hours by the water, listening to the velvety whisper of the sand under her footsteps, until the sea reflected the sky. She sat on a trunk and watched the world wake up: dew painted the houses, trees stretched out their branches, and creepers knitted lace on the sand. The sleepy azure was streaked by herons and brown bobby birds on their way for fishing. Whitecaps sprayed perfume in the air. Watching the sun cast its golden net on the waters, Marisa saw beauty until then ignored. Saw it within and without. Heard it within and without.

That was when she took a deep breath and let the sorrow flow without clinging to it any longer, for sorrow was a rock that dragged the soul to the bottom of the sea. And without resisting it either—accepting and facing it without fear. Sorrow thus flowed, it flowed out of her like a cloudy river clearing up as it followed its course. And, when she least expected, the last cloudy drop drained and Marco finally occupied his place in the past.

The day broke. In the ocean foam, Cocteau Twins' verses twisted and untwisted and dispersed. *A Kissed Out Red Floatboat*. Want, indifference, love, hurt. The words diluted in the foam. Marisa no longer needed to conjure a prince charming to complete her.

The prince was inside her.

The prince was her.

The learning now would continue along other paths.

That was all. Everything was fine.

Follow your own self and the rest will follow.

When she returned to the city, the journalism course at college and new friends provided a welcomed change to routine. Life regained color. The situation at home, in the meantime, had greatly improved too. Marisa's mother, already adapted to widowhood, was visiting relatives and getting together with her lady friends. The apartment became airy, and in the fluttering of the curtains there were no more shadows.

The Wheel of Fortune spun faster, faster…

One day her mother broke the news: an irresistible bargain, an intensive program. And she registered Marisa in a summer course in Miami for perfecting her English during two weeks. Unable to refrain herself, she persuaded Valentina's mother to register her own daughter too (Ms. Adélia's dislike had shifted to unconditional approval since Valentina helped her during Marisa's nervous breakdown).

Valentina was studying sociology and, as they went to different colleges, the two saw each other less often. Still, they talked on the phone every day. Lately, as expected, the cherry in the conversation was the trip: they raved about the possibilities of study and personal growth.

In order to sharpen their English, they had decided no method was more efficient than on-site practice on Miami Beach. They dreamed of sea and margaritas in the shade of tiny paper parasols. The two entertained visions of Latinos with mysterious eyes and sculpted bodies swaying in salsa clubs. And their visions became even more calientes once they produced fake student IDs and got self-promoted to respectable twenty-one-year-old damsels, the legal age for alcoholic stupor in the United States.

They would travel in the second week of July. At five days from departure, while Marisa still frazzled to find the perfect bikini, Valentina had already packed: she temporarily put aside her anti-capitalist convictions and surrendered to the temptations of tourism. Valentina carried enough luggage for a whole semester, besides a minilibrary with dictionaries and tourist guides. She would come up with elaborate itineraries and submit them to Marisa's appreciation.

"On the first Saturday, we leave early to visit the Hemingway House in Key West. In the afternoon we go shopping at the Bayside. In the evening, we do the round of the club circuit in Miami Beach until dawn. Then we have breakfast on the street and spend Sunday on the beach. That way we can get a tan while we sleep. Is this brilliant or what?" She would leaf through a guide and go on: "Hey, there's a sex museum in South Beach! We can go there after our beach session."

On that particular day, they idled in Valentina's bedroom, which looked rather like a pop art gallery. In contrast with the colorful posters on the walls, a large black-and-white print hanging on the door depicted Marcel Duchamp's work *Fountain*. Sprawled on fake leather yellow puffs, the two girls ate popcorn and listened to an old Roxy Music album. Brian Ferry sang how good it would be to fall in love. *Could It Happen to Me?*

"Oh, I wish I could find me a boyfriend there." Marisa sipped her long-neck beer. "I'm tired of being single. To make things worse, it seems I only see couples everywhere I look. It's sickening. Do you know what I miss the most? A man who gazes at me with gleaming eyes. All that first-date thrill, the first discoveries…"

"Yeah, there's nothing like a first date. To spend the whole afternoon busy with clothes, accessories, makeup…"

"… to have your nails, hair and waxing done, exfoliate your body and apply a hundred different creams… cram yourself into a pair of jeans one size smaller than the regular, torture your feet on seven-inch high heels…"

Valentina turned up her activist nose.

"I refuse to wear anything uncomfortable just to please a guy. That's pure lumbar thought."

"Lumbar thought?"

"It's a courtesy by Umberto Eco. He noticed the loose frock worn by medieval monks allowed them to forget their bodies and concentrate on the intellect and spirit. Compare that to yourself shoved inside a pair of pants that glue to your rear end. While medieval monks question the mysteries of the universe, you think about your pants."

"What do you mean? I also question the mysteries of the universe."

Marisa acted offended, to which Valentina clicked her tongue with a condescending *tsc-tsc*. It was so heartfelt it bordered obscene.

"Honey, you may even question them. But in the back of your mind are those pants."

"Why in the back of my mind are those pants?"

"Because they squeeze everything and it's impossible to forget them." Valentina rolled her eyes at Marisa's failure to realize such an obvious fact. "So you think about the pants and the pants brand, about your association with that brand and with the people who wear it. You belong to a tribe now and feel suddenly… oh so adventurous, rebellious, sophisticated, romantic, seductive, or whatever it is that the brand slogan dictates. You transfer your discernment and decision power to stylists and admen. And all that chain of gibberish constitutes the lumbar thought."

"And what's the conclusion?"

"You no longer think with your head. You think with your butt."

Marisa stared at her and blinked a couple of times without knowing what to respond. At last she said: "I guess it's a social phenomenon. Women want to be attractive at any cost. After all, aren't they raised to get hold of a man? The ultimate goal in life. That's why they compete so fiercely in that terrain. It's the perpetuation of species logic: to get hold of *one* man in order to fecundate *one* egg and help them raise the child."

"By the same logic, men can go out there and fecundate several women, the more the better. Very egalitarian indeed."

"It's the premise of masculine domination, Val."

"Well, in the beginning of the world society was matriarchal, based on the partnership between women and men. The problem started when all tribes quit being nomadic and created private property."

"The supreme religion."

"Yeah. And we were caught in the middle of that. Since men can never tell for sure if a child is theirs or not, it's necessary to repress women to prevent them from generating illegitimate heirs." Here Valentina got inflamed, gesticulating like a sociological wind rose: "We women are second-rate citizens, and to this day our heads are filled with all sorts of nonsense in order to perpetuate that repression. Activist Gloria Feldt noted the repression is already so internalized that today many doors open but few women walk through them."

"It's like a presentation I saw by some British mimes. In one of the sketches, a man in a suit with a briefcase tries to reach a pair of scissors dangling in the middle of the stage. He's held by a string tied on his back and struggles like mad to get the scissors. Finally he manages to grasp them. He smiles triumphantly and opens the briefcase. Inside it, there's a scissor collection."

"That's what conditioning does to people, Ma. And we women are conditioned to believe that the masculine can and should control the feminine. See what's done to *Mother* Nature. In the grand scheme of things, women are consumers and objects of consumption, incubators and a mass of maneuver for the perpetuation of the patriarchal regimen."

"Hmm. Virginia Woolf wrote in *Orlando* that no one objects to a woman *thinking*. As long as she thinks of a man... or pants, apparently." Marisa gave an awkward chuckle. "But can I still wear my skinny jeans? I *really* look good in them."

They laughed and made a toast. Love was beautiful, and so was Valentina when she said: "Yes, you can. If you want a boyfriend, that's gonna be the time. Great possibilities, my dear."

Marisa stared at her with hope. She began braiding a random lock of her hair.

"Why is that, Val?"

"Well, the least you can get in a sex museum is a well-endowed guy," said Valentina with a wink. "If I were you, I'd take those seven-inch high heels in the suitcase too. Maybe your future boyfriend will already be waiting for you across the ocean…"

2. The Light Inside Your Eyes

Books, tablet, camera, MP3 player, speakers, shorts, pants, sweatpants, shirts, T-shirts, swimming trunks, socks, underwear, shoes, sneakers, flip-flops, personal hygiene items, shaver, pocketknife, earplugs, ATM machine, cleaner payment, hotel reservation, car rental, international driving license, congress registration, Jeff's phone number, passport, dollars, a genie of the lamp for granting three wishes…

One single wish, actually, would suffice for Marco: to gain superpowers in order to organize it all in only one hour. It was a shame he didn't even have enough time to find a genie of the lamp.

Marco would be travelling that evening and had just returned home from spending a week inland with his family to look after his mother. She had undergone an emergency surgery for a neglected appendicitis and, after a difficult recovery, was fortunately okay. The good news had been delivered the previous day, but, due to a problem with his car, Marco was only able to take off that morning. Now he needed to run if he didn't want to miss the plane.

He picked a suitcase and opened it on top of the bed. The phone rang. Marco answered, alarmed when he recognized the gentle voice of Aunt Carmina. She was his mom's elder sister, a lady with a cherubic face who liked to dye her short hair blonde and paint her nails pink. Why was she calling? Marco thought the worst and feared for his mother's health. Given the aunt's careless tone, though, he relaxed.

She tended to speak quite a bit—like, a lot. With bovine tranquility, she ruminated the words slowly and would thus chew away many hours before you realized it. As soon as Marco picked up the phone, Aunt Carmina ruminated he had left in such a hurry and she didn't have the chance to say a proper goodbye. She asked if he had eaten lunch, mentioned the hot weather and complained about her rebellious air conditioner. Finally, the aunt said she had forgotten to ask him something, if it wouldn't be a bother, of course. And he replied: no bother at all, Aunt, you can ask whatever you wish.

"Well, Marco, I remembered in the US there's a special baking tray for cakes. It's shaped like small balls, and the dough takes only five minutes to bake. Do you know which one I'm talking about?"

"No, I don't."

"Well, I saw it in a magazine. It's an enclosed tray for round minicakes the size of plums. Then you put a stick into them and they look like lollipops, really cute." She sighed, dreamy. "I saw them decorated with little flowers, little polka dots, little faces… They would be perfect for the children's birthdays. Oh, and did you know you can put filling in them? All you need to do is prepare thicker custard. You can also use chocolate fudge, caramel, nuts—"

Marco bypassed her and said he had never seen such a baking pan but would search for it. The aunt calmly informed that, well, she would need two trays, as each fitted a dozen minicakes. Did he think he could bring them? Sure, swore Marco. His prompt response made her suspicious.

"What if you can't find them?"

"I promise I'll do my best."

Now a higher pitched feminine voice and a closing door could be heard in the background.

"Oh, Marco, wait a minute. Lolo just came in, and I will ask her if she can find the magazine where I saw the tray. It has the name of the manufacturer. It helps, right?"

"Aunt Carmina, I'm in a bit of a hurry, can't you tell Lolo to message me the name later… Aunt? Aunt?"

She was no longer on the other end of the line. Marco listened while she talked to his twenty-year-old cousin (a younger and leaner version of Aunt Carmina with a weakness for fashion). In despair, he opened the closet and started grabbing clothes. *Let's see, shorts, pants, sweatpants…*

"Your cousin is searching for the magazine. The problem is locating anything in her bedroom. You know how Lolo hoards stuff, don't you? I always tell her she needs to do something about it, or else she won't be able to fit even a pin in that bedroom."

"Listen, I'm running late and—"

"Oh my, Lolo is taking so long. You don't happen to have that magazine, do you? It's last month's *Cosmo*… or maybe it's the edition from the month before?"

"I don't read *Cosmo*, Aunt."

She gave a little chuckle that would be lovely if it were not maddening.

"Ah, of course you don't, Marco. What a nonsense I just said. But I thought," she discreetly probed, "maybe your *girlfriend* bought the magazine and left it in your apartment, right? One never knows, that's why it's always good to ask."

As she spoke, Marco tried to concentrate again on his list: *shirts, T-shirts, swimming trunks…*

"True, Aunt. But I don't have a girlfriend," he said, throwing everything in the suitcase.

Since the divorce, it had been basically one-night stands. Many of them. A gentlemen's agreement that included maximum pleasure and minimal strings. After all, the body required some attention and the deal was convenient for both parties. Until Marisa came along: the woman with whom he had wished to be night after night. And then Marisa quarreled with her mother because of him. At that point he still had no idea of what he had gotten himself into.

It was time to rectify the situation once and for all. The circumstances were far from favorable—he had planned a different scenario, a different frame of mind. Now he needed to do the best within his reach. Marco called Marisa's home to talk to her mother and found the line busy. Agitation dominated him. Busy. Busy. Busy. He decided to stop by without warning. The subject at hand didn't sit well on the telephone anyway. In the car, he turned the radio off and concentrated on what he would say, which wasn't too hard. He had already said the words in his thoughts way before that day. The message was clear to him and so it would be to her.

Marco announced himself as a friend of Marisa's to the porter and was admitted in the building. He found the mother waiting for him at the apartment door, her face still marked by tears, her compact frame lost inside a brown pencil dress too loose for her. The resemblance between the mother and Marisa struck him. The eyes were the same, with the color of topaz at twilight and narrow lids that intensified their focus. She stared at him suspiciously and hesitated before inviting him in.

He noticed she lingered on his black clothes, already disapproving of him at some subliminal level. Marco regretted not changing before he'd left his apartment and, as he followed her into the living area, nervousness clutched the pit of his stomach. They sat in opposite armchairs, shielded from each other by the coffee table and an army of ornaments. She offered him water from a silver pitcher, he accepted it, and for a minute both were lost in that automatic game of politeness.

Then he talked about his intentions, financial stability, goals and all the details that composed a good impression. She assessed him with an ambivalent gaze that didn't signal the bent of her thoughts. She wanted to know how Marco and Marisa knew each other. They stumbled into silence—brief but so dense not even the sounds on the street would pervade it. When Marco answered, the good impression he had painted blurred.

"So this is what you do. You get involved with students," the mother summed it up, and Marco felt the stab in her voice.

"Certain things are not planned. It has never happened before, and I didn't intend—"

"But it's a fact."

Marco found himself before a wall. She continued piling up stones meticulously—one more minute and she would disappear behind them. In an effort to keep calm, he searched for a breach and attempted to translate the untranslatable. He needed to think fast and find the vulnerable point in the foundation—find the word Marisa's mother wanted to hear, the one word that would bring down the wall. One mistake, and she'd pile up the last stone.

"I want to make your daughter happy. Marisa is very special to me. More special than anyone I've ever met." Marco saw his words crumbling on her gaze and felt the grasp in the pit of his stomach. Then he remembered *Red River*. "There's a poem by Cora Coralina that says a river is the windowpane of the sky, clouds and stars, a photograph of the moon when it dresses the city in white... To me, that's what Marisa is. A reflection of beauty."

Her smile came unexpectedly.

"I know that poem. You have good taste. No wonder you teach the love for letters."

"Then you understand."

She had to.

The mother helped herself with water from the silver tray where the pitcher rested with three crystal glasses. She adjusted with a mechanical gesture the white cloth on the bottom of it, took a drowsy sip and laid the glass on the table. Her face was almost dreamy when she commented: "I used to read a lot of poetry when I was young. That reminds me of a poem from a book I was given long ago. Pablo Neruda. Do you like him?" And since he assented, she went on. "It's the *Sonnet LXVI* if I'm not mistaken. It speaks of the measure of love, when even if you don't see your loved one, you love them like a blind man."

"That's it. When you find the reflection of beauty, it stays with you wherever you are."

She understood.

Poetry.

Such a simple and complex, magical and obvious thing. As he looked at Marisa's mother, Marco thought of the poem *I(a* by e. e. cummings, which contained a leaf falling within the word *loneliness*. In condensed lines, an entire life. No one could remain immune to that.

And, without realizing he'd clenched his hand on the chair, Marco relaxed. He found a breach, and with it came relief. The mother was a harsh and difficult woman, just like Marisa described. But she had loved. She understood. That was all he needed: an opening. With that step taken, everything would fall into place.

On the other end of the table, the mother meditated for a moment.

"Neruda used to say he was a public service poet, but you must already know that. I've reread him many times. He has also another interesting poem in *The Attempt of the Infinite Man*," she said. "Entitled *I Am Afraid*. About a gray sky that opens up like the mouth of the dead, about a heart that holds the weeping of a princess forgotten in the depths of a desert castle. That's the reflection after the reflection, Marco. Now you say you see beauty. What happens when you're no longer able to see it?"

Marco shivered as the last stone was settled. Not on the wall, but in this heart.

In his gaze passed the river.

"That's never gonna happen. Beauty increases with time." Copious, scintillant, crystalline waters. "You learn to know and love each leaf of each tree, each grain of sand. And when you think you already know it all, the light shifts and the seasons go changing.

"And eventually the eyesight tires. You're still young, but not a boy anymore. You should know better."

"I do."

Ignoring Marco's categorical tone, she smiled again. This time with condescendence.

"Someone once told me pretty words like yours." She fell into a pause that swelled until it burst with a gush: "Flowers in the church and gifts, marriage, children, a shared life and happiness until death do us apart. I believed it. And it meant nothing. *Nothing.* You can regurgitate a thousand poems. Words are just words. Sounds that vanish in the air without a trace."

"Sounds that anchor thought so it becomes action."

"Oh, but of course you can also take action. You can bring me the sky, the clouds and stars tomorrow. And the day after tomorrow. And next week. And it will mean nothing. Only that you're doing your best to fool me, because it's not real. A cardboard sky, insubstantial clouds, cheap stars. I know your kind. Your sweet tongue. You like young flesh. It's firmer and easier to maneuver. Then, when it gets boring, you just move on."

She took a deep breath and leaned forward. Her voice now sounded surprisingly calm.

"I waited five years to have Marisa and carried her in my belly for another nine months. The day she was born was the happiest of my life. You can't imagine what it means to have such a strong bond, what it means to hold a child that transforms a dream in reality and becomes a piece of you. Our relationship may not be perfect, but it's my duty to protect Marisa and ensure only the best for her. That includes a decent companion. I'll never allow a *pedophile* to take advantage of my daughter. Ever." On her glacial countenance, the irises changed color. A deep brown like the entrails of the earth. Almost black. "And don't you even think of setting Marisa against me. This conversation stays between us. If you don't disappear, I'll report you to the school director. I swear I'll make sure no respectable school ever hires you. I'll…"

Marco no longer listened. He was willing to fight to the end of the world, and no threat intimidated him. But in that moment he understood. In the mother's eyes he met hardness—a rock protecting a very fragile core. The issue was not with him, his age, or the fact he'd gotten involved with Marisa at school. No matter what he said or did, the mother would still cling to her own truth. Not for Marisa. For herself. Admitting another truth meant accepting a different reality from the one she embraced. It meant accepting the failure of her engagement as a result of her flaws. She couldn't survive that. She had been raised under her father's protection and the illusion of being perfect. Perfection was her very identity, and she had no choice but to defend it with walls and stones. Without that identity, she was an empty shell. Nothing.

And all of that Marco saw in her eyes when he gazed at her. The mother wouldn't yield. Neither would Marisa. Parallel lives. How many years would be lost until a death in the family reunited them? Marco saw a repeat of the situation with Lorena. Everything was replaying, even the threats behind closed doors. He wasn't indeed a good guide to be followed.

Marco had never told Marisa about his meeting with her mother. Instead, he asked himself a question.

What is life?

Paradox.

Hence, he ended the conversation. Rising to his feet, Marco headed for the door while Marisa's mother accompanied him at a tense pace. Then he turned to her and spoke: "Parents are the most important reference in a person's life. They're the source and the base that stays forever engraved in one's identity. Lovers and friends come and go. Parents are irreplaceable. I'll do my share and you'll do yours. Marisa is in dire need of your support, don't be so harsh. Remember, she's already lost a father. She doesn't deserve to lose a mother too. I will stay away—not for your sake but for hers."

He said it at the exit. The mother stared at him, disarmed—there was a crack in the rock and, inside, pain and confusion. It lasted just one second. Her face shut. Next, the door.

Two months later Camila showed up, insisting to be with him at his weakest moment. She was in for the thrill, for the fantasy she had built in her head. The relationship never reached beyond the surface. When it did, it drowned.

"How come you don't have a girlfriend?" the aunt pressed against his silence. "A young man so handsome like you. You need to marry soon and give your mom a little grandchild. You know nothing would make her happier. And, after what happened to her—"

"I'd love to keep chatting, but I can't talk right now. I haven't even packed—"

"—we must think about that, right? After all, you've already reached the age for starting a family. You can't remain single forever—"

"Aunt, I can't—"

"—I *worry* about you, you know? A man needs a woman to look after him. When I think of you over there, all by yourself—"

Marco now grew utterly desperate. He interrupted her in an emphatic tone: "Aunt, I can't talk now. *I'm very late and I'm gonna miss my flight!*"

She muted for an instant. When the aunt spoke again, she sounded as if she was walking on eggshells. "Gee, I'm so sorry. How silly of me. Well, I won't keep you... Oh, wait a second... What was that, Lolo? Hold on, Marco, your cousin is talking to me..." For what felt like an eternity, the two women talked in a highly specialized jargon. "Lolo is asking if you can get her a bottle of nail polish. She can't find it anywhere, and it's called Sea Breeze. Lolo says there's one similar named Ocean Breeze, so don't get them mixed up, okay? Thank you and have a safe trip, dear. Enjoy your vacation and take care."

"You take care too."

Marco hung up quickly and shoved the remaining items into the suitcase. In his memory he stuck a yellow Post-it: *bring two plum cake baking pans for Aunt Carmina and a bottle of Ocean Spray for Lolo*. While he printed booking confirmations and picked up his passport, Marco thought if one day he found a genie of the lamp, he must remember to wish Aunt Carmina never, ever called him again when he was running late to catch a plane.

He departed to purchase dollars and faced a line at the currency exchange and traffic on the way to the airport. He had half an hour left for checking in and now began to worry about missing the plane. São Paulo's traffic was hell on earth. On one occasion, it took him three hours to reach Guarulhos International Airport, only sixteen miles away from Downtown. In a rainy day, the travel time could go up to four hours.

The expressway clogged almost to a halt. He had twenty-eight minutes left... twenty-six... twenty-five... Now he squeezed through the bottleneck, almost reaching the exit to the highway. Done! Seventeen minutes left to arrive at the airport. He flew, dropped the car at the parking lot, ran to the airline counter. Luckily there were no queues at that time. Marco managed to dispatch his suitcase exactly thirty-six seconds before the check-in deadline.

He rushed to the boarding area. At the security check, he was detained. The X-ray showed a suspicious object in his luggage, and a bored gate agent asked if he was carrying any liquid in it. Marco had no idea. They turned his backpack inside out: book, papers, sweater, an inexplicable roll of string, and at the bottom, the villain—a bottle of aftershave lotion he had forgotten to check in. The aftershave lotion tossed in the garbage, all the rest entangled back into the backpack, the zipper wouldn't close, pull it, pull it... okay.

Free to go, Marco walked fast, increasingly fast through the endless corridor in the boarding area. His gate sat on the farther end. When he saw it, he also saw the employee from the airline company, a brunette in a navy-blue uniform who was stepping away from the gate.

The gate had already been blocked with the security ribbon.

Marco ran the last yards to it and, almost out of breath, called the airline employee: the flight... the flight to Los Angeles... could he still board? He had been stuck in traffic... terrible traffic... She anchored an appreciative gaze on his face and resisted the temptation of fixing his hair. Then she smiled, shaking her head.

"This afternoon the Federal Police conducted an inspection of the airplanes," she informed. "Several flights went out of schedule and some had to be canceled. The takeoff runway is jammed."

"Excuse me?" Marco blinked, bewildered.

"You're lucky. Your flight has not been canceled, but it's going to be two to three hours late," she clarified, always smiling.

Marco thanked her and turned around, now in slow motion, while the girl continued to stare at him. He walked away with his head suddenly empty, leaving behind a trail of discarded thoughts: suitcase, check-in, aftershave lotion, boarding gate. His steps led him to the bookstore, where he purchased the first crime novel to fall into his hands. He had brought along *Coldness and Cruelty*, a highly complex study by Gilles Deleuze on the works of Sacher-Masoch, but he doubted he would be able to read a single line of it now.

He proceeded to the VIP area, planning to have a cup of tea and read his bestseller in a peaceful corner. The spacious room held cream-colored granite floors, lights built into the ceiling and a crowd of passengers that, like him, waited for their messed-up flights. Marco passed by a central area with green armchairs and a counter destined for notebook users. He kept going straight to the buffet when a miracle happened: he neared the massage chair right when its occupant stood up to leave.

Making himself comfortable, he selected the Smooth massage mode and plugged earbuds into his cell phone. He searched for a relaxing track and found *Above Ground* by Norah Jones. Perfect. Marco sighed and shut his eyes for a moment.

Ahhh...

One last flash of light danced inside his closed eyelids, tracing forms and filling them with an invisible paintbrush. The forms flickered in a blur and, at each flicker, a new landscape was drawn.

Sunlight, moonlight
Twilight, starlight
Gloaming at the close of day

Elf-light, bat-light
Touchwood-light and toad-light
And the sea a shimmering gloom of grey

And a small face smiling
In a dream's beguiling
In a world of wonders far away

3. Serendipity

A welcomed surprise. That's how serendipity is defined: you look for one thing and find another by chance. But you must keep an open mind and allow fate to flow... and to surprise. *Serendipity*: such a fashionable word, perhaps because it translates that magical instant when Lady Luck knocks at the door. That instant of suspension when the mind puts in check its conditioning to the cause-effect principle—thus having a glimpse of the hand of God.

Serendipity bears a grain of magic cleverness. Sometimes it comes disguised as a dwarf carrying a pebble, whereas in fact it is a giant silently moving a mountain to change the landscape. Sometimes it hides in plain view, and one day you discover serendipity where you never dreamed it existed. *What if a much of a which of a wind?* e. e. cummings would ask. But then what if a why if a whiff of a flick?

So much for God, serendipity and bikinis.

Or maybe not.

Marisa set off to shop and drop. She dropped but never really shopped, because she couldn't find her precious bikini. Frustrated, with sour mood and swollen feet, she brought home only a leopard-print scarf purchased as a consolation prize. Upon arriving, Marisa saw that her mother was out and headed straight to the bedroom. Carrying with her, unbeknown, a small token of serendipity inside the shopping bag.

Ah, Miami! Well, Miami. Marisa selected an MP3 to get in the mood (*Quando te Veo* by Mo' Horizons, a duo with German blood and Latin penchant). She shoved a mint into her mouth and danced her way to the computer. Hmmm, Latinos with mysterious eyes and sculpted bodies...

Baila, baila morena
Dame de beber de tu fuego
Quiero arder en tu cuerpo
Porque cuándo te veo...

She drifted and drifted in the ocean of pages... *Baila, baila morena...* Social media and email... *Con la espuma del mar...* From click to click, route diversions... *En tu piel voy a pasear...* Stores, travel blog, BDSM site with lots of photos... *Porque cuándo te veo...*

Hmm, BDSM. That four-letter acronym for rituals of discipline, submission and sadomasochism translated into images of fetishes as far as the imagination would venture. They mingled to create new forms or remained true to tradition, such as bondage, the millennial art of tying up your partner for maximum pleasure...

Marisa did a very long detour before returning to a beachwear store.

Then she heard—*beep!* Someone had initiated a chat on the neighboring browser tab. It was her best and very excited friend. Subject: the usual.

Valentina: *how are preparations goin?*

Marisa: *so so. still no bikini. u?*

Valentina: *all set. countdown mode :)*

While Marisa steered the keyboard, she jumped from one tab to another, checking out beach hats or her email inbox. If she heard the beep, she'd click on the chat window. Marisa and Valentina discussed hats, caps, and bandana color codes for preferences in bed (found on BDSM site). And then...

Marisa: *wait, i got email. omg.*

Valentina: *what is it???*

She had to reread the incoming message. It was so unexpected, at first Marisa couldn't quite absorb it. In disbelief, she shook her head and quickly typed.

Marisa: *did u check ur mailbox?*

Valentina: *no. why?*

Marisa: *wait a mo. ill call u right away.*

When she picked up the cell phone, Marisa found the notification for a voice message and accessed the message service. She waited impatiently to hear the recording in the hopes it might bring good news. It didn't.

Meanwhile, Marisa read the email for the third time.

Dear Marisa,

I tried contacting you over the phone but was unable to reach you. I am sorry to inform you that your English course has been canceled, as it did not meet the minimum number of students required.

Your credit card charges were reversed. We still have several summer courses that may interest you, though. Please check out our website for more details.

I apologize for the inconvenience. Should you have any questions, please don't hesitate to contact me.

All the best,
Priscila Fontes
Courses Coordinator
www.newhorizon.com.br

Marisa didn't waste time. She went to the school website and, as she scanned the pages, she called Valentina.

4. Wear Flowers in Your Hair

"Miami. Born in 1896, this is the only major city in the United States founded by a woman: Julia Tuttle. When a harsh frost destroyed the plantations in Northern Florida, she sent to the head of the Standard Oil Company, Henry Flager, a basket of juicy oranges from the region where today lies Miami. She thus persuaded him to extend the railroad from the state's central area to the south, creating there a sumptuous hotel and a town. Miami's name derived from the local Indian tribe living around Okeechobee Lake, which the natives called Mayaimi, 'Big Water.' The city features the largest cruise port on the globe, and many pirates, such as Black Beard, buried their treasures in the area. On firm ground, it offers more than 800 parks, including the Everglades swamps with their unique ecosystem—not to mention a paradoxical snow skiing club. As for the sunny island of Miami Beach, where suntan lotion was born in 1944, it shines with the largest collection of art deco buildings in the world. Elected the best city in the United States for finding a new love, Miami is…"

Valentina tried to snatch the leaflet from her, but Marisa held to it with both hands. A brief tug-of-war ensued.

"Let it go, Ma. I don't even know what this leaflet is still doing here. Get rid of it."

"But I *like* Miami," whimpered Marisa, shuffling a grimace and a smile. "It's all your fault! You filled my head with dreams of South Beach, the sex museum—"

"Forget it. All courses in Miami are filled up."

The two of them released the leaflet at the same time. It planed gently, oscillating to the right and the left, until landing on the rug with a discreet *ahh*.

"Why did my mother need to seize such a bargain?" Marisa threw her hands up. "We'll never find a course for such a good value in another school. Everything seems to cost twice as much! "

"Yeah, your mom talked to mine and both insisted we get something in the same price range. Bummer."

"Can you imagine that my mom proposed we go to Disney World if we can't find anything suitable?" Indignation stirred every muscle on Marisa's face.

"I know. What an indecent proposal. My mom suggested the same after the two spent over an hour on the phone," said Valentina. "I liked it better when they wouldn't speak to each other."

She had come to Marisa's place so they could find a solution to The Vacation Crisis. She had taken charge of Marisa's notebook and, logged into the school website, analyzed the options available. *Orlando, the world capital of theme parks...* No. *Fort Lauderdale, "The Venice of America," a sailing paradise with more than a hundred marinas...* No. *Tampa, home of the Republican National Convention in...* No, no.

They had been browsing for the past two hours. Valentina wouldn't give up and kept evaluating the school branches. *Jacksonville, an important golf destination...* No. *Saint Petersburg, nicknamed "The Sunshine City," with an average of 360 sunny days per year...* Yes, yay! ... *and a refuge for retirees...* No, dammit. That was getting impossible. There must be an alternative. Valentina reread the long course list like a maniac.

Marisa, sitting by her side on a foldable stool, leaned her chin on her hand with an air of deep boredom and melancholy. With her free hand, she tried to pull out a loose thread from her top. Her face suddenly brightened up: why didn't they try out that link to courses in other states? They could change their plane tickets, or else travel to Miami and then get a flight to another city. There were always last minute deals. Valentina cheered up too—finally there was a light at the end of the gloomy Disney World tunnel.

And in that light, the situation soon turned out more favorable: Seattle, Boston, New York, Dallas, Atlanta, San Francisco, Los Angeles. Once they have combed out the list, the girls elected Los Angeles, New York and San Francisco, in that order. The first two choices were all filled up. What was left was San Francisco. Next to the name of the course starting on July 8th, a link in red letters warned: *Last openings, register now!* Valentina and Marisa exchanged a look. They clicked.

Open, Sesame: and the door to paradise opened.

Later they went out to celebrate at a bar, drinking and blabbering like Ali Baba must have done at the sultan's party. The Vacation Crisis had been averted! How lucky they were, what a relief! Miami, its beaches and water sports were history. Now the focus was the West Coast metropolis, exponent of the green movement and hometown of indie band LoveLike-Fire (*What happened to you, la-la-la-lah*). Exhilarated by their choice, they turned on Marisa's tablet and read the page of a popular travel portal:

"*San Francisco.* Founded in 1835, the city was originally named Yerba Buena due to the presence of wild mint, or 'good herb,' in its territory. It's one of the most visited tourist destinations in the world, with the iconic cable cars on the slide of its slopes, the picturesque Victorian houses, and the fog brought by the Pacific Ocean, which bathes most of the city. Its postcard is the Golden Gate Bridge, stretched out for almost two miles, such a long structure that its paint job never ends: as soon as it's completed, it's already time to start it all over again. In the 19th century, San Francisco staged the Gold Rush and attracted many Chinese immigrants to work in the mines of the area. The city was hence the cradle of the denim jeans and Chinese fortune cookies—the latter being actually introduced by a Japanese citizen. In San Francisco flourished the counterculture of the beatniks in the 1950s and of the hippies in the 1960s. Today, spread across 43 hills, this progressive city embraces cultural diversity, technology, art, ecology, and liberal customs."

"Sweet!" the two girls exclaimed in unison.

5. The Kashmir Lounge

The veil of the night fell slowly over San Francisco. As the rosy sky began to swoon, the city lights woke up little by little and the temperature changed. All it took was for the sun to set, and the Pacific blow would claim the streets all to itself, with its icy breath that shook teeth and made window panes grow pale. It came in a rush, sneaking unceremoniously into coats, tickling the tips of noses and biting heels. In despair, not few pedestrians sought shelter in the nearest cafe.

Up above, the Airbus A322 coming from Los Angeles pierced the clouds in the fiery sky, preparing to complete flight 940. Instructed by the flight attendant, passengers kept their safety belts on and their chairs in the upright position. The local temperature, according to the captain, was mild: 55º Fahrenheit, or 13º Celsius. The aircraft flew over the lit-up structure of the Bay Bridge and Alcatraz Island, skirted the Golden Gate Bridge and executed a U-turn over open waters, setting off to the runway by the bay. Minutes later, it landed perfectly on time at the San Francisco Airport. It was 7:45 pm.

On the other side of town, Marisa watched the nightfall spectacle through the bay window in the living room. The glass panes were already becoming hazy when she backed off and studied the room perfumed with flower potpourri. Before the home theater wooden armoire, a huge beige sofa waited patiently for the next movie session. The coffee table, upholstered with the same suede, filled the role of faithful squire and transitory home for two boxes of assorted chocolate.

Marisa smiled to herself. It seemed like everything was ready for Saturday night. Judging by the roasted pork and cherry pie smells that escaped the kitchen, her hostess had prepared a special dinner for her husband, who would soon be back. After the meal the couple usually socialized with two Siamese cats on the sofa, watching TV all night long.

Her hosts made a funny couple, thought Marisa. A large lady, Mrs. Stevenson was a woman in her sixties, short blonde hair, rosy cheeks and blue eyes full of sparkle. Mr. Stevenson was her opposite, a pale, small and circumspect man, with snow-white hair and timid gray eyes that tended to stray away. She liked comedy, he liked drama. They always ended up watching reality shows.

Wrapping the leopard-print scarf around her neck, Marisa smoothed out her new pair of jeans and buttoned up the red jacket she had bought in a sale that afternoon. She picked up her shoulder bag.

"Goodbye, Mrs. Stevenson!" Marisa said as she descended the staircase that led to the street.

"Goodbye, honey. Have fun!" replied the hostess, her hoarse voice coming from the back of the house.

The English course was finally over, and not a moment too soon. For the past couple of weeks, Marisa and Valentina almost drowned in a radically immersive marathon, with practical and theoretical classes that extended from morning to evening. The immersion had continued over the previous weekend, with the usual sightseeing routine under the teachers' supervision: visiting Alcatraz in a guided tour; taking a cable car ride to Fishermen's Wharf to eat fried fish, watch Pier 39's sea lions and buy *I love San Francisco* T-shirts; exploring the exotic gardens of the Golden Gate Park and the De Young Museum, with a promenade on the sands of Ocean Beach in the end; and, of course, driving along the Golden Gate Bridge for a strategic stop at the hill on the other side—along with a group of Japanese tourists—to admire the stunning scenery of the bay, with the metropolis backdrop and the silver waters crisscrossed by sailboats... *click, click, click.* And take lots of pictures.

Now, on their first free Saturday, the girls were determined to make up for the lost time: they still had the weekend to raid the city before they left for Brazil on Monday. Valentina was staying at a flat in the Castro with a gay couple, not very far from where the Stevensons lived in the Mission.

So the two friends agreed to meet at the subway station on 16th Street, halfway between their temporary homes.

Marisa stepped onto the sidewalk and shivered when the wind disheveled her hair. Turning on the MP3 player, she adjusted her earphones and crossed the backstreet with Victorian houses squeezed in the middle of the block. The whispered lyrics by Belgian group Hooverphonic told the story of a girl in a space capsule who found a cowboy on the moon. The slowly orchestrated basis of *Plus Profond.* set the rhythm to Marisa's steps and transformed the landscape into film: traffic lights changing into green-yellow-red; pedestrians in transit on the sidewalks, in and out establishments; live window paintings of store clerks, waiters, clients who laughed, talked, circulated, yawned; cars that passed by, stopped, took off. A kaleidoscope of movement… A girl in a space capsule and a cowboy on the moon.

Slowly she grew
Till she filled the night
And shone
On her throne
In the sky alone…
The queen of the night

Meanwhile the passengers of flight 940 disembarked from the Airbus A322 and moved through a succession of tunnels covered in glass, gliding walkways, and stairs. A man in a brown jacket gesticulated as he spoke on his cell phone. A girl in a yellow jumper dropped a teddy bear on the floor, and her mother paused to collect it. Some in a hurry, others slower, they advanced unremittingly until all had reached carrousel number 7 in the baggage claim section. There, they waited for their suitcases like an assembly of clad flamingos, with their telescopic necks distended to the maximum at each piece of luggage materializing on the carrousel curve. It was 8:05 pm.

Marisa walked for ten minutes and found Valentina waiting for her in front of the subway station. Her friend, dressed in purple velvet pants and an extravagant orange sweater, was reading the Variety section of *The Bay Guardian*.

"There are several bars and clubs close by," Valentina announced, showing her the newspaper.

"Let's go eat something. We'll decide what to do over dinner," said Marisa as she dropped the MP3 player into her purse.

The two wandered in the vicinity until they reached Valencia Street, where a small Thai restaurant decorated with typical lanterns captivated them. The luminous sign above the door informed the place was named Suriya, and a wooden elephant statue greeted them at the entrance. The girls picked a table by the window, tasted a Thai beer and checked out the menu.

Twelve miles away, Marco was leaving the airport with his friend Jeff. As far as looks went, the two men couldn't have been more different. Marco smiled placidly, tanned skin, ripped jeans and a white tank top. His friend maintained a rigid posture, pale in his black trousers and light-blue shirt. His blond hair was stiff with gel, which seemed to have plastered his blue eyes to make them stiff too.

"How was LA, Marco?" Jeff asked while maneuvering his black SUV.

"Great. I did some very interesting networking at the congress. Then I went to a party in Venice Beach and visited Carmel. The usual. What about you? How is the remodel of your apartment going?"

"It's a nightmare. I'm camping in the storage room. The contractor opened a hole in the wrong spot, the painter left more paint on the floors than on the walls, and the electrician vanished from the face of the earth without finishing his job."

Jeff shook his head and laughed to avoid weeping. He paused at the parking exit and tuned the radio into Paul Black's *Down on Me* fast-paced blues. Singing under his breath, he sped into the night.

In the meantime, on the other side of town, the girls waited for their food and ordered more beer. Valentina reached into her purse for *The Guardian* and scanned the Variety section, while Marisa entertained herself trying to read the upside-down words.

"Hmm, let's see. Bars, clubs… indie rock… electronic music… Latin beats…" She ran her index along the text columns. "Oh, there's a bar five blocks away that looks interesting: Kashmir Lounge… tonight, reggae and Arabic fusion music."

"Let's go!" Marisa blurted out in a sluggish voice.

The black SUV rolled smoothly on the freeway. Inside the vehicle, the air freshener spread a smell of tutti frutti that enveloped their laughter as Marco and Jeff revisited old stories. The two had met through mutual friends during Marco's PhD in San Francisco. Jeff was an electrical engineer crazy about bossa nova and jazz. He and Marco hit it off over a shared Miles Davis album.

"I'm starving," Jeff said at one point. "Where are we gonna have dinner? I suggest a classic restaurant in Chinatown. Best Peking duck ever. There's also a new Indian in the Mission."

"I'll leave the choice to you." Marco brushed off a lock of hair from his forehead and uttered a sigh. "Anything but Mexican food. And later, drinks are on me."

They decided for the classic in the good ol' Chinatown of pictorial red flags and shops stuffed with Oriental statuettes on perpetual sale. On their way there, however, a slight problem arose. As known, Chinese restaurants are designated according to a set of a dozen or so keywords, scrambled and randomly combined two by two: *golden, red, jade, imperial, temple, garden, palace* and so on. Thus are born names such as Golden Palace, Red Dragon and Jade Temple. Which can also turn into Jade Palace, Golden Dragon and Red Temple. Jeff couldn't remember the name of the classic restaurant even if his life depended on it. In the end, he and Marco headed for the Indian restaurant. Traffic flowed with ease, so they soon arrived at the Mission. Dropping the car in a parking lot, the two strolled along the sidewalk. The restaurant was located on Valencia Street.

Five blocks ahead, Marisa and Valentina took great delight in their exotic meal. Crispy kratong tong pastries, pumpkin curry, and black rice with coconut ice cream. Marisa told the joke about a man who would repeatedly shout the name of a woman, thinking she was deaf, when in reality she had already answered all of his calls, and he was the one deaf. *Ah, ah, ah, ah!* Hysterical, so hysterical. *Ah, ah, ah, ah!* The girls hit their third round of beers.

Block after block, Marco and Jeff walked past ethnic restaurants, bars, Hispanic food markets, laundromats, convenience stores with neon signs on their windows. They came to a halt one block away from the Suriya and disappeared through a door finely carved with arabesques. A half-hour later, they started on their opulent chicken biryani and malai kofta dishes and washed down with Indian beer.

In the meantime, Marisa and Valentina paid the check and stepped arm in arm onto the street. They walked two blocks and... *Ooops...* Wrong way. They turned around and kept going, tripping here and there. That's how they came to pass twice by the restaurant where Marco and Jeff were dining. The girls gesticulated and laughed hysterically at a joke now told by Valentina.

(In his evening off, James, the butler, returns quite late to the mansion and tiptoes inside. Milady calls him and he obliges, tail between legs. She motions for him to come closer. "James, remove my shoes." Caught by surprise, James hesitates. "But, Milady..." She reinforces the order, and he obeys. Then she asks him to remove her dress. He reddens and begins to sweat. "But... but, Milady..." And she repeats in a soft voice: "James, please. Remove my dress." He complies. Her necklace, pantyhose and bra follow. When it comes to Milady's panties, James is very reluctant. She insists, though. "James, please... please. Remove my panties." And gone are the panties too. At last, Milady says in her usual phlegmatic tone: "Now, James, I want you to promise me that you will never wear my clothes again.")

By the time Valentina finished the joke, she and Marisa had made their second pass in front of the Indian restaurant. Marco and Jeff were seated at a table farther in the back. Nevertheless, through the window framed by a curtain of transparent beads, Marco caught a glimpse of the duo: the top of Marisa's head, her profile, and then an orange sleeve that waved like a windsock in a gale. He frowned, intrigued, and thought he was seeing things. The fleeting image paraded before his eyes like the trail of a dream.

Outside, the two girls trotted happily among hasty pedestrians. Valentina applauded that no man had hit on them on the streets since they arrived in town, to which Marisa replied that Americans were definitely reserved, to which Valentina retorted that reserved was not the word but rather *civilized*.

"Whatever, it's just weird not hearing anything on the street. It's like there's something *wrong* with you," said Marisa.

"Can't you see what's going on? It's the Latino macho culture that does this to women," Valentina roared with fire in her eyes.

As if they guessed the subject at hand, two Mexicans across the street waved at them: *¡Hola, guapas!*

The two girls cracked up. They were still laughing when they finally reached their destination, a club with a slim peacock blue frontage, a glass door and a large rectangular window. As soon as they entered, a cloud of sandalwood incense surrounded them.

How could the Kashmir Lounge be described? If an animal, it would be a rare bird. If a country, the Wonderland. And so on and so on. Perhaps the best way to define it is: a gate to another dimension. Past the threshold, an unaware visitor would immediately land on the Summer of Love of 1967— just like that, nonstop flight. In the square room, Indian lamps flickered among Oriental tapestries. The bar stood to the right, and a few tables were crammed near the entrance. In the back, a low platform served as a stage. The central portion of the room doubled up as an auditorium and a dance floor. So far, so good. Now the patrons…

A psychedelic, blinding profusion of kurtas embroidered with tiny mirrors fluttered around the room, matched with long hair and faded jeans. In the same vein, the four members of the band (two Jamaicans boasting dreadlock plantations and two Arabs with taqiyah caps) sat cross-legged onstage playing guitar, flute, sitar and tabla. The sounds that emanated from the platform created an indescribable amalgam of Bob Marley and Cheb Khaled. Depending on the point of view, it could be deemed pure genius or the undigested leftovers of a second-rate restaurant.

While the audience chanted *ooohmmmm* in tune with the band, a girl in an *I Dream of Jeannie* costume circulated in the room distributing bonbons wrapped in multicolored cellophane. They were magical bonbons, she explained, giving one to Marisa and another to Valentina. Why magical? they asked, and the girl smiled behind the transparent veil that covered the lower portion of her face. She was about to say something when a group approached her asking for bonbons, and the question remained unanswered.

Marisa and Valentina exchanged a look and shrugged. Both unwrapped the bonbons, examining them with interest. Small and spherical, they exhibited a peace symbol in pink icing. They seemed like regular milk chocolate but left a funny aftertaste. Definitely not the sort of item found at the posh candy stores in town.

The two lingered at the bar drinking beer and watching the show, which after all didn't turn out too bad. The music, in fact, proved to be irresistible. Soon pairs of shoes lay in the corners as bare feet glided everywhere to better connect with the telluric energies from the flooring.

Then something happened. All of a sudden, enraptured by the collective trance, Valentina and Marisa removed their shoes too and let the slithering rhythm carry them away. In reality they removed more than just their shoes. Marisa, feeling hot, got rid of her jacket and kept a light top on. Valentina yanked off her sweater to reveal solely a black bra, and that's what she kept on.

"Hurrah!" she whooped with a spin.

Along with the crowd, the two whirled and threw their arms up in a psychedelic epiphany: it was the Summer of Love and everything was in harmony with the Cosmos—oh, yes, and the fusion of reggae and Arabic music was the most *transcendental* thing in the whole universe... how come they'd never listened to anything like that before?

Standing on the sidewalk, Marco and Jeff observed the scene.

"What the hell is that?" Marco asked his friend.

He hadn't spotted Marisa, or he would be really puzzled.

"I have no frigging idea," said Jeff.

"Wanna go inside?"

At that moment, the music stopped for intermission and the audience started dispersing toward the bar. By the stage, a man with a long blond braid continued to dance, unperturbed. He jiggled like a faun... or a rabbit, it was hard to tell. He would bend his elbows close to his sides, forearms raised and hands pointing down, mimicking paws. He'd hop and twirl; then would stand on one leg, perfectly still, and move his head like an Indian dancer.

Jeff scratched his chin and hesitated for a second before answering: "Nah."

Chuckling, he and Marco moved away. They headed to a sports bar across the street.

Inside the Kashmir Lounge, Marisa and Valentina took a seat at one of the tables. Flushed and euphoric, they fanned themselves with the drink cards. A girl in a lilac tie-dye dress with a cowboy hat paused before them. She beamed: "Don't you feel *awesome* tonight?"

And they both beamed back: "*Yeah!*"

6. A New Day

She felt like *crap*. The daylight hurt her eyes with the force of a thousand spears. Marisa blinked a few times, trying to adjust her sight to the brightness. Then she covered her ears to silence the time bomb set in her brain. It did not work. *Tic-tac, tic-tac.* Another attempt. Hmmm. *Tic-tac, tic-tac.* The problem, she reasoned, was her overeating the night before. She shouldn't have ordered dessert.

"C'mon, honey, breakfast is ready!"

It was Mrs. Stevenson calling her again. Oh, God. Just the thought of food. But maybe a cup of coffee would exorcize the Thai demon that had possessed her stomach. She tripped out of bed, put on a sweatshirt and pants, and zigzagged to the bathroom to make herself presentable. The next stop was the kitchen. As Marisa entered the living room, she covered her mouth and almost jumped back when her helpless nostrils were assaulted by a lethal mix: food smell and the flower potpourri Mrs. Stevenson insisted in scattering around the house.

Marisa held her breath and ran to the kitchen. There she found the hostess frying blueberry pancakes while her husband read the newspaper. The cozy room featured white appliances, cherry wood cabinets and, in the center, a square table set with jars of jam, butter, a bread basket and a thermos bottle. Potted violets and voile curtains adorned the window. The two cats, rubbing up against Mrs. Stevenson's legs, meowed nonstop, their upward tails flowing around her like silent interrogation marks.

Marisa saluted the couple and bent down to pet the animals, which usually were quite affectionate. This time, though, their affection had been sequestered by the mound of pancakes growing on the cooktop. Mrs.

Stevenson glanced over her shoulder and asked if Marisa had a good time. Making an effort to ignore the time bomb and the Thai demon, Marisa summed up her evening while helping herself to a double coffee. Then she sat at the table with Mr. Stevenson, who, wrapped in a checked robe, concentrated on the Sports section of the newspaper. He raised his eyes from the page.

"Oh, the Kashmir Lounge. It opened in the seventies. The crowd there is… *interesting.*" With that, he enigmatically took a sip of coffee and returned to the newspaper.

Mrs. Stevenson, on the other hand, sprinkled words in Marisa's ears with the same liberality as she sprinkled berries over the pancake dough. At one point, she wiped her hands absented-mindedly on her yellow apron, decorating it with a large purple stain. It resembled a Rorschach test.

"Such a shame you're leaving. There are wonderful places around. Lake Chabot, Point Reyes, Yosemite… Well, at least you can enjoy the weekend. Didn't your classmates want to join you girls?" Since the cat climbed on the chair to steal a pancake from the table, she brandished the skimmer: "Smokey, get off that chair *now!* Bad, bad boy!"

"They'd rather go back to Fishermen's Wharf, Mrs. Stevenson. Valentina and I decided…"

Marisa interrupted the sentence to fish for the phone ringing in her pocket. It was Valentina, the very one and only.

"Good morning, America! Ready for more?" Without waiting for a reply, she announced: "Richard and Brian are taking us to a fetish fair. Do you have the *Guardian*…? Great. Read the article on page 15. We'll be stopping by at noon to fetch you."

A fetish fair. Marisa recalled the website she had visited before the trip. She hurried to grab the latest edition of the *Bay Guardian* on the kitchen counter, opening it to the mentioned page as she spoke with Valentina.

The fair's description conjured suggestive images: *A showcase of products and services for the boldest erotic fantasies on the planet. Gastronomy, music, role playing and over 50 exhibitors. The Leather Dream Fair promises to bring to town unlimited possibilities of pleasure. Moreover, its grand closing party will be the perfect excuse for test driving the fair's arsenal.*

Marisa chatted a little longer with Valentina and hung up. Then, suddenly thrilled, she attacked the pancake on the plate before her and finished reading the article.

Two miles away, at a hotel in the historical Haight-Ashbury neighborhood, Marco enjoyed breakfast in bed. His room was located on the upper floor of a Victorian mansion, with a bay window offering a view of the hills in the distance. Decorated in antique style, it sported mahogany furniture, cream wallpaper with green stripes and pleated curtains the same color. An oval mirror, a blue armchair and a frosted glass chandelier rounded the time travel.

With the food tray on his lap, Marco nibbled the last piece of toast and emptied a glass of orange juice. Then he put the tray aside and stretched himself from head to toe like a cat. He smiled contentedly, caressing his stomach under the white T-shirt. It was wonderful to indulge in the luxury of escaping routine. At home, before he rushed to work, he would usually have a fruit and a cup of coffee while standing by the kitchen sink. Truth was he had always cherished his sleep far more than the morning rituals.

He zapped through the channels on the small TV set on top of a dark wooden rack. Along with the minibar fitted under it, the TV was the only modern item in the room. Oh, and there was the phone too: Marco stretched his arm to reach it on the nightstand and dialed Jeff's number. He wanted to check if his friend had survived their evening out in one piece—judging by Jeff's hoarse voice and cranky tone, there was not much left of him.

"I haven't drunk like that in a long time," Jeff grumbled. "What happened at the bar?"

"A girl made you a man."

His friend silenced on the other end of the line. A burst of hammer blows could be heard in the background. Then the vigorous scratching of sandpaper.

"Don't kid me," he said. "What happened yesterday? When I try to remember, there's this blank."

"You really wanna know? I warned you to go easy on the drinks, you drowned yourself in alcohol and I had to take you home in a cab. For some obscure reason, you wouldn't stop singing *La Marseillaise*." Marco averted his gaze from the TV and contemplated the blue sky in the window rectangle. "At some point you'll have to explain to me this morbid association between whiskey and the national anthem of France. But enough of that. It's a beautiful day. Why don't we go to Monterey?"

"I can't leave. I don't trust this painter. Right now, he's fitting all cabinet doors back on."

Marco looked at the TV again, switching channels and pausing on a news program. He frowned and asked why the painter had removed all the cabinet doors. In response, Jeff exhaled a never-ending sigh.

"I don't want to talk about it. It's a long story."

"Well, take care. If you need anything, call me."

It was all Jeff wanted to hear. He glanced at the pile of boxes that waited for him in the back of the living room covered in dusty sheets. He cheered up for the first time that week.

"Truth is, my neighbors are out of town and tomorrow I'm assembling the bedroom furniture at the end of the day. I could use some help."

"I'll stop by around six, then."

"Thanks, buddy. You have my eternal gratitude."

"I'm happy with a pizza," Marco replied right before another burst of hammer blows.

As soon as he hung up, Marco leaped out of bed. He wasn't sure about going to Monterey by himself and decided to clear his head in the shower. He took off his T-shirt and started to remove his sweatpants when the TV program drew his attention. It was the end of the news, and the presenter offered leisure tips for the weekend.

Apparently, there were many options in town—maybe even more inviting than a day out in Monterey.

7. The Leather Dream Fair I

Under a sunny sky, the fly flew up and down the empty backstreet. *Bzzz, bzzz...* Much to its delight, it found a banquet of pizza leftovers in an overflowing trash can. While it gobbled pepperoni and stale cheese, the fly saw a couple of highway patrollers ringing the bell at the Stevensons across the street. They wore black leather uniforms, and their eyes hid behind mirrored shades. For a moment, the fly thought they looked like insects too, only huge. Then it shrugged and resumed its meal.

Marisa answered the door and startled at seeing the two men. One of them, with brown hair and a goatee, kept a discreet distance. The other, blond and taller, stepped forward and pulled his shades slightly to stare at her with blue and incisive eyes. After confirming she was "Ms. Marisa Constant," he informed she had committed a series of traffic infractions.

Marisa began to smile, all the while creasing her forehead in perplexity. Maybe she didn't quite understand his English. She opened her mouth, closed it, and finally argued: "But I haven't got a car..."

The man consulted a notepad, flicking through it back and forth, forth and back. The practical gestures denoted skepticism.

"That's not what I've got here... Unsafe operation of motor vehicle... failure to obey the traffic authority... transportation of two Siamese cats without proper carriers... driving under the influence of alcohol..." He interrupted what he was saying, sterner than ever: "You *are* the legal age for consuming alcohol, correct?" And as Marisa nodded vigorously, he went on: "You've committed several violations. Are you aware of the penalties?"

"Uh... no."

"Are you sure?" he insisted in a military tone. "You really don't know what the penalties are?"

Since Marisa shook her head, the agent made a meaningful pause. His face became taut with reproval, and he sentenced: "Ten spanks and twelve months of communal service cleaning, ironing and cooking at my place."

He maintained a grave demeanor for another moment and cracked up, with the face of an angel and a wickedly seductive grin. Then he extended his gloved hand to Marisa and introduced himself as Brian. His companion, Richard, greeted her next, tucking the shades on top of his head to reveal a pair of green eyes.

Marisa laughed too. She *knew* the whole history didn't hold water but gave him credit for being persuasive. Brian exulted: he was an actor. In the corner, Valentina emerged from a red BMW with the hood down and waved. Marisa accompanied Brian and Richard, taking the back seat next to her. She was relieved to see Valentina in black shorts and a T-shirt.

"I'm glad you aren't dressed up, or I'd have to go back and change," Marisa said, indicating her own jean miniskirt and pink top that read *Bodies are made for love* over a big red lipstick mark.

"Relax." Valentina patted her shoulder. "There are all kinds of people at the fair."

They soon arrived. And then a strange world unfolded before their eyes in the South of Market, amid rustling booths, music shows and public flogging arenas. Past the barriers of the Leather Dream Fair, Valentina and Marisa heard *Horny as a Dandy* with The Dandy Warhols and Mousse T. The two felt like they had stepped into a fairy tale from a parallel universe. Its characters included drag queen nuns, Roman soldiers, divas from the thirties, and cowboys in chaps and thongs with their white butts exposed.

Whereas Richard and Brian seemed quite at ease there, the girls nudged each other. Marisa whispered to Valentina that there was a man *naked* on the corner, his body covered solely with tattoos and a harness (the truth be told, he also wore boots). The friend tried to sound blasé and countered that he wasn't *naked* but rather reaffirming his identity (whatever that was). But soon Valentina lost her composure when she saw a guy dressed as a pony carrying a girl on his back: *Ma, check that out...*

For public flogging activities, the Leather Dream Fair offered three main arenas. The first was under the command of two girls who practiced their sway and flogging to the beat of house music. In the second, presided by a man with a military cap and boots, volunteers subjected themselves to spanking sessions. The third arena belonged to a dominatrix and her pet pole.

The four friends paused at the spanking arena to check out the procedure. A volunteer was just bending over a table to receive a few blows on the butt. Wearing glasses and beige clothes, he looked like a first-grade teacher.

"How odd. I'd never imagine a guy like that offering to be spanked in public. Especially by another man with a military cap and boots," Marisa commented with Valentina.

"You know what? After witnessing so many eccentricities, nothing shocks me. I mean, how many more naked guys in harnesses do I need to see before I become desensitized?"

After a moment of thought, Marisa was forced to agree. She lost track of how many naked men they had seen since their arrival at the fair. Marisa, however, couldn't decide if she liked the experience—not all of them were exactly Greek gods. Valentina shrugged and declared that, by now, she found everything quite normal: she even considered volunteering herself.

Marisa then made a point in dragging her away from the arena as fast as she could.

The excursion continued at a stand selling clothes and accessories. Richard and Brian manifested fascination for uniforms and purchased a couple of military caps. The girls, in their turn, focused on a neighboring counter covered in erotic toys. The items that impressed them the most were the following, in this order: 1) large black gas mask featuring a thick cord with a vibrator attached to it, which would haunt them in their nightmares for the next three days; 2) plug for intimate use with the Baby Jesus face on it, perfect for pious fetishists; 3) small, red, heart-shaped paddle, very romantic.

Further ahead, a stand covered in posters with little devils grasping tridents announced: Leather Dream Ball – Tickets for Sale. There, a young man with tattooed arms sold tickets to the fair's closing party to a couple of tourists. Brian cheered up instantly. Richard, scratching his goatee, remained reticent. He worked at the Stock Market and needed to be up early the next day.

"Ricky, don't be a party spoiler. Tomorrow you can have an energy drink and be as good as new," Brian insisted.

"*One* energy drink won't cut it. The way I've been working lately, I'll need at least *half a dozen*."

"Then have *half a dozen*."

Marisa and Valentina looked from one man to the other, praying for Richard to give in. But he shook his head: "It's easy for you to say that because you sleep until late like a diva."

"That's not true, honey. When I have a shoot scheduled, I'm one of the first actors to show up at the set." With both hands planted on his hips, Brian turned to the girls: "You can't *imagine* how *tiring* a filming session can be."

"Yeah, as if the Stock Market were a picnic," his partner replied, annoyed.

Brian kept arguing the girls deserved to spend their last night in town in style, until he wore Richard down. In the end, both men insisted in treating Valentina and Marisa to the party. Continuing their explorations, the group wound up in an arena where a blond man was undressing to get tied to the dominatrix's pole. Brian, always alert, evaluated him with a clinical eye and concluded: with a body like that, they could bet he was a surfer.

When Marisa saw the guy, she couldn't take her eyes off him and paused a few feet from the pole. The surfer boasted a display of attributes: blue eyes, neck-length straight hair and a dragon tattoo on the chest. With denim overalls down to his ankles, he exhibited a tanned skin that suggested more affinity with the wonders of nature than with those of the whip. He seemed strangely out of place there.

The dominatrix crossed the arena with an assertive stride and stood beside him. A mature and attractive woman, she wore a silver minidress, a huge imperial topaz on her middle finger, and boots with very fine stiletto heels, good for poking a man's flesh. Her glacial expression was emphasized by platinum hair hanging from a high ponytail. Marisa and Valentina secretly envied her cold authority that, in an irresistible contradiction, conjured the ardor of fire. Ice can also burn.

Without realizing it, the two held their breath as they watched the dominatrix tie the surfer's wrists to the pole with a neoprene strip. Next, she grasped the whip by the handle and the end, tugging at it with a vigorous crack—that sound alone was enough to stir one's nerves. The dominatrix released the whip end, ran her black nails on the surfer's back and, giving him a light tap on the waist, began the session.

The whip hissed like a rattlesnake as it sliced through the air... *Slap!* The surfer shut his eyes and gritted his teeth, stoically swallowing a moan. *Slap!* He flinched. *Slap!* He flinched further, his face red. *Slap!* He tried to relax to ease the discomfort. *Slap! Slap!* In rhythmic cadence, six were the blows applied, which the surfer took in silence. The dominatrix smiled and caressed the whip's fingerprints stamped on his back. Then, without warning, she gave him a harder lash on the buttocks... *Slaaap!*

"This is for you to remember me," she said in a satin voice, concluding the session.

The surfer addressed an ambiguous stare at her as she released him, and it was difficult to tell if it signaled relief or if he wanted more. When the surfer finished pulling his clothes back on, the dominatrix kissed him goodbye on the cheek and summoned the next volunteer. As he was leaving the arena, the dazed surfer scooted past Marisa, and they collided violently. He apologized as he patted her arm.

At his touch, Marisa was visited by the proverbial electric current, which caused her an odd tingling from the toes to the last lock of hair. Very light, very brief, it came, spread, dissolved... *Oh-ohhhh...*

"It was nothing," she said. And, as a better answer occurred to her, she brought one hand to her arm: "Actually, it's hurting *right here*."

"*Here*, yeah?"

The surfer brushed his fingertips on her arm—sun, salt and wax on his slightly rough skin. And another electric current. *Oh-ohhhh...*

"Judging by your accent, you're not American, right?" she asked, a tad light-headed.

"I'm Australian. Queensland," he clarified, with music in his voice and pearls in his smile. "Where are you from?"

When Marisa told him she was from São Paulo, Brazil, the aquamarines in the surfer's eyes glittered: he wanted to go to Brazil for the World Cup. He had a friend from São Paulo, Fabio Lima, maybe she knew the guy? Marisa wrapped a tress around her finger and said no: São Paulo had a population of twelve million. He felt silly and, changing the subject, asked her name. She said it. So he repeated it slowly. *Ma-ri-sa*. And she asked his. *My name is…*

And then Marisa's friends approached, Richard dragged her away and the spell was broken.

"Let's have something to drink. It's hot like hell today," he said.

"Yeah, a drink would be nice," Brian agreed, averting his eyes from the fat bald guy now being tied up to the pole. "I think we've seen enough."

The surfer hesitated and nodded goodbye. Marisa followed him with her gaze, until he vanished on the street. On the way to the beverage stand, Richard, Brian and Valentina talked about the fair and Russian cinema. Marisa would never know what one thing had to do with the other, for she barely listened. She thought of pearls, musical notes, aquamarines—and a way of meeting the surfer again. As the group strolled away, a song played across the street.

> *I wake up and think of you*
> *I can't seem to find you anywhere*
> *Not even in the other hemisphere*
>
> *You're my Technicolor dream*
> *Such a cool blast of sta-ars*
> *Fireworks from Ma-ars*
>
> *You're my dream in Technicolor*
> *Yeah my dream in Technicolor*

"Good afternoon, everyone! Where is the surfer with eyes as blue as the Pacific? Where is he? Marisa is really impressed with him and wants to… *ahem*… get closer to check if the dragon tattoo has blue eyes too… *ah-ah-ah!* So where is the surfer? Where is he? Is he going to test that spank arena owned by the macho guy with the cap and military boots? Is he at the beverage stand? Or is he on his way to the airport to catch a plane back to Australia? Will Marisa find the mysterious surfer? And if yes, will she finally learn his name? Will it be perhaps Tom, Dick, Harry…? *Ah-ah-ah!* How about one more electric current? *Oh-oooohhhh…* Don't miss the exciting upcoming chapters!"

That wasn't exactly what the MC said as he promoted the fair's attractions.

But it was what she heard.

(music fades in)

> *Day and night let's dream on*
> *Oh sweet dream in*
> *Techni-Techni-Technicolor*

8. The Leather Dream Fair II

Marco passed by the arena where the dominatrix was tying up a fat guy with shiny bald head, on whose back crawled a tarantula of hairs. That natural upholstery would render the whip job more difficult, thought Marco. He did not stop. Further ahead, he spotted an arena playing loud music, where young men lined up waiting for their turn to be flogged by two girls in shorts and white mini tops. Both were attractive, Latina bio-type with long hair, sculpted buttocks and pierced navels. A commotion took place there, for one of the girls shook the flog and asked, puckering her lips: *Who's gonna be the next victim? Who, who?* Curious, Marco paused.

All guys raised their arms, except one. And it was precisely the owner of those limp arms that the hostesses chose for volunteer: a nerd in a pastel yellow shirt with glasses featuring a frame as black as his hair, who was simultaneously pulled by the girls and pushed by a couple of friends that sided him. There he stood with his twenty years of age, paralyzed by a smiley and raging shyness, on the verge of initiation on the mysteries of the flog—it was almost as thrilling as the *Dungeons and Dragons* game in which he got stranded on an island full of demons and… well, but that's another story.

The girls decided to work together on him. One unbuttoned his shirt and the other removed it. They made the nerd place both hands on the backrest of a silver chair and carried on. Their bracelets twirled like happy hula hoops while the two wrote zeros and eights with pink-thread flogs, zeros and eights that began in midair and ended on the volunteer's milky back. The girls took turns, swaying their hips as madly as their wrists during the entire song they played for him.

So now it's all in the clear
I can't wait another minute
Baby, you know I'm in it

You're my Technicolor dream
Streaming in colorful places
With oh so many faces

Sweet dream in Technicolor
Techni-Techni-Technicolor

The nerd's visage (puffy, red, sweaty) now offered an excellent object of study for facial expression. Analyzing it, a scientist would write an essay under the title "The epistemology of public flogging in modern times." Or something like that. Introversion, awe, rapture and all sorts of emotional road forks paraded on the boy's previously anemic countenance. Behind the glasses, his eyes rolled in sync with the flogs. *Rap, rap, rap! Smack, smack!* In the end, his mouth gaped wide and delivered the smile of a skinny yogi in the arms of nirvana—both girls flogged him with their own hair and wrapped up the session with a peck on his cheek. The audience applauded, and Marco moistened his lips. All that enthusiasm had made him thirsty.

While cruising along the packed street, he observed people in extravagant clothes. Marco himself dressed as casually as possible, in a jean shirt and pants—discreet, he didn't trumpet his preferences. Marco couldn't help but smile. It was the third time he had attended an event like this, and it still surprised him to see the most intimate desires exposed like a variety show. A certain dose of humor sugarcoated the impact of the taboos spreading throughout the fair.

A man enveloped in a cloud of red feathers fluttered by with a sign that announced: *Jesus loves you.* He walked down the street side by side with Marco and, the moment he and his feathers turned the corner, the sight cleared to reveal a stand where a blonde lay on her stomach on top of a table. The girl, in a cheerleader outfit, was immobilized by a setup of Gordian knots. Marco slowed down to take in her wrists bound to her ankles, the pair of ivory legs, the blue miniskirt and the ponytail with a pink pompom: fetish and innocence united by a respectable length of white rope.

Marco advanced on the counterflow of a shoal of topless mermaids in colorful skirts that swirled around him and swam down the street. Then he saw the electronics stand. And the Electrosex Magic Wand. According to the advertisement on the box, it would take the user to nearly celestial heights. Made of black plastic, it could easily be mistaken for an electric hairbrush. A detailed examination, however, revealed the Magic Wand leaned toward more hedonistic practices, featuring a slot for various glass attachments that had nothing to do with hairstyling. It also included another accessory, a small black plate connected to a cord, which intrigued Marco.

The clerk with a Chanel-style red wig and blue false eyelashes noticed his interest. She informed the Electrosex was a state-of-the-art device for erotic electro-stimulation. Picking up a wand from the display, she attached a sphere-headed tube to it and turned it on. Tiny orangey rays sparked inside the tube.

"The Electrosex can be used on any body part, providing the finest controls for intensity and frequency." She winked. "After all, precision is crucial in certain moments, right? Here, gimme me your arm. I'm gonna make a demonstration."

As Marco stretched out his arm, he noticed a young woman inspecting the devices on the counter. Petite, she had a pale face and copper hair. Her most prominent feature was almond-shaped eyes as green as the airy dress she wore. Marco felt an instant attraction and tried to get closer.

The clerk retained him, holding his wrist as she ran the Electrosex across his arm.

Mmmm...

What ensued was a flux of delicious sensations associated with the sight of the redhead, whom Marco couldn't stop watching. He ought to find a way of getting to know her. Marco was enthralled not as much by her beauty as he was by her curiosity while manipulating the goods—an exciting and promising curiosity.

"That's enough, thanks," he said.

The clerk, however, grabbed his arm with a surprisingly firm grip. She had replaced the tube with the black plate, plugging it to the wand. Then, with a mischievous expression, she slipped the plate into her cleavage.

"Now comes the best part. With this accessory, I'll conduct the stimuli to you. We will both feel the electric impulses. Open your hand."

Without much enthusiasm, Marco did as he was told. And next…

Mmmmmm…

The clerk massaged the palm of his hand with her fingertips, applying light shocks that made his whole body tingle. *True, precision is crucial in certain moments,* Marco thought vaguely. Yet the demonstration was just starting. The girl produced a white feather from a box. She rested the feather on his arm and, before sliding it, explained in an educational manner: "The plate conducts the stimuli to my body and then I can use any object to transfer the electric impulses to you."

"Listen, I really—"

Mmmmmmmmmmmmmmmmmmmmm…

When Marco came to his senses and looked for the redhead, she had vanished. He got rid of the clerk with a definitive yank.

"I like it very much, thank you. I'll come back later," he said, already moving away.

He scanned the vicinity, dribbling the crowd and peering at each stand he passed by. Women he spotted, loads of them, with natural or tinted hair, with a plain face or thick makeup, fully clothed or half-naked. None the redhead. At last, Marco gave up the search and stopped at an arena with a role-playing contest.

A jury formed by two men and a woman evaluated the performance of a young man in a dog outfit. The candidate sported a black vinyl jump-suit, a collar, and a mask featuring a black muzzle and pricked-up ears. His "owner," a gray-haired man with mellifluous hands, conducted the young guy and made him play tricks such as sitting or balancing on his "hinder paws."

At that point, Marco got bored and finally headed for the beverage stand. He was feasting in a tonic water with lemon when he saw her again. The woman with green eyes and fiery hair stood at the opposite counter, busy paying for a fruit cocktail. She returned the wallet to her purse and, when raising her face, met Marco's gaze.

He ventured a half-smile and lifted his own glass in a toast. The girl reciprocated with an unsure smile and left. Marco followed her at a distance. She proceeded to the stand selling tickets for the ball later that evening. The girl joined a long line, and Marco stood right behind her. They made eye contact. This time, the smiles held no inhibition. Soon the two were talking.

9. The Ball at the Devil's Lair

The night sprinkled blue over San Francisco's hills and gold on the bay waters. From the bedroom window Marisa contemplated the Victorian houses on the street, their pastel-colored façades standing out against the last spiral of magenta in the sky. She would miss the cable cars, mushroom omelettes and twilights like that. Pushing the glass pane, she inhaled the air permeated with a subtle hint of salt. Marisa lingered there a minute and then turned around.

The guestroom set for her was compact and comfortable, furnished with a double bed and nightstands topped with lilac lamps and tiny baskets of lavender potpourri. The ambiance brought echoes of sentimentality in a vintage poster of the Golden Gate Park above the headboard and in the oak wardrobe that had belonged to Mrs. Stevenson's grandmother.

Marisa approached it and opened its doors. Time to get ready for the Leather Dream Ball. Brian and Richard's invitation had been unexpected, and she didn't know what to wear. It was the typical nightmare of every woman. Marisa prayed aloud: Oh God, inspire me with the best color match…

And then she removed a black minidress from a hanger.

Putting it in front of her body, Marisa tried to analyze it with scientific objectivity. She grimaced. And, in a frenzy, started to go through the wardrobe contents, erecting on the bed a mountain of discarded clothes that would make Mahomet jealous. Returning to the black minidress, she decided to wear it with a set of silver jewelry and a black satin mask. She studied herself in the mirror. Hmmm… Satisfied at last, Marisa jumped into the shower.

An hour later, Richard and Brian arrived to pick her up in the red convertible. It seemed like a replay of that afternoon, but now the vinyl hood was closed and the hosts dressed more casually. Richard showed up all in black: jeans, a short-sleeve shirt, jacket and leather sneakers. Brian underscored his Pilates abs with black skinny pants and a tight orange Lycra T-shirt. And Valentina, almost unrecognizable under heavy makeup, wore a burgundy stretch jumpsuit, boots and a leather jacket, plus a police cap borrowed from Richard.

"That's so cool, Val. All you need now is a whip," said Marisa as she slid next to her on the backseat.

"And you don't look bad yourself with that mask. I see you didn't forget to wear the seven-inch heels either. Great possibilities..."

Ah, the Leather Dream Ball: a dream interwoven from leather, such a multipurpose material for alluring the senses—second skin enhancing the animal instinct, whisper and opalescent luster in movement, smell of musk, taste of sin. That evening, leather dressed, undressed, mingled and danced in an underground paradise named Devil's Lair. Owned by an eccentric millionaire from Silicon Valley, the club bordered Downtown and occupied a building with brick façade that used to be a church. Its gothic interiors sheltered an amalgam of scattered references: the scenography of a B movie with a multiple personality disorder.

At the entrance, guests were greeted by a voodoo altar set on a circular table. There towered a wooden cross stud with rusty nails, surrounded by skulls, Orisha statuettes and gris-gris talismans. The visitors then skirted the table to reach the rectangular main room boasting iron chandeliers with flickering lamps. A gallery stretched on each side, topped by the mezzanine and separated from the central aisle by arches and columns. Projectors spread a web of light and shadow on the grayish walls and over the stage set on the old altar.

Valentina and Marisa leaned over each detail exclaiming an *oh!* here and an *ah!* there. Richard told them he knew the club owner. Bob was a big fan of horror movies and manga. Not to mention a terrible dancer. Why, he managed to step on your foot several times in just one go, even when he danced on his own to a disco hit.

Brian eyed him with suspicion.

"*Bob?* How come you've never told me you know Bob?"

"Hey, and since when do *you* know Bob?" Richard retorted, equally suspicious.

Brian put both hands on his waist and came to a halt next to the gallery on the right. His T-shirt emitted a phosphorescent glow under the projectors, making him look like a hunky bottle of orange Fanta.

"Richard, do both of us a favor and explain yourself. When did you go out with Bob? Was it that evening last week, when you said you had to work until late, huh? *Huh?*"

"Don't change the subject, Brian. You're hiding something. Why didn't you tell me you were friends with Bob? *Huh?*"

Another pause. Tension rose with sparks ready to fly while the two stared at each other. Until Brian, tapping his foot, challenged: "*Do you really want to know?*"

Valentina squeezed herself in between the two men, intervening straight away: "Oh my gosh!"

"What?" Both turned to her at the same time.

"Check out this *amazing* décor!"

As she spoke, Valentina took Brian's hand and dragged him away. And, soon enough, Bob and his disco sway slipped into oblivion, for the gallery on the right offered an impressive succession of phantasmagorias: the medieval chamber and the smiling executioner amid iron chains, the room with a hairy creature staring at the moon in the window, the compartment that hid an alien monster, the greenhouse with gigantic carnivore plants, the office where a nurse threatened to stick a syringe in the patient tied to the exam table, the crypt holding an empty coffin and a disturbing question— where was its occupant?

The gallery on the left aimed at practical purposes. Besides the cloakroom, it hosted the bar with tall tables, stools and a counter dotted with electronic candles. The four friends left their coats at the cloakroom and, following the natural order of things, made a stop at the bar. Richard offered everyone a round of blue cocktails embellished with a luminous cube, and they all stood there watching the action. Although the DJ set was still in the warm-up stage, the dance floor in the central aisle had already sprung to life with the lysergic *Anemone* by native band The Brian Jonestown Massacre.

Oh baby
How hard I try
To be truthful to you
Please don't say goodbye

"Let's check out the mezzanine," suggested Brian as his gaze swept the room in search of attractive male specimens.

"Good idea. Maybe you'll find us a little gift up there." Richard produced a wink.

"Anyone in particular?"

A brief silence before Richard answered: "*Bob!*"

And they both couldn't stop laughing.

You took over my head
I see you everywhere
But when I look closer
You're just not there

Marisa also scanned the place, in hopes of spotting someone interesting—preferably the blond surfer. The ball had been regally divulged and attracted a more diverse audience than the fair. Among gay men wrapped in leather paraphernalia, women in vinyl and the usual drag queens, there were also students, clubbers and other tribes.

Marisa noticed a man of strong build in ripped jeans and a red T-shirt imprinted with the watchword *Resist!* He looked like a German actor whose name escaped her, short hair and light-brown eyes, a silver loop on one ear and several rings on his fingers. Not her type. But the stranger stared at Marisa with insistence and moved in her direction. Marisa's gaze fell upon the black letters on the T-shirt, which became increasingly large as he drew closer: *Resist!* She turned around fast and followed her friends, who were already climbing the stairs by the bar.

With access at the galleries' extremities, the mezzanine featured a U-shape configuration, which converged to the front of the main room. Its walls displayed a faint pattern of silver flowers against a black background. Low tables and red velvet couches formed chill-out areas surrounded by Greek statues, suits of armor, gargoyles with flaming eyes, and pale bouquets of withered roses.

The four friends sat in one of those velvety oases, and soon Richard and Brian met a couple of acquaintances that joined the group (Gina and Theodora, two blonde, lesbian-chic lawyers, one in a pinstripe suit and the other in a long black dress). While the two men talked to their friends, Marisa turned to Valentina: "Did you happen to see that surfer from the fair here?"

"As a matter of fact, I saw him earlier downstairs. Forgot to mention. You are really interested, huh?"

"Where did you see him?"

"On the dance floor." And, noticing Marisa's agitation, Valentina smiled. "Can you calm down, Ma?"

"*No!* We must go there *now!*"

(Finally. Oh sea of delight in translucent beads of azure and extensions of complexion gilded by the sun, a dragon on the chest and blazing wheat in the hair... She was so ready to surf—on the surfer.)

10. A Little Surprise

Marisa mobilized the group and they all went down to the aisle. No sign of the surfer. Frustrated, she gave up on her search and decided to enjoy the party, dancing with her friends until she almost dropped. Then, another pit stop at the bar for more fuel. Well, it was just a matter of getting to the counter and having a mineral water and fanning herself for Marisa to spot in the middle of the dance floor... who? None other than the surfer. She stared at him indecisive. In an instant, she returned to the dance floor.

Marisa went on plotting the attack strategy. She would pass by the surfer, feign surprise and, with her best smile, say something witty. Hmm. Like what? Let's see. For starters... *hi*. Yeah, very good. *Hi*. And then... an observation about the ball? that joke about Plato and a platypus in a bar? a comment about the waves in Australia? (That's how Marisa went on plotting, not exactly thrilled with those options—even though the joke was hilarious, by the way.)

At that moment, going from point A to point B required a painful exercise of patience. Marisa advanced with exasperating slowness, looking above the sea of heads to make sure she didn't lose sight of the surfer. She managed to draw closer and went on circling and circling. Almost there, almost... Suddenly, she could no longer spot him. Where did he go? *Where...?* All she could see was heads and arms swaying to the music. When a tall guy moved to the side, Marisa found the surfer again—and realized he was leaving the dance floor. She set off after him.

Like a castaway that crosses the hostile sea, Marisa emerged on the other side of the dance floor and, staggering, neared the surfer. She smoothed her hair and fixed her belt, which had rotated forty-five degrees to the left. Then she squared her shoulders. It was now or never. Or was it? Marisa gazed at him, torn between her attraction and sudden insecurity. There stood the surfer, sunny hair and blue T-shirt, aquamarine eyes and… the horrible truth.

The surfer was kissing the platinum dominatrix (red dress, no whip). Marisa could almost hear them purring. In the face of such a Dantesque scene, there was no argument. She turned around to stumble upon five smiley faces: Valentina, Richard, Brian, Gina and Theodora, who had followed her there in the trail of her impulsiveness. Now the stage whitened with a haze of dry ice, while in the background the projector stamped an indigo sky with clouds that shifted to the electronic beat. The friends decided to stick around.

"I just saw the surfer with the dominatrix," Marisa confided to Valentina.

"I knew it. He seemed too cozy around that whip." She shook her head. "People have their secrets, and at some point they sneak out of the closet."

"What about you, Val? Seen anyone interesting?"

Valentina had made out with a bad kisser she had encountered at the bar. She concluded it was safer to watch the drag queens parading around with their golden-sequin dresses and plastic-fruit turbans. Marisa, annoyed, backed her up: drag queens were more fun than men. She had already decided she was not making out with anyone that evening.

"Uh-huh. What if Jim Morrison rose from the dead to make out with you?"

Marisa shrugged.

"Nope. Not making out with anyone tonight."

If only she knew.

Up above, two cascades of purple fabric unfolded from the sides of the stage. Each was scaled by a ballerina in white, tutus floating in the clouds. The two alternated going up and down: while one twisted herself, upended, to a higher level, the other formed an arch with her body near the ground.

The band stepped into the scene, led by an African-American singer with long hair in black shorts and vest. To her left stood the guitar player with dark hair in an unbuttoned white shirt; to the right, the dark-skinned bass player wearing a suit and sneakers. She sang with a plush voice as they played *Ride* by the LA duo Supreme Beings of Leisure. The clouds dissolved in shreds of gauze, and in the clear sky rose the moon.

The applause cascaded, expanded and softened. It expanded for the moon outside, round as a host, pristine in the perfect day for night sky. It softened when migrating to the moon projected inside each one there. The moon inside lulled spectators into their own daydreams and sensations. Music was a pinch of magic dust tickling up the nostrils and soaking each person in the existing music within themselves. Past, present and future, a walk in the clouds.

Beauty is all in the ride
Every little change inside
Leads to a major fork
On the road
New horizons unfold
In the beauty of the ride

Marisa danced amid the crowd without suspecting that, not far from there, Marco had just ordered a drink at the bar. He watched the show with almost anthropological curiosity and, from time to time, scanned the aisle and the mezzanine. He was supposed to meet the redhead from the fair: Yarina, the Ukrainian immigrant and owner of a delicious accent with whom he had spent the afternoon.

Since Marco's arrival at the club an hour earlier, he had searched for her to no avail. Then he spotted a girl in black right next to the stage. A mass of copper hair escaped from under her Lurex beanie. Marco couldn't see her face. Was that Yarina? There was only one way to find out.

He emptied his glass and burrowed into the dance floor. Marco passed by Marisa at the very moment she turned to gossip with Valentina. A spectator pushed him against Marisa, and their arms touched. She turned in a reflex as he disappeared amidst the crowd. The only person in the group to notice Marco was Brian, who directed an appreciative look at him and concentrated again on the guitar player with the unbuttoned shirt.

It took Marco long minutes to reach the redhead in black. When he eventually neared her, he realized she was a younger girl. Marco glanced at the thick crowd behind him and decided to linger by the stage. The trio came back twice for encores and left under a cloak of strobe light and smoke. While the DJ resumed his position at the turntable to launch a breakbeat set, part of the audience disbanded from the center aisle and Marco returned to the bar. Marisa, at that point, had retreated to the restroom with Valentina.

Marco remained at the bar until the crowd began to thin out. It was almost two o'clock, and he toyed with the idea of returning to his hotel. He was starting to feel tired… His eyes wandered in the vicinity and suddenly he saw, on the mezzanine, the profile of a redhead in a green top. She was out of sight in an instant. This time, however, Marco knew he had found the Ukrainian girl.

He dashed to the stairs and went around to the other side of the mezzanine. He peered at the faces coming and going, checked out the people seated on the sofas. At last, he saw Yarina chatting with a friend beside a vase of fainted roses. Then his attention was hopelessly drawn to a young woman in black leaning over the parapet.

With the camera of his eye, he focused on her, he filmed her movement.

Ballerina legs, short and tight dress, a chain belt. A masked profile and a hazel mantle for hair. Her hands joined behind the nape of her neck, lifting the hair in a wave for her to cool off. Light suffused over it and painted golden strands. The chains in her bracelets skimmed across the tribal tattoo, a stylized rose. It was new. It covered the birthmark.

Yet he recognized her.

11. Dopamine + Pheromone = Nonsense

Time slowed down brusquely until it halted and everything around him went out of focus. In that instant frozen in time, Marco only had eyes for her. The sounds of the music and the crowd muted, the very air stagnated in a vacuum. Amid the silence that reigned, he could hear his own heart beating. It sounded in sync with hers: loud as a drum in an empty room, out of tempo, the rapid pounding merging into its own echo.

Maybe it was just his imagination, Marco conjectured vaguely. Just his imagination. The ghost of her.

He wanted the mirage to disappear. He blinked hard. The mirage persisted. And then he felt thirsty for her. Marco wanted to turn around and step away from the memories. Now wasn't the time to look back; his life had just taken a new turn. But his feet remained rooted to the floor. His body refused to leave. If he had a drop of common sense—but no. Instead of pretending he had not seen Marisa, he stayed. He stared at her. He smiled without even realizing it.

Someone laughed behind Marco, and Marisa looked in his direction. She brought one hand to her mouth to suppress a gasp when, in a flash, time and space compressed: the seven months and one continent that had interposed between them turned into dust. Marisa gazed into Marco's eyes, and it was as if the two had never been apart. His smile remained the same, that smile unfolding springtime…

The illusion, however, evaporated under the club lights. In its place, flimsy flowers shimmered on the wallpaper and dead roses exhaled mold. She no longer knew anything about Marco's life and he knew nothing about hers. They were virtually two strangers now. And, as such, they stood there with the same awkwardness—two strangers on a high wire.

Marisa found him more handsome than before. Lawrence of Arabia. His tan emphasized the heritage of his features and the veins in his muscular arms. The gray T-shirt with a V collar molded his torso and, underneath it, the leather belt showed partially on the low-waisted black jeans. She was exasperated at Marco for still affecting her. Exasperated at herself for still allowing him to affect her.

Until then, she had hoped to see Marco again, if not for them to get back together, at least to cure her pride. Marisa pictured the scene, she all gorgeous with a male companion, irreducible while Marco crawled. Marisa had replayed the scene, adjusting lines with the accuracy of a professional actress. She would conquer fame in her debut. She would earn a round of applause.

Pure foolishness, of course. Certain tremors never pass.

She tried to articulate his name but couldn't. She was dreaming—it must be a dream. Marco took a couple of steps toward her and touched her arm, as if to make sure she was of flesh and blood. Marisa shrunk away, her skin searing. The dark scar of memory, engraved in her body cells, ruptured and throbbed.

Marisa turned to face him without releasing the guardrail. Her legs weakened as an automatic smile spread on her lips.

"Marco, what a coincidence. What are you doing in San Francisco?"

"I was at a congress in Los Angeles and decided to stop by. I'm leaving on Wednesday." Hesitation. His incredulity persisted. "What about you?"

His voice, which used to be so familiar, was now a gap—seven months and still the distance of one continent. Marisa mentioned the English course, told him she would go back to Brazil the following evening, and then kept quiet. She didn't know what else to say. She had anticipated that moment so many times, and when it was finally real, she found herself speechless. No use in preparing yourself for anything, for life was fond of irony and would wait until you got distracted to fulfill your greatest wish. And when it got fulfilled, sometimes it was too late.

He stared at her with such insistence she flushed. The admiration in Marco's eyes was like a physical touch, and Marisa grasped the guardrail. She wondered how she'd react if he wanted to get back together. Just to think of it… No, she'd better forget the idea. She could never trust him. Marco had destroyed many things she cherished. Actually, Marisa thought, she was even grateful for that. She had learned her lesson from him.

Dopamine, pheromones, neurotransmitters. And nothing else. Butterflies fluttering away. Then the clear sky. She smiled, more confident, and removed the mask.

"How great to see you here, Mari." Marco's dark eyes glimmered as he searched hers. He raised his hand, as if to touch her face, and dropped it. "You look gorgeous. Are you here with someone?"

"I'm with Valentina and some friends. They're downstairs, but I'd rather stay here. It's too crowded there."

"Yeah," he agreed with an absent air, his eyes soaking into her. "How's college?"

"Awesome."

"And how did the physics entrance exam go?"

"I made it by a close shave."

Both smiled. The seconds stretched as the two exchanged a captive gaze. People passed by, the music kept playing—nothing but shadows and muffled sounds. The two of them were not there, they were inside each other's eyes. Marco was about to speak when Yarina crossed into view like a line of static. He had forgotten about the Ukrainian girl.

She passed behind Marisa and stood by his side.

"I'm glad I found you. Something came up and I didn't have my cell phone." Yarina acknowledged Marisa and turned to him. "I hope I'm not interrupting."

"Not at all." Dissimulating his discomfort, Marco made the introductions: "Yarina, this is…" An infinitesimal pause. "My friend Marisa."

Marisa smiled out of politeness, while his words rang in her ears. *My friend Marisa. My friend. Friend.* It shocked her to hear that for the first time. Before, she was the girlfriend, but there hadn't been time for him to introduce her to anyone: *This is my girlfriend Marisa.* She had jumped straight to the new status in the introductions. And, at that thought, Marisa couldn't avoid a twinge of melancholy.

She repeated to herself: nonsense, nothing lasts, it's best this way.

Marco acted natural, but his responses were clipped as he spoke to Yarina. She laughed and poked his arm. Marisa didn't hear any of it, paying attention only to body language. There was something going on between the two of them. She directed a side glance at Yarina, trying to guess what Marco saw in her. Although she looked ordinary, her eyes were pretty, Marisa granted with a stab of jealousy.

Dopamine, pheromones, nonsense.

Yarina's smile irradiated from her thin lips to the green in her eyes. Sparkling green. Marco smiled back, his profile cut out like an image superimposed onto the blurry crowd: the strong nose line, the eyebrows slightly arched to make his eyes larger, the mouth curving upward with ease. Yarina held his hand: an intimate gesture that lasted longer than necessary.

Marisa turned her face away.

The scar. The burning sensation invading her chest. No air. She wanted to leave. When Marisa opened her mouth to speak, she had no idea of what to say. Anything that would take her away from that spot. Displaying weakness was out of the question, but watching Yarina flirt with Marco was torture. Why did she have to go through that?

Because life, as a diligent mentor, applies certification tests.

She needed to scream. She needed to think fast.

Any pretext would do. The restroom. A drink. Friends calling her to the dance floor. And then Valentina showed up to save her.

"Oh, so you're hiding here." She ignored Marco. "Richard is very interested in you and insists that you join us on the dance floor. Let's go downstairs before he drives me crazy."

Marisa excused herself and followed her. The last thing she registered was Yarina's laugh. She didn't muster the courage to look at Marco—she knew he was laughing too. Valentina took her hand and led the way. As they descended the stairs, Marisa barely felt her own legs. She squeezed the friend's hand.

"Thank you, Val."

"No need to thank me... What the heck is Marco doing here?" She grimaced, shaking her head. "Whatever. Just do me a favor and forget that jerk."

The two met their friends at the bar and Marisa ordered another blue cocktail. She drank it in one go at the first chords of a remix. The Cure. Marisa laid the empty glass on the counter, cast a last glance at the mezzanine and proceeded alone to the dance floor. Soon the alcohol and the music pulsed within her like fever. She carried on dancing in a farther corner, until a voice called her.

She turned around to face the bold letters: *Resist!* The next thing she faced was his delight.

"Marie, this is unbelievable... it's really you!"

The stranger didn't notice Marisa's perplexity and confided: he had searched for her all over social media... how amazing, it was really her!

Marisa eyed him at a loss.

"You can stop pretending, Marie." A grin spread across his face.

"Pretending what?"

"It's me, Friedrich... Fred."

"Sorry, but I don't think I know you."

He insisted she quit denying. He understood that before she had to pretend she didn't know him because of her boyfriend. But now she was there on her own and... Fred couldn't help himself and ran one hand on her hair before she could protest.

"Wow, your hair is so long. It's really cool. Did you use any special product on it?"

"Well, I usually apply a colorless henna that gives it shine, volume, and—" Marisa shook her head, baffled. "Listen, you're mistaking me for someone else."

"What?" he shouted as a drum solo swallowed up her words.

"You're mistaking me for someone else!" she shouted back over the drums.

"Oh, am I? What about the night we spent together in that resort in Maui? Don't tell me you forgot the insane things we did in my suite. The champagne, the bar counter, the bubble bath in the hot tub... then the bar counter again, the couch, the carpet... *It was amazing!*"

What? Marisa had a hard time keeping track. Hold on. Bar counter twice, hot tub, couch, carpet... That was *five times*—a first-rate service. Marisa stared at Fred with sudden respect. Maybe she should consider...

Maybe he *was* her type. After all, he seemed so adamant…

She came back to her senses: "Will you stop that?"

"If you really don't know me, then why did you answer when I called your name?" accused Fred, his smile paling.

"Because…" Marisa grew exasperated in that pause.

It was hard enough to argue amid the loud music, let alone explain the name coincidence. Only one person in the world called her like that, and for a second she had thought… Well, Fred wouldn't understand anyway.

"Never mind."

"See, Marie? How could you forget that night? You seemed like a wild cat in heat. No woman has ever made me feel that way. Oh my God, the things you did to me…" He sighed. "You were screaming and scratching and having multiple orgasms…"

Fred showed Marisa his arm, where a dark line stretched for a good couple of inches—a scratch scar. He seemed proud.

It was too much for Marisa. She congratulated him for such a *pleasant* night, but the details did not interest her. And with that, she left him standing there and wove her way across the room, all the while dodging kicks and elbow pokes. The demented crowd jiggled in some sort of Saint Vitus dance, and an exalted punk gave her a mighty push as he rehearsed a pogo jump. Like a projectile, Marisa flew to the other end of the dance floor. She landed in the arms of a blond in a white T-shirt passing under the arches.

"Whoa, easy!" he said as he opened his arms with a smile.

Marisa hung on to him to steady herself, and the two wavered together. She apologized. He said that was a pleasure after a bad day. In the lapse that followed, Marisa became aware that his eyes were quite green and reminded her of foliage soaked in rain. He must be about twenty-five, not bad looking at all. The mass of his curly hair, ready to start a rebellion, gave him a teenage air of sorts.

"Problems?" She reciprocated the smile as she straightened up.

"I'd say so. I'm a programmer and just spent the weekend trying to fix the coding for an online game. It's based on the movie *Polar Fire*, did you watch it?"

As Marisa nodded, he hooked one thumb in the pocket of his jeans and narrated the catastrophe: Sam Parker, the game's fearless hero, had only one day left to save the world.

"Now picture the final confrontation scene: Sam finds the enemy's hideout in the Arctic. The supervillain Ozymandias is about to blow up the Earth so mankind won't spread its trail of destruction to the galaxy. Sam draws his Brügger & Thomet MP9, stretches out his arms and holds the gun with both hands... and then what happens?"

"He fires."

"No! Sam twirls around and breaks into a tango."

"*A tango?*"

Exactly. A hacker had sabotaged the game code, and he didn't know how. It was maddening.

"Each one to their hard nut, eh?" Marisa thought of Marco and let out a sigh.

"Problems?" he asked.

"Yeah, but it's not worth talking about it."

They exchanged a sympathetic look.

"My name is Eric. You?"

"Mari," she answered in an impulse.

"You have a distinctive accent. Let me guess... French?"

"Brazilian."

Oh, how interesting. Brazil. Eric gazed at her in admiration. His green eyes conveyed warmth when he touched Marisa's forearm. He told her the previous day he had left the office so late and so wrecked he slept in a hotel just to avoid the drive home. He needed badly to decompress. Would she care to dance?

When Marisa acquiesced, a flash of inspiration hit Eric: "Let's dance a tango, Mari."

"But I don't know how to dance the tango. Do you?"

"I guess so. I learned it from Sam Parker..."

On the fringe of the dance floor, they improvised cheek to cheek in between laughs, making faces because in tango what counted was the attitude. They danced together that entire track and the next, which oddly matched their steps. When Eric held Marisa and she arched back, they stared at each other, suddenly serious, still panting. The two kissed. In that moment, the rhythm mellowed down with Thievery Corporation's. *Take My Soul.* The room began to spin and spin in sync with the music. A long, long tingling…

Guide me along
This winding road
Of truth and illusion
Give me cure

12. The Devil Laughs

"What's with the water?"

Gina looked inquisitively at Valentina, drank a sip of mineral water and brushed the sleeve of her pinstripe suit.

"It's not a *renewable* commodity," Valentina retorted in a heated tone, "and one day the world's gonna end in thirst and filth as corporations privatize water. Why do you get a huge glass of water everywhere you go, without even asking? Think of how much water would be saved if people got it only when they actually *asked* for it."

"Well…" Gina thought for a second and exchanged a glance with Theodora. "This is designed to offer more for your money and beat the competition."

"Money? The glass of water is free," insisted Valentina.

"Exactly."

Around a table by the bar, Valentina continued her spirited conversation with the two women, while Richard and Brian sneaked out with a boy in a fallen angel costume. In the aisle, Marisa still danced with her new friend, a fact that could be interpreted in many ways according to different perspectives. To the people in the center aisle, the pair was just another anonymous couple. To Marisa, Eric was a pleasant consolation prize. To Eric, Marisa was a stereotype of tropical sensuality.

Now to Marco, ironically, Eric was Richard. While Yarina burrowed into the restroom with her friend, Marco proceeded to get drinks. Upon arriving at the bar, he couldn't help but scan the room for Marisa. He searched the fringe of the dance floor near the stage, not knowing for sure what he expected to find.

He found Marisa amid a kiss. His eyes flared in tempo with the laser, the music hammering his temples and irrational thoughts thundering even louder in his brain.

Then he lost sight of her.

"Hey, if you're not buying anything you'd better get out of the way," said a guy at his back.

Marco gave him a long stare. Without a word, he turned to wave at the bartender.

The central aisle sizzled with a drum 'n' bass set. Pushing them toward the middle of the dance floor, the crowd closed in around Marisa and Eric. The two tired from the bedlam and decided to make a pause at the bar. Eric took her by the hand and the two threaded their way among the clubbers. They had hardly advanced a few feet when a man blocked Marisa's way. In spite of his solid build, he had the air of a lost puppy, which made the watchword on his T-shirt look pathetic.

"Friedrich!"

"Marie, don't do this to me, please. I can't get you out of my mind. Let's go somewhere else and relive that night. For old times' sake." He gestured helplessly. One of his rings, the one with the skull, flickered with a grimace.

As he tried to get a hold of her arm, Marisa wrenched herself from him with an abrupt move. Fred, however, grabbed her wrist. She lost it: "Apparently you've had too much champagne in that hot tub and it affected your brain. Leave me alone. *I'm not Marie!*"

"Mari, is there a problem?" Eric intervened.

"Ah, what did I just say? I knew it!" The lost puppy had become a rabid Rottweiler. Fred growled: "Who's this guy? You're too good to be with me, but don't have a problem being with *him*, huh? At least be a woman and stop pretending you don't know me."

"Let her go!" Eric demanded, pushing him.

Eric positioned himself in between the two of them and covered Marisa's back. Fred planted both hands on his shoulders to get him out of the way. Eric reacted with a shove. Fred aimed a violent punch at him.

"*Eric, watch out!*" Marisa yelled.

Eric ducked. Fred's fist full of rings landed on a man with his back to them. The furious guy lashed at Eric's chin. The three tussled to the electronic beat. *Boom-boom.* A rapper tried separating them. Got into the fight. A crossdresser tried. Into the fight. Then a guy who was neither a rapper nor a crossdresser tried too. *Boom-boom.* The scuffling bodies merged into an odd animal of many legs, arms and fists. Bruise on the face and taste of metal in the mouth. *Boom-boom.* The animal grew and spat chains, feathers, neon necklaces, plastic cups. *Boom-boom.* A vase hurled from the mezzanine and withered roses raining on the dance floor. *Boom-boom.* Glass shards. *Boom-boom.* Blows, grunts, gasps to the electronic beat. *Boom-boom-boom-boom…*

And the trail from hell spread in the Devil's Lair.

Red, yellow, blue, under crazed laser beams, *pew, pew, pew.* To the rhythm of *Supergrass* by DJ Marky, Carlito and DJ Addiction." Drum 'n' bass, the perfect soundtrack for a good bar fight. *You know I crave you, so come closer, yeah closer-closer, let's get to the beat, yeah get to the beat-beat…* Red, yellow, blue, *pew, pew, pew.*

It looked like one of those movie scenes when a large bookcase thrown out of balance knocks over another, and another—and the only thing left to do is watch, in fascination and horror, as the whole library comes crashing down. Some ran away, others cheered. Violence, a virus: strifes on the mezzanine, smell of tension and acrid sweat, people rushing to the stairs. *You're finished, you bastard.*

Boom-boom-boom-boom. The DJ booth became a godforsaken territory, a Crystal Method remix adrift on the turntable. Steppenwolf with its *Magic Carpet Ride… One, two, three, four… Let's make the most of the night, floating in mystical delight, come with me baby in this magical ride…* Cheek-to-cheek dance with no love. Dumbfound security guards. Jam-packed restrooms. In the gallery, the nurse rolled over the patient and dropped the syringe on the floor. A Carmen Miranda drag queen hid inside the empty coffin, her plastic fruit turban crushed with a hollow mourn. Across the room a stench of alcohol: punks plundered the deserted bar, pouring down a stream of bourbon on the counter and knocked-over stools. In the midst of confusion, the voodoo altar finally collapsed.

Marisa shook broken bracelets off her wrists where black bruises would soon bloom. *Eric... Eric!* She attempted to pull him from the fight with two men. She clasped his arm, then his shoulder, her hands slipping, slipping... She was dragged away by the human tide that overflowed onto the street, blind to the bouncer gesticulating with a thousand arms. In the exit bottleneck, Marisa fell over a mound of overturned stools by the bar. The pain burnt when the spear of a splinter sank into her thigh. Desperate, she attempted to lift herself up, but the pile gave in to her weight. The wooden legs cracked and crossed to form an obstinate grid, trapping Marisa's legs.

"Somebody help me!" she cried into a vacuum. *Boom-boom-boom-boom. Pew, pew, pew.* The more she struggled, the more the grid tightened. For a long minute, Marisa remained dazed in the surreal ocean of fleeting feet and destroyed furniture. She tried to reconcile the brusque transition between such distinct moments: the calm and the storm... *One, two, three, four... C'mon baby, the night is calling for this magical ride...*

She had plunged into the guts of a mad beast. She needed to get out. A man in a bat costume approached with his transparent wings flapping. Marisa managed to seize one wing. For an instant the iridescent fabric was her salvation, glistering between her fingers like a trembling butterfly, a magic carpet into the starry night. The crowd absorbed the man, and Marisa was left with a tatter in her hand. Trembling butterfly, it flew away, alighted on the ground and turned into a crushed carcass.

The mass thickened toward the exit and now it almost brushed up against her. Soon she would be trampled, Marisa thought with horror. The wooden skeleton imprisoning her also worked as a precarious barrier, but not for too long. *Help! Help!* The electronic beat chewed up her screams. In a flash, she watched images parade in her memory. It was not the retrospect of her life though. It was the fire.

The disaster at a nightclub in the south of Brazil earlier that year... Most patrons, students like herself. A flare ignited by the band released sparkles to the ceiling devoid of fire resistant insulation. In three minutes, the flames took the house. A nightmare of people stampeding blindly. Crying, falling down trampled. Dying. Security agents blocked the exit, for they thought patrons wanted to leave without paying. It was the third worst nightclub disaster in the world. Almost 250 casualties. So many corpses they had to be transported in ice trucks.

And the whole time, the macabre symphony of the dead victims' cell phones, ringing, ringing, ringing… Marisa had a click and groped for her purse. Straining to pull it amid the snarl, she finally managed to extract her phone. She called Valentina. Nothing. One more try. *You've reached Valentina. Don't wear fur. It's cruel wearing the corpse of an animal that was skinned alive only for human vanity. This is my message, now leave yours…* Marisa tried to explain the situation in a coherent manner and, with a heavy heart, put the phone back in the purse. Then a fierce bump shook her, and another, and another. She screamed.

The crowd had spilled into the bar area. In panic, she fought to free herself, only to sink deeper into the quicksand of shattered wood. Two tears budded in her eyes.

Someone gripped her arm and attempted to extricate her: Marco. But in vain. It still took him precious minutes to break the stools and release the pivot piece holding everything together. He had just released her torso when two drunk punks started a quarrel and wrestled on top of the counter—a Mohican with purple spiked hair, in jeans and vest; the other bald, dressed in black leather, an eagle tattooed on his head. The two tumbled over the stools, in a wheel of spikes and tattoos and boots. They wobbled up, ready to resume their fight, and suddenly paused.

They eyed Marco. Then Marisa. Eyes glaring.

Boom-boom-boom-boom.

"We'll get you, slut," the bald one vociferated.

The punks now joined against a common enemy. They were drunk with bourbon and a generic rage that clamored for a target. Any target. Their faces were ghostly masks with dark eyes and twitching mouths. With a battle cry, they forged a trail amid the crumbled tables.

Grasping a piece of wood, Marco jumped in front of Marisa. She now stood six feet behind him. The attackers, sixteen feet ahead—fifteen, thirteen, ten, nine…

"How about a chat with me first?" Marco defied.

They were two against him, but no one would lay a finger on Marisa.

Determination conferred him a blind strength that exploded from his brain into his whole body. A torrent of adrenaline inundated his veins.

The purple-haired Mohican tripped, the bald guy behind him climbed onto the counter and glided over a pool of bourbon, seizing a broken bottle on the way. He fell over Marco and forced him to drop the piece of wood. Hands around throats, the two oscillated on dodgy terrain until Marco brought the bald punk to his knees.

But now the Mohican closed in on him.

"You son of a bitch."

"Impressive vocabulary," Marco retorted, clenching his fists.

"Shut the fuck up!"

The punk lashed out with such furor he lost balance. He quickly recovered. Marco rebuffed him with a punch. The bald guy retrieved the bottle and lashed a frontal assault while the other applied a chokehold from behind. Marco struggled, the jagged glass nearly ripping his face. The three of them rolled to the ground with a crash of fractured wood. The Mohican stuck one knee on Marco's chest. The bald man to his side raised the bottle in the air.

A stool flew to the Mohican's face. Marisa. She grabbed one more stool and flung it. The Mohican collapsed. Marco twisted his body and delivered a blow in the bald guy's jaw, sending him against the counter. He hit his head. The eagle swelled with one goggle eye.

There was no time to waste. Marco pulled Marisa and took her by the hand as both staggered away. With a quick exchange of looks, they dove together into the stream of people that gushed toward the exit. It was like spurting inside a lightning bolt, swimming in a broken wave. They gained the street, air, space. The two then ran and only stopped when they found themselves at a safe distance. Breathlessly, they rested against a wall, still squeezing each other's hands. Far away, the sirens of police cars howled into the night.

"Are you okay?" Marco asked Marisa, alarmed as he took notice of the injury on her leg and the bruises on her arms.

Until then, adrenaline had numbed the pain. Now, the sight of blood on her torn pantyhose triggered a wave of nausea in Marisa. The cut began to throb. She grimaced and leaned heavily on Marco.

"Take a deep breath, Mari."

She obeyed him.

"Can you walk further?"

Marisa nodded, fighting back the tears. Marco supported her weight and circled her waist with his arm. They started walking toward the avenue to get a cab. With her head down, Marisa let him lead the way. She watched the pairs of feet advancing in sync, her pathetic high-heeled sandals, his black leather shoes, the firm hand against her body. On the smoothness of the pavement, anonymous façades irradiated placid circles of light for blocks that seemed to never end.

In a given moment, she realized he was raising his arm. Next, a yellow blur stopped by the curb. Marco helped her enter the vehicle and joined her on the passenger seat, giving an address to the driver. He then wrapped his arms around Marisa and finally relaxed.

13. Nostalgia

On the way to the hotel they remained quiet, Marisa with closed eyes and her head on Marco's shoulder while he stroked her hair and watched the landscape through the cab window. In the eerie stillness of the streets, houses dozed off wrapped in a sheet of mist. They passed by the Golden Gate Park in the light of lethargic lampposts, and the howling of a dog pierced the white air that smelled like pine and salt flower. Soon they arrived. In the warmth of the room there was silence, the gentle dimness from the bedside lamp—and the two of them.

Exhausted, Marisa collapsed in the blue armchair by the window. Marco grabbed a tonic water from the minibar and filled two glasses. They drank avidly, then stared at each other unsure of what to say. So many words. Or nothing… Marisa's cell phone emitted a beep and she averted her face with a startle. She reached for it in her purse and, finding many missed calls from Valentina, phoned her friend. They talked for a few minutes. Valentina told how she had searched for Marisa in the club and finally left, thinking Marisa had managed to escape in one piece. Not finding her outside, Valentina tried to go back inside, but the bouncer wouldn't allow it.

Marisa, in her turn, told what happened to her without much detail. She said goodbye, claiming to be exhausted, and did not mention Marco. Before putting the phone back in her purse, Marisa decided to send a short message to Mrs. Stevenson. As she finished typing, Marco approached her: "Who was that? Richard?"

She hit the Send key and raised her eyes, puzzled with the question. Then she understood. Marisa began laughing, and her laughter became hysterical. She let the cell phone slip onto her lap. Her laughter faded and her eyes filled with the weeping she had suppressed.

Kneeling before her, Marco held her hands.

"Hey… don't be sad. It's over. Everything is fine now."

"Don't pay attention to me, Marco. I'm just emptying my chest. I was so scared. What frightened me the most was the frailty of everything, you know? All of a sudden, everything changed…"

"Things change, Mari. I've never seen such a havoc either… Look, I have something that will help you relax." He sighed. "Actually, I think I could use some too."

Marco caressed her cheek and pushed Marisa gently against the chair backrest. He reached the chest of drawers, inspected one of the compartments and came back with a homemade cigarette in his hand. He sat on the edge of the double bed while lighting it up, and explained it had been a gift from a friend who lived in town. For the next few moments, the two smoked in silence and enjoyed the quietness in the room. It was like a balm, away from the crowd and the fierce music. Away from the screams.

When they finished smoking, Marco offered to take Marisa to the emergency room for her leg to be checked. Marisa thanked him but declined, she only needed a hot shower and a good night's sleep. She would get a cab and go home. Marco insisted she stayed until she recovered: there was a clean towel and a robe in the bathroom, she could shower and afterwards he would take care of her injury. Marisa hesitated and finally agreed.

They exchanged a look, and the air around them grew denser. Now it wasn't that evening's incident that consumed their thoughts. It was the waking memories that brought to surface desire, feelings, non-spoken words. Marisa bowed her head and, not knowing what to do with her hands, returned the cell phone to the purse. She forced herself to rise from the chair and dragged her feet to the bathroom.

She heard Marco's voice behind her: "Let me know if you need anything."

Marisa slowed down imperceptibly and, nodding, locked herself in the bathroom. The prolonged showering relieved her restlessness and her sore muscles. She slipped into the hot water's embrace and rubbed herself with the soap at leisure, washing off that evening from her body and feeling her clean skin. The flower of the skin. Her hands pressed her own flesh, sliding, sliding, climbing mounds, lingering in concavities… Now they were no longer her hands but his, like in the past… Marisa closed her eyes.

She lost track of time—she could have been there for one minute or one hour. Once finished, Marisa wrapped herself in the white robe and made a turban with the towel to cover her wet hair. Running her hand across the mirror, she traced a clear circle that showed her reflection. She stared at her own image with incredulity. Was it all a dream? Was she really there with Marco? Life could be strange sometimes. Suddenly she felt like laughing. Her laughter stifled as the mirror steamed up, blurring her reflection. Her eyes blurred too, and she dried them with a quick gesture.

Back in the room, Marisa found Marco seated on the bed texting. His gaze darted to her and rapidly steered away as he interrupted his message. With a constrained expression, Marco left the phone on the nightstand and massaged the nape of his neck. He sighed, paused, and all his attention turned to Marisa. The almost black eyes registered every detail of her, from the face flushed by the warm water to the pale skin near the collar line, from the figure that the robe hid to the hands and legs it exposed. Marisa felt vulnerable to his proximity. She pretended to busy herself with the robe belt.

"Aren't you gonna shower?" she asked with false ease.

"Yeah, I'm taking a shower now. Try to rest. Wanna listen to some music?"

"Good idea. I miss Brazilian music. Do you have anything by Céu?"

Marco handed his MP3 player to Marisa. She scrolled down the screen, surprised at the playlists.

"You still have my selections?"

He gave but a smile and disappeared into the bathroom. Marisa soon heard the water running behind the closed door. She picked a track, fitted the player onto the speakers and curled up in the armchair. Shutting her eyes, she was lulled by the lyrics of *Legend*, about a misbehaving prince turned into a frog.

She dozed off with a heavy head, all the while acutely aware of Marco's presence just a few feet away. So near and so far. His wash was quick, and Marco came back with a white towel wrapped around his waist. Marisa woke up to the sight of his tanned torso. Against her will, she found herself admiring his strong arms and the trail of dark hair that started on the chest, shadowed his well-defined abdomen, and advanced underneath the towel…

He stood next to her with a vanity case in his hand. Helping her get up from the chair, he led Marisa to the bed in order to tend her injury. Listless, she sat down with her back against the pillow and her legs stretched. She tightened the turban, closed the robe and kept her hand flat on the collar. Marco sat beside her and in a second undid everything, removing the half-collapsed turban and opening the robe at her thighs.

Marisa followed his gestures with her gaze and a quiver. Marco cleansed the wound with cotton drenched in hydrogen peroxide. He examined it and applied pomade with a circular motion. The cut didn't seem too deep. He asked if it hurt when he put the pomade on, and she replied no, not much. In a practical manner, Marco cut a large piece of bandage and covered the area.

Then he smiled.

"Mari, for goodness' sake, take it easy."

"I *am* taking it easy, Marco."

"*Shhh…*"

He picked up a flask of cream on the nightstand and moistened his hands. Marisa concentrated on them—big, tanned, shiny—and recalled when they had first trailed her body in that rainy afternoon belonging to another life. She stared at Marco. In his eyes, she found the same recognition. The dark irises scintillated for an instant, captured hers and steered away as he held her ankle. Marco encircled it and descended to the foot, nestling it between his hands. So he began to massage it with self-assured, deliberate movements. He paused on the tension points. Then on all points. Gradually, his gestures became voluptuous, marked by another kind of precision: the kind that escaped reason.

As much as Marisa intended to resist, she found it impossible to remain immune to that touch. Slowly, she succumbed.

14. Frontiers

Exactly as he remembered. The damp hair and the luminous skin that he loved to feel. The smell of soap when she came out of the shower after they had spent lazy hours in bed. The warm gaze that conveyed the embraces and words of long ago. It was as if Marco had leaped back and the needle of time returned to that period. Now it wasn't the rational thought guiding his hands: it was nostalgia. And they followed familiar paths, identifying the details on the way. A freckle, a mark, peach velvet, contentment. His hands remembered, they rejoiced in landing there once more.

Continent, harbor, home.

They first wended along the feet that were the anchor to the ground, the toes one by one, the arch in the middle and then the ankles, climbing the legs until circling the knees to linger delicately behind them, on the sensitive crook where she liked to be touched. And then they would glide back to the ankles, focusing on the feet and again on the legs.

Now his hands expanded toward the frontier of the intact thigh, enveloping its full length. They moved with the possessiveness of a traveler well-acquainted with the route. Going up and further up, at times smooth, at times more assertive, always right. The palms caressed, the fingers pressed, triggering ardent sensations in their wake. The surface of her skin bristled against Marisa's will, her flesh revived.

Marisa drifted between reluctance and desire. She closed her eyes, unable to stop Marco or venture to touch him, without knowing if she shut her eyes to protect herself or dive blindly in the sensations. His hands brought back all they had shared. The way Marco deciphered her body, and transcended it, awoke in Marisa such a profound yearning it was almost pain.

His hands also vacillated, revisiting joys and fears. They wanted to surpass the limits. They feared getting lost. And so they halted before crossing another frontier, the one that held the most secret delight. Abruptly, they returned to the present and the reality of those four walls. Then they stopped amid an incomplete motion and began another: to close the robe, retreating with modesty.

The firm, tender hands now deserted Marisa. She opened her eyes in confusion. Marco was wiping his hands on the towel as he stared at her with a strange glint in his eyes. Marisa shivered. Dawn filtered through the curtains with a weak light. The temperature in the room had dropped. It was the coldest hour of the day.

Marco slipped into a pair of jeans underneath the towel, then tossed it away and put a white T-shirt on. He would get them something to eat at a twenty-four-hour diner around the corner.

"I'm having a continental breakfast. What about you?"

"Pancakes. With all the toppings," she replied without looking at him. She was hungry, frustrated, somehow discouraged.

It didn't take him too long. When he returned, the two sat at the table and had their meal without saying much. Marco flipped through the TV channels until he found a piece of news about the aftermath of the Devil's Lair mayhem: no fatalities, 116 patrons with no major injuries, a club destroyed. The drag queen that had hidden in the coffin stated in tears: "I feared for my life. It was *so scary...*"

Noticing Marisa was about to doze, Marco turned off the TV. He stretched his arms in front of him and let them drop, then suggested they have some sleep. Marisa nodded, and the two went to the bathroom to brush their teeth. Too tired to pay attention to any awkward feelings. Side by side, just like in old times.

While she returned to the bedroom, Marco switched from the jeans to a pair of white sweatpants hanging on the bathroom door. Then he joined Marisa and proceeded to search the chest of drawers, producing a white T-shirt and a pair of gray swimming trunks for her.

"I'm not used to wearing clothes for bed, as you know... but you can have this," Marco said apologetically as he handed her the clothes. Sensing

Marisa's indecision, he added: "You keep the bed and I'll take the armchair, is that okay?"

"You won't be able to sleep over there," she pondered, shaking her head. "I'd better go home."

Marisa felt the warmth of Marco's body when he held her hand. They stood too close. She lowered her eyes. She saw a bruise on his wrist from the fight and wanted to touch it. Saw an imperceptible tremor in his other hand. Saw his thumb brush her skin in a caress.

"Mari… I'd like you to stay."

The sincerity in his voice disarmed her. Marisa searched Marco's face for a moment and assented. She approached the bed and slipped under the covers without removing the robe while he took a blanket from the closet and tested the armchair. Before turning the lights off, Marco spotted the clothes he had picked for Marisa on top of the nightstand. He insisted she change into them, but Marisa skirted the subject: it would be only for a few hours, and she was exhausted. In truth, Marisa wanted to avoid contact with his clothes. And the memories.

As soon as the lights were out, however, her sleepiness evaporated. Marisa remained stiff with her eyes squeezed shut. Everything there triggered an odd feeling in her. She should be in her own bed at the Stevensons, not in that room, not with that man. Things were not going according to plan.

They didn't always.

Marisa heard him trying to make himself comfortable. Sound of fabric rasping, stirring and rasping again. She couldn't help herself: "Marco?"

"Yes."

"I won't be able to sleep knowing you're in that chair."

Marco reassured her everything was fine. No, objected Marisa, he'd better come to bed. A silence followed, and when Marco spoke, it was in a playful tone. He'd better not, as he feared she would take advantage of his innocence. The voice, husky and somehow feverish, vibrated in the dark with forceful joviality.

"Will you stop it and come here already?" insisted Marisa.

Marco vacillated. His tone changed: "Are you sure?"

"I'm sure."

Marisa gave room to him and, turning to the wall, shrank to the edge of the mattress. She could not see Marco's cautious expression when he lay by her side. Neither the smile that at last came to his lips.

"You're almost falling out of bed, Mari. Don't be silly. Come here."

Marco pulled Marisa near him, wrapping his arm around her waist. Their bodies fitted together, their breathing adjusted. Exhaustion finally won the two. The warmth under the covers lulled them and the dimness switched everything into a blank screen. In a minute, they were fast asleep.

Just like in old times.

15. Vertigo

Through a gap in the curtain crept filaments of light and fog. The day sneaked gently into the room, gently into sleep. A sleep devoid of dreams but populated with impressions old and new. The mind a caravel adrift, the body a sore sheaf of muscles. Sore mind, body adrift. It lasted one hour. The two woke in the same position of falling asleep. Marisa was disoriented at first. Then she remembered.

"Take off the robe," Marco asked in a soft tone, smoothing her hair. "I want to feel you."

She stared at the thick dark-green stripes on the wallpaper—solid, symmetric, aseptic. Straight on their path. She wished her heart was like that too.

"Why, Marco?"

"So I can be closer. Does that bother you?"

In response, she clumsily removed the robe and cuddled up next to his warmth. She kept her back to Marco, eyes alert, erratic pulse. He removed his white T-shirt and curled his arms around her. And thus they lay in dimness, as their breathing flowed again in the same rhythm. Then Marisa turned to Marco. She followed the outline of his face with her fingers, feeling the roughness of the unshaved chin. She lingered on his lips. It had been a long, such a long time… He stroked her hair once more and she copied him, brushing off a dark lock of hair that insisted to fall over his forehead. She had ached to be in his arms and now scrutinized his face, afraid to trust, afraid to discover cowardice there. She found none, though. The intensity she met was genuine.

"Did you ever wonder…" Her voice trailed off away with her thought. "Why is it that when we want something so badly it doesn't happen? And as soon as we stop thinking of it, it does?"

"It must be because, if you want something that badly, you're not ready to have it."

She meditated for a moment.

"What do you mean?"

"This… thing we want so much has the purpose of filling a void. When we stop thinking about it, it means we're ready to have it because we're whole."

He threaded his fingers through hers, and there was infinite tenderness in that gesture. In an impulse, Marisa stamped her lips on his. When she started to retreat, Marco retained her, tightening his embrace and looking into her eyes. His gaze shifted from second to second. She sensed in Marco the same ambiguity that now paralyzed her. Fear and longing. But what would he fear?

On his face, she recognized the expression she had detected in their last encounter. This time, however, Marco didn't leave. He sought her mouth instead. The kiss was tinged with familiarity from the past and the strangeness of the present, expanding into faltering caresses that gradually gained steadiness and purpose. They trailed each other's bodies in no hurry, on those paths already known to them and on others yet to be explored, persisting on the spots where pleasure emerged.

When they finally paused, her desire mirrored his.

"Did you bring the die?"

"Yeah."

"Aren't you gonna use it?"

"Not now."

She smiled intrigued.

"It's our first time without a script, Marco."

"In a way, it's my first too."

Marco smiled, and then he was no longer smiling. He kissed her with hunger, and with hunger possessed her in his hands, lips, tongue, teeth. Marisa pushed Marco against the mattress, her hair a dark stream around him. She yanked off the remainder of his clothes and fondled his body with her own, breasts skimming on chest, belly against belly, the tongue on the skin and then a whiff...

They wanted to prolong that moment, yet against their will urgency budded in those gestures. Marco's hands ran over her breasts and encircled the nape of her neck. He lifted himself to devour her mouth, she sank her nails on his arms. And the unleashed animal side surfaced. Unveiled flesh. Scent of skin. The smoothness in the hair. Taste of kiss. Whisper.

As they fused into each other, their barriers dissolved one by one with no further reasoning, no further questioning. They joined the same cadence and lost themselves in the same vortex, spiraling faster and faster, eyes locked, eyes cloudy, the darkness of surrender like an infinite veil in the arch of space, the splendor of vertigo, the vertigo, the vertigo...

Now close your eyes and forget all thought. Feel it. Feel it. Inside.

So to learn by heart the rhythm of the heartbeat.

16. Speaking of Love

Silk handkerchiefs. Fine, strong, malleable. On her ankles, wrists, mouth, eyes. In his hand. Immobilized, Marisa felt the whisper of the fabric. The touch of silk. Around her breasts, strolling down her arm, playing on the palm of her hand and between the fingers... Levitating to the inner thighs. Lying down on the navel, descending a bit further, pausing once more... Her skin tingled for the more incisive touch that silk would only foretell.

Her body spread out like a cross on the bed, at *his* mercy—and vulnerability offered a cup of aphrodisiac to be slowly sipped with a question mark. Marco turned the music on and played a selection she had made for him when they first met. The sounds in the room were muffled by the soft melody. Marisa, however, could hear Marco fiddling with the contents of his suitcase, zippers being opened, the crumpling of clothes, paper, plastic. Then steps dampened by the carpet, and again his proximity.

The characteristic smell of the fabric, faint, fresh, with a note of bitterness, got mixed with another more poignant and musky. The leather strips of the whip—the whip now gliding on her skin just touched by silk. The caress of leather triggered a different reaction, and Marisa anticipated the moment in which, without warning, it would leave its footprint on the flesh. It was like balancing on the edge of a cliff: the fear of falling and the urge to dive into its depths.

Marisa breathed heavily, clenching her teeth. She remained there trembling, in wait, her flesh exposed like a flower that blossomed for him. One petal, two petals, three petals. Her body, her frailty, her soul. And the play. The guessing game. Where the next touch? How?

Soon she learned the answer.

The leather strips delivered shocks, which started light and then intensified. Leather pet, and suddenly sharper lashes on her belly and thighs. Imperious sensations hurled her into a vortex, fire and electricity mingled, neither one nor the other but something new. The whip petted her once more. Marisa squirmed in fitful moans, unable to tell when one stimulus ended and the next began. Her whole body pulsed in a diffuse flame, simultaneously becoming numb.

Hot and cold, hot and cold, undulating with the music… The strips climbed her legs, bit her nipples and descended to the junction of her thighs. They paused there, instigating electric currents that expanded throughout her body like flares and returned to her loins with double potency. And they came and went until she was nearly subdued with pleasure. When the electric impulses ceased and Marco removed the silk from her lips, Marisa was still shaking from an endless spasm.

Marco kissed her mouth for a long moment, waiting for her to quiet down. And quiet down she did. The flares had dissipated, but now the unsatiated desire devoured her. She craved Marco. And he knew it. He untied her wrists and ankles, brushing his parted lips on them. Next came the weight of his body over hers. Marisa received him with a heave. She breathed in Marco, sought his mouth again, wrapped her arms and legs around him. Still blindfolded, she had her senses awoken to what the eyes could not see. Marco's liquid voice, his perspiration diluting into hers, their desire that would not stanch even after the powerful climax.

He continued to thrust into her in rough motions while stimulating her with his fingers, until she was sobbing as a chain of orgasms ensued. Then Marco took off her blindfold and they remained lying down with their bodies still united. He leaned on his elbow and kissed Marisa's forehead. Girdling her by the waist, he rolled to the side and let his head collapse on the pillow.

Marisa cuddled in his arms and caressed his chest, playing with the fine hair on it. She enjoyed being like that with Marco. In the past, they had abandoned themselves to that same languor, sometimes talking, sometimes in the gentleness of silence. It was always good.

She closed her eyes and paid attention to the song—she hadn't listened to it since their breakup. Portishead. *It Could Be Sweet*. Before she met

Marco, the song evoked to her the sweetness of a possibility. Now it gained a different meaning. Loss. Like dawn in a dream.

"Why did we break up, Marco?" Marisa asked bluntly. "Be honest. You don't need to make up excuses." She no longer believed she hadn't met his expectations, but something still bothered her. Something she couldn't change. "Was it because of my mom? Because you thought she would cause a stir at school?"

Marco avoided her gaze. He hated evasions. But he would honor his word and omit the conversation with her mother. It was no good telling the truth anyway. She'd resent her mother, who, in spite of everything, deep down only wanted Marisa to be happy. Just like he did.

"It's complicated, Mari."

"Then explain it."

"You're too young, still have a lot to live."

"And you don't?"

He remained silent. Marisa, nonetheless, needed to know. To share. Gushing came the memories of what they had lived together and what she'd gone through afterward—lonely, confused, shattered. She wanted to share her being so happy and so unhappy... and the fact that he, Marco, was the magician of it all. He was the sun that awakened, drew, colored, enlivened, warmed. And burned. Burned, seared, carved the raw flesh until it turned black. He was the sun and the darkness. There were so many words choked inside her, Marisa didn't know how to express them.

"I loved you, Marco. I didn't love you more because you refused it."

And that said it all.

"Mari... please..."

His face contracted and his body recoiled. The words wounded. He had also loved Marisa. He didn't love her more because he couldn't. And the situation now was even more complicated than before. He needed to persuade her of the futility of it all. Needed to persuade himself. Marco resorted to the sole defense he had left: the one found in books. A rational wall around a sad castle. If she could be convinced, if she hated him, everything would be easier.

"That was a fantasy," he forced himself to say with a gesture of contempt. "The myth of ideal love exploited by mass culture. Then, when couples realize daily life is not made of perpetual fireworks, comes disappointment. And they ask themselves what went wrong: why can't they have a relationship like those in the movies and soap ads? Why, because it's just an idealization impossible to sustain. How could you possibly love me? You don't even know me that well."

Marisa sat up, on the brink of anger. She bent her knees and hugged her legs, taking a deep breath. When she spoke, it was in a soft tone.

"Are you sure? I know that you enjoy you meat rare but won't tolerate grease, that you'd rather go to the countryside than to the beach, that you never miss a Woody Allen film. I know that you and your brothers were so naughty, you had to be set straight with a quince stick on one occasion. That your uncle used to tell stories around the bonfire while he roasted corn and, to this day, when you smell roasted corn you remember those stories. I know you sometimes have insomnia and get introspective and don't feel like talking…"

"It doesn't mean you really know me. It surely doesn't mean you loved me. You had an infatuation and will have others. *Love* is too strong of a word, Mari. You didn't have enough time for that."

"What I didn't have was a chance. You wiped me off your life just like that."

Marco sat up too, the sheet sliding down to his waist. He grasped it in exasperation—in his memory he saw again the relief on Lorena's face, the crack in the gaze of Marisa's mother. All he could do was move in circles without touching the center.

"Do you really want to talk about love? We can comb through an endless list of authors who devoted themselves to this subject. Comte-Sponville, Marilena Chauí, Octavio Paz, Bauman, to name just a few. Bauman shows that today love is liquid because everything changes too fast, and so it runs through our fingers like water. Everybody wants immediate pleasure for filling their own void. What you call love is that lack pointed out by Comte-Sponville: the passion that makes us think day and night about an object of desire because we need to consume it in order to be fulfilled. Does it even deserve to be called love? It's a self-centered feeling that won't stick around nor withstand the first storm."

Here, he smiled with an edge of bitterness, then went on: "Take Roland Barthes on the tautology of love, this tautology seizing us when we try to describe the object of our desire: *adorable*. That person is adorable because is adorable because is adorable… We can't escape this definition, and if we tried to explain it, we would need an infinity of adjectives, all incomplete, until we reached a standstill again: *adorable*. A pretty word that says everything and says nothing. Then one day we notice a tiny mole on that person's nose, a mole that in our blindness we had never noticed. Our object of desire is no longer perfectly adorable. And that's the beginning of the end." He folded his arms, shoulders slightly rounded. "It's not worth it, believe me."

"What are you talking about, Marco?"

"I'm talking about your passion for me. Hollow as the wind, although you swear it's eternal, sublime, deeper than deep."

"So I'm a liar?"

"All I'm saying is you haven't lived long enough to know better."

"I haven't lived long enough to read all the authors you just quoted."

They remained silent. He averted his eyes to the barely touched food on the table. It exuded a sweet smell. A shiny strawberry jam trail on the white porcelain. Like a razorblade gash.

"After we broke up I went into therapy, you know?" Marisa insisted. "And my therapist said I was just going through some sort of cold turkey. Then I researched the hormones that act upon the brain in order to manufacture love… Testosterone, which activates the sexual urge, dopamine for stimulating passion. Oxytocin and vasopressin, responsible for the maintenance of the relationship. See how many agents intervene in the body system to create love."

"Exactly. All of that serves to ensure the survival of the species. When the offsprings grow up, the reproductive cycle concludes and the biological tendency is for love to end."

"That's it? Love is just a hormone cocktail, an addiction that leaves you cold turkey?" Marisa shook her head, reflecting. "No, there must be more to it. A spiritual side. Each of us is a matrix, with a path to follow and a learning curve to complete. When we encounter someone with a matrix that resonates with ours, we start walking side by side. So we learn to love in depth, with more understanding and respect for differences, with more generosity... being each other's mirror, sharing, teaching and learning."

She stared at him resolutely but her hands trembled when she said: "We've lived that, Marco, even if for a short time. And I ask again: what is time? Some people spend years half-heartedly with their partners in auto-pilot. Our time together was intense and whole. What we had was special. You know it. I went through a lot of pain with our breakup, and it would be easier to justify my feelings based on biochemistry. It would be reassuring. But it wasn't that... it wasn't *only that*."

"It's a natural reaction. When you start a relationship, you stop being an autonomous entity to structure yourself as part of a couple. After separation, you go through the pain of having to restructure yourself again." As Marco spoke, a shadow clouded his eyes. The words now stirred up memories. "And there's grieving too. Igor Caruso said with separation we die little by little in the mind of the other person, and it's a two-way process. You're no longer the brightest star in their constellation and begin to fade... It's death in life. Can you imagine anything worse than that? To be metaphorically buried alive—"

Marisa placed her index finger on his lips, imposing silence. "Let's forget the theories, otherwise we'll end up walking in circles. I know what I've lived. I know with my heart. Now answer this: were you happy with me?"

He opened his mouth, then his lips sealed up again without a sound. Of course he was, Marco said at last.

"And are you happy with me now?"

"Mari... Yes, I'm happy. More than I should." He fixed his eyes on the ceiling. "I missed you, I craved to be with you but thought it would be best to spare us. We went our separate ways when we were at the summit, and we'll always remember good things. A flower cut in full bloom is better than a dry plant with its roots clutched to a grave. That's the most depressing thing."

"So to break up is less depressing than to think of all wasted possibilities of a relationship? Do you know what I think? You're afraid."

"No, Mari, I'm not," he responded, stiffening almost imperceptibly.

He remained quiet. So quiet, she inquired what he was thinking. Then she laughed self-consciously for asking such a typical woman's question.

Marco ran one hand on his hair and said he was trying to remember the time of her flight. Eleven, Marisa replied. He checked the clock on the nightstand: they still had a few hours, it was only half past three. Marisa remembered to call Mrs. Stevenson, as her hostess thought she had spent the night at Valentina's.

Ah, the same old excuse—Marco curved his mouth with a smile that did not reach his eyes. He hesitated and enveloped her in his arms, regretting she must leave that evening. Marisa hugged Marco by the waist and interlaced her legs in his. Resting her head on his shoulder, she listened to his heartbeat. The soothing evidence that he was close again.

"We can meet when you return to Brazil," she murmured. "Your flight is in a couple of days, right? Wednesday."

Marco nodded with feeble conviction and stared at Marisa. His expression was somber. He cupped her face in his hands, entangling his fingers on loose tresses while his thumbs caressed her temples. Then he slid his lips on hers very slowly and deepened the kiss with a gentleness tinted with an emotion she couldn't quite define. Melancholy. They kissed for a long moment. When they parted, Marco cradled Marisa's hands in his and continued to gaze at her.

"What's the matter, Marco?" she asked, alarmed. "You look disturbed."

He pressed her hands, exhaled a sigh, released them.

"Mari, there's something I need to tell you."

Marco now twisted the end of the sheet with an absent air. Marisa felt each fiber of her being petrify. The room grew cold as they stared at each other and time dragged in endless silence. Both vacillated: he reluctant to speak, and she reluctant to listen. Amid that glacial silence, the cell phone on the nightstand rang with the eloquence of a scream. They startled. In a reflex, Marco reached for it without averting his eyes from Marisa. When he answered the call, she heard him say a name.

Yarina.

17. Two Ships Sailing the Night

The curtains remained shut, keeping the gray afternoon away. But inside it was gray too, and the vertical stripes on the wallpaper drew the bars of a prison cell. The prison of her own anguish, Marisa thought as she listened to Marco talk on the phone. She observed him from the corner of her eye, trying to guess the emotion moving him. Marco was tense and only muttered monosyllables. On the other end, Yarina seemed to be narrating her adventures with a friend in the restroom of the Devil's Lair until the police rescued them.

Finally she asked him a question and Marco made a pause.

"Yeah, I saw your message but I didn't have a chance to reply... Sure, sure... Don't worry, everything is fine." He shook his head as she told him something. "Tonight I can't. I've promised to help a friend tidy his apartment."

Yarina resumed talking and Marco restarted delivering monosyllables.

Marisa consumed herself. She took a seat at the table and pretended to read a brochure with San Francisco's attractions and a million ads. The Golden Gate Bridge, a burlesque show at Fort Mason, restaurants, diamond rings. Colorful photographs paraded before her eyes while her numb hands flipped the pages and she tried to guess what Marco wanted to tell her. Maybe he was involved with Yarina? What a silly question. Of course he was. Marisa had noticed the way they stared at each other. The way Yarina touched him. She wondered where the two had met, how long ago...

Beep. Her conjecturing was interrupted when Marco said goodbye and turned off the phone.

As much as Marisa consumed herself, when he shifted to face her, she feared that moment. It was a black well sucking in all colors until everything turned into darkness. How would it feel to lose his love for the second time? Theoretically, she was stronger now. But was she? The weight in her heart became unbearable. She had found, lost, and found Marco again. In that reencounter, she was struck with the certainty of the love uniting her to him. The love that, in a minute, she would lose once more. Marisa sensed it in her heart and in the way Marco gazed at her. She didn't want to believe it. She could fool herself, but there was no denying—his gaze was one of farewell. Gathering courage, she inquired what he had to say. Marco asked her to sit next to him and waited for Marisa to settle down.

"Mari," he began in a restrained voice, "I can't see you anymore."

"You can't or you won't?" Marisa clenched her hands on her lap. "You're in a relationship with Yarina, is that it? Then why didn't you just leave me alone? Before it was already hard enough, and now..." She found no point in finishing the sentence and silenced.

Marco knew he was responsible for the pain he saw in her gaze, and the pain became his too. For an instant, he wished he had never reencountered Marisa. So to never see that gaze.

He shook his head.

"She's just an acquaintance that I'll probably never see again. I don't know what to say. Of course I'd love to meet you. But I won't be going back to Brazil. At least, not straight away."

"You plan to extend your vacation?"

"It's not that, either." He averted his eyes, as if in search of words, then stared at her. "I have a business meeting in Toronto."

It took Marisa a few seconds to assimilate the implications of what he had just said. She expected anything but that. He'd never manifested an interest in Canada. The news unsettled her in such a way she detached herself, like it wasn't happening to her and she was only a spectator. She watched her own incredulity as Marco admitted his surprise at the turn of events. On the first day at the congress, he had met the director of a much-respected Canadian school. They needed a head coordinator urgently, and his preliminary interviews with the director and later through videoconference had gone quite well. So Marco changed his plane ticket and, before going back to Brazil, he would be travelling to Toronto to visit the school and discuss the contract.

"You'll be moving to Canada, then," Marisa concluded as she straightened herself up, her body icy cold.

"That's the idea. I'm tired of the school politics and Belvedere. Even though they offered me a seat on the board of directors, I had already considered resigning at the end of the year to start a business. And then I was offered this opportunity. A unique experience that will help open doors for me on many levels. Besides, I'm already living far away from my family."

He had no ties to São Paulo indeed, Marisa conceded with an apathy that failed to conceal her hurt. Maybe he never had. Now she knew exactly what it was like to lose his love for the second time. Like bleeding.

Bleed.

Bleed.

Bleed.

Each breath a drop. Until it aches so much you get numb. Or not. Or else. Then it throbs and throbs. Then you wish blood red would become oblivion black. Colorless death. White despair. Until one day it's gone.

But the scar remains there—always there.

She started to rise to her feet. Marco retained her.

"Where are you going?"

"Home."

"You're upset with me." His tone revealed regret.

"It's going to pass, Marco, like it did the first time." Marisa cast a stern glare at him. "My mom was right: at the first difficulty, you've discarded me like an old toy. And now you're discarding me again. You know what? I don't need any of this."

"Mari, you know very well why I retreated," Marco countered firmly. Yet he sounded weary. "That 'first difficulty' triggered a family crisis. And I told you I didn't want to wreck your life. Can't you see? I tried to protect you."

"You abandoned me, Marco. That's not protecting." She stood up and barely refrained from snapping. "Since you're so fond of quotes, check out

Laurie Anderson's *My Right Eye*. It's about the eyes and their tears. Tears of love in the right eye. Tears of hate in the left eye."

It wasn't clear whether hate or exasperation. Despair. Disappointment. Maybe all of it, thought Marisa. For everything that hasn't been. For the nothing it had become. Tears held their own logic in contradiction.

She sighed, feeling suddenly empty. Her eyes wanted to cry. They didn't dare.

"Thanks for your help yesterday. I mean it. Now I need to go." And, without giving him a chance to reply, she proceeded to collect her clothes.

Marco quickly slipped into his sweatpants and went after her. In consternation, he paused at the bathroom door while Marisa slid the dress over her head with a jerky motion. She picked up the torn pantyhose, started to fit them and changed her mind, tossing them in the trash. Her hands struggled with the fastener of her sandal.

"Mari, you've got to understand I didn't plan any of this. The trip to Canada had been scheduled before I even met you yesterday. I've never imagined we…" Marco made a helpless gesture. All the reasoning he had so carefully built disintegrated. It was fragile anyway, and he knew it. "You think I'm made of stone? I have feelings too, in case you haven't noticed. This situation is harder for me than you can possibly imagine. Things got out of hand in the first place because *you* invited me to bed."

"You insisted that I stay, and I knew you wouldn't be able to sleep in that chair." She stood upright. Her defensive mode switched to accusation: "Then you asked me to undress the robe."

For a moment, he said nothing.

"Why did you kiss me, Marisa?"

Silence.

Why did he insist and accept and request, why did she stay and invite and caress? The answer was simple yet complicated, for now between the answer and the question there were two continents.

"You're happy in college and have plans for the future… and you finally get along with your mom," Marco said. "It would be beyond selfish to expect you to give up everything and embark with me on an enigma. I may never move back to Brazil."

Marisa became rigid. Marco's hesitation to mention her mother had not gone unnoticed. That was the real problem, just as she'd suspected. Words were not enough. Marco could come up with as many excuses as he wanted and pretend to be concerned about her well-being. But he didn't care. It was her mom that had bothered him in the past and still bothered him now. Marco wanted a relationship free of complications. He wasn't even willing to give it a try—and that betrayed the exact measure of his feelings.

"It's okay. I get it." Marisa quickly braided her hair, ignoring the mirror. "Good luck with your meeting."

"Please, let's not say goodbye like this."

She didn't want to wait any longer, she already knew all she needed. Marisa signaled for him to give her way, but Marco did not move. She tried to push him, holding back the tears. She would never see him again. Would never hold him nor feel the warmth of his smile. What Marco had said about death in life during a separation was true. In that instant, she was already dying within him. Marisa swallowed a sob and pushed him once more.

Marco held her hand, which she retracted impatiently. On his face there was discourage. But what did Marco expect? she asked herself with bitterness, and on a sudden became exasperated. That was life, period. And Marco failed her again. They were two ships meeting in the ocean and then following their separate paths.

Just two ships in the night.

In her memory flashed the scenes that composed their story. The first time they had a cup of coffee, that afternoon with silver in the mirror and on their bodies, the strolls in Downtown, the graduation evening, the dreamed picnic in the park. And then Marco in this room from the present, lying by her side as if they had never been apart. But there were the blooming cherry trees to denounce the illusion—the cherry trees they would never see together.

She made a point to leave. He put his arms around her. She tried to resist but gave up, the inert hands did not obey her, and her eyes closed as a knot tied her throat. He wanted to say the world but had to repress the words. Wanted to say that when he looked at her, he saw a soulmate. That her tenderness brought him comfort and made him happier than he could possibly express. That her qualities would fill pages and pages but fit in one single word.

Adorable.

He would not impose on her the same situation he'd imposed on Lorena. *You have destroyed my life.* He made a promise not to ever hear those words from Marisa's lips. It was hard enough to forgive himself for Lorena, for something he'd done in a moment of blindness. With Lorena, he had been obstinate. Later, he couldn't handle what his own obstinacy sowed.

He wouldn't do that again. He couldn't live with it.

His heart sunk into melancholy. Fractured, always fractured. Marco closed his eyes to breathe in her perfume and retain that tiny fraction of Marisa, just a little longer—and at each second his sorrow grew heavier. Her perfume was air. And in his chest it became lead. Heavy metal, the poison of lost memories.

Marco also remembered.

The first Sunday lunch in his kitchen, seated at the table, so beautiful in a white bodice, her hands eternally playing with her hair in an unconscious tic (she did that when she was anxious or excited). The rosy mouth on the glass, the rosy mouth chatting away with no worries, and all of her filling the kitchen with her gestures, laughter, voice.

"Last year I attended a lecture about Buddhism, Marco. To me, reincarnation makes total sense. We come into this world to learn, and keep changing bodies until we perfect our soul and complete the learning process. What I found the most interesting is the absence of the concept of sin. If you make a mistake, it's your responsibility to improve yourself and you simply delay your learning process."

"So what's to be learned?"

Marisa thought for a moment while he finished preparing the tiella. She followed his hands with a distracted gaze and chewed her lip. Finally, she answered: "I think each of us comes into the world with a personal challenge to overcome. It can be arrogance, weakness, greed, fear. Anything. But ultimately I think we come into the world to learn to love. Because love is the greatest virtue of all." She made a pause to admire the green-yellow-red layers he was crowning with a dab of olive oil, and then smiled. "It looks delicious. If you keep doing that, you'll find the way to my heart through my stomach and I'll never leave you..."

And then—then one day the kitchen was empty again.

Marco opened his eyes and found Marisa's. She pushed him softly, and this time he didn't retain her. The hours remaining were not enough and never would be. It made no sense to postpone the inevitable. Marco retreated to fetch his jacket on the back of a chair. He reached Marisa when she was opening the door and offered her the jacket. She ignored the gesture.

"Don't worry, Marco. I'll grab a taxi in front of the hotel and soon be home. I won't feel cold."

Without another glance, Marisa left. Before her unfolded a monotonous succession of doors and pale sconces. As she walked away in the carpeted hall, the thick stripes on the wallpaper shattered in an explosion of iron bars.

No. It wasn't freedom.

It was wreckage.

18. Denial

We're just ships in the night
No more pretense or ties
Just ships in the night
Sinking goodbyes
In the night
In denial
Die

19. Full Circle

Books, CDs, LPs, notebook, tablet, MP3 player, valise, family relics, abstract painting, Woody Allen DVDs, clothes (include ripped jeans and Armani suit), shoes, soapstone pot, resignation letter, moving company, storage, donations, car sale, tenant for apartment, power of attorney, work visa, Candomblé priest for reading the future in whelk shells...

No, the Candomblé priest was a joke.

Marco left his suitcase by the door, dropped the backpack on the coffee table and stretched his sore body on the sofa. He had gone on vacation without expectations and had returned with his hands full. The plans for opening his school postponed indefinitely, maybe forever. His mind now in turmoil. His heart fractured again. Air, lead, poison. Marco closed his eyes.

He thought of the cells in an organism regenerating until the complete renewal of the body. And one day everything woke up anew and paradoxically the same. Marisa was the same, he was the same, and yet the two were different persons from those meeting the previous year. If he were to be honest, he would have to admit the first time he'd relinquished her due to guilt and—yes—fear. The paralyzing fear that one day Marisa would be Lorena and walk away to leave him with a collapsed world in his hands— and the doubled, tripled guilt of hurting her precisely because he didn't want to hurt her.

Her wound reopened. The cut throbbed in him too, it throbbed to the same pulsation, with the same intensity. Because there was the same cut in him, exactly in the same spot, like a black mirror, like a sad Siamese twin. Wound: an island amid the healthy skin, red and sticky, sending infection to the blood current, infecting everything. Dirty river. Venom. The phantom pain of an amputated limb.

He couldn't stand to go through that again.

The first time had already been such an effort, for he needed to fight not only his own will but hers too. It would have been easier if Marisa was the one breaking the bond. Every time she called, it was an ordeal to remain firm in his decision. Every time he hung up, doubt haunted him. When he slept she visited him in his dream. When he woke up, she wasn't there.

He couldn't stand to go through that again.

Living with the doubt of what could have been. This time around something within Marco resisted with all might the idea of being away from Marisa.

He wanted to *happen* with her.

Unfold.

Unwrap life and its gifts.

Each ordinary moment, each surprise.

Exist.

Every day.

With her.

But.

Sharp blade.

Such a short word and fierce cut.

But.

What could he offer to Marisa? Literary quotes, theories. A valise full of useless accessories. And an existence away from everything and everyone— an existence she might come to hate. Marisa loved the sun and the beach. She obviously wouldn't adapt to Canada. From afar everything exuded the perfume of adventure. Up close there was the stench of adaptation: cold weather, lack of family and friends, uneasiness to communicate in another language.

Pessoa said language was the true homeland, and indeed it was—like a soft blanket, motherly food, comfortable shoes. Marisa would have none of it. Then what?

He had already watched that film. It was as predictable as a Pavlovian experiment. You conditioned a dog with a bell before feeding, and soon the animal would salivate every time it heard the bell. The same happened to people. If you put them in an unpleasant situation, they started associating you with unpleasant feelings. Marisa would associate him with the cold, the loneliness and her frustrations. And would hate him for that. So it was best that she hated him now without the burden of a broken dream.

He took out the MP3 player and portable speakers from his back-pack. He searched for the playlist. Why, he didn't know—maybe fleshing the wound to the bone would help him get used to it. Marisa's selection resumed playing from the point where it had been interrupted. Still Portis-head. *Revenge of the Number.* Verses about deceit and loneliness, profanity and silence, an unbearable silence in the throbbing wound…

Marco pressed Pause. He needed peace and quiet to think. A list of pros and cons would help him evaluate the situation with more clarity. So he took a sheet of paper and drew a circle, dividing it into four numbered parts. In one of the sections he wrote *Brazil* and in the next *Canada*. Then Marco repeated both words in the remaining spaces, now adding a name to each.

Marisa.

Much to his surprise, the pen ran without hesitation as he wrote. Once he was done, Marco studied the equation he'd created. Four quadrants, nineteen lines. The result, a question mark. But he ought to make a decision soon. The clock was ticking. With no compassion.

Thirst, headache. He headed to the kitchen for some water, taking the sheet with him. He left it on the counter while helping himself, took a sip, put the glass down. Tangled up in his thoughts, Marco knocked it over when he reached for the paper sheet. All the water spilled, and he quickly grabbed a cloth on the counter. That was when he heard an incisive noise and saw it. He dropped the cloth with a startle. For an endless moment, Marco stood with one hand in midair and his eyes locked to the counter.

Next to the sheet of paper lay the ivory die.

Collecting it with caution, Marco examined it and frowned. He must have seized it along with the cloth. Marco shrugged and threw it back to the counter.

The die hit a jar twice and bounced back to the edge of the paper.

A sudden gust of icy cold air. A chill. He retrieved the die and the sheet, then sat at the table placing the piece of paper before him. With one hand, Marco drummed his fingers on the tabletop. With the other, he held the die. At last, he left it in a corner. The ivory cube, however, seemed to watch him with inscrutable eyes.

Marco tried to tuck it away in a drawer—he was unable to complete the gesture. He remained with the die stuck between his fingers, searing his flesh. Until he uttered a sigh and surrendered. Marco cupped his hands in a mechanical motion, afraid of the number to be revealed. His whole body was shaking.

A phrase echoed in his head before he closed his eyes. Sartre: *The sole power of the past lies in the future.*

And with his eyes closed Marco breathed deeply. Even deeper. He remained like that, perfectly still with the ivory cube nestled in his hands. Inhaling, exhaling, until the inner turmoil gave room to… nothing. There was nothing in that infinite space. Just him and his breathing, the here and now, truth and peace. Forget about the past, forget about the future, here and now happiness. His shoulders relaxed, his hands turned limp, and the die fell on the paper sheet. Marco's eyelids fluttered open. The circle and the ivory cube started to slip into focus.

Then something happened.

He averted his gaze from the table, without checking the result. A slow smile spread on his lips, and all of his exhaustion melted away at once. There was so much to do: the future was just beginning. He returned to the living room and put his jacket on: in his hand, the cell phone and car keys. Impatiently, Marco waited for the elevator and, with growing impatience, reached the street.

Already activating the cell phone, he strode on the sidewalk like a king. Marco kicked a puddle just for fun, saluted the street sweeper in an orange uniform, and smiled at a tall rubber tree rustling in a garden bed. He felt a tingle of excitement. He felt suddenly invincible.

Free.

Like a mantra, Marco went on reviewing. Books, CDs, LPs, notebook, tablet, MP3 player, valise, relics, painting, DVDs, clothes, shoes, pot, resignation, movers, storage, donations, car, tenant, power of attorney, visa... Maybe.

But.

Double-edged sword.

A chance for atonement.

But.

The certainty of three words.

I love you.

On the avenue, a thunder roared. Then came the rain.

Red is the bed where extremes are born. Blood flower dispersing its petals in the wind of time. Dusk, dawn, eclipse, sunray. Shadow and light.

The first color captured by the eye.

The last feeling to remain.

Red.

APPENDIX: POEMS & WORKS

In order to avoid copyright infringement, I have created my own lyrics for this novel. I love music and used it to comment, reinforce, contradict or ironize scenes, so I invite readers to listen to the tracks mentioned here. I myself listened to those songs a million times while writing and rewriting scenes. "Anemone" by The Brian Jonestown Massacre sets the mood for this book. "La Femme d'Argent" by Air, although not included in the story, is an integral part of it: it got my writing juices flowing, and I've listened to it countless times while hammering at the keyboard.

All quotes are from Brazilian works and public domain material. Here is a list of works quoted, as well as all original Brazilian titles, for credit and reference:

Part 1: White

7. Tropical Rain

"Storm Ending" by Jean Toomer in *Cane* (1922)

8. Rolling the Die

"Pluvial" ("Pluvial") by Augusto de Campos in *Viva Vaia*

"Tempoespaço" ("Timespace") by Augusto de Campos in *Viva Vaia*

"Eis os Amantes" ("Here Are the Lovers") by Augusto de Campos in *Viva Vaia*

11. Close Encounter of the Third Kind

"A Verdade Dividida" ("The Divided Truth") by Carlos Drummond de Andrade in *Contos Plausíveis*

12. Duet Story

"Se te Agarro com Outro te Mato" ("If I Catch You with Another Man I'll Kill You") by Sidney Magal in *Sidney Magal*

16. The Graduation

"Hesperus: a Legend of the Stars" by Charles Sangster in *Hesperus, and Other Poems and Lyrics* (1860)

17. Behind the Peephole

"Ain't Nobody's Business" by Porter Grainger and Everett Robbins (1922)

"Canção do Dia de Sempre" ("The Everyday Song") by Mário Quintana in *Canções*

"O Seu Santo Nome" ("Its Sacred Name") by Carlos Drummond de Andrade in *Corpo*

Part 2: Black

1. A Well Stares at the Sky

Philosophy in the Bedroom by the Marquis de Sade (1795)

Part 3: Red

2. The Light Inside Your Eyes

"Rio Vermelho" ("Red River") by Cora Coralina in *Poemas dos Becos de Goiás e Estórias Mais*

"Dream-song" by Walter de la Mare in *Peacock Pie* (1913)

5. The Kashmir Lounge

"The Wind and the Moon" by George McDonald in *Good Words for the Young* (1872)

14. Nostalgia

"Lenda" ("Legend") by Céu in *Céu*

ACKNOWLEDGEMENTS

I would like to thank Wattpad for offering such a wonderful platform to connect writers and readers, and every Wattpad community member who honored me by choosing to read my story in its unpolished form. You gave me invaluable feedback, incentive and support. Without you, I would never have been able to fulfill my lifelong dream of becoming a writer. You know who you are, and some of you have become dear friends, too. My heartfelt gratitude goes out to each of you.

I am immensely grateful to Something or Other Publishing for materializing my dream and making me so proud of my book. To Wade Fransson for believing in *RED*. To Andrew Doty for beautifully editing it and for his infinite patience with my quirks. To Eleanor Leonne Bennett for her feat of capturing my story in one gorgeous cover that I absolutely love. To Michael Schindler, Christian Lee, Valerie Simons and Rachel Abou-Zeid for teaching me and helping me to spread the word. To Jake Russell and James Monroe for wrapping up my work with their special touch. You all make an awesome team, and I feel blessed to have you by my side.

Thank you, my good friend and talented writer Gwendolyn Valerius, for your great contribution in the initial copyedit and for your suggestions for improving this story.

Marcelino Freire, word magician whom I so much admire, you honored me by reading chapter one and opening my eyes.

Writer and editor Gavin Wilson, you gave me support on Wattpad and are such a nice guy. And Bronwyn Hemus from standoutbooks, your advice counted.

My dear Abeera Dilawar, I could not have done it without your Urdu translation.

Carlos Adolfo Schmidt, you helped me cross quite turbulent waters while my novel was in the making. Your generosity is much appreciated.

Myla Cyrino, Carlos Aguena, Isabela Meirelles Tavares, Yolanda Bastos, Andrea Moraes, Laura Aguiar, Stephen Kanitz, Renata Fontana, Cristina Silv, Lorena Salgado, Rosângela Maschio, Margareth Procópio, Márcia Grande, Schirlley Azevedo… you were my "victims" by reading my manuscript in its embryonic stage. Thank you for allowing me to perform a little literary BDSM on you. I know you're not submissive by nature and only did it for love.

Last but definitively not least, thank you so much to my wonderful family and friends for always being there for me. I love you. You are my harbor in this world, you fill my life with color and make it worth living.

A WORD FROM THE AUTHOR

Thank you for reading *RED*. I hope you had a good ride. If you enjoyed it, please consider posting a spoiler-free review online. The events in the ends of Parts 2 and 3 will be our little secret…

I would love to hear from you. If you want to say hi, stop by at:
www.nicolecollet.com
Facebook: www.facebook.com/NicoleColletAuthor
Twitter: @NicoleCollet

God bless & até breve
Nicole

COMING SOON

RED 2: Mirrors

www.ingramcontent.com/pod-product-compliance
Lightning Source LLC
Chambersburg PA
CBHW051334020726
47501CB00007B/2082